THE FATAL FRONTIER

by
Matt Vancil

Bearfoot Media
Tacoma, Washington
USA

Published by Bearfoot Media, Tacoma, WA, USA

Edited by Daniel Greeno

Cover art by Jacob Blackmon
Cover design by Kevin K° Wiley and Seth Davis
Book design & layout by Kevin K° Wiley

Printed and bound in the United States of America

Acknowledgements

Many thanks to everyone who made this project possible, especially:

The Captain's Council: James Herbert, John Kozlowski, Brent Phillips, Benjamin Mobley, and Qimmortal;

Paxamo, for writing, narrating, and animating the pitch video; Maggie Doyle, for managing the campaign; Jacob Blackmon, for the cover artwork; Seth Davis, for the cover design;

Leslie Sedlak and Red, for keeping the lights on during the darkest days of 2020;

Danny Greeno, for cutting his editorial teeth on this manuscript; Rob MacLennan, for his eagle-eyed typoslaying; K⁰ Wiley, for shepherding the script through layout and fulfillment, and giving to airy nothing a local habitation and a name;

All the Kickstarter backers and Patreon patrons, for your trust and patience;

And to Dan Vining, my first year AFI screenwriting mentor, who, after reading the script upon which this novel is based, said that I was a better writer than I appeared on paper.

for Dorothy

THE
FATAL
FRONTIER

Chapter 1
Omnes Nos Morituri

Forty thousand kilometers above the planet, Webb tuned out the red-shirted crewmen buzzing about like panicked hummingbirds. She shimmied into her pressure suit, chanced a glance at the device she'd affixed to her console. Its screen remained blank.

"Come on, people." She slathered her face and head with pitch-black gel only slightly darker than her skin. "If we're doing this, it has to be *now*. Seven, where's that reading?"

Yolanda Seven's fingers flitted across her console. "Core is stable, and you're insane."

"So noted. Frankie?"

The teleporter tech looked up, her teeth clenched, her shaved brown scalp beaded with sweat. This close to the core, no amount of shielding could hold back all the heat. "We have teleporter lock. You really don't have to do this."

"That's subjective." Webb hit her activator. The suit vacuum-sealed around her.

"At least put your helmet on."

Webb shook her head, clamped on some goggles. "Have to see what I'm doing." Though if this took more than a few seconds, no amount of gel would matter.

"Plus one to your insanity."

"Noted. Everyone behind the dead line." Red shirts glued themselves to the far wall or ducked behind heat shields. Webb made sure no one was in desiccation range, let out a long breath, and opened the core.

Klaxons roared. Alarm lights painted Engineering red. Emergency force fields sprung up to prevent the heat from the star—the living star compressed to the size of a basketball in the heart of the ship—from vaporizing the crew.

The heat still hit Webb hard enough to curl her eyebrows. The super-heated air would have baked organic lungs; she could feel the regulators in hers whirr and spin to keep the air merely hellish.

The gel on her face was already boiling off—the tip of her ear screamed where she'd missed a spot. Not much time now. In a few seconds, the temperature shield would fail and stellar radiation would dust them all across the ship.

Webb hefted her pizza board. She slipped the frozen pizza onto ceramic support ribs in the cooling tower and gave a thumbs up.

Yolanda Seven hit a button. The core slammed shut.

Webb yanked off the goggles. Her protective gel gone, she could barely see through the steam billowing off her suit. But she could see well enough—within the cooling tower, the pizza had already begun to swell.

Seven squinted at the drive core. "Is it supposed to cook that fast?"

"Theoretically." Webb killed the alarm on her console. "There's not really regs for this. The *Heartland* crew estimated fifteen seconds."

"*Cog!*" came a yell from the hall. The red shirts exchanged a collective glance before bolting back to their work stations.

Webb snatched up the device at her console. On its screen, a green dot was blinking right outside Engineering. "Lerd." She looked to the cooling tower. The pizza had swollen to the size of a beach ball. "*Lerd.*"

A door on the upper floor slid open with a pneumatic hiss. A cog marched in with mechanical precision, its stony white eyes peering down at them from a marble face.

Webb and Frankie stood side by side to block its view of the pizza.

"Which one is it?" Frankie whispered.

"Security or Engineering," said Webb. "If I had to guess. Based on the response time."

"We detected a core breach," said the cog without inflection.

"A minimal breach, sir," said Webb. "Barely registered. Three seconds, tops. No damage or leakage, all levels within acceptable parameters."

"We detected no power surge."

"There was none. Routine maintenance. Reset it myself." She indicated the pressure suit.

The cog froze for a beat. Proximity to the core sometimes futzed with their data streams. "No maintenance was scheduled."

"It just came up. Stabilization rib slipped out of alignment."

"If containment is lost, the ship is lost," said the cog.

"Containment was never at risk, sir."

A wet pop from behind them. Webb looked up to see exploded pizza guts caramelizing in the cooling tower. The red shirts let out a disappointed sigh.

"We've lost teleporter lock," reported Frankie.

The cog stared at the contaminants. "Explain."

Webb looked from the dead pizza to Frankie to the cog, and rolled the dice. "Space bat."

She could almost hear the processors catch behind the cog's Roman face. "Please repeat the statement."

"Space bat." Webb ignored Frankie's huge-eyed stare. "Must've flown in through the vents."

"No such creature exists."

"New discovery," said Yolanda Seven. "It just hit the journals."

Webb nodded. "I'm sure the Xenobio cog knows. You should ask him. You want me to close the vents?"

"We will remind the technicians that the Collective Operations Group functions as a single entity. Individual vessels carry no compartmentalized knowledge."

"Thanks, cog. We'd all forgotten."

"There is a high probability your statement was sarcastic."

"Psych cog," Webb said to Frankie. "That's the one. See that chip in his hairline where Dalbert hit him with a table?"

Another hiss. In trundled Dewey, the chief engineer, her hair gray, her badge gold, her shirt as red as the rest of theirs.

3

The cog spun her way. "We responded to a suspicious minor core breach. There is a high probability one or more technicians inserted contraband into the drive core."

"Jesus teabagging shitblisters," said the chief.

The cog actually blinked. "We recommend the cooling vents be sealed to prevent further space bat incursion."

"The fuck are you talking about?"

The cog went rigid again. In these paralytic moments, their resemblance to the classical statues they were modeled after—Roman busts on Greek bodies—was uncanny. As uncanny as the valley that made mistaking them for human impossible.

"Hello?" Dewey knocked on its forehead. Sighed. Glared at Webb. "What have I said about screwing with the cogs?"

"Never unless it's necessary."

"So was it?"

"Subjectively so."

"Disregard previous statement," the cog said abruptly. "We shall be making a full report."

"And I'm certain the captain will read it." Dewey squinted at the cog. Pointed. "There's a crack there under your hairline. That's a distinguishing feature."

"We shall have it repaired immediately." The cog's eyes went blank. Its head drooped, lolling limp as a blacked-out drunk, while its body walked it out of Engineering.

The chief took the lift down. Red shirts parted around her as she approached the cooling tower. She looked up at the blackened remains of the pie. Her sigh could have filled a zeppelin. "A fucking pizza, Webb?"

"A mondo supreme," said Webb. "We were saving you a slice."

"I don't even know what the code is for detonating contraband in the drive core. Harsh, I'm guessing. What's wrong with you?"

"Food pellets, Chief. They've had us on pellets since we ran out of meal creds last crunch."

"God help you if you fabbed that."

Webb looked incredulous. "Why would I fab a *frozen* pizza?"

Dewey eyed Frankie. "You've got a teleporter tech right here."

Frankie shrugged. "I like pizza."

"No one's trying to get brigged here, Chief."

Dewey grunted. "That better have been the only one."

The shift change pealed through Engineering. Red shirts meandered off. A few cast longing looks back at the tower.

Including the chief. "I'll be on the bridge," she told them. "Captain wants us up to oversee the bombardment. Now clean that lerd out of my core, or I'll make sure he does read the report."

"You think he won't otherwise?"

"With that bit of alien strange on board? His only priority's making another... how'd you put it?"

"Diplomatic connection," said Frankie.

"With his dick," Yolanda Seven clarified.

"Thanks, Chevalier," said the chief.

"Are they even compatible?"

Dewey scoffed. "Has that ever stopped him before?"

⊘

From his panoramic cabin atop the starship *Independence,* Captain William Seagrave watched agrichem torpedoes streak into the atmosphere and detonate with ship-nudging force. Each burst blossomed into a swirling atmospheric storm, a tempest heaving with lightning and torrential rains. "Beautiful."

His companion regarded him curiously. "You find beauty in destruction, Captain?"

"I find beauty in life, Ambassador." He eyed her appreciatively. "Among other things."

She didn't catch the pass. No matter. Universal translation was still in its infancy. And according to the report, the Sorl were especially difficult to read. They emoted not with their faces but with their hair-like mane of feathers. Like cats with their ears. The ambassador's feathers remained folded behind her neck.

He wasn't discouraged. If there was one thing he knew, one thing that didn't require computer-assisted translation, it was how to speak woman—even to waifish blue beauties like this one. He put on a smile, gazed up into her too-big eyes, and pictured her naked.

"You didn't answer my question, Captain."

"It's not destruction." He walked to the window, looked out over the storms enwrapping the planet. "It's development. A year from now, that planet—that dead, barren rock—will be supporting life. Civilization."

"And a year after that, you will have stripped and abandoned it."

"There's no stopping progress."

"You take stars to power your ships."

He chuckled. "The wonders of advancement."

"You deprive entire systems of light and life. You consider that advancement?"

"Not intelligent life," he corrected her. "Just bugs and algae."

That got a ripple of feathers. "And forests."

"We harvest the timber before we take the star. We're not monsters." He filled a pair of champagne flutes. "To the fruits of our labor."

"Our stomachs cannot metabolize alcohol."

He chuckled again. "Touché."

Another ripple. "I don't believe that translated."

"Maybe not verbally." It was just a matter of time now. He ran a hand through his luxurious locks.

Her eyes went to his hair. "There is a substantial amount of ointment in your keratin, Captain. Is it ill?"

"So!" He downed both flutes. "How can I convince you to include us in your little galactic union?"

"It's as we said in the communique. Was it not clear?"

"It's clear your organization doesn't think we're ready. That you're hostile to our expansion."

"There is no hostile intent, Captain. We merely wish—"

"You don't approve of what we're doing down there. Developing our resources. If you decide we don't belong in your union, haven't you've effectively chosen to compete with us?"

She spread her hands—an unpracticed gesture, one no doubt gotten from her own behavioral briefing. "There is no hostile intent, nor intent to offend. I am here merely as an amicable observer. I have been instructed to be accommodating in all ways."

"Interesting." He licked the rim of his glass.

Her feathers didn't move. "As was said in our communique, a sufficient level of technological advancement is not the sole criterion we consider."

"Ah," he nodded. "I see. You need an assessment of the human spirit."

"That is not remotely correct. The concept is immeasurable."

"Damn right it is." He rose, tugged his violet uniform taut. "The human spirit is what carried us through wars and across oceans to carve nations out of the wilderness, to raise ourselves from savagery and climb to the heavens to write our names in the stars. You'll find no finer examples of humanity than on this ship. Exemplars of the species, every one." He took her hand. "All at my command."

She blinked both sets of eyelids. The report said that was an indication of a heightened emotional state—clearly arousal.

He caressed the back of her hand. "We began this discussion on beauty. Surely that's as immeasurable as spirit. Yet you didn't challenge me on its existence."

"I did not."

"Ambassador. Would you care to join me on a trip through the immeasurable?" He sat on his chaise before the stars, patted the cushions next to him.

She sat. Her feathers stood up and she looked a question at him when he slipped his arm around her waist.

"For stability," he told her. "Indie?"

A chime from the ceiling. "Yes, Captain?"

"Take us into the atmosphere. Cruise pattern Seagrave Delta One. Let's go sailing."

"That will take us into the planet's gravity well, Captain."

"Well, yes. That's entirely the point."

The ship chimed compliance. Ahead, the planet rose and slinked towards them. As smoothly as slipping into a pool, they slid into the top layer of the stratosphere. A bump, and the air ignited around them. Great curling sheets of fire peeled away around the windows like burning fronds.

Seagrave glanced at the ambassador. Her feathers stood up in an Elizabethan frill.

He indulged in an inward scoff. Xenobiology had been so insistent he read the entire report. As if he required instruction in a language he spoke fluently.

He leaned towards the ambassador. She languidly turned his way.

Her frill dropped when his badge chimed. She turned back to the windows.

The captain mashed his badge. "What?"

"Sir," said some crewman, "we've got a torpedo lodged in a starboard tube. It's keeping the port from closing and we can't fire in atmo, so we need to pull out or evacuate the—"

"Then evac."

"But sir, if the torpedo over—!"

He clicked off his badge, readjusted his smile. "Now, where were we?"

❧

Webb and Frankie waded through a corridor choked with red shirts to slip into their quad. Judging by the sounds coming from behind her bunk panel, Chelse and her husband were taking advantage of the shift change. And judging by the sudden silence, they hadn't been expecting company.

"Don't mind us." Webb pulled a couple fine-geared instruments from her locker. "Won't be more than a sec. Though I suspect you're used to hearing that, Chelse."

"Choke on a spanner, techie." The sound of bunking resumed. Ah, the things you could get used to living on top of each other.

Webb sat on her bunk, pulled out her device from Engineering. A half-dozen blips registered on its screen. "Huh. Seems to be working now."

Frankie seated herself in the full lotus and closed her eyes "Any guess why it didn't pick him up?"

"They may have changed frequencies. Or just stopped talking. I can only pick them up when they're interfacing."

Frankie slowed her breathing. "Any more of that pizza in your locker?"

Webb narrowed her eyes. "Aren't you supposed to not want anything?"

"As Siddhartha himself once sagely observed, 'pizza is pizza.' So how about it?"

"Like I'm gonna keep contraband in my locker when we quad with a cop."

"I'm right here, you know," said Chelse. "I *can* hear you."

"And we could hear you," said Webb. "Both of you."

"From the hall," added Frankie.

Chelse's bunk fell quiet. "Rob's not here."

"Oh?" Webb picked up half a uniform. "Then whose pants are these?"

"Seven's," said Chelse.

"Mine," admitted Rob.

Chelse sighed. "God damn it, Robbie."

"There's such balance in nature," said Webb. "You let me do my side projects, I keep quiet about all the times you break visitation."

"Whatever," said Chelse. "Don't touch my guns."

Webb saluted her bunk, went back to fiddling with her cogfinder. "If I could figure out how track them when they're quiet, then I'd have something."

"Something worth fabbing?" Frankie mused.

"Are you trying to get me brigged?" Webb tossed the device in her bunk, climbed up to flop on the mattress, and rubbed the double shift off her face.

The quad fell quiet. Apart from the bunking.

"What do you think the chances are the captain's exploring a new frontier right now?" Frankie asked.

"Even odds."

"It seems like it should be impossible, doesn't it? All the aliens we've met looking pretty much like us? Just with slightly different foreheads."

"You're meditating rather loudly today."

"I mean what are the chances that *every* intelligent starfaring people we'd encounter would be... how to put it..."

Webb eyed Chelse's panel. "Bunkable?"

"Right? You'd think the infinite vastness of space would have produced more than one basic body type."

"Never gave it much thought, really."

"Ideal form theory," said Rob. "Advanced evolutionary convergence. Like how seals and sea lions have the same basic body shape but evolved from completely different ancestors? Every environment has a form that's ideal for it, right? And steers evolution in that direction. For space, that form appears to be bipedal humanoid toolmaker."

"Honey?" said Chelse. "Shut up."

"Sorry. It's kind of a hobby. The probability of it is like astronomically against. But that's just one theory!"

"Rob," said Webb. "Shut up."

"One of the more compelling counterarguments is that there are *way* more forms out there—incalculably more—but we've only seen aliens who look like us because, psychologically, they're easier for us to accept, and they've been sent here to help ease us into—"

Frankie tapped her comm badge. "Fuller to Alameda."

Rob shut up. Webb heard his badge click. "Uh… yes?"

"I think your wife was looking for you."

A thump against the panel. The sound of a struggle. Rob squealed indignantly.

"That was mean," Webb told Frankie.

"Can't hear you," said Frankie. "Inner peace. *Om.*"

"*Chelse.*" Rob's voice was strained. "What are you…?"

"Nurse, you're out of uniform. That's a Class Two violation."

"I can't move."

"I'm gonna need you to come with me."

"Oh." Rob lowered his voice, added a dash of syrup. "What are you gonna… *do* to me, officer?"

"I think I'm gonna have to… take you *in.*"

"Oh my *God.*" Webb glared at Frankie. "Look what you've done."

A half-smile. "*Om.*"

Webb bounced her cogfinder off the panel. "Keep your stupid sex games to yourself!"

"Get promoted, you won't have to hear them," said Chelse.

"That's a burn," said Frankie. "Also: *om.*"

An explosion rocked the ship, sending Rob and Chelse tumbling out of her bunk. Klaxons screamed in the sudden red light.

"Red alert," the *Independence* said without passion. "All crew to crisis stations."

Rob held up his wrists. "Untie me first?"

The captain strode onto the bridge. "Situation report."

"Explosion in the starboard torpedo bay," said Security Chief Sivos. "Severe structural damage. We're shedding heat tiles left and right."

The ambassador's eyes were locked on the ribbons of fire racing over the bridge. Seagrave grimaced. This was killing the mood. "Emergency shields."

"Up but ineffective."

"The damage exceeds their dimensions," Dewey called from the engineering station. "They're stretched too far. We need to get back to orbit or we lose the whole battery."

Reddening, the captain gritted his teeth. Heads would roll for this. He smiled an apology to the ambassador. "Take us out of atmo. And find out who's responsible."

"Aye, sir," said the helm.

The ship turned for the cold darkness of space. Then a thump, a shudder like the cracking of a suspension bridge, and the lights went out.

"Shit," said the helm.

"Warning. Main power offline," said the ship.

Space dropped from view. In its place swirled crackling terraforming storms. The ship dipped towards the atmosphere at a dangerous angle.

"Uncontrolled descent," reported the ship. "Critical failure in ninety seconds."

"Barbara, get me power!" he shouted at the chief.

Dewey mashed her comm badge. "Talk to me, Webb."

To prevent damage to the stardrive, all consoles in Engineering were rigged to blow away from the drive core. Which they tended to do with alarming frequency. And little provocation. When the ship was in actual danger, they popped off like fireworks.

A pair of red shirts with extinguisher packs hosed down the sparking slag of Webb's console. "Drive core's offline," she commed the chief. "We're on emergency power."

"I can see that. What's with the main?"

"Initial explosion took out a conduit. Main went off like it's supposed to, but the breakers blew on restart."

"Reboot shouldn't have fried the breakers."

"Well, no, but the sequence wasn't specced for atmo during an electrical storm." Webb yanked the radiation shield off a backup console. "The hell are we doing in the stratosphere?"

"Focus, Webb."

"Yeah." Webb punched a few buttons. The readings made her flinch. "Lerd. Seven, can you confirm what I'm seeing?"

"Hang on, my console melted." Yolanda Seven peeled a panel off the wall behind her burning station. Behind it buzzed a swarm of angry lights. She whistled. "Yep, that's a lerd."

"Barbara, where is my power?"

"It's here, Captain," said Webb. "We just can't get it to you. Conduits from Engineering are burnt out."

"How many?" asked the chief.

"How many?" echoed Webb.

"One of them?" Seven picked her way over and through the wreckage, scanning. "All of them? Hard to tell with no console."

"*Focus!* Options?"

"Get lucky and repair the right conduit," said Webb. "Or..."

The ship lurched. Red shirts hit the floor like bowling pins.

"Bunk this." Webb tapped her badge. "Webber to Seagrave. Captain, recommend we abandon ship."

"Denied with prejudice."

"Forget the conduits." The chief's voice was tinny—the storms were interfering with the comms. "Patch power directly into propulsion from the main vein."

Yolanda Seven—the senior electrical technician—went pale as chalk.

Webb lowered her voice. "Chief. Whoever does that's getting fried."

"Only if you send in a body, lead head. Jesus fuck."

Webb snapped her fingers, checked the cogfinder hanging from her belt. Her grin split her face. "Captain, there's a cog right outside Engineering! Don't ask how I know. Permission to send him in for repairs."

"*Denied.* Cogs are too sensitive."

"He means expensive," said Seven.

"But, Captain—"

"Warning," said the ship. "Critical failure in thirty seconds."

"Captain." Webb didn't recognize the voice that cut in, but he sounded young and sure of himself. Clearly an officer. "A direct patch from the main power vein to propulsion would give us the power to clear atmo. We could complete repairs in orbit."

"Tremendous," said the captain. "Proceed."

Seven's eyes went wide as saucers.

They heard the chief's badge engage. "Chevalier." She sounded defeated. "Grab a cutter and some tri-wire."

"Oh God," said Seven.

"Make the patch."

Seven whimpered.

Webb hit her badge. "Webber to Fuller."

"I'm here," said Frankie.

"Get me a pri one lock on Seven's badge. You may have to teep her out of a conduit."

"Copy." Some clicking. "Lock set."

Yolanda Seven numbly looped a length of tri-wire around her torso. Webb took her by the shoulders. "You can do this."

Her gaze went distant. "I was gonna call my mom tonight."

"*Look* at me. This is routine. You've got this."

"We had some good times, didn't we?" Her eyes swam. "I almost made the full six."

"Knock that shit off. Frankie's got you. You'll be *fine*." Webb forced a smile. "Now go save the ship."

With a nod and a sigh, Yolanda Seven wriggled into a crawlspace. Webb's heart tried to claw its way out of her chest to follow.

Terraforming storms bathed the bridge in hot electric light. Not even the advanced stabilizers could keep the section from shaking. Officers exchanged worried glances and looked to their captain for deliverance.

Seagrave glanced to the lantern-jawed officer whose suggestion might just save his ship. "Better hope you're right, Lieutenant."

He'd also better hope this didn't damage his chances with the ambassador. She'd braced herself on his command chair and was blinking every eyelid she had, her frill of feathers at full peacock.

Good. The threat of imminent death was a powerful aphrodisiac.

"I'm there," a technician said over the comms. "Patching in now."

"Critical failure in fifteen seconds," said the ship.

The ship shuddered. So did the captain's gut—both glasses of bubbly had been a mistake. "You have ten seconds, technician."

"More than I need." She didn't sound convinced. A whir and a puncturing clamp. "Patch complete."

Dewey relaxed her death grip on the rail. "Get out of there, girl."

"Critical failure in ten seconds."

"Backing out now."

Explosive lightning pulled the captain's eyes to the storm. Those cells were close. Too close. His stomach lurched.

"Nine."

"Captain." The lieutenant indicated the storm with his eyes.

The captain's stomach did a somersault. He clamped a hand to his gut.

"Eight."

Screw this—no way he was puking in front of his conquest. The captain nodded at the lieutenant.

Dewey saw it. She straightened in alarm. *"Captain?"*

"Almost there," said Seven.

The captain set his jaw. "Energize."

🪐

The core lit up like a magnesium flare, sending trillions of zettajoules of stellar power coursing through the ship—and a plume of raw plasma sparking out of the crawlspace.

Webb's breath deserted her. It took two tries to hit her badge hard enough to engage. "Frankie?" Her mouth had gone dry. "Tell me you got her."

The line was quiet. Frankie choked out a sob.

Webb's heart fell. "No."

"The storm... it broke the lock." Frankie was barely audible. "Ten seconds. He *gave* her ten seconds."

Webb covered her face. Sank to the floor. Pressed her hands over her ears to drown out the cheering over the comms.

🪐

On the bridge, officers whooped and hollered as the ship pulled safely back into orbit. Hand raised, the captain acknowledged the praise. He pointed to the young lieutenant—Blackwell, that was his name. He'd remember him.

Seagave motioned for silence. He turned to the ambassador. *"There. Human spirit, on full display. Crisis leading to innovation leading to success. You just saw who we are."*

"Indeed I did." She blinked both sets of eyelids.

The captain seized her, dipped her, and kissed her right there on the bridge. The officers cheered anew.

Caught off guard by the mating display, and not wishing to appear rude, the ambassador deposited a clutch of eggs in the captain's stomach.

Chapter 2
Sic Semper Plebibus

Command spaced an empty casket. They'd have had a better time justifying that to the crew had Seven's remains been truly irretrievable. If the body had caramelized to the conduit and couldn't be removed without damaging the ship, well, sometimes that happened.

But Command opted not to retrieve the body because it would have put them behind schedule. They'd have had to shut down the stardrive to allow it to cool enough to handle her remains. The captain agonized over the decision—publicly, it was required viewing on the monitors—before ultimately declaring that neither time nor tide waited for any man and ordered them forward towards their next destination. Which just so happened to be Amornomax, the pleasure world where half the officer corps were in danger of losing non-refundable reservations.

So they draped a flag over an empty box, the cost of both deducted from Seven's final payout to her family, and shot her off into space. Caskets were normally fired out of a torpedo tube with the crew gathered in the lounge to watch it pass. But with the starboard torpedo bay shredded, they'd have had to take their other main battery offline—a risk Sivos, their unsmiling security chief, was not about to approve. So the cargo bay it was.

The captain hadn't attended. Neither had any of the officers. The regular no-shows, that is; Winesborough, the Science Officer, was there, though he never looked up from his data pad. And Sivos was present, as always. He had to be anywhere that many red shirts were gathered.

And a lot of red shirts there were. Far more than could have packed into the lounge. The unassigned crew were housed there in the cargo bay, in rows of tents that they had to rent at a cost almost as great as a quad berth.

Most of them hadn't known Seven. For the unassigned, the only way into a quad was when someone got brigged or died. They knew the risks, and the morbid turnover rate. Still they volunteered in swarms—service was the only way off the toxic sauna that used to be the Earth. They volunteered, racked up massive debts in training, and arrived in the cargo bays of the fleet in droves.

And that's where they stayed: an unassigned, highly trained, highly indebted labor pool sitting in tents in the cargo bay, subsisting on meal pellets and accruing more debt while waiting for an opportunity to start working, knowing full well that any such opportunity came over the steaming corpse of someone just like them. And yet, fabbing anything to ease the tension or pass the time—especially food—would get you brigged faster than if you'd suggested unionizing.

The funeral's first speaker had been an Armstrong. He spent his time praising the captain, marveling over how Seagrave's quick thinking and pragmatism had saved the day, yet again. He only brought up Seven to say how happy—nay, how *proud*—she must have been to give her life for the ship. That's what they'd all signed up for, he reminded them.

The captain's hologram appeared at the podium to deliver one of his pregen homilies. The red shirts muttered the words of his speech along with his recording: blah blah duty, blah blah character, now is not the time to politicize this tragedy but to come together as a ship.

"And remember," the captain and his disposable crew said together, "true heroes are those who give their lives to something greater than themselves."

His image turned the wrong way—had the funeral been in the lounge, he'd have been looking out over the torpedo battery—and addressed the wall. "As we commit the earthly remains of our beloved crewmate—"

His image froze.

"Senior Technician Mary Chevalier," said the ship.

"—to the vast depths of space," resumed the captain. "Grant—"

"Her."

"—inner peace and tranquility until that day when—"

"Senior Technician Mary Chevalier."

"And all who believe in You will be raised to the glory of new life promised in the waters of baptism. We ask this through the mercy of Jesus Christ, our Lord. Amen."

"Amen," said the cogs flanking the hologram.

The captain flickered and vanished, leaving the crew to meander back to their stations.

Webb hadn't spoken to anyone after the ceremony, or back at the quad. It was quiet there now, and seeing it empty, she was struck by how truly tiny it was. By how uncomfortable its bunks were—they capped the women's beds at 1.6 meters to save space; Webb had to contort herself to fit and still wound up cracking her head a couple times a night.

By how the shower unit at the back timed your water consumption and charged you every minute you went over. If you fell behind your payments, it would just shut the water off.

By how they'd removed the foodports from the quads when the crew had started hacking them to fab items not on the menu. Now they had to retrieve their food from the mess where your transactions could be properly monitored.

By how this little tin box had been her home for over a decade, and how a hundred women in the cargo bay were waiting for her to die.

The Naked Eye Observation Stations resembled the belly gunner turrets on those ancient warplanes. The ship didn't need them and the crew didn't staff them, but as much as Engineering wanted to shave them off and seal the hull, they were forbidden from touching them. They were a mandated throwback to the earliest days of starfaring, when a moth's fart could knock out the sensors and you had to rely on crew with telescopes floating in zero gravity to see what was out there.

The fleet's current sensors could brush the edge of a galaxy and were more reliable than the sun. But the NEOS remained, obsolete as the internal combustion engine. The contractors who built them in the gerrymandered districts back home had their reps howl at the brass every time they tried phasing them out. As a result, every vessel leaving the Coalition shipyards looked like it had a bad case of boils.

If you needed a quiet place to disappear to, though, you could hardly do better than a NEOS. They offered spectacular panoramic views. Whenever the ship settled in orbit, the planetside stations became popular retreats. And makeout spots. They were a bit like parks that way.

But when the ship was off in the vast, as the *Independence* was now, its NEOS network lay empty. It was one thing to look down on a world from the vantage point of a god. Quite another to stare off into infinity dwelling upon your own insignificance and how your friend is dead.

Webb sat there in the dark, clutching a frozen pizza, blaring power metal at ear-bleeding volume. She was probably doing irreparable damage to her ears, but what the hell. The Coalition would give her new ones. At a crippling interest rate, sure, but it's not like she was ever getting out of debt anyway.

She resisted the urge to slap herself. What the hell was she doing thinking about finances when another quadmate was gone? No, not gone—baked into the circuitry because the officers couldn't be bothered to delay their boner sessions. Perspective, woman.

A tap on her shoulder. She turned to see Frankie shouting her name.

Webb turned the music down. "Sorry. Helps me think. Also drowns out the comm badge ads." Those played at regular intervals when you weren't on duty. And sometimes when you were.

Frankie settled into the seat beside her. "I don't know how you can concentrate with that."

"It's not so much about concentration as annihilating thought."

"Does it work?"

"I hardly hear it anymore, but yeah. When I need to not be in my head, I put on the classics."

"I don't know that I would consider Powerwolf the classics."

"That's Nightwish. Philistine."

Frankie eyed the pizza. "Is this where you keep them?"

"In the lining." Webb rapped on the rim of the NEOS's tiny airlock. "Vacuum of space makes a pretty good freezer." She could hardly feel her hands.

Frankie noticed. "Gloves, maybe?"

"Thought some real food would help. The crew, you know? Seven was popular." She drummed numbed fingers on frozen cheese. "Lost my appetite, though. Indie, that's enough. Cut the music."

"You will be charged for the full hour," said the ship.

"Fine."

Silence fell. The quadmates stared out into the universe.

Years ago, back when Webb was less desensitized to the fatalities, this was about the time Frankie would offer to sit with her, to meditate, discuss, listen if she needed to rant, rave, whatever. It's how they'd met, in the support group Frankie ran where Webb had been sentenced after the shuttle incident. The inner peace Frankie promised never materialized. A friendship had, along with a respect for boundaries staked out around old wounds, the caution tape around pain. So Frankie waited.

Webb felt tears rise up, briny and sour, to catch in her eyes. That's as far as she could allow them—any farther and the dam would burst, and there was no safe place for that. Break down in the wrong spot and a cog would drag you to the infirmary, where they'd pump you full of serum and pills until those unproductive thoughts dissolved along with your personality and libido.

The libido going wouldn't be so bad, though. It's not like she was using hers. She chuckled. And it *would* be nice to see the doctor again…

"I don't want a ship anymore." Webb waited for a reply, cued up counterarguments for what she expected Frankie to say. Probably some variation of "What's changed?" or a reminder of how she always says that.

Frankie just nodded. "Okay."

"I'm serious. It's different this time."

Frankie didn't nod, didn't disagree. She just waited. And watched. The quiet little bitch.

"I'm not kidding," said Webb. "I'm done this time. For real. I'm leaving all this bullshit behind and damn it why won't you contradict me?"

"It makes sense," said Frankie. "Why would you still want your own ship?"

"I don't!"

"I get it."

"Who would, though? Huh? Who'd want to run a ship for an organization that does nothing but stake mineral claims and terraform rocks to sell to settlers?"

Frankie didn't reply.

"But that's how they pay for space travel," Webb said for her. "I know that. Like that's the greatest calling of humankind, finding more shit to sell to each other. It's not bad enough we used up our own planet, we've gotta strip bare everything else we find? Uninhabited worlds, sure, but… *fuck!*" She stared out the transparent triluminium dome. "We know they're out there! The Sorl, the Kixlpik, the Ord. We are not alone. The ultimate question, the one that maddened us for centuries, answered, and on a scale no one could have guessed, and somehow joining that great society has *not* become our main pursuit? What is *wrong* with us?"

Frankie looked amused now. Webb considered slapping her. Not hard, just enough to knock some words loose.

No time for that. She was on a roll. "We trade with them, we host their ambassadors... hell, people get xenoglyph tattoos they think are espousing some profound alien truth but probably just mean soup. You know, I've heard you can get work out there. As a contract freighter, shuttle pilot... some xenos are willing to hire humans. They find us novel. Anyway, there's just... *so* much more out there we don't even *know* we don't know, just worlds of cultures and shit we're not exploring because it's not *profitable,* and... I just... Christ, what a waste. We finally got off the planet but we brought our worst shit with us."

Webb's comm badge chimed.

"Your next lung payment is due," said the ship. "But now is the perfect time to refinance! With offers starting at the low, low interest rate of—"

Webb slapped it off. Sighed. Stared off into the infinity at her fingertips. "I want my own ship."

"There you are," said Frankie.

"Never gonna happen, though."

"You can't know that."

"Shut up, Frank."

"I thought you wanted me to talk. The future hasn't been written, and the past is gone, but most people still figure out a way live in one of the two. You are who you are *now*, at this moment, unbound either by the setbacks of your past or your expectations of what's to come, and *that* person has achievable goals. And a performance review tonight."

Webb blinked. "Lerd. Totally slipped my mind."

"Dewey thought it might have. She asked me to remind you. While we're on the subject of reviews..."

Webb shifted in her seat. "I'm not ready for the hearing. Same God damn result, just you watch."

"Most likely."

25

"They won't find cause for trial."

"Probably not."

"So why even do the dance?"

"You're asking like I have the answer."

Webb reconsidered slapping her. "What would you do? And don't say meditate."

"I won't, then."

"It just never took for me, you know? I can't just *be*. I figure things best out by doing them."

"While doing them, often. You want my advice? There's gotta be a better way of getting out of your head than deafening yourself. Hit the gym. Go to the Arcade. Do what Chelse and Rob do whenever they get a free minute."

Webb snorted. "That's a two-person gig. If you haven't noticed, I'm a body short."

"About that..." Frankie dug a data stick out of her pocket. "Here. Seven used to fire this up when she needed some time out."

Webb raised an eyebrow. "Is this an Arcade scenario?"

"One of her romance novels."

"Come on, Frank. Those are banned."

"And with good cause. They're dumb, certainly, but enjoyable under the right circumstances."

"And tacky as hell."

"You can customize your partner," said Frankie. "They've got a whole bank of images if you want to reskin the sprite. Maybe you could model him after a certain doctor?"

Webb flushed. "I cannot believe you're advocating for this."

"Hey, I practice non-attachment, and this is strings-free. It's also safe—zero chance of disease or pregnancy. And the best part? If you tell him to stop talking, he actually shuts up."

Webb eyed her flatly. "You sound like you're speaking from experience?"

"Or so I've heard." Frankie slipped it into Webb's pocket.

The door to the corridor rolled back. A soldier with their visor down poked their head in. Webb didn't know which to hide first: the pizza or the data stick. She settled on the stick.

Chelse lifted her visor. "Hey." She checked the corridor. "I reported my comm not working so I've got maybe five minutes." She tossed a red-wrapped parcel to Frankie. "I didn't see that contraband."

Webb stashed the pizza away as Chelse clambered between them. The NEOS was a cozy fit for two; with three, and one of those in blast armor, they were squeezed like too many books on a shelf.

Chelse pulled off her helmet, dumped some data sticks into Webb's hand.

"Seven's?"

Chelse nodded. "She wanted them spaced."

"Did you already…?"

Another nod. "Streamed her data to her mom. Security frequency. They don't check those for bereavement violations." Soldiery had its privileges.

Frankie unwrapped the parcel. Inside were the contents of Seven's locker—books, pictures, assorted ephemera—all tied together in her spare uniform. Coalition policy was to ship the effects of dead crew back to their families at enormous cost. So enormous that most crew hoped their quadmates would space their belongings to spare their families the hit.

Chelse held up a dense ball with a heavy seam down the center. "The hell is this?"

"Cricket ball," said Webb. "We played half an inning the last time the Arcade had a sale. She scored so many runs I never even got to bat."

The quaddies retied Seven's uniform around her belongings, slipped it into the airlock, and waited for the latch to read secure.

"Mary Chevalier," said Webb. "We commit your remains to the stars." She opened the lock.

The package drifted out and unfurled, spilling Seven's personality out into the tides of the cosmos. Along with a shimmering frozen disk.

Chelse pointed at it. "Wasn't that your pizza?"

Webb blinked. Slumped. "God damn it."

$\mathcal{O}$

Any officer-involved crew death automatically triggered a review hearing. On average, that meant one or two a week.

For a junior officer, their immediate supervisor was supposed to oversee the proceedings. For a senior officer, such as Lieutenant Blackwell, the captain himself would preside.

Webb took her seat in the crew gallery. Aside from the men in violet below, the officer section was empty. Winesborough was there, his face still anchored to his data pad. Webb wondered if he knew the funeral was over. She wouldn't have been surprised if a cog had carried him here.

Sivos was also there, his gaze already distant. It was his duty to escort any officers found liable to the brig to await trial. He'd never had to break out the cuffs. And based on his body language, he didn't expect to today.

Webb's section—the upper deck reserved for the enlisted crew—was packed tighter than a sardine tin. Her contingent was supposedly composed of the finest members of the crew, individuals renowned for their merit and civic virtue. All of them, to a man—and they were all men—had been hand-picked by their commanding officers. On a totally unrelated note, no officer had ever been found liable for the death of a crewman—a fact the officer corp trumpeted as part of its safety record.

The crew reps were all Armstrongs: a sub-faction of red shirts who revered the officers, informed on the crew, and who were usually left in charge. Narcs, all of them. The rest of the crew called them officers in red, something the Armstrongs didn't take as a slight. Why would they? They all expected to be officers themselves some day—despite promotions out of the enlisted ranks being vanishingly rare—and defended the officers like they were protecting an investment.

The Armstrongs were easy to identify, even without the undeserved swagger. They all wore those stupid secondary badges—technically a uniform violation—of an inverted drop of blood over the moon: a reminder of all the good men who died taming space. *Caelum Nostrum,* their badges proclaimed. *Space is Ours.*

A much bolder motto than the one on the red shirts' badges, *Alius Ascendet—Another Shall Rise.* Usually from the cargo bay.

The Armstrongs got the easiest shifts and completed their advancement requirements at duty stations rather than on away missions, which meant they were rarely in harm's way. Which meant they never died, which meant there was almost zero turnover in crew representation. The Armstrongs made up maybe ten percent of the crew, but over ninety percent of the panel. Webb—the panel's only crew-elected representative, and the only one without a blood drop badge—represented five percent of the vote.

The cog by the stand broke stasis to tap its comm badge. "All rise."

Everyone except Winesborough stood.

"The Incident Review Panel of the starship *Independence* is now in session," it intoned. "Captain William Seagrave presiding. Be seated."

Everyone sat. Except for Sivos, who resumed his bored pacing.

The captain's chair was empty, Webb noticed. She tapped her badge.

The cog turned towards the balcony. "Technician?"

"Will the captain be attending?"

"He's not feeling well," Blackwell told the cog. "He sends his regards."

"In light of the captain's absence," said the cog, "we shall defer to the highest present authority: the *Independence* herself." The cog's head shuddered and dropped only to rise again just as quickly.

"Calling the inquiry into the incident involving crew person 10507," the cog said in the ship's voice. "The Justice Chair will initiate the proceedings."

An Armstrong at the rail smoothed both his hair and uniform as he stood. "Jack Jacobs, if it pleases the court. Hey, L.C. Dig the new pips." He made snap guns at Blackwell.

Blackwell nodded back.

"Alright!" Jacobs turned to the crew contingent. "Let's see if we can't wrap this up early and get out of here. I've got a hot date or three waiting in the Arcade."

The Armstrongs chuckled.

"Okay, somber face. Look, as with any crew fatality, we are shocked and saddened by this senseless tragedy. Our hearts and prayers go out to the family of the deceased and her mates at her duty station. It's easy to savor your anger and hunt for someone to blame in these circumstances, but let's not lose sight of the fact that we are alive right now because of the captain, and because Lieutenant Commander Blackwell's quick thinking gave him the insight he needed to save the ship."

Nods and grunts from the Armstrongs. Webb raised her hand.

Jacobs' smile drooped. "Yes?"

"Did I hear that right? Lieutenant Commander?"

"I was promoted." Blackwell sat up straighter. "For meritorious conduct."

"In saving the ship," added Jacobs.

Webb sucked her teeth. "I love a fair trial."

"So!" Jacobs clapped his hands. "Unless there's any compelling reason to keep us here, the crew panel finds no cause to indict. Move to absolve. Officers?"

Winesborough raised his thumb but not his eyes. Sivos made a face but didn't speak.

"Officers approve. Crew?"

A chorus of ayes as the Armstrongs stood.

"All opposed?"

"Nay."

A battalion of too-similar faces turned to glare at Webb. Jacobs shook his head. "I guess we're doing this. Fun."

"Are we going to have any testimony?" asked Webb.

"The committee's spoken," said Jacobs. "It's unanimous."

"Not quite."

Sighs and hisses from the Armstrongs. The half that were already out of their seats plopped back down.

Jacobs' smile was strained. "The captain would prefer a unanimous decision. He wouldn't want the Lieutenant Commander's promotion tarnished because the crew rep is holding a grudge. We know you and the deceased were close."

"Quaddies," said an Armstrong.

"If that's true, you should recuse yourself," said Blackwell.

Webb looked around Jacobs to the cog. "May I address the defendant?"

"There is no defendant," the ship said through the cog. "Lieutenant Commander Blackwell is not on trial."

"The subject, then." She picked her way to the front of the gallery and stared at Jacobs until he moved. "Lieutenant Commander. Why were we in the atmosphere?"

Blackwell regarded her with professional disinterest. "That's classified."

"That may be so, but planned maneuvers typically aren't. The crew needs time to prepare, and according to the logs, skimming atmo wasn't on our schedule. Unless it's official policy now to make environmental maneuvers without alerting the crew?"

"I've answered the question," said Blackwell.

"Isn't it true that only the captain could have ordered us into—"

"I'm sorry," interrupted Jacobs, who clearly wasn't, "but where exactly is this going?"

"Please keep your inquiries relevant the incident involving service member 10507," said the ship.

"She has a name," said Webb, "and Chevalier's death was the direct result of a having to manually patch a vein after the ship lost power, which itself was a direct result of an unscheduled, unprepared dip into atmo. One the captain ordered without properly alerting the—"

"Excuse me—" Blackwell's face tightened. "—are you *blaming* the captain?"

"The captain is not on trial," said the ship.

"No," Blackwell shushed the cog. "No, I want to hear this. *Clearly,* you have some evidence or you'd never level such an accusation."

Webb could feel Jacobs' stare burning into her back. "The loss of power was caused by a catastrophic failure after an explosion in the starboard torpedo bay."

Jacobs threw up his hands. "Well, there we go. If it's anyone's fault, it's the torpedo crew's. Why are we even talking about this?"

"A good question, and one I'm not qualified to answer." She turned to the cog. "Indie, I would like to call Torpedo Technicians Sandoval and Waretini to testify."

"Denied."

Webb blinked. Her mouth felt dry. "Whatever for?"

"They are in the brig."

"Without trial?"

"They were tried and found guilty," said Indie. "I presided."

"What exactly were the charges?"

"That is classified."

Jacobs leaned into Webb's field of view. "Yeah, so the brigged don't get to testify against law-abiding members of the crew? Because of how they're criminals? Where exactly were you going with this?"

She gripped the rail to avoid punching him. "It isn't obvious? Negligence."

The Armstrongs snorted and started talking among themselves. One mimed jawing with his hands at Webb.

"Shut *up,*" Sivos bellowed over the comms. "This is a serious accusation."

"The captain is not on trial," spat Blackwell. "He kept the loss of life to a minimum. To *one*."

"You could have sent in a cog," said Webb. "The surge wouldn't have killed it."

"That's true," Winesborough said without looking up. "Well. Depending on the voltage."

"You could have *repaired* it. Or *replaced* it! But no, you sent in a body and now Chevalier's gone forever."

"Replaced it?" Jacobs smirk could have split his face. His eyes said *I've got you*. "And *how*, pray tell, would we have replaced it? Hm? How *exactly*? Were you going to say fabbing? You were, weren't you."

Armstrongs were all looking her way. Same with the officers. Even Winesborough.

Bunk it. She had the floor and a platform any crew member could watch. "In times of crisis, the Coalition allows emergency fabrication of critical equipment *so long as* the costs are covered, at interest, once the crisis has passed." The jeering was so loud she couldn't hear herself finish.

"Sure," said Jacobs, "and let's just torpedo the whole economy while we're at it."

Webb rolled her eyes. "Are you that bunking dense?"

"Language," warned Blackwell.

"We have the technology to turn *energy* into *matter*," said Webb. "We have a stardrive that provides nigh infinite energy. So *why* exactly is fabrication illegal if it could save crew lives?"

"I don't know," said Jacobs, "Jobs, maybe? You've heard of those?"

"Which we don't *need*. When we can create *matter*. At *will*."

Blackwell chuckled like an amused professor. "As much as I'd enjoy debating basic economic theory with a technician, is this in any way related to your questions about the atmosphere or torpedo bay? Or are you just taking a moment to shill for a thoroughly discredited agenda?"

The Armstrongs whooped and applauded.

Webb felt the tears rising again, briny and hot. No—not happening here. She narrowed her eyes. "Chevalier is dead because the captain damaged the ship and refused to use a replaceable machine to fix the problem. And now my friend is dead."

"Just vote," said Jacobs.

"You're going to vote against me, aren't you?" A muscle in Blackwell's jaw twitched. "For something I had nothing to do with."

"Damage to the ship and equipment comes out of the officers' lay of profits," said Webb. "You'd rather spend our lives than risk your income. I've said what I came to say. I abstain."

"Wow, what a protest," said Jacobs. "Vote carries with one abstention. Absolved?"

"Absolved," said the ship. "You are free to go, Lieutenant Commander."

"Not just yet," said Blackwell. "I want that technician censured for verbal abuse."

Webb couldn't even summon the energy to scoff. "Are you even serious?"

Lifeless white eyes swung her way. "Senior Technician Webber, you are hereby under censure. Your sentence is sixty hours extra duty."

"Lerd."

"And another twenty for vulgarity," said Blackwell.

Webb dropped into a seat. Out of the corner of her eye, she saw Jacobs whispering into his Armstrong pin.

Blackwell smiled. "I like that." He rose, tugged his uniform taut. "Technician, seeing as how your grandstanding cost your peers their reservations at the Arcade, I think it's only fair you clean it out when they're done."

34

The advent of nearly limitless power, coupled with the technology to convert energy into matter, had mutated entertainment into an unrecognizable new experience.

The ship's various Arcades tapped the stardrive to create immersive fantasy worlds indistinguishable from reality. The Arcade could put you anywhere, at any era, in any situation, with anyone. If you could imagine it, the Arcade could bring a nearly perfect approximation of it to life: a dream, any dream, come true.

But unlike a dream, you could *touch* it. Images in a scenario stayed intangible until they came into contact with a guest, at which point angled force fields sprung up to create resistance and texture and weight—and for the guests, as long as contact was maintained, the grass running through their fingers was as real as the hands touching them. Customizable reality, indistinguishable from the real thing.

It was immediately co-opted for porn.

The downside of the Arcade was the downside of any fantasy: when it was time to wake up, the dreamworld faded. But anything organic left behind by the guests remained. Sometimes in glazed layers.

The Arcade had an auto-sanitizer, but it had been permanently disabled. Not because anything was wrong with it. The auto-scrub got the axe because one of the most disheartening forms of punishment on the ship was cleaning up after someone else's humpfest.

Webb scrubbed the floor of the Arcade with pissed off determination. And a toothbrush.

She shouldn't have gone off during the hearing. Like she hadn't known what the result would have been. Bastard Armstrongs didn't even consider themselves red shirts. Just temporarily embarrassed officers.

She hadn't done herself any favors this close to her own performance review. Accusing the captain of negligence would come back to bite her.

Clean up didn't take that long—this wasn't her first trip to the spunkbox—but she couldn't leave. They'd locked her inside until her off-duty hours were over, and with the Arcade shut down for punitive measures, she couldn't boot up anything better. When it wasn't spinning a fantasy, the Arcade was downright ominous, all harsh angles and deep shadows.

Webb needed a shower. She wouldn't have a chance for one until after her performance review. She considered hacking the Arcade to run a scenario, any scenario, so long as it had a decent bathroom. She couldn't think of one that did.

She dug Seven's data stick out of her pocket. Arcade porn had never been Webb's thing—she'd never even been curious—but Frankie had called it a romance novel. And, most third party scenarios were designed to get around the Arcade's restrictions. Maybe there was a shower in the setting.

The Arcade was locked offline for the duration of Webb's punishment, but you don't get to Senior Technician without a few workarounds in your pocket. She set the Arcade on a phantom diagnostic cycle, made sure the door was locked, loaded the scenario in the main holo-emitter, and double checked that the door was locked.

"Impressario," she told the room. "Load the program on the data stick."

Indie chimed a warning. "Unsanctioned scenario detected."

"Override," said Webb. "Authorization code Dewey, Barbara, KSD-9118."

The Arcade's brutalist contours dissolved into pastoral hills. Hedgerows adorned with roses sprung up, conveniently arranged to keep her in the center of the room. She followed the hedges' vanishing lines towards an old European manor with ivy climbing a castle-like tower.

The place looked cozy and inviting. It also didn't look like it had indoor plumbing. No shower for her.

She was about to pull the plug when she heard a whinny, turned, and spotted a manly paragon riding her way. He was gorgeous, market testedly so, his face carved from a block of solid handsome. He reined his horse to a stop beside her, his open shirt rippling in the wind. He smelled of leather and woodsmoke and autumn apples. The Arcade's pheromone subroutines must be working overtime. With a sigh, he turned piercing blue eyes her way.

Webb felt a flutter. Whoever programmed this had read a few of these novels.

"Forgive me," he rumbled in a pleasant baritone, "but when my game warden reported a trespasser, I never expected to find one so lovely. What business have you here?"

"Hey." Webb gave him a tiny wave. "I don't suppose you've got a shower in that pile of rocks back there?"

He threw is head back and laughed, his perfect hair streaming in the wind. "So forward! I must inquire: what family would raise a daughter to be so bold in the presence of her lord?"

"Um..."

"No, don't tell me. I'm keen to guess."

"Look, is this part skippable? I'm really only interested in the shower."

"Surely you know me, the widowed lord of this manor." He gazed off towards the pain in his backstory. "How lonely my home has been since fate took her away from me. *Please!*" He thrust out his arm. "Do not bring her up again."

"I didn't say anything."

"I shall speak of it no more."

"Okay."

"Careful!" He bellowed. "You'll startle him!"

Webb blinked. "Who?"

The nobleman didn't move.

Webb pointed toward the horse. "Did you mean the—"

The moment she moved, the horse performed a completely scripted action, rearing and stamping down in a convenient puddle. Mud spattered Webb's dress. Webb also noted she was wearing a dress.

The nobleman chided his horse. "Forgive me, dear lady! Casanova only rears when he fears I am in danger of being hurt. Clearly, he is mistaken. For what pain could you inflict upon me greater that what I have already suffered?" His gaze went distant again. A single tear welled in his eye. "I shall speak of it no more."

"Jesus," said Webb. "Spring for a writer next time."

"Your dress," said the nobleman. "You are sodden. You must accompany me back to the manor. I shall have my handmaidens draw you a hot bath and launder your clothes."

"You had me at bath," said Webb. "Wait, you have handmaidens? Are they naughty?"

He nodded gravely. "Persistently so."

The sky turned crimson as the sun dipped below the horizon. Webb was pretty sure it had been noon a minute ago.

She regarded the sprite. He was far better looking than she'd expected—whoever'd programmed this had put in amazing attention to detail. And it *had* been quite a while since her last dive between the sheets. But he was way too pallid for her taste. "Impressario, what are the customization options for this character?"

"You may choose from the bank of pregenerated skins or customize individual features," said the Arcade. "Full customization averages 3.6 hours."

"No thanks, I'd probably get caught before that. What are the pregens drawn from?"

"Historical figures and celebrities."

"Well." She glanced at the frozen nobleman, considered who to overlay him with. There was that one guy… what was his name? Her sister had a poster of him in high school. Twenty-first century movie star. Something Elbow. Ignis? Ignis Elbow? That didn't sound right.

She snapped her fingers. "Idris Elba. Have you got him?"

The nobleman refreshed with a ripple. Now his locks were leonine, with more salt than pepper. He gazed upon her with mahogany eyes in a forestwood face.

Webb's heart still skipped a beat. "Oh, *shit* yeah. Okay. Resume program."

"It is late, my lady," cooed Idris in a voice distilled from honey and sex. "Too late to return to your village. I fear the wolves prowl at night. For your own safety, you must accompany me back to the manor. I insist." He extended his hand.

Webb's pulse quickened. She scoffed at herself—this was ridiculous— and motioned for him to lower his hand. "Okay, so… I haven't really decided if I'm into this? Or if this is tacky or not? So as tempting as a bath sounds… and anything that might follow it…"

"My lady!" He recoiled, aghast. "Never would I dream of taking advantage! Although the only room large enough for the bathtub is my bedchamber, and my study *is* nearby, but never would I inadvertently traipse in upon—"

"Shut up. What I'm saying is, I'm not entirely sold."

"What would convince you of my sincerity?" He sounded genuine enough.

"That's not what concerns me," said Webb, "I haven't determined the quality of your programming. Are you high lit or schlock?"

"Come again?"

"Like, is your story an actual good read, or are you just a bodice ripper?"

He shook his head. "You've lost me."

As if he'd have been programmed to answer out of character. Nothing to break the immersion. "Let's start simple. Why don't you tell me your name?"

He straightened in his saddle, framing himself before the setting sun, which had just sprung back up, and threw back his hair. "I am Ablehard Mountworthy. Heir to the duchy of Eversex."

"And we're done," said Webb. "Impressario, end program."

"My lady!" He reached for her and was gone, along with his castle and hedgerows and sunset. Along with her dress.

Webb sighed, waited until her heart had stopped pounding, and sat in the corner. She strained her ears—no thump of approaching cogs. The scenario had gone undetected.

She smiled. Chuckled. Damn Frankie had gotten her out of her head alright, at least long enough to set the grief aside for a while. Long enough to prepare for her performance review in a few hours. Long enough to catch a nap.

The floor of the Arcade wasn't particularly comfortable, but at least she could fully stretch out.

Chapter 3
Futue Fragrariam

"So the review panel didn't go well."

"I heard." Dewey stubbed out a cigarette. "Everyone heard. It was all the talk on the bridge. Belowdecks as well, I expect." She wrinkled her nose at Webb. "You smell like ammonia."

Webb shrugged an apology. "Had to clean the Arcade. Didn't leave time for a shower." She sniffed her armpit and winced. Her dress uniform would have to be laundered, and like every other service on the ship, that wasn't cheap.

She didn't dare sit, even though it was just her and the chief. The moment she sat would be the moment they showed. She felt sticky, unbuttoned her collar. "Don't know why I bothered getting dressed up."

"It's one of the hoops. All part of the pageantry. So jump."

Webb wanted to sit. Why wasn't she sitting? It's not like it'd make a difference. "I'm not getting the job. Not after today. No one gets promoted out of the enlisted ranks."

"Sivos did."

"And the red shirts hate him for it."

"The *Armstrongs* hate him." Dewey lit up again. "For the unpardonable crime of getting promoted without kissing purple ass. They don't count. Have some tar." She blew smoke into Webb's face.

Webb inhaled. The aroma was acrid and sweet and took her back to her youth. Then her lungs kicked in and filtered out the nicotine. The letdown was similar to having a sneeze dissolve right before climax. "God, I miss smoking."

"Does the secondhand help?"

"Not really. I appreciate it, though. I wouldn't mind sanding off the edge a bit."

"You *can* sit, you know."

"The moment I sit is the moment they show." She'd only just stopped pacing. "I wish they'd get here. I just want this over with."

Dewey pulled a couple shots out of a cabinet. "Your lungs can't keep you from drinking."

Webb scoffed. "Great plan, Chief. Get blitzed at my own review when they're already pissed at me." Though the thought was tempting. She looked towards the door again. Worry curdled her stomach and sent ice through her veins. "Do you think word got back to the captain? About how…?"

"You basically accused him of negligence?"

Webb shifted her weight. "There wasn't really a basically."

"He's guilty. He juiced the conduit early so he wouldn't ralph on the ambassador. I was there." Dewey's face tightened. "Xenofucking horndog."

"I'm so bunked."

"Don't worry, he's not even coming. He hasn't been feeling too hot; something with his stomach. Serves him right, the festering throbcock. Would you sit down, please? Your tension's infectious."

Webb sat, set her forehead to the table. "I hate this."

"I know." Dewey patted her on the back and slid her a shot. "Drink."

"I haven't eaten in ten hours."

"Fine, we'll go down to the Horizon afterward and you can binge on protein. I just thought you'd want to pregame before we celebrate."

Webb slowly lifted her head. She found Dewey wearing a lopsided grin. "Celebrate?"

"Oh, yeah. That *is* the word I used."

"Chief." Webb's heart wanted to race. She held it back. "Do you know something I don't?"

Another grin. "*So* many things."

"Like…"

"Like who's getting promoted today." She raised her glass. "Congrats, techie."

Webb sat upright. "No way."

"I'm serious."

"You've seen an order?"

"I signed it myself." Her grin slipped. "This is my last trip. I'd been considering it for a while, but after Chevalier… that cemented it." She popped the top off her shot and threw it back. "Anyway. I've hit retirement age, they can't deny me my pension, and as much as I love you kids, I'm not sticking around this shitshow any longer than I have to. I'm gonna head back to Yellowknife while I can still ride, maybe teach my granddaughters how to tap dance. Uncoordinated little shitgoblins. God damn, I miss them."

Webb could only gape. "You're retiring?"

"Which means the *Independence* is gonna be in need of a new chief engineer. One who already knows this bird and has patched her up almost as many times as I have. There's only one tech who fits the bill, and she's not drinking her shot."

Different emotions fought for control of Webb's voice. She settled on an interrogative whimper.

"It's one of those unwritten rules," said Dewey, "like 'don't stick your junk in a teleporter.' Chiefs get to pick their own replacements. Technically, it's just a recommendation, but it's a bone the brass is willing to throw. No one in purple wants to work that close with the crew anyway. And the red shirts need an upper level advocate, and I can think of no one better. Close your mouth."

Webb clicked it shut. "I'd be an officer?"

"Not an ensign. It's not that track. If I'm being honest, I don't know if you'll ever get to the bridge. And your shirt would still be red. But your badge would be gold, and you'd get your pips—along with everything else that comes with being an officer. I entered the recommendation this morning and Young signed off for the captain." Dewey raised her glass again. "Congratulations, Joni."

"Holy bunking lerd."

"Just act surprised."

43

"That won't be hard."

"Good. Now you gonna drink with me or not?"

Webb didn't have time to open her shot before the door to the wardroom slid open. She jumped to her feet.

In marched a cog. And an officer who made Webb's blood go cold.

Dewey hid her surprise better. "Lieutenant Commander." She rose, chanced a glance around him towards the corridor. "Is Commander Young on his way?"

"He has the bridge," said Blackwell. "I'll be presiding. Please take a seat." He locked eyes on Webb. "You're out of uniform."

Webb buttoned her collar, looked to Dewey for an explanation.

"Is something wrong, Technician?"

Webb slipped the shot in her pocket. "Just a bit taken aback, sir. I can't say I was expecting you."

"Neither could I," said Dewey.

"A performance review with potential for promotion requires the presence of a senior, yes?"

"It does indeed, sir." Webb should probably shut up. "It's just…"

"You think I can't be impartial," he said flatly. "That I'd let your accusations from earlier affect my judgment. They won't. Officers don't have the luxury of allowing personal feelings to affect their duties."

Dewey leaned in to point to his data pad. "No judgment is necessary. See? The form right there—"

"Your recommendation has been noted." He tapped some keys on the pad. "Senior Technician Joni Webber. Fifteen years distinguished service. Nine unit commendations. One meritorious unit commendation. You will stand at attention."

Webb stood straight as a rod.

"Certified operations specialist. Certified shuttle pilot. Certified mechanical engineer with specializations in… well, that's quite the list."

"Thank you, sir."

"I see you've kept your sidearm certification up to date. Not that you need combat training in Engineering. Crew representative, twice elected. And stellar recommendations from your commanding officer. Impressive. Your promotion is denied."

It fell quiet but for the creak of Blackwell reclining. Webb could almost hear herself deflate.

Dewey stabbed a finger at the data pad. "This has already been approved."

"*Submitted* for approval," corrected Blackwell. "Final say is the captain's."

"I choose my own replacement."

"Is that a regulation?" he asked innocently. "One I'm not aware of?"

"It's a norm," hissed Dewey. "Well known on the bridge."

"Source?" He offered her the data pad. "Show me the reg. I'm happy to be corrected."

Dewey slammed it on the table. "It's tradition. Recognized on every ship in the fleet!"

"Ships that are commanded by captains. Who make the ultimate decisions, I believe."

"But..." It was all Webb could manage with her heart pounding and throat desert-dry.

Dewey glanced at her. "Let me handle this."

Blackwell cocked his head. A smile played at his lips. "Something to add, Technician?"

"Sir. I am the most qualified candidate on the ship."

"She damn well is," said Dewey.

"I've logged more hours on duty than anyone but the chief. I'm proficient in every technical department—I train the replacements, for God's sake."

"Language." Blackwell steepled his fingers. "Your technical qualifications are impressive. There's no denying that. But we are simply not in the habit of promoting individuals who show no initiative."

45

Webb and Dewey gawked in unison. The chief went red as her uniform. "In what *conceivable* way—?"

"In the time you've served, you've been on…" He tapped at the pad. "… a grand total of *three* away missions. And the last of these was over a decade ago." His expression said checkmate.

Webb hoped she came across confused rather than irritated. "Away missions aren't required for promotion."

"But they are highly encouraged."

"You're penalizing me for not volunteering?"

"I needed her in Engineering," said Dewey. "I'm gonna risk losing my best hand to grunt work?"

Blackwell was not moved. "Red shirts volunteer all the time."

"The Armstrongs do," said Webb, "but not for away missions. If there's any level of danger involved, crew are assigned. There's no volunteering involved."

"I certainly see none on your record." Blackwell set the pad aside. "You don't believe in risking your skin, I get it. But you need to own that, and its consequences."

"Easy for you to say," Webb spat. "You're an officer."

Blackwell darkened. "Meaning?"

Dewey looked a warning at Webb.

"Red shirts die on away missions," Webb blurted. "Officers always come back."

Fuming, Dewey rose and tugged her uniform taut. "I'll be taking this up with the captain."

"How you waste your time is your call," said Blackwell.

"Sir," said Webb. "Please. Every year I've served, I've served with distinction. The officer corp needs people the crew trusts, and I'm the crew representative."

"Oh, I remember."

"I have a list of accolades as long as your arm. I've been here longer than half the officers! I know this ship inside out—I've worked in every little nook and rat hole—and I can navigate it with my eyes closed. I did it once on a dare. I've applied for this promotion *every year*—"

"With the *same result,*" he cut in. "You need to wake up, Ms. Webber. You will never be an officer. *Dismissed.*"

Webb was trembling so much she almost didn't feel Dewey's hand on her shoulder. "This isn't over," the chief lied.

But it was, gone as quickly and completely as an early morning dream. Webb was so crestfallen she almost didn't hear her badge chime.

Ø

Blackwell waited for the doors to his quarters to slide shut before letting out a sigh. For a precious handful of moments, his time was his own again.

His quarters weren't large, but he'd grown accustomed to living under spartan conditions. There was just enough room for his bed, his couch, the reading chair, his wardrobe, and a few art pieces. He'd converted the utility room into a personal gym; what entertaining was expected of him as an officer he kept to his kitchen and dining room. Apart from the bathroom and its jacuzzi tub, that was all the personal space he was allotted. And it was all he needed—he was used to going without.

The space in his sleeping quarters was a bit reduced due to the private holo-emitters he'd set up in its corners. Those weren't against regulation, but they weren't exactly common. Most officers could get by entertaining themselves in the Arcade.

Not Blackwell. His tastes ran towards the authentic, the more intimate. The more private, certainly. Unlike the Arcades, all officers' quarters were teep shielded—no one could teleport in unexpectedly. The Coalition had learned the need for that the hard way after the string of mutinies a generation past.

Blackwell turned off his badge, peeled off his jacket, and gazed out the window, which offered an unobstructed view of the starboard nacelle and the shredded torpedo bay beneath. He let out another sigh, this one irritated. He'd have to crack the whip down in Engineering. If the crew didn't want to work 100 hour weeks, they could get the work done on schedule.

His view wasn't the most romantic on the ship. But it was private, and it was practical. Just the way his lady preferred.

He checked to make sure the teep shields were up. He could feel his pulse quicken as he styled his hair, and couldn't suppress his smile. Just thinking about her made him giddy.

He placed himself at the foot of the bed. "Indie, execute private program Blackwell 3, version 331, authorization code Blackwell, Jared, KNU-1664."

The air shimmered. She appeared before his bed, kneeling in her silken kimono. She blinked as if she'd just awakened, looked into his face, and tightened her robe.

Blackwell's heart leapt. "Hello, Sunshine. Did you miss me?"

She smiled. Looked towards the window. "Where are we now?"

"Still at space. On our way to Amornomax." He couldn't keep the distaste out of his voice. What other officers did with their own time was their own business, but paying for intimacy was simply undignified. What were you learning, about yourself or the fairer sex, by paying for a performance? It was demeaning, hardly any better than bedding one of the pixies in the Arcade. All fantasy, zero substance.

At least here, with Sunshine, he was practicing with a semblance of real femininity. A woman you had to win. A woman you had to woo.

She blinked at the broken torpedo bay. "What happened? Is the ship in danger?"

"Hardly. The damage is all structural. One torpedo bay offline."

"It looks worse than that."

"The section depressurized, but we'll be fine." He sat on the bed and patted the comforter.

She sat, folded her hands and legs.

Blackwell felt a twinge of annoyance. "The teep shields are up. For privacy. As always. It's just us."

She noticed the wrinkle in his brow. "Something's bothering you."

He chuckled. She knew him so well. "Am I that transparent?"

She smiled again. He felt himself mirror her. Their relationship had had its fair share of bumps—every longterm romance did—but they'd really turned a corner when she'd learned to recognize his cues. Like when he just needed to vent. It was affirming, validating, to be heard, and not just because the uniform gave him that right.

"It's been a hell of a day," he told her. "I had to answer for a crew death."

"Oh, no."

"All part of the job. And I was happy to. Any chance to show I care."

"It didn't go well?"

"It was a disgrace. A—forgive me—God damn sideshow. A red shirt— the crew rep, if you can believe it—accused me of murder, dragged my name *and* the captain's through the exhaust 'cause she was mad her friend was too dumb to exit a live conduit. And now my promotion—something I've worked *so hard* for, my whole career; you know that."

"I do."

"Well, it's tainted. Her dissent is on my permanent record. Why the hell do we even give them that power? Huh? Oh, and then? You won't believe this, they had the gall to submit *her* for promotion." He scoffed. "You'd better believe I shot that down."

"The crew rep?"

"Honey, I'm not done."

She paled and shrunk a bit. "I'm sorry."

The twinge returned. Every time he thought they were making progress. "It hurts when you react like that. Like I'm going to punish you."

"I'm so sorry."

"We've been over this. I was simply correcting for politeness. Forget it." He back-flopped on the mattress.

49

She stiffened. Laid down beside him. Started stroking his hair.

"That's nice." He shook his head. "They hate us, you know. They really do."

"They?"

"The crew. It doesn't matter what we do for them, how many opportunities we create. They always find a way to make their own misery our fault. Like we're supposed to feel bad they don't have the wherewithal to improve their circumstances? Boggles the mind. You know what they are without us? Without the structure we offer? A mob. An ungrateful, ungovernable mob we still need to keep the ship running. Until we can get cog production costs low enough."

He turned towards her then, looked deep into her eyes. A test, to see how quickly she could read him. Of how their relationship was doing. Silent communication, anticipation of your partner's needs. Something he'd tried that she'd failed before.

Understanding dawned in her eyes. "I suppose you'll be wanting to…"

He rolled away from her with a grunt. "Do you have to put it like that?"

She flinched again. "I'm sorry."

"You don't understand the stress I've been under. This is *not* where I need strain. This is where I need understanding and acceptance."

"You're right. I'm sorry. Do you want to try again?"

"Now? Not really."

Her eyes began to shine. "Please don't restart me."

"Oh my *God*, can we not do this?" He sat up. "That's not fair. That is not what I need right now. I need you, here in the moment, with me."

She silently rose, wrapped her arms around him from behind. Kissed him gently on the cheek.

"Better," said Blackwell. "Getting there."

She turned his head to kiss him. Smiled into his eyes. The smile seemed strained.

But there it was: silent communication. Or at least the start of it. He pulled off his shirt.

She began to undress.

"Stop."

She froze.

"Face the window. I want to see your reflection in the stars."

She bit off a sigh and turned around.

A bearded face appeared on the wall monitor. "Lieutenant Commander?"

Blackwell nearly yelped. He spun to cover himself and Sunshine. "Commander. You caught me indisposed."

"I can see that," said Commander Young. "We've received a pri one message from the Admiralty. All senior officers to the bridge. That includes you now, Mr. Blackwell."

"Aye, sir. I'll be right there."

"You'd have received the message earlier if you hadn't turned off your badge." His eyeline shifted to Sunshine.

Blackwell's pulse increased. "It's nothing, sir."

"We take security very seriously, Mr. Blackwell. This is an encrypted channel."

"Sir, she's not even... Indie, end program."

Sunshine's face curled in horror. She sucked in breath to scream but didn't get it out before she vanished.

Young looked decidedly unimpressed.

"Sir, I—"

"Your own time is your own business. So long as it doesn't interfere with your duties. Now turn on your badge and get back to the bridge." The monitor went blank.

Blackwell knelt on the bed, burning with embarrassment. He cast a longing look at the nearest holo-emitter.

He hadn't had time to save her progress. She hated when he did that. It's not like she'd remember though; those memories—and the communication progress they'd made—were gone. Although she would try to interpolate what had happened the next time he summoned her. A bug he had to fix.

Later. He turned on his badge and tugged on his uniform. Its familiar weight closed over him. Back to work.

𝒟

Every head turned as Blackwell entered the bridge. There were fewer there than he'd expected. None of the ensigns or lieutenants who normally manned the duty stations were present. Senior officers only. He muttered an apology and took his place at the ops console.

Young nodded to the communications officer. "Patch it through."

On the main screen appeared a regally paunchy admiral with a fruit salad of medals on his chest.

"Admiral Self." Young saluted. "Thank you for your patience."

"Good to see you, Commander," replied the admiral. "How's life on the frontier?"

"We've just seeded our final planet, and we're on our way home. Minus a minor stop for leave."

"It'll have to wait, I'm afraid." The admiral looked toward the captain's empty chair. "Where is Seagrave?"

"Taken ill, sir. He's confined himself to quarters. Shall I forward your message there?"

"No, you'll do. And the Sorl ambassador?"

"She's in the diplomatic suite, I imagine." Young looked to Sivos, who gave him a nod. "Yes, the suite. We haven't seen much of her in the last couple days, though the demonstration did go according to plan. Mostly."

"Fine. Keep this to yourselves. We have an urgent new mission, and the *Independence* is the closest ship."

Young seemed baffled. "We're on edge of the territory."

"The mission's not in the territory. We're sending you into No Man's Space."

The officers exchanged glances. "I should get the captain," Young said.

"He can review once you're underway. A month ago, we lost contact with the *Flagstaff*, a deep space vessel. A scout ship, searching out dead planets for terraforming and colonization."

"I know the *Flagstaff*," said Winesborough. "Fontana's ship."

"She vanished with all hands," said the admiral. "We'd given her up as a total loss until we picked up her distress beacon this morning. It's coming from Acheron something something in the outer fringe. I'm sending you the coordinates. We presume she crashed. Locate the wreckage before any xenos get any ideas about claiming salvage."

Young frowned. "May I ask why this is priority one, sir? Wreckage retrieval... it hardly seems to warrant this level of encryption."

"Just get there, Commander. Time is of the essence. Seagrave will receive updated orders once you've arrived. Out." The monitor went blank.

The senior officers all looked to Young, who could only shrug. "You heard the admiral. We're bound for a crash site beyond the frontier. I'll brief the captain. Mr. Winesborough, what do we have on our destination?"

"One sec." The science officer's hands flew over his data pad. "Acheron 117. Looks like your standard piece of shit rock. It's within its star's habitable band, but there's no bodies of water. Slightly bigger than Earth, gravity 1.2... huh."

"Care to share?"

"Breathable atmosphere. Don't see many of those unclaimed. That'll speed up terraforming for sure. Otherwise, unremarkable."

"Noted. Anything that would have caused the *Flagstaff* to crash?"

"Those ships are bricks," said Winesborough. "Whatever knocked it out of the sky, it must have taken a *lot* of it."

Young turned to Blackwell. "Lieutenant Commander, gather volunteers for an away mission. Standard survey and security detail."

"Volunteers, sir?"

"Is that a problem?"

Blackwell bit back a glare. "No, sir. But wouldn't it be simpler to assign hands?"

"Not unless you want to spook the crew," said Young. "We'll need them calm and functional. There's no hiding the course change, and they'll also notice we didn't give them a reason for it, so they'll be on edge. Asking for volunteers communicates that we don't expect this to be a dangerous mission. We can always mandate if we're understaffed."

"Aye, sir." Blackwell turned so his peers wouldn't see him redden. He couldn't stand being talked down to. He tapped his badge. "Blackwell to crew."

Throughout the Event Horizon, the ship's central commissary, lounge, and bar, red shirts in various stages of inebriation looked towards the ceiling.

"We are changing course," Blackwell continued over the comms, "for an undisclosed location beyond the frontier."

Some of the crew started to sweat. Others to tremble. Some put their heads to the tables and moaned.

"Details will be provided upon our arrival. An away team will be assembled for the mission. You are highly encouraged to volunteer."

The rest of the message was lost to derisive hissing. Someone hurled a beer at the ship's emblem on the wall. That unleashed a torrent of alcoholic missiles against the Coalition symbol.

Slumped on the bar, Webb watched the cog bartender trace the arcs of the bottles back to their throwers. "All vandals have been identified and fined."

A new salvo of bottles smashed into the cog. "All fines have increased," it said through the beer and glass streaming down its face.

"Hey." Webb tapped the bar. "I need about six more of those."

The cog swung its gaze her way. "You are out of uniform, Technician."

Webb fumbled her clasps back together. "There, happy? How about now?"

It set a half-dozen bottles in front of her. She twisted one open, mock saluted, and undid her clasps.

"You are out of uniform, Technician."

"Holy shit, you're right." She chugged half a bottle.

"Further violations will result in a citation and fine."

"I cannot take you seriously covered in Coors."

Frankie slid onto the stool next to her. She didn't say anything. She didn't really have to; she could glean enough just taking in Webb's wrinkled uniform, slack expression, and the cluster of empty but precisely arranged beer bottles in front of her. "Well. I suppose the good news is Chelse and I won't have to get a new quadmate. Another one, I mean."

Webb snorted. "Yeah."

"What do you need right now?"

Webb wagged the bottle at her and downed it.

"Is that all?"

"Hardly." Webb twisted open another. "I'm doing a full psychological diagnostic. Step one: flush system prior to reboot. I've got plenty of solvent." She belched.

Frankie waved to the cog. "A pitcher of water, please?"

"I don't even particularly *like* alcohol," Webb slurred. "But I can't smoke out anymore 'cause my bunking lungs filter out the good stuff before it hits my bloodstream, so this waste of rice and formaldehyde it is. Thanks, Coalition! So glad you saved my life." She drank the bottle dry.

Her eyes on the cog, Frankie leaned in. "I get the self-medicating, but you don't want to be implying drug use in front of that."

"Right," said Webb. "Might hurt my promotion prospects."

"Your push for next year starts now, so maybe reel it in a bit? Did they even say why?"

"Apparently, I lack initiative."

Frankie was incredulous. "You what?"

"Because I won't go get myself killed on an away mission. And I'm too competent to get killed on the job, so they're stuck with me on the review panel, and 'cause they can't just order me to go get killed, they're gonna kill my career instead. Did you know Dewey was gonna retire?"

Frankie slid an arm around her shoulder. "Let's get you to your bunk."

"No way." Webb shrugged her off. "I paid way too much for these beers and I'm damn well gonna finish them."

"You'll be hungover your next shift. You could get flagged unfit for duty."

"Lerd. I'd only be at the standard level of crew competence."

"Okay, yeah. Let's get you out of here." Frankie made another grab.

Webb deflected it. "Look at these people."

"Webb, you're not yourself."

"Half are just unplugged. Can't even admit how bad they have it. But do they protest? Vote or complain or try to better things at all? *No.* The unassigned do, but these assholes in quads? They just cling to the little bit of security they have and do nothing for their fellow crew. No wonder the officers despise us. Can you say they're wrong?"

"Wow." Frankie shook her head. "Maybe keep your voice down? You're the frigging crew rep."

"Oh, no. I might lose all my power."

"What has gotten into you?"

Webb couldn't look at her. "I quit, Frank."

Frankie grunted. She slid the unopened bottles away. "You've been working too hard. We all have. I've got a few days of shore leave saved up. How about we cash some in when we're back home? Go backpacking somewhere. We could go fishing on Enceladus. I hear the cod finally took."

"I'm serious." Webb undid another clasp. One more day and she could take off that scratchy hellblanket forever. "Signed the papers and everything. My last shift is tomorrow. Earliest withdrawal date I could get."

Something in Frankie's eyes died. "Webb?"

"Don't." She didn't need this right now. "Don't you guilt me. I'll just flush it out with beer anyway." She took another drink and winced. "Christ, this is awful."

Frankie slid back onto the stool, slumped over the bar. Webb had never seen her with bad posture. "So... what happens now?"

"First thing? You'll have to reconsider the whole Yolanda naming convention. Like... will whoever gets my bunk be Yolanda Nine, or Webb Two? If it's another Yolanda, do you alternate, go odds-evens, or...?"

"I don't find this funny."

"I'm not joking. Check it out, I need your help." She surreptitiously showed Frankie the unopened shot in her pocket. "I wanna fab the hell out of this to raise some retirement funds. Since I could never get the cogfinder working consistently."

Frankie looked aghast. Then she looked towards the cog and its all-recording eyes. "You can't be serious."

"Gotta pay for passage home somehow. And for these fucking lungs. I'm a civilian now."

Frankie clenched and unclenched her fists. "I understand getting blitzed. But to leave? Over *this?* You weren't even expecting the promotion, so how did not getting it break you?"

"Because the last one of them died." Bottle halfway to her lips, the tears ambushed her, hot and sour and too close to the surface. Webb shook her head and ground her palms into her eyes.

When she took them away, Frankie was staring a question at her.

"From the shuttle," she said. "The last one. He fell into a ravine on some half-terra'd world without guardrails in place."

Frankie had gone very still. "How did you find out?"

"They fucking told me."

Webb slapped her badge on the bar, hit recall. Up popped the holo-image with the death notice. Webb felt another stab watching his translucent face rotate above the Coalition symbol.

"They sent me all the notifications," Webb told her. "Every one, over the last dozen years. So that I'd know that, no, I didn't actually save anyone. That every red shirt I took off that imploding rock didn't make it, not in the long run. Because they hate me." The tears were coming now. She couldn't have wiped them away fast enough, so she didn't try. "They hate *us*. And they wanted me to know they could undo what I did just by *waiting*. And so I'm just fucking *done*. They win. I'm out. "

Frankie put a hand on hers.

"I don't even know if I can miss this place." Webb scrubbed her eyes, took a deep steadying breath. Looked around the room. All she could see were morose folks in red, all trying to disconnect before taking their next turn in the machine and trying not to get crushed.

Her eyes found their way to the corner of the lounge, where a strikingly handsome officer sat in starlight in his medical blues.

"I was going to introduce myself today," Webb said softly. "The words just came to me, just popped into my head when Dewey gave me the news. 'Hello, Doctor, I'm the new chief appointed,' I was gonna say. 'Engineering sends a lot of crew your way, and I'd like to reduce that number. We should meet, talk about ways our departments could work together more efficiently. Maybe over dinner?' Corny, yeah, but all I needed was an in." She turned back to her thicket of empties. "I was almost somebody today. I almost got to talk to him."

"What's stopping you?" Frankie asked. "He's sitting right over there. See? There. Go on, it's easy. 'Hi, Dr. Marwazi, I'm Webb. Want to spike each others' endorphins?'"

"He's an officer," Webb said flatly. "I'm a crew—no, worse, a *civilian*. A nothing."

"If you're a nothing, what's that make the rest of us? You're always going to be disappointed when you set unrealistic goals."

"Easy for you to say. You don't want anything."

Frankie sighed. "That's not what non-attachment means."

"I don't care." Webb was tired, so damn tired. "Lend me a hand with these beers or piss the hell off. Either suits me."

Frankie stiffened. Studied her. Seemed to nod to herself. She leaned in. "A man traveling across the countryside encounters a tiger. He runs. The tiger gives chase."

"Oh, God." Webb covered her head. "Is this another parable?"

"The tiger chases him," Frankie continued, "all the way to a precipice. The man grabs onto a vine and swings down over the edge, out of reach. Trembling, he looks down and what does he see? Another tiger!"

"Really. Two tigers, in the same range. And they're not fighting."

"Shut up. The tiger below looks up with hunger while the tiger above sniffs down. There's nowhere for the man to go. If he falls, he dies; if he climbs up, he dies. Only the vine is keeping him from a drop into snacktime. Then he hears it: squeaking. He looks up and sees two mice—one white, the other black."

"Yin and yang, I get it. Not even subtle."

"—shut *up*. Two mice gnawing on the vine. They'll chew through it soon. But as he looks at them, he sees a strawberry growing out of the cliff. Grasping the vine with one hand, he plucks the strawberry and pops it in his mouth. How sweet it is!" She sat back and set her hands in her lap.

"So…" Webb shrugged. "I need to live in the moment. Is what you're telling me."

"No!"

The shout made Webb lean back. She hadn't seen Frankie angry in a long… well, ever.

"That's not what it's about at all! Everyone always gets that wrong. It's not about ignoring crises and being in the moment, it's about *not getting distracted by pleasure."*

"So… wait." Frankie was losing her. "What *are* you saying?"

"I'm saying, fuck the strawberry! There are tigers!"

Webb shook her head. "You've lost me."

"And you've lost yourself." Her disappointment was palpable. "You're throwing away your career—and your power to advocate for a crew that trusts you—in a moment of self-pity. That's your strawberry."

Webb's anger flared. "How about you get lost? 'Cause you're really not helping me." She turned away. "Stupid strawbuddhist berry story. Tigers and mice and who gives a shit."

When Webb turned around again, Frankie was gone. Her anger melted into sorrow. Had she been sober, the moment might have been one of self-reflection. But as it was, the half-thoughts that careened around in her head couldn't stick to anything, couldn't form into the chain of a plan, so they all just floated around, loose bits of guilt bumping into each other on a tide of depression. She wanted to cry again.

No. Not here. Never here.

She took another beer from the bar. It held absolutely no appeal. She was, quite literally, full; there was no amount of additional liquid she was interested in ingesting. Anything she added now would only be contributing to tomorrow's throbbing regret.

She saw Dr. Marwazi rise from his table, bid his companions goodbye. He headed towards the hall.

Webb found her feet on the floor. Looks like she'd decided to follow. To show some initiative, even. Why not? What's the worst that could happen? It's not like they could fire her.

She followed Marwazi into the lift. Wherever he was going, she wouldn't have more than a minute before the ride reached its destination. Stupid lifts and their stupid efficiency.

"Bridge," said Marwazi. The lift whirred and began to rise.

He looked at her. Her pulse quickened and the words died in her throat. A nod, and he looked away.

Webb eyed the navimeter. Time was burning. So much to cram into a few stolen moments.

"So I'm leaving the Coalition," she blurted.

"Oh," said Marwazi. "Thank you for your service." His accent was so savory smooth she could have sipped it. "Have you served long?"

"Fifteen years." Her heart fell. "We've served together for twelve." And he didn't recognize her.

"Have we?" He looked embarrassed. He glanced at her badge. "Ah, Engineering. That would be why we haven't met."

"You've treated me nine times."

His cheeks went from bronze to rose. "My apologies."

"Nine times."

"I'm terrible with faces."

"You put my lungs in."

His raven eyes widened. God, his lashes were luxurious. "Yes. *Yes,* the biomech ferrofibers! How are they?"

"Oh, can't complain." She nodded too quickly. "I mean I could, but they'd filter it out."

He blinked at that.

Webb flushed. "The lungs, I meant. That was a joke."

"Ah. Yes, I see it now." He chuckled. "Very droll."

She flushed harder. "I was going to take over for Dewey. But not anymore."

"Oh, is she's retiring?"

"I won't get to now, though. I'm leaving the Coalition."

"Yes, you already said. Best of luck." He gave her the polite nod that signaled the end of a conversation.

Webb screwed her eyes shut. She swallowed the lump in her throat and went for it. "Do you like fishing?"

He seemed taken aback by the question. As taken aback as Webb was that she'd asked it. "Come again?"

"I'm all out of plans, but I was thinking, hey, if you've got some planet leave maybe we go encing on Fisheladus. Or something. I hear the cod are really… there."

He looked confused. Then he looked at the bottle she hadn't realized she'd carried out of the lounge. "I can't, unfortunately. I have to prep for the away mission. I'm leading one of the teams. But thank you."

"No, it's…" Her opportunity was fading. "What I meant was—"

The doors opened with a pneumatic hiss. Marwazi ducked out onto the bridge—the sleek, elegant bridge, with its unobtrusive workstations, luxurious seating, and gorgeous view of the cosmos.

Webb leaned against the frame of the lift and gazed out into the stars. She'd never seen such a view, not even in a NEOS. One must feel like a god up here.

"Ms. Webber?"

Her blood went cold again. A smile she didn't know she was wearing fell from her face and smashed on the floor.

Blackwell was staring at her. "May I ask what you're doing on the bridge without permission? And out of uniform?"

"I…" Webb saw a knot of senior officers watching at her with a range of expressions. The one Marwazi wore was curious.

Initiative. Webb slipped the bottle behind her back and flipped her clasps shut with one smooth motion. "Sir. I came to volunteer for the away mission."

Chapter 4
Vita Incerta

Webb's brain awoke before the rest of her, and as she lay there in the oddly chatter-filled darkness in her head, wincing at her blossoming hangover, she wondered where the whispers were coming from. Distant whispers, but not too far, like a crowd of gossipers gabbing in the next room. There was an urgency to their conversation, an edge of panic that gave way to a rhythmic pounding in her skull. That pounding gave way to the actual pounding coming from behind Chelse's bunk panel.

Webb groaned. Her body was awake now, and it had more than a few complaints to lodge. Her brain had grown spikes that were stabbing out in all directions. How one could drink so much and yet awaken dehydrated was one of the great mysteries of the universe. At least the lights were off.

She looked down toward the spot between bunks where Frankie usually meditated. Frankie wasn't there.

A twinge of guilt wove through the brain-spikes. Frankie must have left for her shift early. Which would probably make Webb's last day easier, not starting with another fight and all.

Guilt and regret clawed at her. Webb hadn't known yesterday that today would be her final day in uniform. She hadn't even told her station mates yet. They likely knew by now. Doubtless Dewey did. There was a reaming she wasn't looking forward to.

Webb looked to the ceiling of her too-short bunk and realized, with a jolt, that she'd just slept her last night in it. Where would she be after today? In the cargo hold, dodging looks from unassigned crew who couldn't believe she'd given up a quad berth.

Whatever. Issues for later.

Chelse's bunk panel was down. Rob had gotten his shirt half on before he'd noticed her. "Oh. Hey." He flushed, nudged Chelse. "Webb's up. Hope we didn't wake you."

Webb tried to speak. It came out in a dry heave. Her mouth tasted like she'd eaten a cardigan. "Come again?"

"I'm good" said Chelse.

Webb swallowed her mouth clear. "Rob. Hey. I've heard you guys have some magical rehydration spray?"

"The hangover pill?" He finished pulling his shirt on. "Yeah, that's not part of the crew medical package. Sorry."

Webb grunted. She eyed the door to the bath chamber. She still needed that shower. And she could drink the water—she had about a week's worth of hydro rations to cash out.

She dropped to her feet, put a hand to her temple to steady herself. Her hair was plastered into a plate on the side of her head. "When did Frankie leave?"

"About thirty seconds before I commed Rob," said Chelse.

Webb didn't have the energy to glare. "You bunked when you knew I was here?"

"You were passed out," said Chelse. "On the floor."

"Unresponsive," added Rob. "Chelse thought you were dead. You weren't, though. We tucked you in."

"Left your uni on, though."

They had. Dress uniforms did not make comfy pajamas. "Did Frank have an early shift?"

Chelse drew the covers over herself. "I don't think it's as early as you think it is."

The door slid open. Light from the hall stabbed Webb's brain. She shielded her eyes with a whimper. "Frankie? That you?"

It was not. At the door stood a mousy woman with a key card and a duffel over her shoulder. She looked surprised that the key card had worked. "Is this 1262-B?"

"Yeah," croaked Webb. "Hey."

Mousey held up her quad assignment. "Good morning. Hi, I'm—oh." She went pale—well, paler—when she saw Chelse's uniform on the floor. And the half-naked man in her bunk. "Uh. I can come back."

"You're in the right place." Webb waved her in. "We quad with a cop."

"Officer Alameda to you," said Chelse. "This is Rob. He's not here."

"Hi," said Rob.

"Honey? Pants."

"Right." Rob retroused himself. "I was just leaving."

Mousey looked no less confused. "I thought soldiers were berthed in barracks?"

"We're supposed to be," said Chelse. "But there aren't enough lady grunts to fill our own garrison, and housing us with the men is a scandal just waiting to happen, so they stick us in the quads. I'm as happy about it as you are. Could you get the door, please? I'm naked."

Mousey flushed. And hiccuped. She closed the door. "Sorry. Strange morning. Okay. Let's try this again." She checked her housing order. "Hello, Chelsea, Francine, and Joni. And Rob."

"Hi."

"It's nice to meet you. My name is—"

"Your name," interrupted Chelse, "is Yolanda Eight."

Eight blinked. She opened and closed her mouth a few times. "Sorry?"

"If you're still with us after six months, you get your real name. In the meantime, we're not getting attached. Welcome to the quad. Don't touch my guns."

"Um." Eight looked from quaddie to quaddie. Webb could see her doing the math in her head. "Hold on. *Eight?*"

"You're wondering what happened to the rest."

"I wasn't a moment ago."

"I'll go," said Rob.

"You'll stay." Chelse started buttoning her jacket. "If you were at the funeral, you heard what happened to Seven. She almost made it the full six. We were pretty shook up about it. Now *Six*—"

"Can we not do this now?" said Webb. "It's my last damn morning and I've got a pulsar of a headache."

"Oh." Eight searched for something else to say. "It was a pleasure meeting you."

"Don't let her fool you," said Chelse. "She's not going anywhere."

Webb regarded Chelse flatly. "I resigned, jarhead."

"And I'm sure it'll stick. This is the only home you know."

Webb's anger surged. "You know what?"

"I can come back," said Eight.

"Shut it, noob." Chelse shimmied into her pants. "Let's start from the top, it'll be easier. The first Yolanda, Yolanda Prime, was our original quaddie. Great lady, total infotech nerd. Loved her to pieces. She got scattered in a teleporter accident."

Webb scoffed. *"Accident."*

"There were warnings of solar flare activity, but the brass ignored them so they wouldn't fall behind schedule. One erupted while she was in midstream, dispersed her signature, and they could never put her back together."

Eight recoiled. "That's horrid."

"Right? You'd never even know what happened to you. Energize, poof, atoms everywhere. Rob, I'm hungry."

"Yeah." He gave her a meal pack, a peck, and hopped down from the bunk. "Nice to meet you. I honestly hope you're the very last Yolanda." Out he went.

"Two was here less than a week," said Chelse. "She got crushed in a shipquake. Bulkhead dropped on her when the inertial dampeners failed. That's kind of where the tradition began. The rest of us couldn't remember her name."

"Megan," said Webb. A woman with hair so red her head looked on fire. One who'd wanted to hang a Utah State pennant above the door. That's all Webb remembered of her.

"Three was cool," said Chelse. "She lasted a couple months before she got herself brigged for stealing rations. That's the official story. Scuttlebutt was she wouldn't sleep with the officer who took her to dinner so he reported the food stolen, and as far as we know she's still in the meat locker."

"Jesus." Eight sank to the floor with a hiccup.

"Chelse," said Webb. "You're freaking her out."

"Good, that means she's paying attention. I'm doing this to help you, Eight. I hope you understand that. Where were—? Right. Four's the current record holder. Two days in, her shuttle lost pressure when it hit atmo and burped all the passengers to soup."

"Jesus *fuck.*"

"That's what we said. Now *Five—*"

Webb and Eight's badges chimed in unison. They exchanged a look: Webb's resigned, Eight's alarmed.

"Away mission crew, report to shuttle bay," said the Independence.

Webb checked her chronometer. Ten minutes to departure. Her shower would have to wait. Again.

"Good luck, Eight." Chelse waved once. "Try not to break the record."

❋

With a clap and a bump, the ship dropped out of hyperspace. The stars went from blinding streaks to dots on the main screen of the bridge.

The ship settled into orbit above a sickly yellow planet with swirling storms blanketing its atmosphere. It was the color of an aging banana with moving spots.

"Acheron 117," announced the helm officer. "Aptly named after a river in hell."

"Thank you, Mr. Metz." Commander Young rose from his chair beside the captain's. "Scan for signs of the *Flagstaff.*"

Winesborough tapped a few keys at the science station. "The sandstorms are interfering with the scans. Too many silicates in the atmosphere."

"Even for a ship that size?"

"They're bouncing the signal everywhere, Pat."

"All right. Let's go visual. Look for signs of a crash."

The view zoomed towards the surface through the storms, losing resolution as it went. It came to rest on a strange black grid zigzagging out from an equatorial mountain range.

Young squinted. "Can you enhance?"

"A little," said Winesborough, "but we'll have to extrapolate the planet's topograph... wait. Break in the storm." Some rapid key tapping. "Here we go."

The zigzags jumped into focus: stone construction of some sort. The pattern was too geometrical to be natural.

"Closer," said Young.

Their view slid in again, gliding along enormous ruins weathered by time and erosion, stretching for kilometers in either direction.

Young approached the screen in awe. "Ruins? On a dead planet?"

"That appears to be the case, Commander."

"Was there anything about this in our files?"

"Nothing." For once, Winesborough seemed more curious than annoyed. "And nothing from the *Flagstaff's* reports."

"Commander, we need to reshuffle the away teams," said Sivos. "Possible xeno presence requires an expeditionary force."

"Scan for biosigns again," said Young.

"Scans are negative," said Winesborough. "And that's not just storm interference. There's a distinct lack of organic matter in the atmosphere and in what we can scan of the soil."

"Then who built those?"

"A mystery soon to be revealed," the captain said over the comms. The door to his cabin slid open.

Blackwell rose from his duty station. "Captain on the bridge."

The officers all rose in surprise.

Young greeted Seagrave with a salute at the command dais. "Captain. Good to see you on your feet again. How are you feeling?"

"Right as rain," said the captain, who was paler than usual.

Young nodded. "Will you be monitoring the mission from the bridge?"

"From far closer, Mr. Young. I'll be leading it."

Young flicked his eyes to the doctor and back. "Is that wise, sir? You've been on medical leave."

Seagrave narrowed his eyes. "There's nothing wrong with my backbone, Commander."

"I'm merely concerned about your health."

"Shall I scan you, Captain?" offered Marwazi. "It wouldn't take but a moment."

Seagrave shooed him away. "If xenos are involved, my own discomfort is a minor sacrifice."

Young leaned in. "That's very noble, sir. But the doctor hasn't cleared you for duty. We don't know what was causing your gastric distress."

"My withdrawal was voluntary," said Seagrave. "I was not placed under medical leave."

"You haven't set foot on the bridge in two days."

"And you've gotten used to that, have you?" He said it with a smirk, and louder than necessary. "The chair's not yours yet, Mr. Young. The crew needs to see their captain in action." He didn't take his eyes off Young as he sat. "Status update."

"Getting to the surface will be an issue," said Winesborough. "We're—"

"Thank you, Wino, but I didn't ask you," said Seagrave. "I'd like to hear it from the commander."

Young stiffened. "Sir. Due to the particulates in the atmosphere, any teleporter signature we attempt to send down is in danger of being scattered."

"I'm hearing problems. What I want are solutions"

"Well, for one, we could—"

"We should send a team down in a shuttle," said Blackwell. "Have them drop a teleporter anchor. It should strengthen the beam enough to allow for teleportation."

"Very good," said Seagrave. "See? Was that so hard? Proceed."

Young looked a warning at Blackwell. "Sir, sending a shuttle through that storm is an unnecessary risk. Wouldn't it be wiser to wait for it to clear?"

"Time is of the essence," said the captain. "You recall the admiral's words, Commander?"

"I do, sir," said Young. "But even if we strengthen the signal enough for teleportation, if the storm's intensity increases, the anchor may not be enough. At which point we may have more crew on the surface than can fit in the shuttle."

Seagrave rolled his eyes. "Yes, I'm aware of the passenger capacity of our shuttles, Commander. I've been in those a few times." He rose, tugged his uniform taut. "Lieutenant Commander, proceed with the plan and meet me at the teleporter. Commander? The bridge is yours."

Young froze. "You want me here?"

The captain regarded him languidly. "You had other plans?"

"I was going to lead an away team."

"Yes, in the vanguard exploring the ruins. Commander, it is unbecoming of a senior officer to put his personal interests above the needs of the ship."

"Sir, I—"

"I'm sure there will be plenty of time after the mission for you to collect artifacts. In the meantime, you can stay here next to that chair you haven't earned."

Young pressed his mouth into a line. "Aye, sir."

ℚ

Webb clutched her head as if that could steady the shaking. It did nothing to blot out the roar of the thrusters. Riding a shuttle down through a continent-wide dust storm wasn't doing wonders for her hangover.

She wasn't going to puke. Not here. Not in this tiny space in front of her peers. Definitely not in front of that lanky Armstrong who hardly looked old enough to shave.

"I heard there were ruins on the planet!" Eight was still trying to make conversation. "That's pretty exciting, right? We'll get to see them first!"

Webb ground her eyes shut and gripped her harness. "I'm sure sending us first has nothing to do with making sure they're not booby-trapped."

"You think the officers will come down?"

"For a chance to loot the ruins? Are you kidding? You know how much xeno artifacts go for at auction?"

"Brace for the storm," said the pilot.

Webb looked up in alarm. "Wait, *for* the storm?"

"We haven't hit it yet," said Eight. "That buffeting was all stratosphere."

Webb's heart sank. Her stomach followed, tripped, flipped, and tried to empty itself.

No. Not puking here. She tamped it back down.

The storm hit them with the force of a tidal wave. Webb held her harness in a death grip as the shuttle bounced around like a ping pong ball in a shop vac.

She wanted to shout at the pilot to pump the stabilizers. She could hear her excuse—they needed to get through the cell first, couldn't afford to slow momentum and linger in the winds. Not that that would matter if the ailerons snapped.

Grit soup sprayed against the viewscreen. With a stomach-punching lurch, the shuttle dropped a kilometer in a heartbeat. Everyone screamed before it stabilized again.

Eight, quivering like a Chihuahua, reached out to touch Webb's arm. "It's okay." Did Webb really look that distraught? "We're okay. Statistically speaking, we'll live through this."

"Statistically? Not everyone," said the prematurely gray tech in the harness across from her. Adler, that was his name. "Statistically, someone in a red shirt's going back tits up."

"Not just one," said a tech with mismatched eyes. Judging by the scar, the right one was an implant; he probably couldn't have afforded the matching color. "Casualty rate goes up with mission size."

"How'd they rope you in?"

"Shuttle maintenance." Eye Guy thumped a panel. Swank, that was it. Webb remembered now. "I go where this turkey goes."

"Supply," said Adler. "Four missions a year or we lose our health coverage."

"Wasn't Koumontaros in supply?"

"Was," said Adler. "Rack of shelves fell on him. Smashed him flatter than a pancake."

"That's like what got Foley," said Swank. "Right here in the shuttle, going through turbulence. Her harness held, but the one holding the demetrium didn't, and splat."

"I'm in agriculture." Eight forced a smile. "It's my first mission!"

Alder and Swank blanched. "Our condolences."

Eight looked alarmed. "What?"

"Nothing," said Adler. "I'm sure you'll be fine."

"Fresh fish always come back," said Swank.

The pilot snorted.

Eight hiccuped.

"You'll be *fine*," said Webb. "You're in frigging agriculture."

"So was McSherry," said Swank. "He popped a pod by mistake and choked out on the chems." He glanced at the pallet of agripods lashed to the floor. "Those look secure, though."

"I don't know," said Adler. "That's where the demetrium was."

Eight sank deeper in her seat.

"What about you, chatterbox?" Adler asked Webb.

Webb let out a long breath. Screw it, it hardly mattered now. "I volunteered."

They looked incredulous. "What, were you drunk?"

"Murphy drunk-volunteered once," said Swank. "He bought it on Primea from a massive skull fracture."

Adler nodded somberly. "Like a leaky red coconut."

"Enough," blurted the Armstrong. "That's enough chatter. Let's keep it down." Poor guy was even paler than Eight. Looks like it wasn't just her first mission.

"Let me guess," Webb said to him. "First away mission?"

"So?" He glared at her. "They told me not to talk to you."

Webb leaned in to Eight, nodded at the Armstrong. "See that acne farm over there? Armstrongs don't risk their own. If he's here, you know what that means?"

"What?"

"It means we'll be *fine.*"

And just like that, the shuttle popped out the bottom of the storm.

⊘

The pilot set the shuttle down atop the stony outcropping of a gentle slope. "Checking atmo. Breathable," she confirmed. "Temperature, eleven degrees. Welcome to Planet Shithole." She lowered the back hatch.

At the base of the slope, packed earth stretched out beneath a dirty yellow sky. The xeno ruins squatted ominously on the desert plain below, looking like a series of entrances to cathedral naves, their pattern repeating over and over as far as the horizon stretched.

Webb and the other red shirts waited for the Armstrong—their appointed leader—to realize they were all looking at him. When he finally did, he flushed. "Shut up." He flushed harder when he realized how stupid that sounded. "Try comming the ship."

The pilot hit her badge. "Shuttle to *Independence*." There was no reply. She cast her eyes up at the storm swirling above them. "Storm's eating the signal."

"I can hear that." He unbuckled his harness. "Let's get that stuff unpacked and set anchor."

"Copy." Swank unfolded the gravjack and offloaded the gear.

Webb took her first step onto an unsettled planet in years. The last one had also involved a shuttle, one she'd been flying. It struck her that she'd never see this again, the majesty of this moment, those towering ruins extending off under an alien sky. She regarded their distant arching curves in sadness and wonder.

The ruins seemed to echo the feelings back at her. Her head swam. She considered raiding the shuttle's medkit for a rehydrator.

Eight lowered her binoculars. "Huh."

Webb looked a question at her. Eight handed over the binocs, pointed to the plain.

Through them, Webb saw a series of rotten circular fields in the near distance, stretching in a line from the plain towards the ruins. "What am I looking at?"

"Barley. Sorghum. That first one was wheat. The others are too far away to tell given the decay."

Webb lowered the binocs. "How long have they been here?"

"Not long. Since whenever the *Flagstaff* was here. But they've taken a lot of damage in that time."

"The storms?"

"Most likely," said Eight. "But take another look at the breakage. If it were just the storms, they'd all be flattened in the same patterns. Those look broken."

Webb handed the binoculars back. "What's that mean?"

"It means this place might not be as promising as Settlement assessed. They flag any rock that ticks all the right boxes, yeah? Climate, atmo, within the habitable band…"

"Water." Water was at the forefront of Webb's mind. Her throat was dry as the Mojave. "So what's wrong with it?"

Eight handed her a canteen. "Could be the soil isn't hospitable to the bacteria in the pods. If that doesn't take, you get no grow cycle." She hefted one of the globe-headed agripods. "These are optimized for high-yield harvests, but they get those by sucking a ton of minerals out of the soil. They don't bother replacing those, because why would they?"

Webb eyed the fields. "Is that why we're burning through so many resource worlds?"

Eight nodded. "On a hospitable rock, they'll extract all nutrients from the soil in a few cycles. Once there's a downturn in yield, the settlers pull up stakes and go to the next planet. Colonizers only stay long enough to turn a planet into food or ore or whatever else until their transports are full." She stooped, crumbled a pinch of soil between her fingers. "Could be the crops failed because they're all aggressive strains. You can't pull out what isn't in the soil."

"Does that explain the breakage?"

"Not really." She looked out over the broken fields. "Sure seems a long way to go for another load of soybeans. Makes you wonder why we don't just fab everything."

"That sounds like dissident talk, technician," said the Armstrong. "You can get yourself brigged for that."

"Sorry, sir. Just thinking out loud. Won't happen again."

Webb regarded her frankly. "I might come to regret not knowing you, Eight."

"That's not my name. Six months, right?"

Webb's grin faded. "Right." She'd be well gone by then.

Yolanda Eight picked a pair of agripods from the pallet with the care of an artist choosing her brushes. "I need to repeat the experiment, see if I can determine why the test fields degraded so quickly."

"What've you got there?"

"Corn and beans," said Eight. "I'm gonna jury-rig a milpa, see if getting them to grow around one another will help. It mixes the crop, but the structures support each other and are more stable than a monoculture. If it holds, I'll add squashes and tomatoes."

Webb's mouth watered. The promise of real, fresh vegetables… "That sounds amazing. I'll go with you."

"You'll stay with the shuttle," said the Armstrong. "Make yourself useful and get that anchor set."

Webb watched Eight tread down towards the fields. The mousy agri-tech seemed to have gotten over her fear. Webb couldn't really remember what that felt like—not so much being over the fear, but not being jaded. She kind of envied that Eight still had the spark.

The teleportation anchor was metallic mesh stretched out between translator pylons. The moment she turned it on, their badges all chimed in unison.

The kid tapped his badge. "Bilson to *Independence*. Anchor in place."

"Copy, technician," Blackwell commed back. "Stand by for transport."

The air shimmered before them and seemed to split. With a whiff of ozone, Blackwell appeared, and then the captain, and then most of the rest of the bridge crew: Winesborough, Sivos, Osei the communications officer… and Dr. Marwazi. Webb felt her heart shimmer and seem to split.

Marwazi noticed her. His brow furrowed.

Webb realized her hair was still a plate-like protrusion on the side of her head. She flushed, mentally kicked herself. Too late to grab a handful fo grease to plaster it down.

A flash from the flatland, a burst of blue light veined with yellow, and a circular corn field unfolded on the plain. The storm seemed to worsen in reply.

The captain shook his head, looked sidelong at the new field. "That's one of yours," he told Winesborough.

The science officer leisurely looked Eight's way. "The one operating independently?"

"She acted without orders. Get your tech under control."

"Oh, you mean the one I'm not micromanaging?"

Webb snorted. Too loud, because Winesborough looked her way. He shot her a nod and the snap guns.

Webb hid her smile, which wasn't hard, drowned as it was by the annoying realization that her last day was turning out well. Because of course it would, damn it. Alien ruins, stimulating conversation, the actual officers she liked in play… Maybe she shouldn't have given up on away missions for all those years. Maybe it was just karmic balance for the hangover.

The captain strode to the top of the ridge and struck an unnecessary pose above the officers. "Somewhere in this system, the *Flagstaff* vanished. While locating the ship is our highest priority, we owe it to the Coalition to map this planet and explore its ruins. You'll recall that we are outside Coalition space, so salvage rules apply."

Ah, thought Webb. That explains all the bridge crew. No one wanted to miss a chance to pad their retirement.

"You'll also recall that your lay is one-fiftieth of any profits acquired over the course of our deployment, with forty percent going to the Coalition. Which, of course, doesn't apply if you don't happen to find anything." He winked. Knowing chuckles from the crew. "Now, let's go expand the realms of men."

The officers whooped and ran towards the ruins, their escort of soldiers following at a trot.

✺

Blackwell had told her to stay with the shuttle. Since it was her last day, he'd explained with a smirk, there was no point putting her at risk. "At risk" meant seeing the cool stuff in the ruins, an actual fun perk of the job.

Webb didn't mind. It gave her a chance to put some work in on the cogfinder. She hadn't given up on the idea of selling copies if she could work out the kinks.

And it wasn't like she had much else to do. She couldn't stay outside with the storm worsening. Ever since Eight had popped her agripod, the winds had picked up and the temperature had dropped to single digits. Grit was pounding the sides of the shuttle in a miniature hailstorm. Only an idiot would be out in that.

Bilson was out in that, puking vodka and regret against the side of the shuttle.

Webb had never seen the Armstrong initiation ritual before. The Armstrongs who'd teeped down with the officers had encircled Bilson and told him to claim the planet. He'd done so, planting the flag—the Armstrong one, not the Coalition's—urinating a circle around it, and bellowing "Caelum Nostrum!" The Armstrongs pinned their blood drop badge on him and made him drink about a quart of alcohol from a pump.

Now her unit commander was hunkered down in the storm, retching out his last few meals and, by the sound of it, several childhood memories. She almost felt sorry for him. She couldn't, though, since he wouldn't even have a hangover. They'd given him the rehydrator.

So distracted had she been by Bilson's heaving that she hadn't noticed the cogfinder light up.

She studied it in surprise. Its monitor couldn't draw an accurate background—the heavy metals in the planet's bones were preventing that—but there was activity on its screen. Blips. Several of them.

That was odd. No chance there was a cog out there. Cogs didn't go on away missions. The risk of loss was too costly.

Webb dialed down the scope of her scan. The blips were coming from the ruins. The finder must have caught a signal echo bouncing around in there. That would explain the multiple hits.

But not what originated it. Maybe a cog had wandered into a teleporter stream and gotten whisked down? Teeping sometimes futzed with their neural circuitry. It was possible one had come down by accident and wandered off. Hell, maybe she could claim it as salvage and sell it back to the Coalition. She chuckled.

A runner popped his head into the shuttle. "Unit commander?"

Webb jerked her thumb towards the wall. Bilson puked on cue. "What's up?"

"Comms are down," said the runner. "Command wants us to regroup at the fields."

"Out in that?"

"Affirmative. We're running the message team to team."

"Efficient." Comms didn't go from comm to comm; they had to go to the ship first to be logged. The storm must be interfering with things again. "Need a breather?"

"Please." The runner collapsed into a harness. "You want Wino or Marwazi?"

Webb's heart leapt. "Oh, I guess I'll take the doctor? Where is he?"

The runner gestured towards the ruins. Towards the area where her cogfinder was blipping. Two birds with one stone it was.

Webb stepped out into the storm. "I'm leaving my post," she told Bilson. "If that's okay, don't say anything."

Bilson didn't. He wasn't in much of a position to, not lying against the shuttle in a puddle of his own vomit. Webb laid a blanket over him. He muttered a thank you and lost consciousness.

❶

Webb hustled overland towards the ruins. They were farther away and far larger than they appeared at a distance. Their tapered entrances towered above, their surfaced pitted by age and erosion. Any writing or decorative work on the stone had been lost to time.

Webb couldn't get a real sense of their scale. Too much of the ruins' interior was buried in sand. The dunes and an eon's worth of wind had filled the chamber leading back to the plain. She wondered, not for the first time, who built the place, and why.

Not her concern. Her mission was having a sober conversation with Marwazi before she mustered out.

She followed the little glowing tags the away team had left to mark their path into the ruins. Those were required by the reg, but few of the teams followed them. It was tedious stopping to log your position every hundred meters. Plus, if you did stop, you were wasting precious tomb-looting time and inviting another team to lap you.

Webb was glad to see Marwazi had marked his way. It was one of the things she liked about him, his adherence to regulations. Those kept the crew safe.

She left the light behind her and entered a high-ceilinged chamber with corridors that went off at angles through the ceiling. It was too dark to tell if that was the intent of the design, or if an upper floor had collapsed and been buried in the sands. Some sort of stony air ducts, perhaps?

In the shadows behind her, something skittered across the sand.

Webb whirled, heart thrumming. She saw nothing there, could hear nothing but the rumble of the distant storm.

The Armstrongs were probably pranking her. Stupid assholes. She wished she were armed.

Another skitter from the ceiling this time. It startled a yelp out of her. The chamber echoed the yelp back at her from all directions.

Screw it, Marwazi wasn't that hot. She turned and ran, tripped over something solid and found herself sliding down a slope, she couldn't tell how far, until she hit a stony floor.

Webb rose on unsteady feet, felt back at the slope. Its angle was steep. She couldn't see a damn thing.

Panic settled over her. The comms were down, she hadn't seen a tag in a while, and she had no light. She'd fallen into these ruins and oh god they were never going to find her why had she thought the day was turning out well—

A beam of light turned a corner. She whirled towards it. "Hello?"

A glowing bolt like lightning threw her against the slope. For a moment of blinding pain, she couldn't move, couldn't breathe—her guts all seized at once. She pitched forward and convulsed.

Marwazi, staring in shock, lowered his sidearm. "Oh, dearest God, I am so dreadfully sorry."

"Quite the seizure there. Up we go." She felt Adler take hold of her arm. He helped her up. "Good thing that was on stun, Doc."

"Morrison took a close-range stun on Imbar 6." Swank lit up the chamber with his hand lamp. "Internal hemorrhaging did him in."

Webb's guts burned. "You shot me," she managed.

Marwazi holstered his sidearm and took out his scanner. "Please tell me where the pain is."

"Pretty much where you shot me. Isn't that a direct violation of your oath?"

"I'm afraid you don't look so good, Technician."

"That's probably the hangover," said Adler.

Webb's head finally stopped spinning. Her stomach didn't, though, and made a motion to adjourn. Her esophagus seconded.

No. Not here. Not in front of her crush. She clutched her guts and vomited copiously.

Swank stepped back and let out a low whistle. "Morrison barfed too. First symptom, really."

Webb slid onto her butt. "I'm fine." She wasn't. "Really. Just let me sit here for a few weeks. I can't believe you shot me."

Their badges chimed in unison. "… postponing search and survey," Blackwell said over the comms.

Webb snorted. "Of course they're working now."

"Reconvene at the teep anchor."

Marwazi tapped his badge. "Copy. Sir? We've had an accidental weapons discharge."

A pause. "Is everyone alright?"

"I shot a technician."

"At least no one was hurt. Blackwell out."

Marwazi handed a data pad to Adler. "Please increase the brightness of the tags upon your return. I'll escort the patient back."

With a nod from the doc, Adler and Swank disappeared around a corner. She heard the clap of boots on stairs. There were stairs? Of course there bunking were. She glared at the slope she'd slid down and blinked in surprise at the vomit pooled at its base.

"Do you need help to stand?" said the doctor.

Webb ignored him. Her eyes had adjusted enough that she could watch her spew spread across the floor. Across the oddly smooth, almost polished floor. Two lines of the liquid suddenly darted off to the side, in perfect parallel, terminating at a section of wall.

"Technician?" Marwazi stooped in front of her. "Are you hurt?"

She shushed him. "Look." She pointed. "Those are tracks."

"Tracks?"

"Yeah." Slim and shallow, but there. Clearly engineered.

"For what?"

"If I had to guess…" She teetered over to the wall, found a stony outcropping, and pulled.

A stone door slid out of the wall along the tracks in the floor. The corridor beyond glowed an eerie blue.

Marwazi's jaw dropped. He stared down the glowing corridor in childlike wonder. "Oh, Technician. What have you found?"

82

Webb could only shake her head. This could only happen on her last day. "Want to find out?"

Chapter 5
Mors Certissima

Beyond the door lay a tunnel that extended a dozen meters before dropping down a hexagonal shaft. Webb braced herself against the wall of the passage and peered down. The shaft was about three meters across and choked with boulders. A soft blue light cast an eerie glow up from its depths.

She felt Marwazi peer over her shoulder. Her pulse quickened, not entirely from the discovery. "What do you think this is?"

He held his scanner out over the shaft. Its lights were harsh in the near darkness. "These rocks are of a different material than the ruins."

Webb checked the ceiling. It ran solid and smooth with no signs of distress. "This wasn't a cave-in. These were moved here."

"My conclusion as well." He turned her way. The blue glow limned his jaw with starlight. "But who would do that? And why? This is quite exciting."

"Shit yeah, it is. My hands are shaking." She made a few fists to get her pulse under control, took a few deep breaths the way Frankie always told her to. Don't overwhelm yourself. One thing at a time. "Pardon my language, by the way."

"I was thinking along the same lines. Do you think the *Flagstaff* put these here?"

"Can't say for sure, but I wouldn't bet on it. If they wanted to plug the shaft, blasting the ceiling's the easiest way. These were brought from elsewhere."

"Teleported?"

"Unlikely. Not with all the interference. We're lucky our scanners are even working now." She ran hers above the pit. "None of these rocks are larger than about half the diameter of the shaft. But still, the effort involved in moving them by hand would've been... huh."

"What is it?"

"They're soundly arranged. Structurally so, almost engineered. Look." She kick-pushed a smaller stone. It didn't budge. "Good balance points, consistent weight distribution. Room enough between stones for ventilation. And solid as a rock wall."

Marwazi stooped to shove at a rock. "What does that mean?"

"It means whoever did this knew what they were doing."

"They clearly wanted to seal this shaft."

"But they didn't." His silhouette turned her way. "Not entirely." She pointed towards the far side of the pit, where the blue light glowed with the greatest intensity.

Marwazi clicked on his light and aimed where she pointed. A gap in the stones lit up, a meter-wide shaft within the shaft. "Seems they missed a spot."

Webb shook her head. "No, that's deliberate." The mat of boulders screamed broken ankle, especially given her hangover, but Webb's curiosity got the better of her. "Hold the light out if you don't mind. I can't believe I'm doing this."

"What *are* you doing?"

"Can't get a good look from here." She stepped gingerly onto the first boulder. It was porous enough to provide a good grip.

"Be careful, Technician."

"We have names, Doc." She hopped to the next stone. "Webb's fine. Fix me up if I break something?"

"Seems only fair, considering I shot you."

"Deal." She skipped across the topmost boulders and peered down the gap. It plunged at least twenty meters to a polished floor. While the arrangement of stones ringing it was hardly uniform, the width of the shaft remained consistent. As did the glow from below. She let out a low whistle.

"What do you see?"

"An access shaft." Made of stacked stone, but she'd been through enough maintenance hatches to know what she was looking at. "A way down through the wider shaft they blocked."

"They?"

"I mean, somebody did it. And they balanced these stones with mechanical precision while leaving an effective ladder to another level."

Marwazi leaned forward as far as he could without stepping over the shaft. "Why leave access if the point is to block the shaft?"

"Maybe they were just trying to narrow it." A chill ran over her skin. "Or keep something from getting through."

"There's that 'they' again."

"Nice alliteration, Doc."

"Dr. Marwazi will do. I think we should start back. This is fascinating, but as you point out, the ruins have been interfering with our instruments. If we get lost or hurt we've no way to call for aid. And we've already been called to reconvene."

Webb looked down the eerie blue shaft. If she went back, she'd never find out what was causing that glow or who stacked these stones. Discoveries—the big ones, ruins and races and the like—were the purview of officers, as were the accolades and book deals and naming rights that flowed from them. Leaving now would be intentionally waking herself mid-dream. There'd be no slipping back into it, and she'd always be left wondering. "Don't you want to see what's down there?"

She heard his weight shift. "Of course I do."

"We're literally *right here,* Doc. Tor Marwazi, sorry."

"We're hardly equipped for it."

"No, but… we've got a chance for real discovery here." She'd never had that. She hoped she didn't sound like she was whining. She scanned below. Her device groaned in protest. "I'm getting a ton of magnetic interference."

"More so than from above?" He sounded closer.

87

"Way more. You know, that might have been what made my... personal device wig out." She couldn't call it her cogfinder without raising eyebrows. "We should at least find out what's causing that glow."

"We can flag this point for further exploration."

"If it's electronic, what's its power source? If it's not, well... what *is* it?" She was thinking out loud now. Walk through it. Everything has a mechanical explanation. "We didn't pick up any tech from the ship's scans. Or heat, for that matter. Light equals heat, even in low amounts. We should have picked up the heat. Why was there no heat?"

Marwazi shook his head. "You're going down, aren't you."

She had already descended halfway. "There are natural handholds. I mean, not *natural,* these stones were arranged. But still. It's an easy climb."

"Technician?"

"Webb. I'm just getting enough for a full report. The chief likes it when we're thorough." She alighted quietly at the bottom and turned to find herself in a chamber of stars.

The passage below was hexagonal, carved through the stone at the same width as the shaft. Glowing blue streaks in patterns she couldn't identify ran the length of the tunnel in veins and dots and whorls. It was as though the passage had been wallpapered with a Van Gogh sky. "You *really* want to see this."

A grunt of effort, a slap of boots on stone, and the doctor ducked into the passage. "Oh, my." He straightened, gaped with the slack-jawed wonder of a child seeing their first stars. "Oh, *my.* Oh my, oh my."

He looked ready to cry. Or to dance. Unmade, like his ego had dissolved in the presence of ineffable splendor. He put his hand to his heart, a gesture Webb repeated. Whatever happened above, wherever she wound up, she'd have this little moment, this glimpse into the soul of her crush. "Beautiful."

He nodded. He thought she meant the patterns. Which she also did, but not exclusively. "I'm no expert, but it almost looks like... bioluminescence."

"Biological light?" She wiped at a streak of it with her sleeve. The color didn't smudge. "Like the deep-sea nightmare fish?"

"Not just those. And not just in the sea." He scanned a particularly dense patch of color. "Fireflies, glow worms… though in the latter case, it's used to attract prey. They dangle sticky nets of it to ensnare insects. And those examples are of chemical reactions, ones that consume their fuel over time."

"I thought you said you weren't an expert."

He slapped his scanner. "I can't get a reading. Interference is too strong. We should get a sample for Phillips."

The ship's Head of Xenobiology. Baron Freakbomb to the crew. She'd never had cause or desire to learn why. "We could try scanning some on the surface. The interference wouldn't be as strong there."

"I didn't bring my sample case." He sounded apologetic. "If I'd known. If I'd suspected! Life signs were negative."

They stood there in the near-dark, faces lit by softly glowing streaks of mystery. Their eyes found each other. They shared a smile.

"Thank you for coming down," said Webb. "I'm really glad I got to see this." She left out *with you.*

"As am I," said Marwazi. "Thanks for taking the initiative."

"Do you really want to go back?"

"I really don't," he said. "But protocol is protocol. And the longer we linger, the more likely a search party comes after us. One not in a pleasant mood."

"Seriously. I don't want to get court-martialed." She toed the floor. "They're just looking for an excuse to come down on me with both feet."

Marwazi tapped his badge. It spat out static. He tapped it off again. "With the comms down, we hardly could have gotten the message to reconvene."

Webb shifted her feet. "Except I was sent to tell you."

"And you did." A smile crept up his face. "And then I enlisted you for a side mission. Let's at least see where this tunnel goes."

89

Webb returned his grin. "Aye aye, Doctor."

"While we're here, just the two of us? Call me Haroun."

Her whole body smiled.

⌀

The passage turned to open up into a much larger chamber, also hexagonal, with cryptic bioluminescence swirling up its vaulted ceiling. Their glow wasn't enough to light a space so large, and the heart of the chamber lay dark.

"Could you share your light?" Webb asked him.

Marwazi handed it to her. "I don't think it's enough for the chamber."

"You'd think." She popped the bulb out of it housing. "Little engineering trick." She set the light to diffuse, clicked on hover mode, and tossed it into the chamber.

The bulb traced a high, gentle arc through the air before plowing into the floor with the grace of a drunken star.

Marwazi raised an eyebrow. "Was it supposed to do that?"

"It most certainly was not." Webb was glad it was too dark to see her flush.

"Is this still part of the trick?"

"It's supposed to... it was gonna hang up there and... never mind." She retrieved the bulb and held it up.

To Webb's eye, the room was obviously engineered, though whoever had done so had taken pains to preserve the natural contours of the cave. More hexagonal tunnels snaked off in different directions, but none had nearly as much bioglow as the one they'd come down. Flat areas had been carved around lumps of raised rock in the floor. Near those, other stones of different material had been set on stony bases, moved here for unclear purposes.

Webb scanned the nearest lump. Her instruments went haywire. "Whoa."

"What have you found?"

"An overloaded scanner. Hang on." She tugged a metal switch off the scanner and dropped it in the air. It snapped to the side of the stone. "Just what I thought."

"Which was?"

"Lodestone. Magnetite."

His face was blank.

"Natural magnets." She climbed over a mound of brown stone to examine a lump that didn't match the rest of the chamber. The switch stuck to it as well. "These others have been moved here. Look, even in this light you can see their sediment. The layers are different. Someone's been collecting magnetite, and bringing it to a chamber that already had a lot of it."

"Is that what kept the bulb from hovering?"

"No, that was gravity."

"Such cheek."

"Thank you. But yeah, the magnets probably knocked it out of the air."

Marwazi stepped back to get a wider look. "These are arranged in a pattern. In concentric hexagons. And... oh. *My.* "

Webb turned the bulb towards the doctor. It found him staring at a stump of stone Webb had mistaken for a tall lump of rock. With the light right, she could see its angular contours. And stony limbs.

Marwazi turned his head her way but not his eyes. "What do you make of this?"

Webb circled around to its front. It was a statue, glittering with metallic pinpricks, of a creature she'd never seen: a xeno octoped with slim, armored limbs, slightly shorter than her, with six legs folded beneath it. It looked like a great stony insect sitting in repose, like some thoughtful hybrid of ant and mantis. It wasn't a perfect comparison; its abdomen was not separate from its thorax, and Webb saw no wings. Its forelimbs, longer and thicker than its legs, were raised skyward. And its head was missing.

"Wow," said Webb. "Now *that* is ugly. I'll bet not even the captain would have sex with that."

Marwazi checked the statue's neck. "It appears to have been decapitated. Sliced clean through." He framed it with his data pad and started recording.

Webb scanned the statue. Her device blipped and flatlined again. "Magnetite. Possibly solid." And certainly powerful. It was trying to pull the structural mesh in her lungs right out of her chest.

A wave of dizziness hit her. Her thoughts started to drift. She put a hand to her head as if she could sweep them back in, but it was like fighting the tide with a broom.

Her thoughts went from the falling starlight of her bulb to the starlight outside the NEOS to looking out over so many worlds—which wasn't accurate; she never used a planetside view—and then she was falling out the NEOS airlock and drifting towards a sickly yellow planet until she shook herself back to the present.

She wobbled and had to sit.

"Webb?" Marwazi appeared above her. "Are you alright?"

"Yeah." She had to blink a couple times to put herself back in the chamber. "Just… really disoriented all of a sudden. Vertigo out of nowhere."

He clicked on a light pen. "Let me check your eyes."

She suddenly felt cold and scared. "I think we should go." She rose in a turn towards their tunnel and her spine turned to ice.

The stone she'd climbed over was gone.

No, not gone. Standing. Looking at her, at them. A xeno, a hulking shadow the shape of the statue but towering above, a line of black orbs rimming its wedge-shaped head—eyes, like a spider's, each the size of Seven's cricket ball.

On reflex, Webb switched her bulb to specular and aimed the beam at its head. The creature's eyes went from black to silver. It didn't turn away.

She couldn't scream. She couldn't breathe. But she could run, so she did, scrabbling breathlessly as though through a nightmare, as if she could outpace the thought that they'd just discovered exactly why the shaft had been sealed.

𝒪

She'd never run so fast, or with so little attention towards what lay in her path. She flew up first the chimney and then the stairs, her pulse thundering, her lungs straining to pull enough oxygen out of the air, and streaked across the sands inside the ruins. She didn't even hear the sandstorm outside until it knocked her off her feet.

She shielded eyes blinded by the light with bloody fingers torn in her scramble up the shaft. The world swam around her as her senses reoriented, and she nearly vomited again. Running for your life was inappropriate hangover activity, especially when the lizard part of your brain wouldn't stop screaming.

Marwazi dropped to all fours beside her. Webb guessed he didn't do much sprinting in the Infirmary. "You okay?"

He nodded, eyes on the sand, and giggled. "Did you see that?"

She looked back towards the ruins. No towering angular xeno was following them out. No way it was getting through that stack of stones. Not quickly, at least. She knew that intellectually, but try telling that to her amygdala.

Marwazi, still giggling, was on his feet now, and pulling her to hers. "Did you *see* that? Of course you did. What a marvel. What an absolute *marvel!* God is great! I nearly pissed myself."

Webb could only nod. The pounding of her pulse wasn't allowing for much speech yet.

A clutch of soldiers emerged through the sands. Marwazi spotted them and waved for their attention. "Here!"

"Lerd." Webb slumped when she saw who was leading them.

93

Blackwell marched up with fists balled at his sides. "Bilson said I'd find you here."

So the babyfaced Armstrong had ratted her out. And after she'd given him that blanket. "Sir. I was relaying the order to regroup."

"That order went out an hour ago." He gave Marwazi a dirty look. "The rest of your team arrived shortly thereafter."

"Yes." Marzawi grinned back giddily. "You won't believe what we found."

"I'm surprised at you, Doctor. You know our protocols when the comms go down."

"There were extenuating circumstances, I assure you. Sir. Under these very ruins, we encountered the most incredible—"

"*Under?* You went beyond mission parameters?" He glared sidelong at Webb. "Where'd you get that idea?"

"We stumbled upon a great chamber, an *inhabited* chamber further underground. Some sort of den for a truly massive creature!"

Blackwell was nodding—too quickly, not so much listening as waiting for his turn to speak. "Maybe you saw something. Maybe you were jumping at shadows. Life scans were negative."

"Conventional scans." Webb pulled the cogfinder from her belt. "But I've been fiddling with this personal device? It lit up like a holiday tree. I thought it was a glitch, but—"

"Is that a recording device?" Blackwell eyed the cogfinder.

"What? No, it's a—"

"*I* recorded it," said Marwazi. "With my data pad. Which is…" He patted at his uniform. "Oh dear."

"It's illegal to record officers exercising their duty."

"It's not a recorder!" said Webb. "It's a… well…" She couldn't call it what it was without incriminating herself.

"Here!" Marwazi held out his pad and pulled up the footage. "You see this? This was a statue, in the chamber, much smaller than the creature itself."

The end of his sentence was lost to a burst of winds and stinging sands. Just as quick as it had come, the storm abated and retreated into the sky, leaving them in a suddenly calm and quiet column of air.

Blackwell took Marwazi's data pad. "That's a statue, Doctor."

"Yes." The grin finally fell from his face. "I just said that. This was before we saw the creature. It was huge, possibly five meters tall."

"I'm seeing no creature here."

"I didn't get footage of it, I'm afraid."

"You saw a statue, then you saw its shadow on the wall and flipped your lid." He slapped the pad back in Marwazi's hands. "I would have expected steadier nerves from a senior officer."

"There was more than one, though." Webb slapped the side of the cogfinder to knock the sand from its recesses.

"There was?" said Marwazi.

"On my non-recorder. If you'll just let me fire this up..."

Blackwell narrowed his eyes. "Is that an engineering scanner?"

Webb froze. "It's the frame of one."

"Which you got where?"

Webb straightened. "I built it out of salvaged parts, and I don't appreciate the implication."

"Check yourself, Technician. If I check its serial number, will I find this one missing?"

When she didn't reply, he motioned for her to hand it over. When she didn't do that, a soldier wrenched it out of her hands. "Hey! That's mine!"

"Could we *please*," implored Marwazi, "keep talking about the giant xeno arthropod?"

"Engineering scanner," Blackwell confirmed. He tapped a few keys. "And it doesn't even work. Cuff her."

Webb could either scream or chuckle, so she went with the option less likely to get her punched. "Hey Doc, maybe you want to start recording again?"

"Tag their section," Blackwell told a soldier. "If there's an artifact down there, we should retrieve it."

"Sir!" called a distant voice.

Blackwell turned to see a red shirt running towards them. Yolanda Eight, Webb noted, looking even paler and more shaken than usual. She ran up to Blackwell clutching an armful of broken wheat stalks.

The lieutenant commander eyed her. "Yes?"

"Sir, the comms are still down and I need *someone* to look at this."

"At what?"

She held out the wheat.

"Agriculture is not my department. You two," he pointed from a pair of soldiers to Webb, "take her back to the shuttle. Keep her there. The rest of you are with me."

"But sir, I—" Eight balked when she saw Webb cuffed.

Webb waved. "Hey."

Eight recovered quickly. "Sir, we figured out why the stalks were broken."

"Yes, well done. Put it in your report. And we're walking." He strode off towards the new corn field a half kilometer distant.

Marwazi looked an apology to Webb as the soldiers led her away. "I'll take this up with the captain. I'll put in a good word for you. Don't worry! We will discuss this again!" He fell in line behind Blackwell.

Eight looked like she couldn't decide who to follow. "This is important."

"I believe you," Webb called over her shoulder.

"Who do I take it to?"

"Your superior. That's all you really can do."

"But." Eight slumped. "Nobody listens to me."

"You're just getting that?" She'd meant it as a joke, but it felt meaner than she'd intended. Whatever. You grew calluses quick in the service. The cuffs chafed, but Dewey would spring her once she'd confirmed the scanner wasn't stolen. "Good luck. I can't help you. Last day." One she'd be spending at least part of in a cell. She wondered if Dr. Marwazi would visit.

No, not Dr. Marwazi. *Haroun.* She grinned despite the cuffs.

Ø

Blackwell found Seagrave with the other senior officers at the edge of the new corn field. He also found him pale.

The captain gave them a curt nod and turned to the knot of officers. "Now that we're all here."

"Captain," began Marwazi, "I—"

"Nothing in the ruins." Sivos bit into an ear of sweet corn. "Just tunnels on tunnels."

"No leads as to where the ship went down," said Osei. "No luck establishing sub-stratospheric communication either. I don't think we should stop trying, though. These storms have to blow off eventually."

Seagrave nodded languidly, turned to Marwazi. "Took your sweet time, Doctor."

"Captain." Marwazi stepped around Blackwell. "I encountered—my team and I, I should say—encountered an enormous *non-humanoid* xeno in our section. By all signs intelligent."

The officers eyed one another. Sivos picked corn from his teeth.

Before Blackwell could speak, the captain asked "Where?"

"In catacombs beneath the ruins. It was truly massive. Here." He played his footage for the officers. "It looked like this. Some manner of great arthropod, crustacean or maybe insectoid. We didn't get close enough to tell."

"That looks like a statue," said the captain.

"It is," said Blackwell.

"*This* is, yes," said Marwazi. "We found it in a shrine of sorts. A space filled with decorations and magnetite, both natural and transplanted."

97

"Lieutenant!" A hysterical technician—that damn agro tech again—ran up to Winesborough, who was hanging in his usual spot near the back. "Please, this can't wait."

"Technician, are we not clearly in a meeting?" Blackwell bellowed at her.

Short as she was, she still managed to shrink. And hiccup. "You said take it to my superior."

The captain set one hand to his stomach and the other on Blackwell's shoulder. "Wino, get your tech under control."

"I got this." Winesborough took her aside. He hadn't taken more than a couple steps before she shoved the wheat stalks into his hands and pointed frantically back at the broken field. Whatever she said lit a fire under his ass. Winesborough broke into a sprint and ran back towards the field with her.

"That must be some important wheat," said the captain. Everyone but Sivos laughed. "I've never seen Wino move that fast."

"Neither have I." Sivos kept his eyes on the wheat field.

"Let's wrap this up and get back upstairs," said Seagrave.

"Captain, I request permission to return to my section of the ruins with a larger team," said Marwazi. "And security."

"Denied. We'll continue the search for the *Flagstaff* from the bridge. Did you at least tag the statue?"

"I sent a soldier to find it," said Blackwell.

"Good," said Seagrave. "At least today wasn't a total loss."

"*Captain.*" Marwazi seemed equally befuddled and agitated. "We are so greatly downplaying the magnitude of this moment."

"Yes, yes, yes." Seagrave dismissed that with a wave. "We'll send a team to tag and cage whatever critter you think you saw down there. You clearly found something." He squinted at the doctor's data pad. "Shame the head is missing. I wonder what it looked like."

An alarmed shout split the air. Everyone looked towards each other and then towards the ruins.

There, atop a low rise, a child-sized silver ant-like creature regarded them with its wedge-shaped head.

"Like that," said the doctor.

Chapter 6
Ossa Iacta Sunt

Her hands cuffed at the small of her back, Webb followed the soldiers back to the landing zone, where the ship's other shuttle alighted on a ridge near the officers. Probably there to ferry looted artifacts back to the *Independence*. Teleporting their spoils back through a storm was a risk the officers were unlikely to take.

Webb watched a couple red shirts wrestle a gravjack laden with agripods down the second shuttle's ramp. Maybe they were only going to run some more experiments. Maybe double duty, equal parts looting and terraforming. Always nice to give something back.

The sky behind them lit up like a sudden sunrise. Webb and the soldiers turned to see a flare arc lazily under the churning clouds. They followed its trajectory down to the cluster of bridge officers and the silvery little xeno.

Webb went rigid. The soldiers didn't react—they weren't quite sure what they were looking at—until one peered through his binocs and nearly tripped over his feet. "Holy…"

"What?" Webb tried to keep her voice steady.

The soldier passed the binocs to his partner. "The hell *is* that?"

"A xeno," said Webb.

"It looks like a walking pile of fishhooks."

The first soldier eyed Webb. "Is that what you saw?"

"No." It really wasn't. "That one's small. And silver. The one in the ruins wasn't shiny."

A second flare went up, this one red. The troops stiffened. "Comms must be down," said the first.

The other hit his badge and got only static. He checked the charge in his rifle. "Keep on to the shuttle," he told Webb. "You know the way."

They were off before she could reply, bounding across tawny sands. Webb looked to the shuttle. Even from here, she caught a whiff of puke. Her eyes went from the xeno to the dead wheat field where Yolanda Eight appeared to be losing her mind.

ℓ

The xeno tilted its head to watch the second flare burn its arc through the sky. It didn't seem to mind the glare—its eyes had darkened and it didn't look away. Neither did it cower. If anything, it looked curious. Then it turned its rows of eyes back on them.

Blackwell's skin crawled. The oldest parts of his brain screamed for him to kill it, to smash the bug-thing to paste with scream-powered bashings of rock. It was all he could do to maintain his composure.

Sivos mashed his badge again, got the same burst of static. The storm cell must be swallowing the signal. "Firing line!" he yelled over the wind.

A row of rifles knelt in front of the officers.

"Cool it, Chief." Seagrave seemed more intrigued than alarmed. "Fingers off those triggers, boys."

Sivos put a hand on the captain's shoulder. "Sir. We are out of contact with the ship. We are unprepared for—"

"I won't have a first contact massacre on my record." The captain shrugged him off. "Lower those guns. What are you all afraid of?"

Blackwell admired the captain's sangfroid. What he saw was a child-sized metal insect made of jagged shards of chrome. Compound eyes—silver again now that the flare had burned out in the sands light— regarded him from a wedge-shaped head. A head his brain screamed he should be crushing with a stone.

The captain pulled the doctor forward. "Is this what you saw in the ruins?"

"Yes. And no," said Marwazi.

"Well, which is it?"

"The specimen we saw was larger. Much larger, at least five meters tall. This one is tiny by comparison."

"Any idea why?"

The question seemed to catch Marwazi off guard. "I can't possibly say at the moment. A juvenile? Sexual dimorphism? It could be a different species entirely. We simply don't have enough information to..."

He trailed off as Seagrave sighed. "Then why are you even here, Doctor?"

"Medical support." Marwazi shifted his feet. "This was supposed to be a dead planet. We left Xenobiology on the ship."

"What's that on its back?" asked the helm officer.

As if it had been waiting for the question, the xeno held something up for them all to see. Blackwell's blood ran cold.

The captain once again seemed more fascinated rather than concerned. "Is that...?"

"It is." Blackwell watched it unfold like a pockmarked flag in the wind. "A Coalition pressure suit."

✺

Webb trotted back towards the wheat field. She probably should have continued on to the shuttle—not probably, *absolutely* should have—but it wasn't going anywhere. And she owed it to herself to get an un-panicked look at what she'd seen down below.

She was also curious to know why Eight was going bonkers, and Webb could hardly comm her with her hands tied. Had the comms even been working.

She crunched through the edge of the field to find Eight trying to get Winesborough to pay attention to her armful of wheat stalks. His eyes were glued on the xeno-officer interaction half a K away.

"Hey." She nudged Eight. "What's going on? I could see you flailing halfway to the shuttle."

"There's a xeno over there," Winesborough said absently.

"Yeah, there sure is."

"How about that. Is that the, uh…?"

"Same type. Smaller, though. Maybe an adolescent?" The doctor was with the officers. He'd offer a better guess. "So what's with—?"

With a hiccup, Eight shoved the bundle of broken stalks in her face. "Look!"

Webb did. It looked like old wheat. "At what?"

"The grain." Eight was near panic. "The heads."

Had Webb's hands been free, she'd have run her fingers over the stalks. As it was, she could only squint at them through the grit. The winds were increasing. "These look…" They were mostly bare. What little grain remained appeared to be crushed. "How do these look?" There was a familiar pattern to them. "Gnawed?"

Eight nodded, her eyes huge. "They *ate* these."

"Who did?"

"*They* did!"

"Not the xenos."

"*No!*"

Webb shook her head. "You're losing me."

Eight tossed the stalks and knelt. The floor of the field was a tangled mat of dried flattened stalks. She pulled a few aside. Webb's whimper-yelp was enough to get Winesborough to look.

Beneath the stalks lay a desiccated body in red.

"Shit," said Webb.

Winesborough said nothing, though his face twitched a couple times.

Webb's throat felt dry. She forced it to swallow. "You said *they.*"

Eight nodded and hiccuped. She pulled more of the mat aside, revealing a half dozen mummified red shirts.

"Shit, indeed," muttered Winesborough.

The alien waved the suit like a kid with a toy flag.

The captain smiled. He even snorted a chuckle. "Hey, little guy. Where'd you find that?" He took a step forward.

"Sir," warned Sivos. "Please stay behind the line."

"Let's maybe not shit our panties, Chief? It looks like it's made of glass and mercury." He snapped towards the communications officer. "Osei, record this."

"Aye, sir." He started spooling on his data pad.

Sivos leaned in close. Minus the storm, he could have spoken quietly enough not to be overheard. "Sir, we are cut off from the ship."

"Even better." The captain grinned. "Do you know how rare first contact footage is? And here we are, forging ahead, on our own like Columbus and Clark. Look, he's waving it like the flag."

"*Sir.* We have no idea what this creature is, how it evaded our life scans. Or what it's capable of."

"This could go right in the recruitment reel. My face, in front of billions... I'll betcha this gets me in the ambassador's pants." He elbowed the unsmiling chief. "How's my hair?"

"Pristine," said Blackwell. He hit record on his data pad.

Sivos motioned for Blackwell to cut. "Sir, as chief of security, I must insist you return to the shuttle."

"I smell panty shit, Chief. Osei, make sure you get footage from a side angle so we'll have cutting points. Blackwell, get inserts, cutaways. This really has to sizzle. You soldiers keep those guns down. I don't want you looking aggressive." The captain straightened his uniform, took a step closer to the alien.

The xeno reared up, mantis-like, doubling its height.

The soldiers' rifles rose in response. All smiles, the captain motioned for them to lower their weapons. Then he shook his head, his expression sour. "I can do it better. Let's take the approach again. Guns up."

The soldiers eyed one another.

"Come on." The captain mimed raising a rifle. "Let's get those up."

"Sir, please," said Sivos.

The soldiers complied. Seagrave whirled on them, arms raised, as if staring down a firing squad and motioned dramatically for them to lower their weapons. Then he turned, framed perfectly by the theatrical storm lighting, and nodded towards the xeno. "Friend. Do you understand? Friend?" The cameras didn't catch the soldiery eye rolling.

The alien shook the pressure suit. Then it darted back a few meters.

"He's out of frame," said Osei.

"I've still got him," said Blackwell.

The xeno trotted forwards again and shook the suit. It ducked its head, then abruptly rolled onto its back and writhed as if in pain. It sprung back upright, skittered back a few meters, and it ducked its head again, a repetitive scoop-nod.

"What do you think it's doing?" Blackwell asked the doctor.

"I can't," said Marwazi. "Phillips might have a guess."

"Xenobiology's back on the ship. If you *could* say?"

"Well… if we allowed ourselves to be anthropocentric, which isn't advisable, it's almost as if it's beckoning us to—"

"It's beckoning to us," said Seagrave, sliding into the foreground of Blackwell's frame. "It wants us to follow."

"Perhaps," said Marwazi. "But it would be premature to jump to—"

"Beckoning to us," repeated the captain. "And I shall answer his call."

The xeno shook the uniform, dropped on its back and writhed again. It popped up, skittered back, bobbed its head for them them to follow.

"The survivors." The captain snapped his fingers. "The crew of the *Flagstaff*. They're in pain, injured. He wants to lead us to our missing servicemen." The captain took a step forward out of the corn field.

The soldiers fell in alongside him. He shooed them back.

The xeno set down the uniform and gingerly approached the captain. It reached out to tap the nearest soldier's rifle.

"Steady there," Seagrave told the soldier. "It's wondering if that's part of your body."

The xeno returned to the uniform and held it up until the suit's feet brushed the ground.

"Standing height," observed the doctor.

The captain nodded in understanding and cheated outward for the camera. "You found our crew? Our missing friends?" He pointed from the suit to himself.

The alien set the suit on its back like a cape and skittered up the low hill towards the ruins. It hesitated there, set the uniform down in their field of view, and vanished over the rise. When they didn't follow, it poked its head over the hill, skittered back into view, pulled the suit a meter closer to the crest, and disappeared again.

"Sir, we need to *go,*" said Sivos.

"We do," said the captain. He hiked towards the hill.

Cool as a freeze seal, Winesborough squatted to scan the desiccated crew remains.

"What killed them?" Webb asked.

"De—*hic,*" started Eight. "Dehy—*hic.* Damn it."

"Didn't catch that."

"Dehydration. A scan will sh—*hic.* Show you."

"I haven't got a scanner," said Webb. "Or a hand free."

Winesborough's scanner hummed and chirped. He grunted. "She's right. Cause of death was dehydration."

Webb was incredulous. "You mean to tell me they stood in the middle of this field and bunking died of thirst?"

"Looks like."

"After eating the gr—*hic.* Grain."

"Why?" Webb looked out over the circular acre of field. "The hell kept them inside?" When no one answered, she turned to see them both staring across the expanse to where the xeno was waving the uniform.

The color had drained from Winesborough's face. He tapped his badge. "Winesborough to Seagrave."

Static.

He hit it again. "Winesborough to Captain, please respond."

Static. Eight hiccuped.

A sense of dread crept up Webb's spine. She felt like running. Absolutely should have continued to the shuttle.

Winesborough loaded Eight's arms with the stalks. "Get these back to the ship." He ripped something out of the mat and took off at a sprint towards the captain.

Eight and Webb eyed one another. Webb's bonds felt especially tight. She also felt jointly cold and laser alert. Her hangover seemed to melt away.

A quick break in the clouds brightened the sky. Not for long, just a single burst of light, but enough to reflect off the horde of shiny carapaces arrayed behind the hill.

Webb saw it. And, going off the rapid increase in hiccups, so did Eight.

𝒪

The wind whipped Seagrave's carefully coiffed hair into his face. He flicked his eyes clear, annoyed. They'd have to fix that in post. He smoothed his hair into place as the soldiers fanned out towards the hill.

Sivos stepped in front of him. "The storm's picking up and we have no eyes in the sky."

He couldn't say what he wanted to with the cameras rolling, so Seagrave put on a smile. "You seem determined to impede this moment, Chief."

"A dead planet. That's what the scanners told us. We are not equipped for this." As if on cue, the sky darkened. Thunder pealed.

Perfect drama. Possibly the lead clip in the recruitment reel. "Agreed," he said somberly. "We need to report this unexpected turn. Lieutenant Commander."

Blackwell hustled over. "Sir."

"Make plans for a basecamp. I'm sending you back on the shuttle. Tell Young to organize an away mission for a biome with neutral alien life."

"You should accompany him, Captain," said Sivos. "Your place is on the bridge."

"My place is with the brave men of my crew. I'm staying here." He put his hand over Blackwell's data pad camera. "First contact with insectoid xenos? I'll sell a million copies of my memoir." His grin slid into a grimace as he clutched his gut. He also slid sideways.

Sivos steadied him. "You're not well."

"Oh, you think, Chief?" His stomach roiled. He felt like he needed to burp for an hour. "We'll edit that part out."

Marwazi scanned him. Seagrave swatted his hands away. "Captain?"

"I don't need footage of that. Just give me a dramamine, Doctor." He blinked. "Doctor?"

Marwazi had frozen. A moment of realization. And based on the brow furrow, not a pleasant one.

Sivos saw it too. "What is it, Doc?"

"The xeno," the doctor said vacantly, as if in a dream. "Why did it bring the suit?"

"To show us he found the crew," said Blackwell.

"If they found the crew…" The doctor turned to look at him. "Why not just bring a crewman?"

The captain blinked. He saw the faces of the officers shift.

A yell from the side made them turn. Through the swirling strands of the storm, they could see Winesborough running their way from the other field, shouting and waving his arms. "Go see what he wants," said Seagrave.

"A treadmill, apparently," said Blackwell.

Winesborough had stopped, out of breath. He held something up.

Sivos pulled up his binocs and grunted. "That's a skull," he said matter-of-factly.

A shout of alarm. The soldiers who'd reached the top of the rise were sprinting back their way.

Behind them, a wave of chrome spilled over the hill—xenos, a swarm of them, moving much faster than the one with the uniform had, their forelimbs held out like cavalry sabres. They rolled over the soldiers farthest back in line, their limbs stabbing through their blast armor as if it were eggshell.

The captain mashed his badge. "Emergency teleport, now!" More static.

The remaining soldiers opened fire. Bolts of colonnaded energy ripped into the alien wave, flinging xenos back. But others kept coming. As did the ones who'd been shot—the ones the rifles should have turned into dust and ozone.

The captain felt his balls try to crawl back into his body. This wouldn't be going in the recruitment vid. "Set weapons to kill."

"They already are," barked Sivos.

Sand exploded before them. Soldiers screamed. There were xenos in their line, bursting up from the dirt like demonic bladed gophers. A few scissor-quick slices and bisected soldiers fell.

"Fall back!" Whatever Sivos said next was lost as the storm dropped and engulfed them completely.

Through stinging grit and whirling winds, Seagrave could discern only chaos and screams and the whump of falling bodies. He swallowed the churning in his gut and scrambled for the shuttle, only to find himself surrounded by a ring of silvery aliens.

It parted around the alien wearing the Coalition uniform like a cape. The xeno who'd waved it like a flag. It rose up to its full height and chittered. Scythe-like blades swung out of its forelimbs like giant switchblades.

"Now, let's talk about this." Seagrave rose, raised his hands. "No one knows more about interspecies communication than me." He straightened his uniform. "There's two ways this can go. One provides a lot of honey for everyone involved. The other—"

The xeno leapt for him.

Webb saw the blood jump up from the captain's neck. A little plume of red, a crimson ribbon from a distant paper doll.

Halfway between the fields, Winesborough reversed direction and pounded sand back towards them. He shouted something that was lost in the storm.

The meaning was clear enough. "Eight, we need to go."

Eight peered through her binocs and whimpered. She held them out for Webb.

Webb saw the wave of silvery xenos break over the soldiers, stabbing and slicing like a tide made of knives. "We need to go *right now.*"

Eight didn't move. She was hyperventilating, the muscles in her neck spasming with each rapid sip of breath.

"Eight. Stay with me."

"*Hic.* I'm just a farmer."

"You can't freeze. You freeze, you die."

"I'm just a glorified—*hic*—farmer. I can't crew this."

"I'd help, but my hands are literally tied."

Eight looked back towards Winesborough. "The lieutenant is coming."

He was, flail-sprinting his way back toward their field. He was close enough for them to see the surprise in his eyes when xenos burst out of the ground in front of him. They darted towards him like arrows. Two halves of him fell.

Panic exploded in Webb's brain, screaming and pounding on its walls, threatening to drown her. *No. Can't freeze.* She poured her fear into anger and anger into movement, and then she was flying over the sands. She'd crossed a couple hundred meters before she realized Eight wasn't with her.

Heart thrumming, she looked back. Eight stood trembling in the wheat field, clutching her damn stalks. The xenos had encircled the field, treading around it like wolves. A few of them looked Webb's way.

Webb screamed and swore as she ran, hating herself with every step, as if she could outpace the guilt. It wasn't her fault Eight froze. She wondered how far distant the memories would have to be before she believed it. Poor little farmer.

Through sand and screams, Blackwell saw the captain's head loll back like a broken thing, his blood spurting in a champagne spray. Seagrave's body crumpled. The caped xeno—the one who'd killed him—turned its clusters of eyes Blackwell's way.

Colonnaded energy split the air beside his head, slamming into the xeno and cartwheeling it back into the horde. Blackwell smelled ozone, felt heat as another salvo of fire punched past him. Aliens went flying like leaves in the wind.

Blackwell staggered towards the laser fire. Sivos had rallied his soldiers into a wedge, an ancient firing line sending a phalanx of rifle fire into the swarm. The line split to allow Blackwell through. Arms pulled and pushed him back until he found himself in a small circle where Marwazi was trying to revive the legless Osei.

Dazed, Blackwell assessed the battle line. It wouldn't hold—their weapons were doing no damage to the aliens, just flinging them back. They were fighting lions with firehoses. He saw a xeno no larger than a child get close enough to the firing line to pull a soldier's head off.

Now Sivos was yelling something in his face, pressing a pair of flags into his hands—ancient signaling devices to accompany their ancient formation; what had they come to?—and now Sivos was turning him towards the shuttles, pointing at the rocky outcropping above the landing zone.

Sivos ducked back into the firing line, shouting orders directly into his sergeants' ears. Their forces shifted—a fighting retreat towards the ridge.

Numbly, by rote, Blackwell went through the signals from that class he'd bitched about—that everyone had bitched about; semaphore in the age of starships?—signaling the shuttles for emergency evacuation.

Webb pounded into her shuttle at a dead sprint, whipping past Adler and Swank on the ramp, who were watching the carnage unfold with forgotten ration bars in their hands. "Get in the shuttle!" she yelled back at them. They jerked and hustled in after her as if the notion hadn't occurred to them.

She threw herself into a crash harness, tried to wriggle in as best she could with her hands clamped behind her back. She looked up to find everyone staring at her. "Uh... yes?"

"What do we do?" asked the pilot.

Webb blinked. "Why're you asking me?"

"You're highest rank," said Adler.

"You're kidding me."

They didn't look like they were joking. Webb scanned the shuttle. No officers on board. No soldiers, either—they'd run for the captain when the xenos showed. "What about the kid?"

The pilot gestured to Bilson, who lying unconscious in a puddle of his own vomit. "You're the highest capacitated rank."

"But he got the hangover spray."

"It doesn't work if you're drunk," said Swank. "You're up."

"Lerd. Okay." Evacuate. They had to evacuate; that should be easy enough. She held her manacles out behind her. "Keys? Anyone? Maybe a sidearm?"

"They don't arm us," said Adler.

"Hang on, I'll do it myself." She slipped her arms and under her legs, the cuffs biting into her wrists, and went to the shuttle's short-range teleporter.

"What are you doing?" asked the pilot.

"One sec." She teleported the manacles into space and turned to the pilot, rubbing her wrists. "What's your name, flygirl?"

"Sherry."

"First or last?"

A thump atop the shuttle. Then three more in succession, like bowling balls on a tin roof.

"Close the ramp!" Webb barked.

Swank slammed a button. The back whisked shut.

Pilot Sherry screamed. An alien had dropped onto the shuttle's narrow viewscreen. Scythe-like blades flicked out of its forelimbs. It hacked at the view plate.

"Nobody freak," said Webb. "That's fifteen centimeters of solid—"

The blade went through the viewscreen and Sherry's shoulder like an icepick through glass. Sherry screamed and threw her hands up to defend herself. The next chop went through her forearm.

Webb grabbed an agripod and thrust it at the xeno. The alien slashed through the canister at its head. A cloud of gas burst out, filling the shuttle with chemical dust. The xeno squealed and fled.

Webb coughed once before her lungs whirred and filtered out the agrichem smoke. The others weren't so lucky—they were hacking and clawing at their throats. Webb threw herself into the pilot's chair—Sherry had slid to the floor in shock—and hit the vents.

"Unable to comply," chirped the computer. "Vents sealed due to atmospheric detritus."

She heard more thumping and atop the shuttle. "Open the back!" She yelled at Swank. "Open it or we'll suffocate!" She grabbed the conn and lifted the shuttle off the ground.

"Warning," chimed the computer. "Shuttle is above maximum atmospheric weight."

Bastards must be heavy as tanks. They'd have to be to punch through the hull. Webb could hear, could almost feel them hacking at the shuttle's dorsal plating. "Drop that hatch!"

Between wracking hacks, Swank hit a switch. The loading ramp dropped open and out roared the cloud of agrichems, accompanied by the bone-shuddering squealing of xenos leaping off the ship. Free of their weight, the shuttle jumped up a good ten meters before stabilizing. Heavy bastards indeed.

Webb checked the viewscreen. It's iridescent shimmer told her the emergency force field had sprung up. At least that was working. She hoped it would hold through the rise through atmo.

The winds had already buried Swank's feet in sand. "Closing the hatch!" he called

"Not yet!" Webb swung the shuttle around towards the wheat field.

Swank looked at her like she was crazy. "We have to get into orbit! We're taking on sand!"

"I am not losing another bunking Yolanda." Webb hit the thrusters. In a single stride the shuttle was there, hovering above a wheat field surrounded by xenos.

"Get that gate closed." Adler put Sherry to sleep with a hypospray. "I'm doing triage here."

"One minute." Webb didn't see Eight in the mess of stalks. Her heart fell.

"We'll be full of sand in a minute!" It was up to Swank's calves.

The movement of the shuttle had apparently been enough to wake Bilson. He sat up, and managed to get a "What's going—?" out before emptying his guts.

Webb checked the monitor. Still no sign of Eight, nor of a body. Other than Winesborough's halves.

Focus, she told herself. *Find your quaddie.* "Shuttle, locate Technician…" Webb blanked on her actual name.

The shuttle chimed. "Please complete query."

If she died because Webb couldn't remember the name they wouldn't let her have, she'd hate herself forever. What did she say? Before Chelse cut her off? Had they even let her get that far? Screw it. "Shuttle, locate every technician within a hundred meters."

A blip appeared on the map directly below.

"On screen and enhance."

She saw Eight there, lying under the mat of stalks, nestled next to the dead. She'd pulled them over herself as camouflage.

Clever little farmer. Webb's slid to the teleporter controls, aimed a lock on Eight's biosign. The ship chimed a negative. "Damn it."

"Could we please hurry." Swank was knee deep in dune. "Those xenos are eyeing me."

"They can't jump that high."

"You sure?"

"Actually, no." She boosted power to the teleporter's signal anchor. Same negative chime. *"Damn* it! I can't get a lock."

"You teeped your manacles," said Adler.

"There's no storm interference inside. The particulates in the wind are bouncing the signal everywhere." She slid back to the controls. "We have to pull her up."

"If you put down, they'll jump on us."

"I have no intention of putting us down. Is the gravjack harness still back there?"

Swank looked. "Yeah."

"Drop it out the back and get ready to hit the auto-winch."

"It'll just flap in the wind."

"Weigh it down," croaked Sherry.

"Back to sleep, you." Adler zapped her again.

"Here." Webb tossed the agripod with the busted head to Swank. He threaded it through the mesh and threw the harness out the back.

Webb swung the shuttle over the field, keeping it ten meters or so above the stalks. She could see the xenos now without the monitor. They'd stopped scuttling around the perimeter and had their eyes trained on the shuttle. A couple poised to leap.

Webb jerked the shuttle up another five meters and clicked on its external speakers. It was probably the first time they'd been used for something other than crowd dispersal.

"Eight!" She couldn't see movement in the field. "Climb on the harness and we'll pull you in!"

She saw movement. Eight pulled the stalks aside and wove her arms through the mesh of the harness.

"Good farmer. Winch her in!"

"She'll smack the gate!"

Webb grunted. "Lerd. Hang on. I mean you, Eight." She hoped Eight's grip strength was up to snuff and hit the thrusters as gently as she could. The shuttle still shot away into the storm. The harness flew out behind them, Eight dangling on it like a kitten from a bough. Swank hit the winch.

The moment they'd cleared the field, xenos started leaping for them. A couple came close, soaring thirty meters up from a sprint. Webb heard a cracking thump from under the shuttle and hoped one had broken whatever passed for its neck.

The winch reeled in the harness along with Eight. Swank slammed the gate after her. Eight lay there, gripping the mesh, her face and uniform a solid orange from the sands.

"You okay?" asked Webb.

She spat out grit. "I don't like away missions."

"Now can we?" Swank pointed up.

"Hell, yes." Webb spun back to the monitors. "Heading back to the ship. Bringing her abou— oh God."

The other shuttle was covered in a crawling blanket of xenos. It shuddered and sputtered as it tried to lift off, its VTOL thrusters straining, before it lost attitude and fell prow-first into the ridge. The shuttle exploded in a modest fireball that flattened the survivors on the plain.

"That's... no." Swank looked like his brain had broken. "How? The failsafes, the hull..."

A second explosion. The flames had crawled to the skid of agripods at basecamp and blown it into a column of bruised smoke.

Webb heard a shrieking like metal on dry ice, louder even than the explosion. The xenos collectively fell back.

"Pilot's stable." Adler slipped into a harness. "What'd I mi— holy fuck what happened to the shuttle?"

"Too many xenos, and their weight..." Webb mimed her fist crashing.

"But it's solid impervium!" Swank hollered. "That force wasn't enough to break the bulkheads, so why did it explode?"

"Not sure it matters," said Webb. "Punctured fuel line? You saw them chop through our viewscreen. Who knows what they cut over there."

"I'd like to go home now," said Eight.

"Look." Adler pointed out the viewscreen.

On the field below, the survivors, flattened by the shuttle's explosion, were just starting to stir. The horde of xenos was likewise reforming.

"They were heading for the shuttle when it went down," said Webb. She took a quick headcount.

"I couldn't help but notice that we're still here," said Adler. "Let's get back upstairs. We've got wounded."

The survivors were regrouping, laying down fire to avoid being outflanked. It was a futile maneuver. Webb could see the trail of xenos extending all the way back to the ruins. They'd be encircled eventually. "We can't just leave them there."

"Sure we can," said Adler.

"It's not like they'd come back for us," said Swank.

Webb gritted her teeth. "Everyone strap in."

𝒪

With a detached sense of dread, Blackwell watched their shuttle explode. A cold grip tightened around the back of his skull. He would leave his bones on this alien world. It was only a matter of when.

Sivos apparently hadn't gotten the message. He was still directing fire as if he hadn't just watched their ride home drop out of the sky. He'd hemmed the survivors against the rocky outcropping where the soldiers could pool their fire against the xenos. The location also kept them from burrowing up under their target soldiers.

Not that it mattered. He was only delaying the inevitable.

Sunshine would never know what happened to him. She'd be stuck forever in the computer of his quarters, wondering why he never came back for her.

The soldiers had switched their rifles from burst to beam. Those flowed out like streams of molten sun to lash the xenos back. And lash them they did—beams were more effective in keeping them away, but they severely drained the charge. They'd have minutes at most before their cells were empty.

Blackwell was so focused on their approaching doom that he didn't notice the other shuttle until the cheer had gone up from the soldiers.

His heart leapt when he saw it. Then it froze as he did the math. The soldiers' joy was premature. Not everyone was going home.

Sivos didn't make the connection. "Just a few more minutes, boys. The boat home is here."

Blackwell pulled Sivos close. "We'll be over the weight limit."

"We'll ditch the gear," Sivos said between beams of fire. "Toss rifles as we board. That'll buy us a couple extra bodies."

It should, but… "Which bodies?"

Sivos regarded him flatly. "That's a command call."

The other shuttle shuddered overhead like a kite in a gale. There was no place for it to set down that wouldn't be immediately overrun. Blackwell watched a stream of xenos peel off to circle around and up the side of the outcropping, moving faster than spiders up a wall. In moments, they'd be within leaping distance of the shuttle. "Chief, we need a landing spot!"

Sivos was already on it, directing soldiers to sweep the rock with their particle beams. Xenos tumbled off and were whisked away by the storm.

The xenos pressing forward from the ground were ducking the particle streams now, clustering together to hold against the beams like boulders in a stream. Or ruggers in a scrum.

Blackwell could see why—the horde was increasing, more streams of silver flowing from the ruins to reinforce them. All the xenos had to do was push on their held positions and they'd be overrun. They were coming from every direction now, reinforcing from every angle.

Except one. He saw it, the gap in the alien horde near the burning remains of the wreck.

Blackwell signaled the shuttle with his flags. The shuttle wagged in confirmation. And then the screen of soldiers was moving, firing and sliding in locked formation towards the shuttle, shielding Blackwell and the doctor and the handful of shocked Armstrongs still standing.

Blackwell noted absently that Osei was no longer with them. The bloodstains on Marwazi's uniform and the blank expression in his eyes confirmed it. Well, one less evacuee to worry about.

He could hardly see the burning wreck through the smoke. "Where's that damn shuttle?"

It dropped like a thunderbolt, crushing a cluster of forward-creeping xenos, and fired its maneuvering thrusters to grind aliens beneath it like a pestle in a mortar. The oldest part of Blackwell's brain approved. He made a note to promote the pilot.

The loading ramp dropped to reveal a red shirt with mismatched eyes. He waved them forward.

The xenos had regrouped by the time the officers and Armstrongs had boarded. Sivos signaled the retreat. Soldiers fought their way back towards the ramp.

Now for the winnowing, the who got to go home. The burden of leadership could be cruel sometimes. Blackwell pulled himself towards the controls and balked when he saw who was sitting there.

𝒟

Blackwell gawked at Webb, his eyes huge in a face caked with sand. Sivos and the first of a wedge of soldiers clambered aboard behind him. Blackwell seemed too surprised to be pissed. "Where's the tech I left in charge?"

"Pickled."

"What?"

She nodded toward Bilson. "Pilot's been injured. I was the only one left who could fly."

Whatever he was thinking about saying, he bit it off. "Stand by for liftoff."

The computer chimed. "Warning: shuttle is above maximum atmospheric weight."

"Jettison the gear," said Blackwell.

"Already have," said Webb.

Familiar thumps drew Blackwell's gaze up.

"That's them," Webb told him. "We don't go soon, they'll drag us down. Hang on." She jerked the shuttle into the air.

Crew not strapped in hit the floor. Blackwell braced himself against a bulkhead. "The hell are you doing?"

"Buying us time." She slid the shuttle over the burning wreck, hit the stabilizers, and blew the thrusters on minimum. Smoke from the wreck billowed over the remaining soldiers. The xenos squealed and fell.

Webb landed the shuttle again. She didn't have time to grin before she heard more thumps from above. "I can shake them off, but we've gotta get airborne."

"Warning," the computer reminded them, "shuttle is above maximum atmospheric weight."

Blackwell looked out the back. The dozen or so remaining soldiers were nearing the shuttle. As was the doctor who must have hung back to treat the wounded.

Alarm lights bathed the shuttle red. "Warning: shuttle is critically above maximum atmospheric weight."

"Sir." Jacobs slid sideways to speak in Blackwell's ear. Webb hadn't seen him since the review panel. "What are we going to do, sir?"

Blackwell's eyes flitted from Sivos to Jacobs. He swallowed, put on his command face. "All junior technicians off the shuttle."

Everyone stared at him.

"You heard him," squeaked Jacobs.

"We'll evacuate by rank," said Blackwell. "Those staying at camp, hold position. We'll come back for you after the storm."

"That's a death sentence," said Webb.

Blackwell stared at her coldly. "You all knew what you signed up for."

Webb spun to the controls. "I can take the deflectors and shields offline, put their power into thrust. Storm's overwhelming those systems anyway."

Blackwell straightened. "Off the shuttle. That's a direct order."

"We can cut out the interior struts!" She pulled up a load-bearing schematic. "Look. Shuttle would need major repairs, sure, and the ship would have to tow us in from orbit, but—"

"Get them off my shuttle," Blackwell told the soldiers.

The soldiers looked to Sivos.

Blackwell's nostrils flared. "Damn it, either some of us die or we all die!"

"So, you admit it's a death sentence," said Webb.

"We'd be dead already if they hadn't come back," said Sivos.

Blackwell glared at the chief. "You wanted a call? I'm making a call."

"We don't leave crew behind," said Sivos.

Blackwell jabbed a finger at Webb. *"She* does!" He spun to the teleporter.

Before Webb could flinch, the shuttle melted away and she was falling. She hit sand with wind howling in her ears. Streaks of heat flashed by over head.

He teeped me. The bastard teeped me in front of the firing line.

Eight hit the dirt beside her. "I—*hic*—*really* don't like away missions."

Sherry appeared and fell. The jolt woke her. She didn't get a word out before a xeno darted in and plunged both arm blades through her chest.

Webb took off for the line, energy waves ripping past. Eight needed no prompting to keep up this time.

The air shimmered ahead. Adler hit the sand, but apparently he'd had time to prepare because he landed in a crouch and caught up after a few strides.

Webb dodged an energy beam and nearly collided with the doctor, who was staunching the flow in a fallen soldier's neck. He seemed shocked to see them. "Webb?"

"Got to *go!* They're gonna leave us!"

"We've got wounded out here!"

"We've got wounded in *there!*" Or had. They'd thrown Sherry out.

The doctor's scanner beeped, pulling his eyes back to his patient. "Oh no." He started chest compressions.

Webb checked his scanner. The biosign was gray. "He's gone, Doc."

"I'm losing everyone." The doctor didn't look up. "I'm losing everyone today."

"You will unless we go."

He looked up, lost and scared, and didn't see the xeno emerge from the sands behind him. Before she could shout, it sliced across the base of his back. Marwazi collapsed onto her, bleeding and leaking spinal fluid.

A directed energy beam flung the xeno away. Webb whirled.

Sivos and a knot of soldiers had come charging back out of the shuttle, roaring with each beam of fire they laid down.

Webb hoisted the doctor and ran back towards the shuttle with the other teeped out red shirts. Sivos stopped her as she passed. "Get that bird airborne." He didn't wait for her to nod before he'd resumed firing.

Webb thundered up the ramp, past soldiers tossing molten-edged struts out the back. *"Move!"* She set Marwazi down. He'd gone white with shock. "We need help! The doc needs help!" An Armstrong she didn't know ripped a medkit off the wall and ducked down beside him.

At the controls, Blackwell staggered to his feet, his eye black, his nose a bloody waterfall. Webb surmised Sivos had disagreed with his decision to leave them behind.

Torch in hand, Swank lasered the last of the cargo clamps out of place and chucked it out the back. "We've cut what we can," he told Blackwell. "Any more and we'll crack like an egg on takeoff."

Blackwell looked back out. The xenos had regrouped and encircled Sivos and his rescue party.

"Vent the smoke at them again," said Webb. "They don't like that."

Blackwell wiped his sleeve across his face. "Close the gate."

The Armstrong at the lift controls—Jacobs—balked. "Sir?"

"The gate," repeated Blackwell. "Close it."

Webb was about to protest when Marwazi groaned.

Jacobs had frozen. "But the soldiers."

Blackwell's jaw clenched. "They made their choice. Now if you can't do what has to be done, get the hell out of the way!"

Jacobs hit the lift. A cry went up from the soldiers outside as they heard the hydraulics engage. Blackwell turned away from them and threw himself behind the controls. And then the shuttle was rising, climbing drunkenly through the storm.

Chapter 7
Per Ignem Caelumque

From the bridge, Commander Young watched the storm swirl across the atmosphere of Acheron 117. It looked a bit like the swirls of milk in his latte. "Any luck?"

"No, sir." It took the tech at the comm several seconds to reply. In a crisis situation, that would have been unacceptable.

Young sipped his coffee. "Can you compensate?"

The tech blinked at his console. "Can I?"

"One would hope." Young bit off a sigh. "It's a basic skill for that station."

The tech had the nerve to look incensed. He sullenly punched keys.

Young had to have a word with the other officers. These Armstrongs... loyalty was no substitute for skill. They were proving that now, in their struggles to perform even basic tasks. Had Young had his way, senior techs would have been appointed to the empty bridge stations. That's what the regs called for. Young could only conclude the captain was punishing him.

He took another sip. The away team had been out of communication since the order to reconvene. Since then, the storm had scattered any messages to or from the ship. Hardly an uncommon occurrence; planetary-to-orbital communication was rarely better than fragile. Had he been left with competent crew, Young could have left them to it and enjoyed his coffee from the wardroom. Instead, he got to babysit.

If Osei were here, this wouldn't be an issue. But the communications officer was down there with the rest of them. Taking the comms officer off the bridge when a storm was brewing... absurd. But he took the best datapad footage, and knowing the captain—and the promise of plunder—he wasn't about to let himself be filmed from non-flattering angles.

Young glanced back at the comm station. Whether out of incompetence or insolence, the Armstrong still hadn't adjusted the signal strength.

"Technician, stand aside. You." He snapped at the cog standing statue-still by the captain's chair. "Take the comms."

The cog moved with disturbing precision to the seat vacated by the red-faced Armstrong now sulking in the corner. The seat sagged under its weight.

"Compensate the comm signal and analyze the storm," Young told it.

"The storm appears to be localized above the landing zone," the cog reported without inflection. It adjusted levels on the console. "The entire region has been lost to our scanners. Compensation has proven ineffective."

Odd for a storm that small. "How long have they been out of contact? And I mean approximately. I don't need it down to the second."

"Approximately eleven minutes, Commander. Any loss of communication with an away team for more than three minutes is considered a crisis."

"Well aware." A light crisis. One no worse than having shit techs on the bridge. He'd be more concerned if scans had revealed any life signs below. Still, Seagrave had been pretty pissy since he contracted that stomach bug. If Young did nothing—as Seagrave himself would have done in this situation—the captain would find a way to hold it against him.

The cog was staring at him. Young hated that. They never blinked. "Could we launch a comm beacon, skip it across the upper atmosphere? Just far enough to get a signal down under the storm before it's blocked by the curvature of the planet."

The cog's eyes twitched as it calculated. "Theoretically, Commander. But it would require modifications to adapt the beacon for atmospheric conditions."

"Do it. Relay it to one of your clones."

The cog went rigid. "Message conveyed."

Boyer, the ship's gangly second officer, hustled over with his brows furrowed. Young fought down a wince.

126

"Is that wise, Commander?" Boyer spoke loud enough to be heard by the Armstrongs. "The beacons are for deep space communication."

"Indeed they are," Young replied. "Hence the modifications."

"But what if we need it for deep space communication?"

"That's why we have six of them." Young wasn't sure which annoyed him more: being saddled with the Armstrongs or stuck with a scion of the Boyer family. "We can fish it out of the atmo once the away team's returned. And converting it back will give the techs something to do."

Boyer nodded. "But what if we need it for deep space communication?"

Young screamed behind his eyes.

Legacy. It was the only thing that carried as much weight in the Coalition as property, and the Boyers were legacy's champion parasites. They were the descendants of some great hero, some admiral who'd won a critical battle a century ago. His multitude of progeny had been piggy-backing on his accomplishment ever since. Pretty much every ship in the fleet had a Boyer now: a legion of mediocre, incurious dullards born into unmerited power. How the Armstrongs envied them.

Young put on a smile. "You know, Lieutenant Commander... the captain's likely to be famished upon his return. Go make sure his cabin is fully stocked."

Boyer looked as if Young had offered him a bag of fish heads. "That's hardly a job for an officer."

You're hardly an officer, Young didn't say. In any fair universe, Boyer would never have risen past the rank of technician. "You want to tell the captain we let a *tech* touch his personal effects?"

Boyer paled. "Oh. Goodness." He hurried off towards the cabin to fail with aplomb.

Young savored a moment of silence before tapping his badge. "Young to Teleporter."

"Fuller here, sir."

Fuller. The Buddhist with the shaved head. "Any chance you've found something to lock onto down there?"

"Negative, sir. Interference from the storm is too severe. It's also not behaving normally."

"Explain?"

"Particulate storms typically have a fluctuating effect on the teleporter lock. A signal will get through microseconds at a time, but it gets lost again before a lock can be established. It's a phenomenon that intensifies and ebbs with the storm."

"But… those fractions of signal aren't even coming through."

"Correct. It's like no signals are being sent."

Young grunted. That certainly wasn't normal. The storm must be particularly strong. "Alright. Keep on it, and keep me updated."

"Aye, sir."

"Commander." The cog was staring with those soulless eyes again. "Beta Shuttle has emerged from the storm."

Young turned to the viewer. "On screen."

When it popped up, Young almost dropped his mug. The shuttle was scarred almost past identification. It looked like it been used for target practice.

"The shuttle appears to be damaged," said the cog.

"No shit. It looks like it lost a knife fight with a garbage disposal."

"Scans indicate the vessel is missing key structural elements," said the cog. "It is also well over its carrying capacity."

A pit formed in the bottom of Young's stomach. "Any sign of Alpha Shuttle?"

"Negative, Commander. Beta Shuttle is hailing us."

"Put them up."

The screen erupted in shrieks and static. The shuttle's interior looked like a train car overpacked with refugees. Screams from its passengers almost drowned out the bursts of sparks popping off damaged conduits.

The woman flying it was not the shuttle's pilot. Young recognized her—the crew liaison. The one who'd stumbled drunk onto the bridge to volunteer the night before.

She didn't look drunk now. Her eyes were wide as saucers. "—*dependence*, we've got injured! We need teep people to the infirmary."

"I would recommend against that, Commander," said the cog. "Teleporter beams may further destabilize the shuttle."

"That's a negative, tech." Young saw soldiers in black, techs in red… but no purple. "Who's in command?"

The pilot moved aside—as much as she could; the shuttle was packed tighter than a sardine tin—revealing a bruised and sullen Lieutenant Commander.

"Mr. Blackwell." Young was relieved to see an officer. "Situation report."

"I can deliver that in private, Commander."

"Where's the rest of the bridge crew?"

"A message best related in private, sir."

Young's throat felt dry. He felt the Armstrongs at the consoles eyeing him. "Where's the captain? Is he with you?"

"We were attacked," said the pilot. "Hostile xenos. Swarms of them, all over the landing site."

"That's classified!" spat Blackwell.

"Secret's out, I'm afraid."

"Xenos?" Young felt baffled. "Life signs were negative."

"They were still negative when they were overrunning us," said the pilot. "We've got wounded."

Young hit his badge. "Triage units to the shuttle bay."

"And security," added Blackwell. "Full strike team."

"Are you being followed?" asked Young.

"They had no tech that we saw," said the pilot.

"Again, Commander, this is information best relayed in private."

"Mr. Blackwell, what the *hell* happened down there?"

"This." The pilot hit a button.

The feed switched to footage from the shuttle's exterior. Through the whirling chaos of the storm, a swarm of silvery mantis-like creatures waded through a fusillade of fire to pull soldiers apart as easily as paper dolls.

Young's head swam. He steadied himself on the command chair and tapped his badge. "Young to Fuller. Keep trying to get a lock on survivors."

"Survivors? What happened?"

"We're still putting that together."

𝒪

Blackwell slapped off the comms. "You will *not* insert yourself into conversations between officers."

Webb didn't look at him. She didn't dare take her eyes off the monitor. "The relaying of critical information is the duty of the commanding serviceman—"

"Who is me."

"—assigned to the shuttle. The tech you left in charge is too drunk to stand, and the pilot is dead. I was next in line. Just following protocol."

The shaking dropped away as the shuttle popped out of the atmosphere. Ahead, the great silvery bulk of the *Independence* loomed into view, traversing ever so slightly to offer the shuttle an angle towards its bay. Webb steered toward the hangar, hit the maneuvering thrusters. The shuttle didn't change its vector.

A negative chime. Webb's console flashed red. "That's not good."

"What's that mean?" Eight's face was a pale mask surrounded by agrichem dust.

"I'm not sure." Webb flipped some switches. "Swank, get up here."

"Yeah." The shuttle tech clambered forward through the mass. "What's wrong?"

"Something with the maneuvering thrusters." She tried turning the shuttle. Her console flashed red again.

Swank tapped some keys. "They're not reading as compromised in the damage report." Which was considerable.

"I can't steer." She tried. More warning lights.

He called up a schematic. "Looks like the flow of thrust is impeded."

"By what?"

"Dust from the storm," said Blackwell. "Obviously."

"Might be," said Swank. "Won't know for certain 'til we look inside."

"We've got more pressing issues," said Webb. They were darting with deceptive speed towards the shuttle bay. They were also arcing to starboard. At their current trajectory, they'd clip the side of the hangar entrance and wind up debris orbiting the ship. She tried the thrusters again. No luck.

Swank noted their trajectory. "We're not gonna make the bay."

Webb stomped down a surge of panic, tried to keep her hands from shaking on the controls. "Everyone? Brace for crash landing."

"On what?" Eight looked back over the sea of wide eyes. "There's nothing to hold onto. We cut out the struts."

"Reynolds was in a crash landing once," muttered Adler, his arm in a sling. "Inertial compensators failed. He wound up soup on the viewscreen."

"Comm the bay," said Swank.

Of course. Webb toggled on the comms. "Shuttle Bay, this is Beta Shuttle. Thrusters are compromised. Requesting immediate tractor beam for tow in."

"Copy," commed the landing crew.

"Hunker down, everyone," Webb called over her shoulder. "This is gonna get bumpy."

Soldiers ducked and covered. The red shirts who could stand braced themselves over the wounded. Even Blackwell steadied himself against his console.

Marwazi, his eyes half-open, didn't seem to react. Webb hoped he wasn't too far gone.

The tractor beam shot out of the bay's emitter. It seized the shuttle, shaking it violently but pulling it into a more central position. "They've got us."

The shuttle abruptly shook. Klaxons blared. A crack opened in the forward bulkhead and raced above the viewscreen.

"Okay, that's bad," said Swank.

"Severe structural damage," warned the computer. "Prow in danger of breach."

"Beam's too strong!" Webb yelled over the comms. "Dial it back!"

"The beam is already at minimum," said the tech.

"Turn it off or you'll tear us apart!"

"Copy."

The beam winked out. Webb hoped they were aligned enough to make it in. The shuttle bay entrance ahead went from the size of a postcard to a book to a house.

Webb's heart pounded like a rabbit's. They were coming in too fast. At this rate, they'd plow into the bulkhead at the back of the bay. "Switch beam from pull to push!" she commed. "One second burst!"

The shuttle hit the bay floor in a grating shower of metal flakes. Had the bay had been pressurized, the sparks would have been incredible.

With a blinding flash, the emitter spat out a tractor beam pulse. It hit the shuttle in the starboard prow, spinning it like a top. The force of the spin pressed crew to the walls and nearly threw Webb out of her chair.

The shuttle careened up on its side before it rocked, dropped, and settled. The shuttle bay airlock whisked shut with a clang. Somewhere behind Webb, someone puked.

At the press of a button, the shuttle's sides slid up. Out tumbled red shirts and a handful of soldiers. The ones who could walk, anyway.

The shuttle had spun completely around and was now facing the airlock. Webb took in the deep gouges and skid marks from their entry. "Not my best landing."

"Any one you can walk away from," said Eight.

"To be fair, it's been a few years."

"You still got us home."

"Yeah." Webb's stomach had yet to stop spinning. "Home."

Medical staff was already there, performing triage on the cargo bay floor: administering hyposprays to the walking, stasis plaques to the wounded, and sheets to the unresponsive. Anyone they stabilized they slapped with a teleporter tag. Those patients vanished in whiffs of ozone, teleported straight to the Infirmary.

She spotted Marwazi among the bodies on the floor. She unbuckled and climbed out, picked her way through the groaning survivors. Rob was administering to the doctor when she made her way over. "Is he going to be okay?"

"He…" Rob's face was slack with shock. Whatever platitude he was thinking of saying died on his lips. "It's bad." He tagged the doctor with a stasis plaque and a teleporter tag.

Webb squeezed Marwazi's hand. "Doc. Haroun. We're home now. Come on back." He didn't return her squeeze. He couldn't, not frozen in stasis. His hand went intangible and vanished as the teleporter stream whisked him away.

"Hey." Swank, limping, was hanging off Adler. Looks like he'd been hurt on the landing. "Thanks for getting us out of there."

"Thought our number was up," said Adler.

"Yeah," said Webb. "Kinda did too. Sorry about the bumps."

"I'll take 'em," said Swank.

Eight was blinking rapidly, as if she couldn't believe she was actually back on the ship. "Are all away missions like this?"

"The ones that are don't make the recruitment vids," said Webb.

Eight's shoulders sagged. "The lieutenant."

"One of the good ones. A lot of folks didn't make it back."

"There are still people down there."

"There are." Sivos and the soldiers who covered their retreat. Some more red shirts. And whoever was left from the bridge crew. Webb wind-milled her arms at the hangar's maintenance crew, who were gawking at the damage to the shuttle. "Hey!"

133

One of them turned, incredulous. "The bunking hell happened? You go through a meteorite shower with your shields down?"

"Xenos," Webb said flatly.

The tech stared at the slashes in the hull. *"Xenos* did this?"

"Don't ask me how." Webb had no idea how to explain it—the arm blades popping out of forelimbs, the sheer weight of them on the shuttle's back. The maddening insectoid chittering. She set a hand on the jagged shuttle hull. "When can this be flight ready?"

"You're kidding, right?"

"Let's pretend I'm not."

"The inside alone will take days to refortify. The hull..." she shrugged.

"There's also something wrong with the thrusters," another tech said from behind the shuttle.

"I noticed that," Webb told them. "Maneuvering thrusters were down when I was bringing her in."

"Where's Alpha Shuttle?" asked the first tech. "Are they circling? There's no room to land with all the wounded in here."

"It went down. Under a xeno swarm." Webb ground her eyes shut. "They must've punctured a plasma line or something, I don't know. It's gone."

"Lerd."

"Yeah."

The techs abruptly straightened. Webb turned, saw Blackwell marching towards her, scowling, flanked on either side by fresh pairs of soldiers. He stabbed a finger at her. "Arrest that technician."

The soldiers started her way. Swank and Adler put themselves in front of her. "The hell do you think you're doing?"

"Guys?" said Webb. "Not a good idea."

"If they don't move," said Blackwell, "arrest them too."

Young shouldered his way through the crowd. "I'm still waiting on that situation report, Mr. Blackwell."

"Sir." Blackwell saluted, indicated Webb with his eyes. "This technician refused multiple direct orders during the evacuation. Her actions delayed us and exacerbated crew casualties."

"That's *not* what happened," growled Adler.

Young looked them over. "The captain?"

"Dead," said Webb. Young and the soldiers stared at her. "Winesborough, too. And Osei. Marwazi was badly injured. I'm not sure about the rest."

Young took in the crowd anew. "Is this all there is?"

"Because of *her,*" hissed Blackwell. "We could have evacuated more of the officers and soldiery had she simply followed—"

Whatever he said next was drowned out by shouting red shirts. An angry press of them carried her forward. The soldiers closed ranks around Blackwell and Young. One looked ready to raise his rifle before Young halted him with a look.

"She got us out of there!" yelled Adler.

"After he teeped us out," added Swank.

Blackwell clenched his jaw. "There is a *clear* order of priority during an emergency evac. Had my orders been—"

"Is this true?" Young stared at Blackwell in disgust. "Did you teleport service members *out* of the shuttle?"

"He did," said Webb. "We barely made it back in."

"We wouldn't have if Sivos hadn't come back for us," said Adler. "He's the hero here."

"And where is he now?"

"Still down there," said Webb. "We were ordered to leave him behind."

"By the L.C. here," said Adler.

Swank smirked at Blackwell. "That's quite the shiner, sir."

"Commander." Blackwell turned towards Young, walling them away from the red shirts. "I made a hard call, under duress, to ensure the survival of the highest priority crew."

Young eyed him flatly. "That's not a denial."

"If we could speak about this in private?"

Young eyed Swank's insignia. "Shuttle tech?"

"Aye, sir."

"Send the shuttle's teleporter logs to my quarters."

Swank grinned wickedly. "With pleasure, sir."

"Commander!" Blackwell stiffened. "This is highly irregular. And completely unnecessary!"

"You're dismissed, Mr. Blackwell." He mashed his comm badge. "Young to Teleporters."

Four techs replied. Webb's heart leapt when she heard Frankie's voice. It sunk again when she recalled how poorly their last parting had gone. Still needed to patch things up there.

"Initiate emergency evac," said Young. "Teleport anyone you can get a lock on planetside directly to the Infirmary. Eighty percent signature threshold is authorized."

A chorus of ayes. Young hit his badge again, twisted it a quarter turn to sends his words through the ship. "Attention, crew. This is Commander Young. We've got people stranded down on that planet, including our captain. Priority one is getting them back. Engineering: can you modify a tractor beam to scatter some of the particulates in that storm?"

"Maybe," Dewey commed back. "But without anything solid to push it'd be like pissing in the wind."

"Can you reroute teleportation beams through that comm beacon we sent into atmo?"

A pause. "We'll get right on it."

"See that you do. Security, full fire team to the shuttle bay."

"Copy."

"Beam weapons," said Webb.

Young looked her way.

"Phototherm did nothing," she added. "Just knocked them back. Beam weapons didn't hurt 'em either, but were more effective at moving them around."

Young looked incredulous. Then he looked to Blackwell, who nodded curtly. "Beam weapons only. Bring extra cells."

"Copy. Fire team en route."

Young swung to the shuttle crew. "How soon can that wreck be spaceworthy?"

The tech Webb spoke to ducked out of the interior. "A few hours, sir. We have to weld in new struts to keep it from imploding when it hits atmo."

"Bunk that," said Young. "Fab what you need. I'll handle the paperwork."

Blackwell actually gasped.

The tech ducked back in as the other propulsion tech poked his head out from the thruster assembly. "We've also got an issue with the thrusters."

Young sighed. "What kind of issue?"

"Something's blocking them."

Insectoid chittering drifted out of the thruster. The tech looked back at it curiously. Something jerked him back in.

Webb stiffened.

Out of the thruster burst three xenos, their carapaces burnt black and cracked like a pattern of celadon glaze. They moved with a skittering, nightmarish ease, apparently no worse for having been bathed in thruster plasma. They skated towards the knot of crewmen like water striders across a pond.

"Security!" Young managed to draw his sidearm before an alien plunged its blades through his chest.

Crewmen scattered. Blackwell pushed his way through the soldiers and bolted for the lifts. True to their training, the soldiers dropped into a rank and fired. Their bolts reflected off xeno carapaces to spark against the bulkheads.

"Get out!" Webb felt like she was moving through quicksand. "You can't fight them!"

The red shirts who'd been on the surface needed no prompting. They were already halfway to the lifts, Swank limping along between Adler and Eight. One of the xenos was right on their heels.

"Close the doors!" Webb yelled at the control station.

The tech there snapped out of his torpor. His hands flew over the controls. Then his hands flew across the room as a xeno waded through him like a wave made of knives. It skittered towards the lifts.

Webb slid to a stop behind the console, slapped the lift controls. Across the room, the overcrowded lifts slammed shut behind the techs. The pursuing xeno slammed into it, rebounded, and started hacking at the shaft.

Webb coolly realized she was the last tech in the room— only she and the soldiers were left in the bay. And given how she could no longer hear rifle fire, she was the only one left standing.

More chittering. Webb glanced over the console, saw the other two xenos skating from the soldiers' bodies towards the lift shafts—the shafts that led directly to the most trafficked corridors in the ship.

She wrenched up the console's emergency panel. Its interface prompted her for an access code. She entered Dewey's.

The console chimed compliance. Up rose the emergency lever.

One of the xenos turned Webb's way. Its compound eyes glimmered. It chittered something.

Webb couldn't come up with anything pithy to say. Or think. Maybe it was good that her mind was blank. She hoped Marwazi would think of her fondly if she saved the ship. It would be a nice way to be remembered. She wondered which pregen homily would be read for her and pulled the lever.

The airlock split open, roaring like a wounded god. Klaxons screamed. The temperature plummeted. Webb gripped the emergency restraints as everything in the bay—the shuttle, the bodies, and the three thrashing aliens—went hurtling out into the stars.

A heartbeat later, her numbed hands gave way, and she too was hurling towards the void.

Chapter 8
Sic Transit Aequitas

Webb sat, lotus-legged, struggling with the breathing techniques Frankie had tried so hard to teach her. Not because she was trying to calm herself down—though that would have been nice—but because she was pretty sure her lungs were broken.

She'd hit the emergency bulkheads that closed over the blown airlock back-first. That had been a bit of luck—she wasn't sure she'd timed things right. A split second off, and she'd have wound up a popsicle orbiting the ship. Or worse, half a popsicle.

She tried to steady her breathing. She could feel grinding in her lungs, the fluttering of parts out of place. The impact must have knocked her alveolar intakes out of alignment. She'd been winded since Security had peeled her off the shuttle bay floor.

She needed a doctor. Or an engineer. Hell, even a bio scanner—with that and a decent console, she could realign them herself.

She wouldn't be getting either here. The brig had a half-dozen cells, two each on three sides. The force fields they used in place of bars didn't have to be charged to hurt—they functioned perfectly well without stinging current coursing through them—but that wouldn't have been punitive enough.

Webb didn't know how long she'd been there. Long enough to be famished. Once she was convicted—she wondered when her trial would be—they'd drop her in an oubliette with the rest of the red shirts who'd fucked up beyond redemption and freeze her solid. Then they'd pack her in the meat locker with the others, whose crimes ranged from assaulting an officer to fabbing a decent hamburger.

Apart from the cog, the brig was empty. It stood there, inanimate, the eyes in its unsmiling white face trained on her, recording everything.

The door whisked open. Dewey stepped in and hung her jacket over the cog's head.

The cog animated. "Obstruction of surveillance is illegal."

"Shut up," said the chief. "I require your assistance."

"Acknowledged, Chief Engineer." It must have recognized her voice-print. "Please state the nature of the assistance required."

"Equipment transpo."

"Please state the nature of the equipment to be transported."

"My jacket," said the chief. "It is extremely volatile. It cannot be touched by limbs."

Some whirring. "Acknowledged. Please state the delivery location."

"Cell Block C, northwest corner. I shall collect the item at…" She glanced at the wall clock. "06:00 hours."

"Acknowledged." The cog dutifully marched into the corner and stood there facing the wall. "Location reached. Would you like to collect the equipment early?"

"That's a hell no." The chief turned her way. "Six hours to kill. You busy?"

"Don't make me laugh," said Webb. "It hurts." Her voice sounded disjointed. Clipped, like audio that hadn't finished buffering.

Dewey frowned. "What's wrong with your pipes?"

"I damaged my lungs." Worse than she'd thought. She sounded like she was talking through a fan.

The chief nodded. "You hit the bulkhead pretty hard. Quick think-ing, blowing the airlock. Don't expect a commendation."

Webb grunted. It sounded like a robotic cat's purr. "What's going on up—? Ugh, I sound like a broken cog. How are things up top?" She almost didn't want to ask. "The xenos. Are they…?"

"Dead," said the chief. "Dead as that planet was supposed to be. We've flagged two of them in orbit around the ship."

Only two? "There were three, Chief."

"I'm sure it's still out there." She didn't seem concerned. "We still can't scan for them, for whatever reason. The two we spotted were out of a NEOS. First time in a century those have been used for their actual purposes. Mind if I smoke?"

"Wish I could join you." With her lungs damaged, the nicotine might actually hit. Her back throbbed. Those final moments in the shuttle bay clawed back up in her memory. The chittering. The burnt xenos, a tarnished silver with the crackle pattern of Frankie's teacups. Arm blades punching through the commander like spikes through a melon. She shuddered. "Young."

Dewey exhaled a plume. "Yeah." Webb had never seen her so pale. "No one knows what to do with the captain *and* the first gone. That's never happened before. We've lost whole ships—show me a navy that hasn't—but one's never been decapitated quite like this."

"How's the crew?"

"Scared," said Dewey. "Angry. Lots of fighting in the mess."

"What? No."

"Oh, yeah." She flicked ash. "Armstrongs, mainly. Big surprise."

"We're not on lockdown?"

"We're supposed to be. Officially, we are. That bloodbath in the shuttle bay certainly constitutes an incursion." She glanced at the cog. "Screw it, it's not like it's a secret. The Armstrongs decided they shouldn't have to be confined to quarters like the rest of the crew, so—"

"They *what?*"

"Oh, yeah. They're doing their own security sweep, going room to room themselves, sometimes with the soldiers, sometimes on their own, spoiling for a fight."

Bunch of idiots. "What are they going to do if they find more xenos? Punch them?"

"It's not the xenos they want to punch. It's just free-floating hostility and they want an outlet."

"And you went alone through that?"

143

Dewey blew a smoke ring. "I've got a security clearance. It has its perks. Lets me bypass the checkpoints."

"There are checkpoints now?"

"Mm hm. Security went full war zone. So I get to dodge them *and* the roving gangs of pent-up Armstrongs. Fun."

Webb clicked her mouth shut. "And Security's just... allowing this?"

"Sivos wouldn't. Too bad he's dead." She stubbed out her cig on the cog's ass. "And what exactly do you expect Security to do? Shoot the Armstrongs? Their most vocal supporters?" She lit up again.

If Webb weren't already sitting, she'd have sunk to the floor. "How'd it get this bad?"

"Young's comm was on." Dewey got a far off look. "The whole ship heard him die. I dunno, something about hearing that *on the ship*, having the xenos hit us here... it's one thing when it happens to crew you don't know fifty kilometers down. But *here*? It broke something. Something structural. The Armstrongs are demanding revenge, ignoring higher ranking techs. Those dumb enough to try to corral them, anyway. And the soldiers are patrolling like they expect us to be boarded."

"What are the officers doing?"

"*What* officers? The bridge crew followed the captain planetside with a raging loot boner. Aside from Young, the ones they left behind were juniors or incompetents. What's left of the command structure has sealed itself in the captain's cabin, God knows why."

"Then..." Webb was at a loss. "Who's in charge?"

Ϙ

The planet looked angry. It was ridiculous to anthropomorphize a celestial body—Blackwell knew that—but if he'd ever had to describe a planet as pissed off, he'd have pictured what he was seeing from the captain's cabin. The storms roiling the atmosphere had broken up, leaving wounded whorls like jagged bruises across the skies.

If the storms were indeed dissipating, teleportation to the surface might be possible again. The lockdown was costing them time to mount a rescue. It was the inefficiency Blackwell couldn't stand. Sometimes, in a crisis, regulations just got in the way.

He took pride in how well he was concealing his annoyance. He was doing a far better job of it than the ship's chaplain, who had clearly been pulled out of bed for the swearing in.

Commander Boyer stood ramrod straight, his hand on the Bible, a smile tugging at the corners of his mouth. Blackwell strangled a grimace. The man actually believed he deserved this, that he'd somehow earned this promotion by merit rather than massacre. The twerp had actually taken the time to put on his dress uniform.

Blackwell barely heard him repeat the Oath of Captaincy. The affair was more than ceremonial—the ship wouldn't allow them access to the captain-only message from the admiralty until it had a captain again.

When it was done, the mussed chaplain lowered the Bible. "Congratulations, Captain." He crossed himself.

Boyer—*Captain* Boyer now; Blackwell couldn't think of it without wincing—fished a wad of paper out of his pocket. "I've prepared a speech."

"Sir." Blackwell exchanged a glance with the chaplain. "There isn't the time."

"This won't take long. It's only a few pages."

"The admiral is waiting, sir."

"Oh, yes. Of course." The new captain pocketed his speech. "*Independence,* open encrypted channel, authorization Boyer ACN-889." That unearned smile again. "By order of the *captain.*"

The chaplain actually snorted.

Admiral Self's glower displaced the planet on the viewscreen. He betrayed a moment of surprise when he saw them. "Where's Seagrave?"

"He's dead, sir," said Blackwell.

The admiral seemed more irritated than shocked. "Commander Young?"

"Also dead," said Blackwell.

"We encountered a hostile alien presence on the surface," said Boyer.

You didn't, thought Blackwell. Your inept hide was on the bridge. "The native xenos followed us back to the ship. We've suffered heavy losses to the officer corp."

"That is… unfortunate," said the admiral. "You said they reached the ship?"

"The threat has been contained," reported Blackwell. "We are conducting thorough security sweeps to make sure the *Independence* is clean."

A curt nod. "I take it you're in charge now?"

"Sir." Boyer clicked his heels together. "It is my distinct honor to serve as the new captain of the *Independence*." He saluted with a flourish.

The admiral flinched. "I forgot your Boyer was your second. Jesus. Congratulations, Captain."

"Thank you, sir." If Boyer caught the diss, he gave no indication.

Self turned back to Blackwell. "What's the status of the Sorl ambassador?"

It was a question none of them were expecting. "The… ambassador?" Boyer looked blankly to Blackwell.

"We…" Blackwell failed to see what she had to do with anything. "We haven't seen her since her private talks with the late captain."

"I see," said the admiral. "And your location is secure?"

"Aye, sir. We're on the captain's private channel."

"Good." Self nodded. "Scour the planet."

A heavy silence descended, one only broken by the uncorking of the chaplain's flask.

Boyer raised his hand.

Self closed his eyes. "It's your ship, Captain."

"Yes. A question for you, sir. Our original orders were to locate the wreck of the *Flagstaff* and any survivors. But if we scour the planet… won't we destroy it? And them?"

Their Boyer actually had a point. Would wonders never cease?

"Given the xeno presence and their unprovoked aggression against the ship, we must conclude there were no survivors," said the admiral. "Scour the planet."

Boyer nodded. "Straightaway, sir." He turned to Blackwell. "See to it, Commander."

"We're still on lockdown, sir." Blackwell didn't miss that he'd just been promoted again. "We'll be unable to carry out that order until the sweeps are complete and we've restaffed the bridge. I would also like a chance to scan for survivors now that the storm has cleared."

"Yes." Boyer nodded more than was necessary. "Yes, that seems entirely reasonable."

Something tugged at Blackwell's mind. A dangling thread. "Admiral… may I ask how you knew about the violent interaction with the xenos? We haven't submitted an incident report."

The admiral looked sidelong at Boyer. "Captain, you do understand that 'captain's eyes only' means you are to respond in private?"

"Yes, sir." Boyer flushed. "Of course." He glared at Blackwell. "You are dismissed, Commander." He looked to the chaplain. "You as well."

The chaplain saluted with his flask. "Religious exemption."

Blackwell saluted, spun on his heel, and exited the cabin. But for the pairs of soldiers doing the sweeps, the bridge lay empty. Blackwell hadn't been out of the captain's cabin ten seconds before his badge chimed. He slapped it. "Blackwell."

"Lieutenant!" The voice on the comm made him cringe. "I've been trying to reach you for some time."

"What is it, Mr. Fr… Phillips?" He'd almost said "Freakbomb" out loud. "I've been in a meeting with the captain."

"Very good, I'll keep this quick. Allow me to thank you for procuring the specimen during lockdown."

"Don't mention it." Blackwell wanted off the call. He needed a break, a moment to recenter and process. Jesus, he was a commander now. He had to tell Sunshine. She'd want to congratulate him. "Anything else?"

"Oh, *so* much. I've made some *amazing* discoveries about our alien assailants. If you would be so good as to join me in Xenobiology?"

Blackwell sighed. Duty first, as always.

⌀

The crew tended to avoid the Xenobiology Lab. They avoided the crew who worked there just as diligently. Xenobio techs were weirdos, they joked, creepy shut-ins obsessed with the bizarre and grotesque. Recluses and geeks, all of them. Buncha weirdos.

This was the accepted reason for shunning the xenobs and their work. It gave power and a sense of control to the easily disturbed.

The real reason, the one only mentioned in counseling sessions or when the drinks were flowing, was dread. For Xenobiology was not the lab where the Coalition studied the other bipedal humanoid toolmakers mankind had met in the cosmos, the folks who looked human but for a few exotic characteristics. The ones you could fetishize; the ones you could bunk. That department was Xenoanthropology, located near the bridge with transparent walls the crew could peer through and see examples of themselves mirrored back by creation.

The Xenobiology Lab was for the species that broke the mold. The distinctly inhuman, the sort the brain couldn't categorize. Creatures that shook the crew on a core level, that caused the screams and psychotic breaks and knee-jerk suicides. The stuff of nightmares.

Xenobiology was nowhere near the bridge. It lay tucked away in the sternum of the ship, its walls thick and opaque, its entrance well away from the main corridors. It didn't announce its presence. If you didn't know it was there, you'd walk right past it. As most crew did.

Blackwell hated it. He hated its enthusiastic director even more; the man could at least have the decency to be disgusted by what he studied. Every cell of Blackwell's being screamed at him to turn around, to head back toward Sunshine's waiting arms. He'd rather scrub the Arcade than take a closer look at the thing that had made a Boyer captain of his ship.

The vault door rolled back, revealing the grinning Baron Freakbomb. "Thank you for coming, Lieutenant Commander."

"It's Commander now."

"Oh." Freakbomb stood aside. *"Congratulations,* Commander."

"I should be on the bridge. What's so important it couldn't wait?" Or be commed to the viewscreen so he wouldn't have to look at it.

"The captain has a standing order that all xenobiological discoveries are to be reviewed in *person.* So as not to disturb the *crew,* you see. How is the captain, by the way?"

"Still dead."

"Ah." Phillips nodded without emotion. "That's right, yes. A shame. *Come."*

Blackwell followed him into an operating room past an array of contraptions he couldn't identify. On the central examination table lay the body of a xeno. Blackwell had to fight down the urge to flee. Or shoot it.

Freakbomb grinned. *"Magnificent,* isn't it?"

"That thing killed a lot of my colleagues today," said Blackwell. "Magnificent isn't how I'd put it."

"In all honesty, Commander—and congratulations again—it is miraculous casualties were not *worse.* A single specimen such as this, with its natural blast armor and formidable weaponry, could have wiped out an entire *platoon.* And on the planet, considering you were outnumbered..." He shook his head in inappropriate wonder. "One is almost tempted to thank God you made it back."

The xeno's wedge of a head lay separate from its body. Blackwell felt the tension in his chest release a bit. He considered its ant-like anatomy, albeit an ant without an abdomen and with a torso closer to that of a mantis. "What did you need to show me?"

"Let us begin with the hide." Freakbomb consulted his data pad. "As you can see here, its cellular structure is extraordinary. Almost *crystalline,* with each cell forming an astoundingly strong latticework that nevertheless retains some flexibility. There are heavy amounts of silicon and selenium coating their cells. And I have detected iridophores in the specimen's dermal sheath."

Blackwell looked up from the xeno. "I'm not familiar with those."

"They can be found in a wide range of our world's oceanic creatures, most notably the cephalopods." Freakbomb paused as if Blackwell should know what those were. "Squid and cuttlefish. Octopuses."

"Octopi."

"What's that?"

"Octopi, Doctor," corrected Blackwell. "The plural of octopus."

"Ah. It would be, were the root of octopus Latin. But it is Greek, *ergo…* " He paused for a laugh that didn't come. His smile faded. "Because ergo itself is…? No?"

"Iridophores, Doctor."

"Yes. They are pigment-containing and light-reflecting cells that cephalopods use to mimic their environments."

Blackwell glanced at the creature's tarnished carapace. "These things didn't use camouflage."

"*Correct.* Their iridophores are without pigment sacs. Theirs are entirely for reflecting *light*—and, hypothetically, weapons *composed* of light."

Blackwell considered the hide anew. Even burnt a tawny silver, it still shone in spots like chrome. "That's why our weapons didn't work?"

"Why the beams reflected off them, yes. Now, this specimen's hide is burnt and cracked, but it took the intense heat of the shuttle's thruster core to damage its exoskeleton. Even then, its iridophores offered protection against energy weapons, as we saw in the unfortunate incident in the shuttle bay."

Unfortunate. A rather disconnected way of putting it. "Anything else?"

"Let us move on to its weaponry." The Baron indicated one of its forelimbs. "The retracting arm blades are a truly remarkable adaptation. I've never seen their like. Observe."

Phillips withdrew the creature's arm blade from its forelimb with a pair of pincers. It took some effort. He had to set down the data pad and pull with both hands.

"It is housed in the exoskeleton," the doctor huffed, "and the interior of the blade chamber is lined with what I would like to describe as organic diamond, except it contains not a single atom of carbon."

"Diamond?" Blackwell wondered at the commercial potential of farming these creatures.

Phillips finished withdrawing the weapon: a silvery, delicate arc resembling the blade of a scythe. "The blades are metal and *remarkably* sharp. I believe the diamonds are to maintain a cutting edge, sharpening them within the sheath. The composition of the blades—and this is *truly* remarkable—is a magnesium-based alloy, light as aluminum, yet stronger than steel."

"It didn't look light when you were tugging it." The doctor had actually broken out in a sweat.

"These creatures are… *shockingly* heavy." He wiped his brow. "Which I attribute to the metallic compounds in their cellular structure. Their weight, and the composition of their arm blades, explain how they were able to damage the impervium of the shuttle." He marveled at the xeno. "I have not yet determined how they are able to cut with such strength, however. I have not been able to examine their tendons, as I have found no easy means of cracking the exoskeleton."

"Good God." No wonder they'd made such short work of the hull. Not to mention the soldiers. "If we can't punch through their hides, how are we supposed to fight them?"

"I am only in the initial stages of my analysis," said Phillips. "With time, I am confident their vulnerabilities will become apparent." He indicated the creature's wedge-shaped head. "I have yet to outline my most *remarkable* discovery."

"There's more?"

"*Oh,* yes." That grin again.

"How were you able to detach its head?"

"No spoilers," said Freakbomb. "As you can see, the creature has eye clusters on either side of its head."

Blackwell nodded. He'd seen as much on the surface. The creatures' silver eyes had gone black when the flare had gone up. They were a dull pearl now. "Why do their eyes change color?"

"I haven't examined them yet." He pointed to the top of the creature's head. "Take a look."

Blackwell spotted a tiny incision in the bulb atop its wedge-shaped head. A slim cable ran from the incision into the table, past another pair of cables attached to the back of the xeno's skull. "You put these in?"

"Oh, yes."

"What kind of cable are these?"

"An optical one. So we could see what was inside. The others are to carry current to a sensory cortex I have yet to identify."

This was precisely the sort of shit that made the xenobs so creepy. "What madness is this, Doctor?"

The doctor grinned again. "Within the bulb of the creature's head is some sort of resonance chamber filled with metallic dust. At first, I thought it was something akin to the melon of a whale."

Blackwell blinked. "You've lost me again."

"An organ used by aquatic creatures that hunt and navigate with bio-sonar. The melon is what receives reflected sound waves and allows the cetaceans to *see* their environment without their eyes."

"But these creatures *have* eyes."

"*Exactly!* Which means this chamber was for something else." He picked up his data pad. "Observe."

Blackwell eyed the head with unease. "I thought you weren't able to crack their hides. How'd you get the cable in?"

"With this." He held up what looked like a miniaturized version of the creature's forelimb and arm blade. "It was the only thing sharp enough to cut through its hide. Like the claws of the Nemean Lion!"

"Where did you get that?"

"I fabbed it. Based on the specimen."

"Doctor!"

"Medical exemption, Commander. It's also how I removed the head. Don't worry, I will unravel the tool once the work is done. Now, please. *Observe.*"

Phillips hit a switch. Above the imaging table popped a hologram of an organic chamber.

"What am I looking at?"

"The inside of the creature's head. Do you see the structures at the back of the chamber?"

Blackwell did. It had been a decade since his biology courses, but they still tickled a memory. "Those look familiar."

"They should. They are the equivalent of rods and cones."

"So… wait." It took Blackwell a moment to parse that. "Those are *eyes?*"

"Of a sort. It's more an *array* of optical sensory organs. But one still in the *interior* of an enclosed cranial chamber."

His curiosity was getting the better of him. "Why would they need eyes *inside* their heads?"

The Baron grinned. "To see *this.*" He hit a switch.

153

Sparkling metallic dust leapt into a rough sphere in the center of the cranial chamber. It slowly rotated there like a fat, sluggish tornado. Blackwell's jaw actually dropped open.

"Magnificent, isn't it?"

"I don't understand what I'm looking at."

"*Galvanization.* The result of running current to the sensory cortex within the chamber."

"Okay. But what's the dust for?"

"If I had to guess?"

"That is your job, Doctor."

Freakbomb shrugged an apology. "I'm afraid I don't have an answer at this time."

A flash of annoyance. "And if you were to speculate?"

That bullshit grin again. "I simply do not have the information. I will keep at it." He turned off his pad. The hologram vanished. "Do you have any questions?"

Hundreds. But one in particular. "How do we kill them?"

"*Ah!* Now *that,*" said Phillips, "is an *excellent* question. We know spacing them works. And with enough pressure and weight, I presume they can be crushed."

"But our handheld weapons are useless against them."

"Quite useless."

Blackwell folded his arms. "What about orbital bombardment?"

Freakbomb scratched his temple. "The ship's gigalasers are the most powerful energy weapons known to man. It's possible even they might not penetrate their shells. *However,* the heat and pressure of such a bombardment would be so *intense* that I cannot see how anything could survive."

Good to know. "And impact weapons?"

Phillips shifted his weight. "Concussion torpedoes would generate enough of a pressure wave to crush anything, even these creatures."

Blackwell nodded. "Keep at it, Baron."

Phillips frowned as he left. It didn't strike Blackwell until he'd reached the lift that he'd called Phillips by his nickname.

Dewey flopped a card beside the board. "Nine."

Webb pointed to the six propped up against her cell's force field. "Fifteen for two."

Dewey slapped another six onto hers. "Twenty-one for two."

Webb raised an eyebrow. "Betting I don't have a ten. Risky." She pointed to another card.

Dewey set it on the stack. A third six. "God *damn* it."

"Twenty-seven for six."

The chief checked her cards. "And that's a go."

Webb pointed to her three. "Thirty." And to her final card: an ace. "Thirty-one for two."

Dewey threw her hand. "You're cheating."

"How'm I cheating? I can't even touch the cards."

"That's what makes it so insidious."

"If I had tech to bypass the barrier, you think I'd waste it on cribbage?"

"Cheating a poor old woman." The chief shook her head. "And one in emotional distress! Prison's changed you." She spread Webb's cards out, set the nine from the cut next to them. "Alright, count 'em. You cheating, robot-voiced holo-fucker."

"Hey, now. I told you about Ablehard in confidence." Webb grinned. It felt good to grin again. "Let's see... fifteen-two, four, six, and a pair is eight."

The door slid open. Dewey heaved herself up with a grunt. "About goddamn time. I've never heard of a security sweep taking so long."

The men who stepped in weren't soldiers. They were far too jittery. And their uniforms weren't black, but red. Red, with Armstrong pins at their collars. And skull masks pulled up over the bottom of their faces.

One leveled a sidearm at Dewey. "Get in the corner."

Dewey didn't move. "The fuck is this?"

One of the three—Webb recognized him from the eyes up—pointed at Webb. "You're under arrest."

"That's right." She tried to keep the panic out of her voice. The distortion from her lungs hid it well. "Kinda why I'm in here."

The skittish Armstrong balked. "What's wrong with her voice?"

"She's scared," said the big one. "Her voice is fluttering."

The chief snorted. "Those are damaged bronchial servos, you fucking goon."

The leader pointed towards an empty cell. "Get in there."

Dewey fixed him with a death stare. "I will have your badge for this, whoever you are."

"We are justice," said the lead Armstrong. "We are legion."

"We are anonymous," said the big one.

"You're Jacobs and a couple fucks from Navigation," said Dewey. "You didn't take off your comm badges, you imbecilic proto-fucks."

The skittish one looked ready to bolt. Jacobs—who hadn't lowered his sidearm—put his hand on his shoulder to steady him.

"Chief?" Dewey looked Webb's way. "Just do what he says. Don't spook them. People do stupid shit when they're scared."

"I'm not scared!" croaked the skittish one.

"Right," said Webb. "Because mask."

"Into the cell, Chief," said Jacobs. "I'm not gonna ask you again."

Dewey stood her ground. "That pin isn't the protection you think it is."

"You can't prove we were here," said the big one.

Dewey yanked her jacket off the cog's head. Its eyes fixed on the newcomers. "Mission complete 4.6 hours early."

The Armstrongs stiffened. The skittish one even whimpered.

"Cog," said the chief, "identity the occupants of this brig."

156

"Chief Engineer Barbara Dewey and Senior Technician Joni Webber." The cog fell silent.

Dewey's smirk slipped. "And who else?"

"No other crew members are present."

Webb could see Jacobs smile through the mask. "Like he said. Anonymous." He gestured towards the cell.

"Chief." Webb felt tired rather than scared. Tired and resigned. "Don't make this harder than it is."

"Fuck that. And fuck them. No way in hell I'm letting them take you." There was pain in her eyes when she looked at Webb. "There are *rules.* This isn't how it's done."

"Oh, Chief." Webb swallowed a lump. "Do you really believe all those mutineers on the *Adam Smith* decided to space themselves? Only the leaders made it to trial."

The chief didn't move. Jacobs fired a blast at her feet. Without breaking eye contact, she took a step backwards into the cell. "This isn't over. Is the record gonna show I somehow sealed myself in here?"

"It'll show what we tell it to." The big one activated her barrier.

Jacobs kicked the cribbage board away from Webb's cell. "You have been found guilty of crimes against the officer corp."

"I don't remember a trial," said Webb.

"You abandoned them." The sidearm was actually shaking in his fist. "Left them there to *die.*" He actually believed it.

"Jacobs." Might as well try reason. At least the cog was still theoretically recording. "Listen to me. There is nothing I, or anyone else, could have done to save them. Okay? They were already dead when the shuttle got there."

"And you're going to join them."

Dewey was yelling something now, yelling and pounding on her barrier despite the current burning her hands. They must have muted her.

"We have the package," the big one said into his pin.

"Come on." Jacobs deactivated Webb's force field. "Justice is waiting."

Chapter 9
Inimicus Ad Portas

Webb was keenly aware that her hands were free.

That couldn't be an oversight. The Armstrongs must not know how to operate the cuffs. Pretty embarrassing for a group that idolized law enforcement. She wasn't about to try anything, however, not with the sidearm in her back. It took no training at all to blow a hole in her spine.

She was also still unsure about her lung capacity. She hadn't been able to get a full sense of the damage in the brig—a few minutes of jumping jacks hadn't winded her—and so far, as they'd marched her through the darkened corridors of the ship, she hadn't found herself wanting for breath. Maybe the damage wasn't as severe as she'd thought.

The corridors lay empty. Not a surprise during a security sweep, but Webb still hoped they'd run into an officer, maybe a patrol, anyone who might see what the skull-faced Armstrongs were doing and put a stop to it. Of course, if they were coordinating their actions with Security, no bystanders would be any help. Sivos never would have allowed it. But he was dead on the surface.

The Armstrongs led her through a juncture, away from the airlocks, and turned her towards the heart of the ship. Maybe they weren't going to space her after all. In which case, she had no idea where they were leading her. She didn't realize where they were heading until they'd arrived.

"The teleporter?" And not just any teleporter. Frankie's. Not that she'd be here.

"You left them to those alien freaks," said Jacobs. "Only fitting you should join them." He hit the controls by the door.

The door slid open on sparks and smoke. Frankie's prayer flags hung askew. Within the room, another skull-masked Armstrong perched sheepishly over the console.

Jacobs pushed her in through the smoke and pulled the other Armstrong aside. "The hell did you do!"

"Nothing!" He seemed genuinely lost. "It was like this when I got here."

Even through the mask, Webb could see Jacobs' jaw clench. "Sabotage. Fucking socialists." He glared at Webb. As if she were somehow to blame. In his mind, she probably was. "How'd they know? Which one of you commed over the comms?"

"Not me," said the one at the console. The others shook their heads. "All talk's been through the pins."

Webb felt an inkling of hope. Maybe the Armstrongs weren't in full control. Maybe some sort of resistance had formed. And maybe they'd just toss her out an airlock now.

A burst of sparks drew her attention to the damage. The conduits leading from the console to the teleporter pad had been opened, their cables exposed, but, by all appearances, still intact. Some had been removed from the main conduit and were now snaking up to a grated section of the wall behind a panel. Webb didn't know the teleporter's power matrix well enough to determine what that might be diverting to. But the pad itself appeared undamaged. If whoever had done this was trying to disable the teleporter, they'd done a piss poor job.

The door slid open again, and Frankie froze in the doorway. "Hello?"

Three sidearms whirled on her. "The hell are you doing here?" demanded Jacobs.

Wide-eyed, Frankie slowly raised her hands. "Indie alerted me that my duty station was active."

"We're on lockdown."

"Protocol is to investigate." Frankie kept her voice remarkably level for the number of guns aimed at her. "I tried comming Security, but there weren't any in this section for some reason."

Webb glanced at Jacobs. "For some reason."

Frankie blinked at her. "Webb?"

"Hey."

"What happened to your voice?"

"Bulkhead."

Jacobs grabbed Frankie and steered her into the room. "You're under arrest for violation of lockdown."

Frankie spotted the open conduits. "What did you do? Why are you all here?"

"They were gonna teep me down," said Webb. "But someone tore up the conduits."

"It wasn't me," whined the Armstrong at the console.

Jacobs snapped for Frankie's attention. He gestured at the console. "Make it work."

Frankie nodded. "I'll need a few minutes."

The door slid open again, this time on a pair of soldiers in blast armor. The Armstrongs turned but didn't lower their sidearms.

In a flash, one of the soldier's rifles was up. The other one froze. "Weapons down," said the first.

Webb almost gasped with relief. Even through the voice scrambler and with the visor down, she recognized who spoke: Chelse.

The Armstrongs exchanged looks. They didn't lower their weapons.

"Weapons *down!*" barked Chelse. The Armstrongs still didn't move. Chelse elbowed her partner. Rather than raise his rifle, he looked at her like she'd broken some taboo.

"What the hell do you think you're doing?" spat Jacobs.

"Security request," said Chelse's partner, somewhat apologetically.

"Sent by?"

Frankie, her arms still raised, gave a tiny wave. "Unauthorized activity at my station. Reported it to Security. Protocol."

Jacobs swore. The skittish Armstrong actually whimpered.

"It's fine," said the big one. "He'll sort it."

"Who'll sort what?" asked Frankie.

"Shut up," said Jacobs.

161

The door slid open yet again, on an officer in his dress whites. Boyer halted abruptly, blinked his bug eyes at the odd array of crew. "What's all this, then?"

"Security sweep, Captain." Chelse didn't take her eyes off the Armstrongs. "Requested by station op for unauthorized activity during lockdown."

"Yes, I was following up on the request myself. Very good." He seemed puzzled by the skull masks. "What are you technicians wearing?" Puzzled and mildly offended. "You're out of uniform."

The skittish one sidestepped behind Jacobs. "Jack?"

Jacobs kicked him. "My *God,* shut up."

Boyer still seemed confused. Could he really not put this together? Webb cleared her throat. It sounded like an alto garbage disposal. "Commander, these men are trying to—"

"It's captain now."

"Captain. My apologies, I've been out of the loop."

"What's the matter with your voice? And which one of you is the station op?"

"I am, sir." Frankie indicate the Armstrongs. "These techs aren't supposed to be here."

"They locked Chief Dewey in the brig," said Webb. "Where they got me. They're going to teep me to the surface."

"But we're on lockdown." The new captain had reached an angry level of confused. "I've authorized no teleportations."

"Captain." Holy God, he still wasn't getting it. "They're trying to send me down there. *Without* your permission."

"Lower your weapons," demanded Chelse. "Not gonna tell you again." She actually nudged Boyer.

Annoyance flashed across the captain's face, then shock as he finally seemed to notice the Armstrongs were armed. "You there. Drop your weapons."

They didn't. They just seemed frozen. Or to be waiting.

Boyer's annoyance calcified into indignation. "Drop your weapons. That's an order. From your *captain.*"

Chelse hit her comm. "Backup to Teleporter 2."

The door slid open again. Blackwell didn't make it a step in before he balked in shock. The soldiers behind him actually bumped into his back.

The Armstrongs slumped in relief.

Boyer looked surprised. "Commander?"

"Captain?" Blackwell looked from the Captain to the red shirts to the single security officer with her rifle raised. He hid his surprise behind a smile. "I'm glad I found you. You're needed on the bridge. I'll clear this up for you."

Boyer narrowed his eyes. "Why are you here, Mr. Blackwell?"

"To watch me die," Webb said flatly.

Blackwell's chuckle was strained. He clapped Jacobs on the shoulder. "You're dismissed, Jacobs."

Boyer turned to Webb. "What did you say?"

"They brought me here to execute me, Captain."

"Extrajudicially," added Frankie.

Boyer stared at her blankly.

"Without your permission," she clarified.

Boyer glared at Blackwell. "Is this true, Mr. Blackwell?"

"Sir." Blackwell tried to take Boyer aside. "It's a stressful time on the ship. These men are passionate supporters of the late captain and his officer corp. Whatever their excesses, you can be assured they were acting in the best interests of the ship."

Boyer pointed at the Armstrongs. "Disarm them."

Chelse snatched Jacobs' sidearm. Her partner didn't move until she kicked him. He reluctantly motioned for the others to give up their weapons.

The skittish one's arm was quivering as he handed over his sidearm. "Sir?"

"Shut *up,*" hissed Blackwell.

"Teleport these men to a holding cell," Boyer told Frankie.

"We were only following orders!" the skittish one blurted.

"Bilson." Webb finally recognized his voice—the puker from the planet. "And after I gave you a blanket."

Boyer frowned at Bilson. "Whose?"

"Sir?"

"*Whose* orders? Whose orders were you following."

Bilson couldn't stop himself from looking at Blackwell. Blackwell's lip curled. "You little shit."

Boyer looked aghast. And furious. "Is this *true,* Commander?"

"Can we just assume it *is?*" cried Webb.

Fuming, Boyer leaned over Frankie at the console. "Why are these men not in the brig?"

"Teleporter's not responding, sir." Frankie actually looked lost. A rare state of affairs. "We have power, but control has been rerouted."

"Where? And why?"

Webb glanced from the exposed conduits to the cables leading to the grated section of wall. Behind the grate, she caught a wet-looking reflection. She felt a twinge at the back of her skull.

Then she heard it. Chittering.

So did everyone else. All eyes turned towards the grate.

Webb's throat went dry. "Xeno," she croaked. "There."

Chelse fired, a small burst that vaporized the grate. Behind it, packed in the recesses of the column, a heavily burnt alien uncoiled from a nest of wires. It was still wearing the burnt tatters of the pressure suit as a cape. It activated a device sprouting with cables.

The air above the teleporter pad shimmered.

"That's not me," said Frankie.

A knot of xenos materialized on the teleporter pad. The first to fully manifest leapt the length of the room onto the guards, its arm blades flashing.

Chelse—the only one with her weapon up—fired as she screamed. Her burst sent the xeno bound for her caroming off the back wall.

The others weren't so lucky. Alien arm blades punched through Chelse's partner, through the soldiers who'd come with Blackwell, and through the newly minted captain, who died in befuddled surprise.

Webb hit the floor in a mad scramble of feet. The air above the pad shimmered again. She scooped up a fallen rifle as something tugged her towards the door. She almost blew Frankie's head off before she saw it was her quadmate pulling her into the hall.

The door to the teleporter whisked shut behind them. Webb blasted the access controls, and the door fused shut in a fart of sparks.

A dent appeared in the door with a massive clang. Then another, then a third before the first blade punctured through.

Frankie gawked at the damage. "That door is solid mag-steel."

"They cut through the shuttle's hull." Webb scrambled to her feet. "Internal doors are nothing." She took aim.

"I thought beams didn't hurt them."

"They don't." She trained her aim on the coin-sized opening the xenos had cut in the door.

"Then what good will shooting them do?"

"I'm not aiming at them."

An arm blade hacked the gap open to the size of a dinner plate. Webb adjusted and fired through it at the teleporter console. Her shot glanced off its casing.

"Lerd." Webb took aim again. A blast roared over her shoulder—so close it singed her hair—and hit the console dead center.

The console exploded with shocking force. The door dented outward from shrapnel and flung xenos. Behind Webb, Chelse adjusted her rifle from blast to beam.

"Nice shot, jarhead."

A nod from Chelse. "We're withdrawing to the Nexus shield. Get behind the e-gates. Move!"

The quadmates fled. Over the alarms echoing through the ship, Webb heard the door wrenched out of it frame and the metallic plunking of xeno limbs skittering down the corridor after them.

Around a corner, soldiers had formed a firing line at a juncture in the hallway—the frame of the first emergency gate, a reinforced set of impervium blast doors. Panicking crew streamed by the soldiers. Frankie and Chelse were a few steps past the gate before they noticed Webb was no longer with them.

"Webb?" Franke called after her.

"One minute!" Webb didn't know if she'd been heard over the din. She darted down a side corridor, away from the gate, past a cluster of soldiers heading back the other way. A couple quick turns, darting around evacuating techs, and she was back at the brig.

Dewey was up against the force field when Webb entered. The chief seemed more shocked to see Webb, and to see her armed, than she was by the blaring klaxons. "Those are boarding alarms."

"Xeno incursion." Webb deactivated the security field. "Ship's lost to the e-gates."

"Fuck," opined Dewey.

"Yup." Webb tossed the chief her jacket.

Webb led Dewey back the way she'd come. The soldiers she'd passed on the way to the brig were already down, gaping gashes in their blast armor.

They could hear the cascade of fire before they turned the corner. Baking beams ripped into a mass of xenos, slingshotting an alien here or there but doing nothing to stem the tide. It was like trying to stop an avalanche with a broom.

"Is there another route to the gate?" Webb yelled over the fire.

Dewey shook her head. "It's a choke point by design."

Chittering behind them. Webb spun and spotted a silvery xeno skating towards their way. It slashed as she fired. Webb's beam flung it down the corridor like a corgi hit by a firehose.

Webb heard a gurgle from the floor. The chief was down. Blood streamed from her mouth and the gash across her back.

Webb went numb. "Chief?"

Dewey didn't say anything. She couldn't. Her breath was shallow, ragged—she was going into shock.

Webb slung the rifle over her shoulder, scooped up her chief, and pounded her way back towards the junction. Her lungs strained. She felt tiny misaligned mechanisms in her chest catch and clunk. Her breath went shallow. She gasped as she ran, gulping down as much air as possible with each breath. It didn't help—her lungs weren't absorbing enough oxygen. By the time she rounded the corner into the Nexus, the ship's central junction, spots were swimming at the edge of her vision.

The soldiers had fallen back past the first of the e-gates. The xenos had already hacked through it. Her vision tunneling, Webb stepped through the rent, shuffled for the firing line that had formed behind the next gate.

The loss of the first e-gate had activated the ship's interior gigalasers. They spattered xenos back in cascades of blinding fire as crew rushed through the closing blast doors.

Webb scuttled for the gate on aching legs. She felt like she was running underwater, like she was drowning—the oxygen flow to her brain had slowed to a trickle. She forced herself forward to hand Dewey through the closing gap to a pair of soldiers.

It was like breaking through the surface. With the chief's weight gone, Webb's breathing eased. The surge of oxygen that hit her brain restored enough of her senses that she could hear hear the deafening combination of chittering and internal laser fire surrounding her.

The doors of the Nexus shield had almost ground shut. Webb took a couple deep breaths, pulled herself into the gap. The spots reappeared in her vision. Beyond the blast doors, behind the soldiers, huddled shocked and wounded crew, many of them armed—including the skull-faced Armstrong aiming a rifle at her.

Webb pushed herself back out and dropped. The blast clipped her ribs, ripping a scream out of her. She heard the bulkheads close behind her and the thrum of its force-field springing into place.

Her side burning, Webb scrambled to her feet. The gigalasers had stopped firing. Ahead, at the end of the hall, xenos skittered into view. They chittered at her.

Webb grabbed a second rifle and darted down a side corridor, a narrow access tunnel. There was an emergency teleporter in Engineering, one meant for evacuation if the section were sealed or the lifts went down. If she could reach it, she could teep to the safe section of ship. Assuming her lungs let her get that far.

A dozen meters distant, the end of the tunnel came into view. So too did the cluster of xenos there.

Webb skidded to a halt. Glanced behind her. Xenos skittered towards her from that direction as well.

The xenos at the end of the tunnel parted. From their ranks emerged the heavily burnt xeno from the teleporter, which appeared no worse for its wounds. It tore off its cape, looked at her—directly at her—and chittered.

Webb yelled back defiantly. She raised her ineffectual rifles and fired beams of destruction into the ceiling.

Through the bulk of debris raining down, she couldn't see the xenos. Something heavy crashed onto her back—maybe detritus, maybe a xeno—and then she saw nothing.

Chapter 10
Quod Nocet, Saepe Docet

Wounded crew lined the floor behind the Nexus shield. The handful of medical personnel flitted between the fallen, administering triage, assisted by the few surviving soldiers.

Blackwell realized coldly that there would be no medical reinforcements. The Infirmary lay several decks down, buried in the infested section of the ship. His half of the *Independence* had limited medical supplies and even less personnel.

A trio of soldiers were standing over him. He realized he had no idea how much time had passed. Or why he was lying down.

He shot to his feet. "What?"

"Orders, sir," said the nearest soldier.

He stared at her blankly. "Orders?"

"You're the highest ranking officer."

"I am?"

"You are," said Dewey, slumped against a bulkhead. "Now that the new captain's sushi." She shooed away a nurse, tried to stand, and fell back down in a landslide of curses.

Blackwell's skin tingled. By the looks of it, he was one of the few who hadn't been injured. "You don't look so hot, Chief."

"I'll be fine." She yanked a medical stapler out of the nurse's kit. "Patch me up. I've got a ship to fix."

The ship. Blackwell took a moment to assess the damage. More of the crew were prostrate than standing. He noted that Jacobs and a number of other Armstrongs were hurt.

His chest tightened. They'd blame him for this. Shit may roll downhill, but blame always rolled up.

The soldier cleared her throat.

Blackwell snapped to. "You." He pointed to the soldier and her partner. "And you, put together a team." He raised his voice. "I need qualified

169

crew at the bridge duty stations. Uninjured or walking wounded only. Hands."

A few weak hands went up.

Blackwell thumped a soldier on the chest. "Get them situated." He looked for the bald Black teleporter tech, and spotted her sitting by the chief. No, not sitting. Meditating. Under these circumstances. "Fuller."

She opened her eyes.

"I want you on the bridge."

She nodded, rose.

A knot of armed Armstrongs formed around him. Loomis—the big one still had his skull mask up. "Take those off."

"Sir." The female soldier again. Alameda, by her name tag. "We have sixteen active personnel in the safe zone."

He felt bile burn at the back of his throat. "Is that all?"

She shifted her feet. "We took heavy losses planetside."

Sixteen soldiers. Maybe twice as many Armstrongs. It would have to do. "Start with security sweeps, make sure the ship's really been cut in half. I don't want to find out there's a burst hatch somewhere those things can fit through. If you spot them, don't engage. Drop force fields and retreat."

"Aye, sir." She saluted and led the soldiers away at a trot.

Blackwell pulled up the ship's schematic on a wall monitor. Behind the blast shields, fully half of the ship lay in the infested decks. "Independence. Activate level ten force fields in every junction beyond the Nexus Shield."

A negative chime. "Unable to comply."

"Explain."

"Main power conduit has been breached."

Dewey braced herself against the monitor. "That direct patch must've burnt out. Probably overloaded." She pulled up a readout of the ship's electrical veins, tapped a red point not far from Engineering. "Yep. Fuck. Surge knocked out the flow here."

Well beyond the Nexus shield. Blackwell ground his teeth. "Can you reroute it?"

A weary nod. "Through the backup conduits, but we won't get full juice. It should be enough to buttress the safe zone, though."

"Good enough. Independence, activate force fields between Decks Nine and Twelve, and in every corridor connected to the Nexus."

A positive chime. "Force fields activated."

Dewey frowned. "Those will lock out any crew in the cut off sections of the ship."

"We have more pressing concerns," he told her. "Those force fields are the only thing we know can keep those creatures back. We need to assess what state the ship is in before we can entertain rescue plans."

Dewey didn't disagree. Which didn't mean she approved.

"Sir." Loomis looked better with his mask on. His thin mustache made him look stupid. "Bridge is manned and ready."

Blackwell nodded. "Chief, see to your people."

"Great, yeah, I'll get right on that."

He set off for the bridge. En route, he pulled the highest ranking nurse aside. "Status?"

She lowered her voice. "Not good, sir. Supplies here are limited. There's only so much we can do without access to the Infirmary."

He looked out over the wounded. "Do you have enough to treat everyone?"

"We do not."

"Priority treatment goes to the Armstrongs. You can identify them by their pins."

She balked. "Sir, the protocol in a situation like this is—"

"Lieutenant." He leaned in. "I know this doesn't fit your agenda, but this is an emergency, and we need to close ranks. And when this crisis has passed, I'll remember who sprung into action, who dragged their feet. I trust I'm understood?"

She nodded stiffly.

✇

171

Webb was burning. She screamed as the stone around her hissed and vaporized. In fell the ceiling on the magnetite chamber below the ruins. The giant xeno was there, staring at her, and then it was gone, dissolving in an ochre wind, screaming without a mouth. Screaming and beeping.

Webb gasped awake in the darkness. Her lungs whirred and grated. She heard the beep again, inside her chest, like a second heartbeat: the low oxygen warning from her lungs.

She grunted. Her head ached and throbbed with spikes of pain. The air was stale and hot. She couldn't feel her legs below her knees, but there was pressure there, heavy, oppressive.

Her heart raced. She started hyperventilating.

No. Stop it. Panic would just suck the oxygen up faster. She tried jerking her legs free from their obstruction and cracked her head on a low ceiling.

Visions from her nightmare rattled around her skull: fire and pain, stone and dust.

Webb twisted again and pulled. Her legs yanked free, and she heard the crash of debris settling behind her. Her legs burned with a thousand blazing needles as her blood fought its way back into them.

She felt a rush of fresher, cooler air. She took as deep a breath as her damaged lungs would allow.

She felt the grate below her hands. That and the one meter of clearance told her where she was: a maintenance tube.

Worse than that. A conduit.

She felt around for her bearings. Definitely a maintenance conduit, but badly damaged. No lights, for one. And she hadn't been cooked to a crisp the way Yolanda Seven had. Which meant something had disrupted the ship's power flow.

As she rubbed the feeling back into her legs, Webb retraced her steps. She'd run for Engineering. She never got there, obviously. The main conduit was a deck below where the xenos had surrounded her. She remembered firing into the ceiling.

She felt around until she found the slagged remains of the rifle. Everything above its lower receiver had melted off. Well, that's a weapons overload for you. Pure luck that it hadn't exploded.

No, not luck. Don't be lazy. Everything had a mechanical cause. Work it out.

The rifle must have kept firing after she'd blacked out. That must have ripped up enough of the ceiling—and the floor when her aim fell—that she'd fallen through the deck and been buried in the shipslide. And if her blasting had ruptured the conduit beneath the floor, that would have triggered a power breach—one that, had it cascaded unchecked, would have filled the corridor with zettajoules of power and burned up the surrounding decks—which in turn would have triggered the conduit's emergency coolant sheath to kill the reaction. Everything had worked as designed, and she'd landed in the debris.

She shouldn't be alive. And she might not be after she had to explain to the chief how she'd fried her main conduit.

A problem for later. She constructed a mental map of her location. The conduits led from Engineering to the upper splitter core, where they branched out to carry power through the ship's various decks. The maintenance ring around the core allowed access to the ship's maintenance tubes.

The route to the splitter core, however, was blocked by the shipslide. She tried shoving the debris. It didn't budge.

Which left only one way to go: towards Engineering.

Webb crawled through darkness, down an ever descending slope towards the heart of the ship. She went by feel, probing ahead with the dead rifle, the only sounds her own breathing and the whirring of her lungs.

It reminded her unpleasantly of the time she'd let Frankie talk her into floating in a sensory deprivation tank in the Arcade. She'd claimed the sensory dep would help clear her mind, but all Webb remembered was feeling cold and pissed off.

173

The conduit leveled out. Engineering wasn't far. She pressed forward, but stopped abruptly when the rifle receiver clacked against something non-metallic.

Webb hadn't passed any damage for some time, no irregularities in the conduit's floor or siding. She felt out ahead of her, found something misshapen, smooth, just a few inches thick, with slagged protrusions sticking out. She felt into where one of the protrusion had given way. Her fingers brushed bone.

She whipped out her hands, choked out a sob. It was her remains. Yolanda Seven.

No, not Seven. Mary Chevalier. Her friend, her quadmate who'd died in a burst of pain and light. Webb's eyes felt hot and gummy. She'd died here, died saving the ship she was now a part of forever.

They'd said her remains were unrecoverable. It was remarkable any of her was left. She'd been baked into the side of the conduit, centimeters away from the main flow of power. Webb felt around for anything she could send to Chevalier's family—a scrap of uniform, a bit of the tri-wire she'd carried to her doom. Her fingers closed around something in the groove at the bottom of the conduit.

It was slumped and dulled from the heat, but she could still tell what it was. She ran her thumb over its Coalition logo. Seven's comm badge.

She gave it an experimental tap. It was dead. Hardly a surprise.

Webb tucked the badge into her toolband. She'd send it to the family. Hell, she'd take it to them herself if she ever got out of here.

Webb let out a shuddering breath. She kissed her fingers and pressed them to Chevalier's skull. "Thanks for saving us."

⏀

Another series of turns took Webb to the conduit's hatch. There was no handle on Webb's side. The Coalition had opted not to include an interior latch, as they'd determined that they'd save more omitting that feature than they'd lose from edge case lawsuits. But the Coalition also tended to contract with the lowest bidder, so Webb had had to fix these hatches more times than she could remember. She knew where the welds were. A hefty crack from the dead rifle snapped the hatch's deadbolt.

Webb creaked the hatch open. Light stabbed through her eyes and punched her in the brain. She shut it with a curse and waited until her eyes had adjusted.

Lights were good. Meant the core still had power. If it didn't, she'd have been halfway to popsicle as the ship cooled.

Webb put her ear to the crack in the hatch. Aside from the thrum of the stardrive, Engineering was quiet. No chatter of crewmates monitoring consoles. No xeno chittering, no plunk of metallic limbs on deck plating. Just the heart of the ship and the whirring of her lungs.

She eased the hatch open, crawled out of the conduit. The drive core still pulsed with power. She saw the caramelized remains of her pizza inside it. Engineering appeared abandoned.

She slid behind a console and pulled up Engineering's emergency teleporter. It was offline. Offline, and with command protocols rerouted to the bridge. "Lerd."

Plan. She needed a plan. If the Nexus shield was still down, the ship could be cut in half. She pulled up a power dispersal display on the console. It confirmed her suspicions. Power had been rerouted through the maintenance tubes. Unwittingly frying the conduit had saved her life.

The power was going to a lattice of force fields below Deck Eight. Every junction and corridor three decks down from the Nexus was locked with a security field.

The ship was indeed cut in half. And she was on the wrong side.

She had to gasp to keep her breathing regular. Calm. Have to keep calm.

She couldn't stay here. The safest way out was teleportation. If she could get in touch with someone in the safe zone, she could request a teleporter evac. She checked the comms. They were down, shipwide.

Webb took out Seven's comm badge. In the light, it wasn't as badly damaged as she'd thought. She might even be able to repair it if she could get the casing open.

But that would take tools, and time. And the tools were in her go-kit back in the quad, four decks away.

Bunk that. There were lifeboats near all the critical systems. Most were clustered around the bridge, but there were some scattered throughout the lower decks. She'd hop one and wait out the crisis in orbit.

She turned for the exit and nearly screamed.

A cog was standing behind her.

"Jesus *fuck*. I thought I was alone." Nothing that heavy should be able to move so silently. "Where's the nearest lifeboat?"

The cog fixed her with its marble gaze. "Identify yourself."

"I don't have my badge." They clued off of those rather than faces. "Senior Tech Joni Webber, service number XF4456H."

It seized her wrist. "You will come with us to the brig."

She tried to jerk away. Its grip was a vise. "What are you doing?"

"Do not resist." It tightened its grip. "You escaped from the brig at 13:47 hours."

"I didn't *escape,* I was taken *out* by people who were gonna *kill* me!"

"Do not resist. Use of force is authorized."

A clang like an axe on a church bell.

Time seemed to slow to a trickle. A massive dent had appeared in the door. Xeno chittering drifted in behind it.

Webb's stomach turned to ice. "We have to *go.* "

The cog swiveled towards the door. "Cease vandalizing Coalition property."

"We have to go *now.*"

Another dent punched into the door. The cog stalked towards the door, dragging Webb behind it. "Cease vandalizing Coalition property. Use of force is authorized."

Webb smashed her rifle against the cog's head. "Indie, drop a force field around the exit to Engineering!"

A negative chime. "Your privileges have been revoked," said the ship.

"*What?*"

"You terminated your service as of 00:00 hours and are no longer a member of this crew. Your permissions and privileges have been revoked."

"Are you bunking *kidding* me?"

A gash appeared in the door. Compound eyes milled in the corridor beyond.

"Engineering is off-limits to civilians," said the ship. "Disperse at once."

The cog had almost reached the door. Webb pounded it harder, chipping off bits of enamel. "There xenos are gonna kill us, you stupid marble fuck!"

"Our scans indicate no alien presence," said the cog. "Cease vandalizing Coalition property."

An armblade cut through the door and into the cog's shoulder. Its arm fell limp, dangling by a nest of spitting cables. The cog actually looked shocked.

More blades punched through and sliced through the cog like a garden claw through tin foil.

Webb jammed her rifle receiver through the wires in the cog's hanging arm and wrenched with all her might.

Cables popped and snapped. The cog's arm hit the deck, the weight of it nearly pulling Webb to the floor. She chucked the receiver and ran for the hatch, dragging the cog's arm like an anchor behind her.

The door gave way as she dove back into the conduit. She caught a glimpse of the cog going down under a wave of xenos as she shut the hatch.

Webb strained to peel the cog's thumb off her wrist. Servos in the arm complained, but she got its grip loose enough to slide her wrist out. She looped the arm through a couple of brackets and bent it around to grasp itself.

The hatch sealed, and the conduit went dark as a tomb. Webb hoped it wouldn't be hers.

𝒟

Loomis snapped off a crisp salute. "Captain on the bridge."

Blackwell returned the salute and looked out over the motley group manning the duty stations of the bridge. *His* bridge. His first command, the first of many if he played his cards right. He'd never felt taller.

"As you were." He strode to the command dais and sank into the captain's chair. "Independence, dispatch all cogs to the bridge."

The ship chimed. "All but one cog is en route."

"All but one?"

"One member of the Collective Operations Group has been destroyed."

"Dear God." Those things cost a fortune. "Damage report."

A series of chimes. "Comms are offline. Teleporter grid is offline. The shuttle bay has been depressurized and has been sealed by emergency bulkheads. The port torpedo bay has been sealed off, but remains destroyed. Disruptions to the conduits have reduced available power to forty percent. Damaged non-essential systems include: the mess hall, the Arcade, the—"

"What about hull breaches?"

"Severe structural damage to bulkheads and doors on Decks 13, 15, 18 through 21, and 27."

All in the infested section of ship. "Scan for boarders."

A negative chime. "No invaders are present."

The xenos still weren't appearing on their scans. Blackwell drummed his fingers on the armrest. "Indie, bring the comms back online. Open a shipwide channel to the crew, including the occupied decks."

A chime. "Comms online. Channel open."

Blackwell rose, tugged his uniform taut. "This is acting Captain Blackwell. We are dealing with a situation. Contrary to any rumors you may have heard, we have it under control. Help is on the way. In the meantime, the ship is on lockdown. I order any crew currently below Deck Eight to shelter in place. Activate security fields around your exits, but remain where you are. Further updates will be made as we approach victory. Blackwell out."

He hit a button, turned to the red shirt at Ops. "Take the comms back offline. I don't want any disinformation spreading."

The doors whisked open. In limped Dewey on a pair of makeshift crutches. She glared at the Armstrong manning the engineering station in the outer command ring until he slinked away and nodded at Blackwell. "Sir."

"Chief." He made a mental note to demote whoever had gotten her mobile again. "Good to see you upright."

"You didn't say anything about the incursion," she said flatly. "Or the ship being cut in half."

"I am well aware, Chief." He thrust out his chin. "I did make the announcement myself." Chuckles from the Armstrongs.

"You don't think the stranded crew deserves to know what they're up against? A bunch of pissed off xenos who can cut through walls… seems an important detail to leave out."

He gave her a glassy stare. "That's what the force fields are for. You saw what those creatures did. Last thing we need is a bunch of panicking crewmen filling ship with more bodies."

"Sir. The crew is trained. They know how to act in a crisis. We get plenty of practice. This is no time to give them incomplete information. And those force fields are an enormous drain on our power."

Blackwell nodded curtly. "Good point. We need all the power we can muster. Juice the conduits."

She looked incredulous. "There might be crew in there."

"And I told them to shelter in place." He spun his chair toward the teleporter tech. "Fuller. Teleporter status."

"We have limited teleporter capability in this section," said Fuller.

"How limited?"

"From the bridge, we can only control the emergency unit. It's short-range, deck to deck and immediate vicinity only. We might be able to reach the surface if we goose the range, but the emergency units just don't have the reach of the main bays. It's still enough to pull any trapped crew out of the infested zone."

Blackwell shook his head. "We don't have room for them."

"We would if we opened the officers' quarters," said Dewey.

"Hard no," said Blackwell. "They're safe where they are. If we start changing our way of life, the xenos have already won."

"*Sir.*" The teleporter tech was talking again. "We have people in the Nexus in dire need of medical assistance. At the very least, we could teep in some doctors and equipment from the Infirmary."

"Solid plan, sir," said Dewey.

Blackwell bit off a sigh. "Apparently, I have to remind you all that the ship is infested *because* the xenos hijacked our teleporters. As far as we know, they've occupied the main bays and they could teep to the bridge if they figure out how. It's a risk I'm not willing to take. Keep all teleporters offline, and lock them down."

Fuller's shoulders drooped. "Aye, sir."

The doors slid open again. In marched the cogs in perfect unison.

Blackwell rose. "Indie, assign the cogs to the bridge's duty stations. Those of you currently at those stations, thank you for your service. Go assist the medical personnel. Armstrongs, you're with me."

"Sir," said the cog at Communications. "We have an incoming message."

Blackwell glared at the red shirts filing out. "I thought I had the comms taken offline."

"It is from the Admiralty, sir," said the cog. "On a private channel, addressed to the captain."

Blackwell nodded. "I'll take it in my cabin."

"Sir," said the cog. "The message is for the captain's eyes only. And while you are the ship's acting captain, you must officially be sworn in and have the ship's command codes transferred to—"

"Yes, yes, let's get this over with. Send the chaplain to my cabin if he's still alive." He tried to keep his expression somber, but it was hard to keep the smile from his face.

He could see the thrill on the Armstrongs as well. Not so on the faces of the retreating red shirts.

Ah, well. They'd learn to love him, in time. Just like Sunshine.

Webb took a branching route away from Engineering through a warren of maintenance tubes. She followed a map in her head towards a service entrance accessible from a lift shaft. There, she popped out of the conduit, peered down the yawning, unlit shaft. High above hummed the force fields barring passage to the supposedly safe decks.

That was all she heard, though. No chittering. She felt for the service ladder.

Below, several decks down, were the quads on the habitation decks. There were lifeboats there. Not enough for everyone—lifeboat capacity had been calculated to include acceptable losses—but with xenos and force fields cutting Indie in half, those were her only way off the ship. So down she went.

Three decks down, she slid a blast shutter away from the viewport in the door. A rack of lifeboats lay at the end of the hall beyond. Most of its pods were gone. Which was good. Some of the crew had escaped.

But not all of them. Of the lifeboats left, one had been carved open like a grisly gourd. A thick red streak led around a corner away from it.

Webb steeled herself. Fifty meters between the shaft and the rack. Two lifeboats left.

But the lifeboats were only accessible to crew. Indie wouldn't let her board, not by voice command. Not with her privileges revoked. Which meant she'd have to blast the lock off the door and manually release the docking clamps from inside the lifeboat.

So she needed a weapon. For the first time, Webb was grateful she shared a quad with a soldier.

She climbed two floors further down to the deck of her quad. Hallway lights flickered there beyond the viewport. The corridor looked empty, the only sounds the flickering of lights and the occasional fart of sparks.

Webb gingerly opened the lift hatch and padded her way down the hallway towards her quad. Its door slid open. She may not have been a member of the crew anymore, but at least Indie still recognized she lived here.

Webb's legs buckled. She locked the door and collapsed on Eight's bunk. Not that the lock would keep the xenos from tearing through the door, but it gave her a bit of mental comfort.

Chelse's weapons locker was, as always, locked. Triple locked: the thing required a voice-print, retinal scan, and handprint to open. Or, as Webb and Frankie had discovered after Chelse's family had sent her a bottle of scotch for her anniversary, you could just pop the hinges off.

She smiled at the memory. Chelse thought her family had skimped and sent her the cheap stuff. No, dear, not cheap. Just watered down.

The smile faded. Webb drew her limbs to herself. She'd rarely ever been alone in the quad. The bunk beneath hers, the bunk she was lying in now, had slept six new quadmates since its original inhabitant. Yolanda Prime—that's how they'd come to think of her, their original quadmate— she'd been the peacemaker. Three strong-willed women living on top of each other—a jarhead with a couple of engineering rats, one calm as a mountain lake, the other the defiant crew advocate—it shouldn't have worked. It wouldn't have without Yolanda.

She'd been the organizer, the one who convinced them to pool their water rations so they could each take a hot shower once a week, who'd worked out the visitation schedule so the women could have a modicum of privacy if they brought home a date. She remembered how hard she and Frankie had teased Chelse when she'd overslept with that stubbly nurse. "Be nice," Yolanda had chided them after Chelse and Rob had slinked out. "That's your future quaddie-in-law."

Webb could still remember her voice. But her features—her heart-shaped face, her thin nose and tapered chin—were getting harder to recall with each month that slipped by. The other Yolandas were starting to blur. Even Seven's features were starting to fade.

They were all gone now. But Webb was still alive. And so were her quaddies, as far as she knew. She felt a stab of guilt for not learning Eight's name. Definitely time to end that policy.

She popped the hinges off Chelse's locker with practiced ease. Inside lay a pair of quellers: sidearms with variable power. The lowest setting was nonlethal, but still pretty excruciating. She wouldn't be slagging through a deck with them, but their max setting would still blow a hole through a mutineer. Or the lock off a lifeboat hatch. They'd be useless against the xenos, but if she found herself cornered again, a maxed shot to her temple would be a quick and far less gruesome way to go. And on the bright side, she wouldn't have to pay off the rest of her lungs.

Webb tucked both quellers into her toolband and fished her toolkit out of her locker. She popped open Seven's comm badge. Its fuses were burnt out, and its power crystal cracked. She couldn't do anything about that, but she could at least replace the fuses. She tugged some wires out of a decoupler she wouldn't be using and wove them into the power casing of the badge.

Her stomach rumbled. She couldn't remember the last time she'd eaten. "Hey, Indie. How many meal credits have I got left?"

A negative chime. "All meal credits are forfeited upon resignation of commission."

She flipped off the ceiling. "Thanks, shiphead." She scrounged for food, but found nothing in the lockers except for Chelse's watered down scotch and Frankie's chalky tea powder. Eight's locker was empty—she hadn't even had time to unpack before the shit hit the reactor—but she'd left a duffel bag on her bunk.

Webb rifled through it. No food, just clothes, a bunch of ag testing equipment, and a disassembled agripod.

There are rations on the lifeboats, her stomach reminded her. And now she could board one without Indie's permission.

Back to the shaft, then. Webb screwed Eight's disassembled agripod together, smacked its reassuring weight in her hand. The xenos might shrug off sidearm fire, but a whack with a six foot pole would ring anyone's bell.

✺

The lift shaft was a longer route to the lifeboats, but it felt safer than taking the corridors. Webb climbed the shaft's ladder back up to the maintenance tube she'd taken out of Engineering. She opened its hatch.

An arc of plasma shot out that nearly tore her from the ladder. It lit up the shaft like a flare from Hell, hit the far wall, and dispersed, sending echoes roaring up and down the length of the shaft.

Webb clung to the ladder like a traumatized squirrel, her heart thundering. They'd juiced the tubes. They'd bunking juiced the tubes to boost power. If she'd been farther up the ladder when she opened the hatch, her ashes would be raining down the lift.

Chittering drifted down from higher above. Webb's heart froze.

Screw it. She'd have to risk the corridor.

She slid down the ladder to the deck with the lifeboats, Eight's agripod slapping against her back in her tool sheath. The corridor beyond the viewport looked empty. She opened the hatch and sprinted down the hall.

She hadn't made it halfway to the lifeboats before the xenos slid into view ahead of her. Three of them, two silver, one burnt with a crackle pattern. The burnt one hissed.

Webb's breath deserted her. She ran back and dove through the lift hatch. She hadn't slid more than a deck down the ladder before she heard the hatch torn open above.

More chittering drifted up from below. She looked down, saw xenos skittering up the shaft like spiders made of fishhooks.

Webb yanked open the shaft controls on her current level and activated the emergency bulkheads. Blast doors slammed shut above and below. She dropped to the new floor, unlocked the hatch onto whatever deck she was on with trembling fingers. The xenos were already beating dents into the ceiling by the time she slipped out of the hatch.

She darted down an empty corridor. There were no lifeboats here, just hallways leading towards the ship's interior. What was on this level? The mess, some labs, the Arcade. Nothing they couldn't chop through.

But the labs had access to the tubes. Hopefully unjuiced ones. She could hide there. She skidded to a stop at the nearest lab, slapped at its door controls. The door didn't open.

She hit the controls again. "Indie, let me in!"

"Your privileges have been revoked."

Webb drew a queller and shot the control panel. It died in a shower of sparks, but the door remained shut.

Chitters echoed down the corridor towards her. Her stomach went hard as a rock. They'd trapped her.

No. Think. You know the ship. She couldn't access the labs, and the mess was too open, but the Arcade... the Arcade was a third party. It wasn't run by the Coalition. She might still have access.

She dashed for the Arcade, her lungs whirring. The Arcade's curtain-painted doors slid opened before her onto its empty grid and slid shut behind her. "Impressario," she gasped. "Private mode."

Locking mechanisms latched. The doors shuddered with impact. She could hear the xenos tearing at the controls, hear the bursting of circuits and conduits. The lights flickered.

Now would certainly be a good time to hide behind a hedgerow. And possibly a castle. "Impressario, load my last program!"

The grid melted away onto a manicured green field. To her horror, Webb found herself standing in the infield of Lord's Cricket Ground, right where she and Seven had left their match months ago. An annoyed Australian wicket keeper glared at her.

"Oh, shit." Her throat clenched. "Shit shit *shit.*" This was her last *official* program. That stupid romance novel was unauthorized.

The two silvers and the burnt xeno burst onto the field from the stadium's media center and immediately froze.

The wicket keeper cleared his throat. "Do you *mind?*"

"Sorry." Webb backed towards the stands, hoping the xenos were too disoriented to single her out.

The xenos bobbed their heads at one another. They chittered. Then they streaked towards the infield and beheaded the bowler.

"Bad form!" called the batsman, whom they disemboweled.

Webb climbed into the stands and backed through the crowd of booing spectators. On the field, the umpire blew a whistle and gave the xenos a red card. They decapitated him. The boos intensified.

Webb sank into an empty seat, shrunk down in the crowd. The holographic fans kept booing as the xenos carved up more cricketers. The sprites must have been programmed with a limited range of responses. Probably for the best; if they had panic in their subroutines, she could have been trampled in a stampede of horrified cricket fans.

The burnt xeno had stopped killing sprites. It traversed its head across the stands and came to looking right at her.

Webb's blood ran cold. If anyone had taken Seven's novel out of the disk port, she was dead. "Impressario, load last program from the *data stick.*"

The sky darkened and the moon shot up as the cricket ground melted away. Hedgerows popped up in its place, obscuring the xenos, as did the manor house in the distance. The far distance, she noted sourly.

The xenos made a sound she hadn't heard before. Par for the course when reality warps around you.

Another sound, one far more welcome: hoofbeats. She turned to see the novel's romantic interest, Ablehard, riding towards her from the castle, his leonine locks trailing in the breeze, his shirt open, his manly pecs glistening with rose-scented oil. She shouldn't have been able to tell the oil was rose-scented from this distance, but the program was really selling it.

She snorted. "Frigging porn programs."

The sprite reined to a stop, gave her a curt nod. "My lady. I see you have returned." He wasn't smiling.

"Yeah, hi. Is that horse a two-seater?"

He blinked. "Are you ill? You sound as if you've swallowed a woodwind."

"Yeah, broke my lungs. So—horse?"

"I must admit, I am perplexed." He examined his hand, pointedly not looking at her. "When last we parted, I had the distinct impression you did not wish to see me again."

The xenos skittered over a hedgerow. "I've changed my mind."

Ablehard spotted them. "My lady. Don't. Move." He narrowed his eyes. "The wolves have returned."

She backed towards his horse. "Those ain't wolves, dude."

Ablehard drew his sword. The xenos regarded Ablehard and his horse and chittered to one another. "Regardless of how distasteful you find my company, I must insist you accompany me. It's not safe here." He extended a hand.

"No shit." She took his hand and straddled the horse behind him. The horse reared cinematically and galloped off towards the manor.

Another startled chitter. The xenos skittered after them.

"We'll be safe in the manor!" roared Ablehard, his musculature rippling beneath his silken shirt. His programmers really knew their audience. "In three hundred years, its walls have never been breached!"

"Yeah, no, they can cut right through those," Webb shouted over the wind. "Or climb over them."

Ablehard laughed, a deep booming rumble. "I've never known wolves to climb, my lady."

"Yes, well, we're discovering the limits of your visual recognition matrix." She looked behind them. The xenos didn't appear to be gaining, but neither were they falling behind. If she couldn't put some distance between them, she was just spinning her wheels. "Hey, man-locks. Is there a river nearby?"

He seemed surprised. And morose. "Are you not one of my subjects?"

"I'm just passing through." She hoped. "Yes or no on the river?"

"Yes." He looked off distantly, his eyes glistening with unshed tears. "The very river where my poor lady drowned, seven years ago tonight: the Sorrowmere."

"Jesus Christ."

"Please!" He looked away, but not so far as to conceal his manly suffering. "I shall speak of it no more."

"Deal," said Webb. "Ride to the river. Preferably a bridge."

Ablehard reined his mount down a hedgerow, away from the manor. The xenos matched their pace.

In the distance glimmered the Sorrowmere, a shimmering ribbon of rapids cutting through the mountain valley. A covered wooden bridge straddled it at an appropriately perilous spot.

"I blame myself," he said somberly. "Had I not allowed my work to consume me, I would have noticed how her affections had—"

"Shut up," she told him. "Cross the bridge."

"'Twas from this very bridge that my poor lady fell!" he gasped.

"Yes, I gathered that from the foreshadowing."

"Please!" He looked away again. "I shall speak of it no more."

Ablehard slowed as the bridge rose into view, its roof sagging in disrepair. Webb could see roaring water through holes in some of the boards. "Um… perhaps we could cross at a bridge with less anguish in it?"

"There *is* another bridge," muttered Ablehard, tears welling in his eyes, "where my childhood love did fall to her premature—"

"Shut *up.*" The xenos skated into view. Webb slammed her heels into the horse's flanks. It surged forward with a dramatic whinny.

Hooves rattled on rotting wood. Webb shoved her agripod into Ablehard's hands and pulled the quellers from her toolband. She didn't know how the discharge would interact with the hologrid, but sometimes you had to test on the fly. She cranked them to max.

Webb slammed into Ablehard's back as he reined to an abrupt stop. "What are you *doing?*"

His mighty shoulders sagged. His gaze fell upon a plaque at a little shrine halfway across the bridge. "Seven years. Seven years since I last saw her face."

"*Wolves,* guy!"

"Never did I think I would return. Perhaps… it *has* been too long. Or not long enough. I remember the night it happened…"

He gazed towards the moon. Letterbox bars appeared on the horizon.

"Do *not* start a cutscene!" Webb fired both quellers at the floor of the bridge.

Timbers exploded and fell. The xenos fell with them, down into the whirling rapids. They tumbled away in the current.

Webb hopped off the horse to peer downriver. The xenos winked around a corner at least a kilometer away.

Except, they weren't that far away. The Arcade wasn't more than thirty meters wide. But as long as she kept the program running, the Arcade would maintain its convincing fiction of distance.

"Perhaps…" rumbled Ablehard, "perhaps it is time I moved on," Ablehard concluded.

Webb had missed the rest of his monologue. No real loss there. The writing had been lackluster for a while. "Hey, so I hope you find some peace or whatever, but I've gotta go."

Chittering. Webb froze. With nightmare slowness, she looked up into the bridge's rafters. The xeno dove for her, blades extended.

"For *love!*" Ablehard smashed it into the wall with the agripod, shattering the globe of agrichems at its tip.

The xeno squealed like the wrenching of rusty gears and literally fell apart, blue and yellow agrichems eating through its metallic plating. Hidden gasses burst from its carapace and vented out. It died a broken slurry on the timbers.

Ablehard was aghast. "What manner of wolf *is* this?"

Webb squatted down beside the remains, looked from them to the agripod's broken housing. "Holy lerd."

Ablehard dismounted. "What have we done, my lady?"

"I'll tell you what we've done." A fierce grin split her face. "We've found out what hurts them."

Chapter 11
Bonum Consilium Quod Mutari Potest

When it followed the death of a captain, the swearing-in ceremony was meant to be a private affair, a somber occasion held in the new captain's cabin with only the most senior officers and chaplain in attendance. But after the events that had shaken the ship, the crew needed hope. They needed leadership, and to see it in action.

And so, Blackwell stood on the bridge in his dress uniform, surrounded by his crew, his hand on the Bible. "And that I will well and faithfully discharge the duties of the office on which I am about to enter," he intoned. "So help me God."

The chaplain teetered, his eyes unfocused. "Eternal Lord God, You have summarized ethical behavior in a single sentence: do for others what you would like them to do for you."

Blackwell nodded, smiled humbly. "Thank you, Father."

"Remind our officers," the chaplain continued, his breath a hot wind of Schnapps, "that they are ultimately accountable to You for their conduct. Lord, help them to remember that they cannot ignore You and get away with it. For we always reap what we sow."

The Armstrongs shifted their feet. Red shirts exchanged glances. Blackwell felt his smile tighten.

The chaplain raised his hands and flask to the heavens. "Have Your way, mighty God. You are the potter. Our officers and we are the clay. Mold and make us after Your will."

"A lovely homily," said Blackwell. "We are, all of us, in your debt."

The chaplain clamped his hand atop Blackwell's, pinning it to the Bible. He had a remarkably strong grip for a boozehound. "Stand up, omnipotent God. Stretch Yourself, and let this crew and Coalition know that You alone are sovereign."

"A*men*." Blackwell made a mental note to move the chaplain's quarters next to the firing range.

"I pray in the name of Jesus. Amen."

"Amen!" shouted the Armstrongs.

The chaplain wobbled a salute. "Congratulations. Captain."

Thunderous applause from the Armstrongs. Polite claps from everyone else. Blackwell seated himself in the captain's chair—*his* chair now, officially—and winked at the Armstrongs. "Status report, Chief."

"The corridors have been juiced," Dewey replied as a pair of Armstrongs forcefully chucked the chaplain off the bridge. "Force fields are holding on Decks 9 through 12."

Blackwell grunted. "That should prevent further incursion."

"It does nothing for the crew in the infested decks," said Dewey. "They need to know what's going on. Without an update, they might conclude no one's in charge."

"The ceremony was broadcast shipwide, Chief." He studied a data pad. "Anyone who missed the broadcast can review it once they're safely back in their quads. Anything else?"

"Yes," she said flatly. "I'm hearing complaints from the crew."

"Oh?" He spun his chair to face her. "About what?"

"The Armstrongs. They're issuing orders. And beatings."

"Yes, I've put them in charge. We're lucky to have a unit so dedicated to maintaining order." Out of the corner of his eye, he saw some of the soldiers stiffen.

Dewey clenched her jaw. "Sir. They're ordering crew of equal rank around and they're sending the injured back to work."

"As you just pointed out, Chief, the ship is overrun. If they can stand, they can work."

"Many of them *can't*," she snapped. "You can't walk down the hall without tripping over a stretcher. But the Armstrongs *can*. Work. But they're not."

Blackwell snorted. "You know, it's funny. The other divisions never see Command as real work."

"*Sir.*" She gripped the command rail so hard her knuckles turned white. "This crew need stability. The Armstrongs—who I must remind you are a group not recognized by the Coalition—have *armed* themselves and are forcing crew *of equal rank* to carry out their duties."

"Fine, fine." He spun his chair to the main screen. "Independence, bring the comms back up. Broadcast the following message throughout the ship."

The comms chimed on.

"This is your captain." He let that sink in. "It's come to my attention that some rumors have been spreading. Divisive rumors about a loss of command structure, about how we've been boarded and overrun. I'll put it plainly. Our command structure remains intact. The external threat is absolutely contained. And we are even now, at this very moment, retaking the ship."

He stood, turned his gaze over those assembled. "Now, I've heard a few of you have been complaining about the Armstrongs. Mainly about how they're taking too much initiative during a crisis." He paused for their chuckles. "I'll be frank. Most of you aren't used to working as hard as is necessary during a crisis. I'd like to thank the Armstrongs for rising to the occasion, and working above and beyond the call of duty. You should look to their example—no whining, no pointless debate, just *action.* They're keeping our ship functional. I'm sorry if that rubs some of you the wrong way."

"That said, I understand some of you don't like the idea of taking orders from equals. Makes sense to me. Hierarchy is good, keeps things nice and clear. So, as of this moment, every Armstrong is considered to hold the rank of Master Technician."

Dewey bristled. The red shirts' eyes went wide.

"You don't want to take orders from anyone but a superior? Fine, the Armstrongs are now your superiors. Keep that in mind the next time you feel like complaining." He watched the Armstrongs swell with pride. "Oh, and one final reminder: remain where you are. You have nothing to fear. We are in complete control. Comms and teleporters will remain offline to assure your safety. Keep your doors shut and your force fields up. Captain out."

He clicked off the comms, sat, and drank in the glare Dewey sent his way.

"Captain," said the cog at ops. "You have a priority one message from the Admiralty."

"Yes, yes, all in good time," said Blackwell. "A couple more fires to put out first. Get me a status report from Xenobiology. Let's see what the good Baron's come up with."

"Aye, sir."

He sank back into his chair. He felt eyes on him, turned to see Dewey's glare hadn't slackened. "Something to say, Barbara?"

"You told them we were on our way."

"We are. Have a little faith in the process."

A negative chime from ops. "No response from Xenobiology," said the cog.

Of course there wasn't; he'd ordered a communications blackout. He tapped his badge. "Blackwell to Phillips."

No reply. Not even the usual static when the system was down.

He tapped his badge again. "Bridge to Xenobiology. Respond."

"Xenobiology's in the infested decks," said Dewey.

"I know the layout of my own ship, thank you." He shifted his weight. "Give me visual in Xenobiology."

The ship's main screen switched to a field of static. The Ops cog stated the obvious. "Xenobiology's cameras are offline."

Blackwell felt a twinge of concern. "Give me the cameras outside the lab."

The view shifted to outside the Xenobiology Lab. Its door remained shut and sealed. But the wall beside it had been peeled open.

Gasps from the bridge, and not just from the red shirts. Blackwell fought to keep his voice steady. "Take that down." The image flicked back to the planet. "Transfer all data from the Xenobiology Lab to the bridge."

"We need to get people out of there," said Dewey.

Blackwell reddened. "The security fields are holding."

"That hardly matters when they can cut through walls."

Blackwell avoided her gaze. "Scan for life signs," he told Ops. "Surround any compartment with a human biosign with a level ten force field."

The cog tapped some keys. A negative chime. "Unable to comply, sir. The internal force field grid has been damaged in several areas."

"The grid runs through the walls," observed Dewey.

"Sir," piped up the teleporter tech, "it's not too late to teep survivors to the safe decks. I could overload and short out the teleporter terminals in the other sections of ship."

"They're expecting us to help them," said the chief. "I don't see how else we can if we can't hurt the xenos."

"We can hurt them." Blackwell clenched and unclenched his fist. "Spacing kills them. Chief, draw up a plan to vent the infested decks."

Her jaw dropped. She blinked rapidly, as if she couldn't process what she'd just heard.

Jacobs stepped up. "We'd have to blow every deck from Deck Nine down. Everything—every hatch, bulkhead, and seal."

"Anyone in a corridor or a breached room would be spaced along with the xenos," said Fuller.

"That is unfortunate," said Blackwell. "But if it's a choice between losing a few people and saving the ship, that's a sacrifice I'm willing to make."

"That would kill everyone," barked Dewey.

"Hyperbole doesn't help, Chief."

"*Everyone,*" she repeated. "In all sections of ship. Bridge included."

He sucked his teeth. "Explain."

"Engineering is in the infested decks. The ship interprets *any* depressurization in Engineering as a hull breach, and that would trigger its emergency failsafe."

Blackwell shrugged. "And?"

She blurted a laugh. "We've got a star compressed to the size of a *beach ball* in the drive core! If the core fails, the pressures compressing it give out, and a new star pops up 20,000 kilometers above the planet. That's bye bye planet, along with any ship within 10 million k's."

Blackwell scoffed. "The ejector pod would spit the star a light year away before it expanded."

"That's assuming the ejector assembly hasn't been damaged," said Dewey. "We don't know the state of Engineering or any of its systems because we don't have anyone there. If we depressurize those decks, and Indie freaks and tries to puke out the star, but the ejector pod fails, the star either kindles *within* the ship, in which case we're dead, or it flings it away at sub-light speed but the star doesn't travel far enough before it blossoms and we're caught in its corona, in which case, also, dead." She crossed her arms. "You might space all the xenos on the ship, and any crew dumb enough to be in the corridors, but you're also risking giving birth to a sun beneath our feet."

Blackwell rapped his fingers on his command chair. "*Is* the core drive damaged?"

"It might be. Someone blew up a pizza in there."

"What?"

"We can't know for certain without boots on the deck. And sending anyone into the infested zone before we've secured the ship is a death sentence."

By their expressions, the red shirts agreed. So did some of the Armstrongs. "How do we prevent the stardrive from failing if we vent the infested decks? There must be some way to keep Engineering from depressurizing."

Dewey wrinkled her face. "Theoretically. But we'd have to seal off Engineering first. Literally, *all* of it. We're talking welding everything shut—doors, vents, conduits. There can't be an unsealed seam anywhere."

"But it's doable."

"Yes, but only from Engineering. Which is in the infested decks. And we can't teep anyone down without bringing the teleporters online, which you've already shot down, and we can't bulldoze our way down there because our fucking guns don't hurt them."

Blackwell fumed. "Is *that* all?"

"Oh, there's more. With our power rerouted around the burnt-out conduit, we're running everything through lower-band systems in danger of overloading. We can only send so many zettajoules through them before the bypasses themselves burn out."

Blackwell let out a low whistle. "Alright. Chief, figure out how to assess the drive core's viability remotely. If its failsafes are undamaged, we can proceed with the plan as is."

"There's also the moral implications of spacing several hundred people you just told to shelter in place."

"They knew what they were signing up for." Blackwell turned back to the viewscreen.

"Captain." The ops cog was looking his way again. "You have a priority one message from the Admiralty."

"My God, fine. I'll take it in my cabin." He stood, straightened his medals. "Master Tech Jacobs, you have the bridge." Protocol called for the highest ranking officer to be given the conn, but he wasn't about to reward Dewey for that bit of grandstanding.

Ø

197

Webb watched the last of the xeno's slagged remains dissolve into the puddle of agricultural chemicals.

Her mind racing. Agrichems hurt them. That's why they ran from the shuttle explosion on the surface—it had been carrying racks of those things. It also explained why those crewmen from the *Flagstaff* had stayed in a chemborn wheat field until they'd died of thirst.

Ablehard held a perfumed hanky over his nose. "I am shocked by the boldness of this pack. No wolves have ever pressed so far into my demesne."

"I think we're to blame for that." Webb felt disoriented. "We dropped a bunch of toxic fields on their planet."

"What manner of sickness makes them rot so, with not even a skin to display? Its body looks like a pool of melted grappling hooks."

Webb shook her head. "I think we've been destroying their habitat."

He nodded knowingly. "If the wolves are sick, the land itself may be ill. I confess, I have been lax in my stewardship, and have not been giving the land the attention it deserves. Not since..." He looked towards the shrine.

"Let me guess. You shall speak of it no more."

A gentle smile. "Thank you for understanding."

This one was dead, but the other xenos were still alive somewhere in the Arcade. Its safety protocols wouldn't let them drown. It would create a sandbar for them to catch, maybe push them to a riverbank. Then again, if the xenos didn't scan as life forms, those protocols might not activate.

No point sticking around to find out. Too bad she'd only had the one agripod. She rose, looked up into Ablehard's chiseled face. "Well, this has been... I'm not gonna say *fun,* but uh... anyway, I'm leaving."

He set a hand to his heart. "My lady, it is near midnight! And there may be more wolves. For your own safety, I must insist you spend the night in my bed. *Alone!*" He blanched with horror. "I meant *alone,* obviously. I would stay elsewhere, obviously. It's just the nicest one in the

manor, and I thought… I assure you, my entendres are entirely single."
Mortified, he mounted up.

"I'm good." She patted his horse's neck. "Thanks for slaying that wolf."

He reined his steed around to block her path. "I must insist. As my
subject, your safety falls to me."

"Dude." She didn't have time for this. "I'm leaving. I'd just end the
program, but there's a good chance those other wolves are just a few real
world meters away."

He narrowed his eyes. "I could *order* you to stay."

She rolled hers and strolled on by.

He bellowed a laugh. "You remind me of her." She heard him dis-
mount. "Your truculence. Your fierce independence, the surety of your
convictions."

"Not playing your porn narrative right now." She had to get word
out, let command know how to fight the xenos. She tapped Seven's dead
comm badge. Without a power crystal, it was just a bulky pin.

"She was also of the common folk." Ablehard smiled fondly. "Like
yourself. A fierce lass with fire in her eyes and venom in her tongue."

"She sounds awesome. Indie, are the comms up?"

"Your privileges have been revoked."

"Thanks, I'd almost forgotten."

"Privileges." His face was a mask of bittersweet memory. "She chal-
lenged me to reflect upon mine. To see that they were due but to the
randomness of birth, pure chance—not merit!—that had put me in my
station." A dark chuckle. "It's how I fell out of favor with my own class. I
regret it not in the least."

"Predictable plot line, all things considered." She picked her way
across the rickety bridge and jumped out onto the gravel.

"It shames me now," he was still following her, "but I was quite in-
dolent in my youth. Foolish. Hedonistic. Given to the pursuit of pleasure
rather than attending to the duties of statecraft. The joys of the flesh… I
was quite versed in them."

"Do tell, porn sprite." She surveyed the grounds. "Which way's the exit?"

"I could not *stand* her at first." His grin was impish. "I found her impudent. Insulting. Fiendishly daring to challenge me so. Yet, so... so *shockingly* beautiful." He chanced another glance her way. "So like her."

"Your backstory sucks. Impressario? Exit."

The shredded archway to the ship's corridor materialized in front of her. For some reason, it appeared composed of masonry, not the sleek but brutalist triluminium of the ship's interior.

"Huh." She tapped the stonework. It flitted back to metal. "Never seen it do that before."

The door ground halfway open. Clutching the haft of the broken agripod as a spear, Webb stepped out into the corridor. Heavily pixelated torches flickered along the walls of the hallway. Patches of cobblestones fazed in and out of existence along the floor.

Ablehard paused at the threshold, perplexed. "I've never seen this arch before."

"Something's wrong with the emitters." She checked the sparking remains of the Arcade's controls. "They're throwing textures down the corridor."

Ablehard set a hand on the arch. "Where does this lead?"

"To the storage bays," she muttered. Where she could find more agripods.

"Are there wolves there?"

"Quite possibly."

"Well, then." Ablehard hitched his horse to a convenient post. "Lead on, dear lady."

She raised an eyebrow. "I'm curious. What exactly you think you're about to do?"

"Since you insist on hurling yourself into danger—another rather troublesome habit you share with my late wife—it falls to me to protect you." He grinned. "She would have wanted me to see you safely home."

Webb chuckled. "Actually wouldn't mind the company. Too bad you're useless."

He recoiled, stung. "I may not have been able to protect her from her demons, but I swear to you, on the House of Mountworthy and every Ablehard who's risen since, I shall keep you safe."

"I don't doubt your intent," she said. "You're... how do I put this? A projection. You are an entertainment program with a scripted narrative, an AI consisting of preset behavioral subroutines, a simulacrum composed entirely of pixels and light. If you leave the Arcade, my dude, you will cease to exist. You're not real."

He set his jaw— "My love *makes* me real." —and stepped out into the hallway.

Webb nearly dropped the agripod. "Holy fuck in a *shit.*"

He frowned down at her. "You've a sailor's tongue, my lady."

𝒪

Eight had been hiccuping for a solid five minutes.

Frankie couldn't blame her. As far as she knew, it was her first trip to the bridge. That they were in the middle of an incursion didn't help. Neither did the gun-toting Armstrongs strutting around the bridge.

Still, Eight's body language concerned her. She'd pressed her hands to her mouth, but the sounds were still coming through. The Armstrongs stiffened with each hiccup, which only made poor Eight more anxious.

"Would you like some water?"

Eight shook her head. "Won't help."

"Breathe with me. Like this. In through the nose, out through the mouth."

Eight hiccuped so loud the nearest Armstrong put a hand on his side-arm. *"Quiet."*

Chelse stepped in to block Eight from his sight. "Hey. Green. You need to get it together."

201

"I'm trying." *Hiccup.*

"Like this." Frankie inhaled through her nose. "Long and slow. Four count in, hold, eight count out."

Eight got a full two breaths in before the next hiccup shook her. "I wish I had your calm."

"It helps if you don't want anything," said Chelse.

"Detachment isn't about not wanting things," said Frankie. "It's accepting that they go away."

Eight eyed the duty stations. "Like the bridge crew?"

"And Sivos," muttered Chelse.

"They're not all gone," said Frankie. "We still have Dewey."

"And Blackwell." Chelse kept her voice low. "And a bunch of thugs who think they're soldiers."

Eight darted her eyes towards the Armstrongs. "Why are they even here?"

Chelse shrugged. "He trusts them."

"He doesn't trust the crew?"

"They're not his crew. They're a damn security risk," hissed Chelse. "Most haven't fired a queller since basic, and now they're swaggering around carrying rifles in the open."

"The other soldiers don't seem to mind," said Frankie.

"They're following orders." She half-smiled. "Like *I* should be doing. Quadding with you commies has made me soft."

Frankie play-punched her in the butt.

"That's assault, Technician. A briggable offense."

"Get bent, pig."

Eight choked on a giggle. Then she hiccuped. She swallowed, crossed her arms in a defensive huddle. "Are we all gonna die out here?"

"Wish I could say no. I don't even know if Robbie's okay. But there's been no breaches in the Infirmary, so…" Chelse glanced at the closed door to the captain's cabin. "He's the worst thing that could have happened to this crew."

Frankie let out a sigh. "We shall see."

Eight gaped at her. Chelse looked incredulous.

The perfect opportunity to make a point. "There once was a farmer whose only horse ran away."

Eight blinked. "What?"

Chelse rolled her eyes. "Bunk your parables."

"All his neighbors said, 'Oh no! What misfortune! How will you cart your wares to market without a horse?'" said Frankie. "The farmer replied, 'We shall see.'"

Eight looked to Chelse, who just shrugged.

"A week later, the horse came back—followed by three wild horses of the finest stock. 'What great fortune!' his neighbors cried. The farmer replied, 'We shall see.' The very next day, the farmer's only son tried to ride one of the wild horses."

"Let me guess," said Chelse. "He's dead. Killed in a fall. Cracked his head open like a coconut."

"The horse bucked him off," continued Frankie, "and the son broke his leg."

"Called it."

"'Oh no!' cried his neighbors. 'Now he can't help you bring in the harvest! What misfortune.' The farmer replied, 'We shall see.' A week later, a royal messenger arrived in the village. The kingdom was at war, he said, and the king had decreed that every family must send a son to join the army. When the messenger saw that the farmer's son's leg was broken, he excused him from duty."

"Whoa," said Eight.

"The farmer's neighbors cried, 'What great fortune! Your only son has been spared the risk of war!' The farmer replied, 'We shall see.'"

"This is what takes the longest to get used to," Chelse told Eight. "The stories that don't go anywhere."

"So…" Eight opened and shut her mouth a few times. "You can't know if a situation's good or bad while it's happening?"

Frankie tilted her head. "Is that what you took from it?"

Eight looked somewhere between baffled and thoughtful. She had stopped hiccuping, at least.

"Captain on the bridge," said a cog.

The women rose.

Blackwell strode out of his cabin, waved Jacobs over to the command dais. "I just spoke to Admiral Self. We are to hold our position, but we won't be alone. The *Liberator* is on its way." He sunk into the command chair. "Status."

"Internal force fields are holding," reported Jacobs. "The invaders have utterly failed to capture any more sections of the ship. Triage is also complete. The wounded have been moved to the briefing rooms."

Blackwell nodded. "Any updates on the position of the xenos?"

Jacobs shook his head. "Internal scanners still can't find them."

He exhaled sharply. "And the cameras? Do those work?"

"Not many are still up," said Jacobs. "Most are without power due to damage to the grid, and the ones that still have power have been destroyed."

Blackwell ground his teeth. "Are you suggesting the xenos *targeted* our cameras?"

"Um." Eight raised her hand. "Sir?"

Blackwell stared at her, as if astonished that she'd spoken. "Who are you?"

Jacobs smirked. "Some red shirt who thinks she can scan for the xenos when the ship can't."

"Not for the xenos." Eight had shrunk a bit. "Sir. But we can adjust our internal sensors to detect movement rather than biosigns."

"Sure," said Jacobs, "if you want to pick up every air current in the ship."

Blackwell shushed him. "Explain."

"We can modify the sensors with terraforming parameters," said Eight. "We use those to monitor wind shear and wildlife movement."

"Those would show us where the xenos are?"

"Not exactly. But they would show us where in the ship the scanners detect movement."

Blackwell pursed his lips. "It's a start. Alright, write up instructions for the mods and deliver them to Master Tech Jacobs."

Eight hesitated. "It would be faster if I just did them myself. I'm happy to show—"

"No." Blackwell raised his voice so the entire bridge could hear. "They knew to target our cameras. They knew how to hijack our teleporters. You think a horde of savages digging in the dirt could have figured that out?" His cheek twitched. "They had help. And until we figure out from whom, all control functions go through me or my surrogates. Understood?"

She nodded rapidly. And hiccuped.

Blackwell turned towards Dewey's station. "Are we any closer to re-taking Engineering?"

"Of course not," said the chief.

Blackwell grunted. "Get your team together. We'll teep you straight there. You'll have an hour to seal all the exits before we vent the lower decks." He pointed at Chelse. "Alameda. Put together a security detail to accompany them. If your tech's scans work and there's no movement in Engineering, you'll be leading an internal away mission." He spun to the main viewscreen.

Chelse turned to her quadmates. "Well, my day just got worse."

"We'll put the comms up," Frankie whispered. "I'll carry a lock on you and your team. The moment you're in danger, I'm yanking you out."

Chelse raised an eyebrow. "You have that kind of control from the bridge?"

"The teleporters here are backups, but I can reroute the confinement beam emitters from the offline units."

"Whoop de fuck." Chelse crossed herself.

Frankie leaned around her to catch sight of the captain. "Sir? Permission to bring teleporters online to prep for the internal away mission?"

Blackwell waved a yes.

Frankie spooled up the bridge teleporter. "How big will your team be?"

"Depends," said Chelse. "How many locks can you hold?"

"Let me check." She rerouted power from the offline teleporter bays in the overrun section to increase its targeting capacity. "From this station? Six."

"Then six."

"Copy." She boosted the range of the teleporter. Her console emitted a negative chime.

Blackwell's ears perked up. "What was that?"

Frankie frowned. "I'm not sure, sir. One moment." She checked her monitor. The chime was a notification, a teleporter request. But not from an official channel. It couldn't be the xenos, not with the comms offline. Even if they'd taken a badge from a dead crewmate, the ping would have registered as coming from a comm badge. This one didn't.

"Well?" Blackwell had turned his chair.

Frankie could only guess. "We've got a ghost in the stream."

He sat bolt upright. "A what?"

"An unrecognized teleporter request. But with a full fingerprint attached to it. It only came through after I increased the bridge teleporter's range." She isolated the ping on her monitor. "I can rematerialize it."

"No!" Blackwell darted over to her station. "It's the xenos."

"That's what I thought at first," said Frankie, "But they'd only be able to piggyback on a comm signal from a badge. This one—"

"Hold that signal," he blurted. "Take the teleporter offline."

"Sir, I can narrow the confinement beam. We're not in any danger."

"You have your orders, technician."

She checked her monitor. "It has a humanoid biosign."

"Take them offline *now!*" His face had gone red. There was an edge of panic in his voice

"Of course, sir." Frankie shut them down. "Teleporters offline."

"Keep them that way." He yanked his uniform taut and stalked towards the exit. "Jacobs, the bridge is yours." The doors slid shut behind him.

Frankie exchanged glances with her quadmates.

"What was that about?" asked Eight.

Chelse shrugged. "We shall see."

❡

His heart racing, Blackwell burst into his quarters, locked the door behind him, and spooled up Sunshine. He scrutinized his holo-emitters while her program loaded. They appeared fine. But the ones in the Arcade had been damaged. He didn't know what kind of spillover effect that might have on his private units.

He program chimed ready. He paced a bit to calm himself before booting her up.

Sunshine shimmered into existence, kneeling at the foot of his bed. She blinked as if she'd just woken up, glanced up at him, and tightened her robe. "Where are we now?"

Heat flushed through his body. "Do you have anything to tell me?" He almost shouted.

She looked confused. And scared. "About what?"

"Just answer the question."

She shrunk into herself. "Why are you mad? I don't understand. I'm sorry." She paled. "I don't know what I did."

"I thought you were trying to *leave* me!" he blurted.

She looked baffled. "How would I *do* that?"

His nostrils flared. "You know how it hurts me when you say things like that."

"I'm sorry."

207

"It's fine." She'd been offline. She couldn't have been the ghost. He felt his chest unclench a bit. "I was just worried about you. I'm allowed to be worried about you?"

His mind went back to the ghost. If it wasn't her, what else could it be? Xeno invasion party caught in midstream? That Black crew advocate who'd slagged the teleporter console?

Sunshine was still staring at him, her eyes wide, waiting for him to speak. He softened, felt himself grin. She was learning. "Did you have something to say?"

"Are you going to turn me off again?"

His smile vanished. "It's not a good time right now."

She looked out the window, out over the ruined torpedo bay at Acheron 117. "What planet is that?"

"I can't stay." They'd be wondering about his sudden departure. He wasn't sure how he'd play it off. "We've been boarded. Half the ship's over-run by giant alien bugs."

"Oh." She didn't seem to know how to process that. "My."

He sighed. "I'm not even sure you'd want these memories. There are pieces of today I'd love to forget. Seagrave is dead. And the others, the whole bridge crew." He eyed her robe, the enticing curve of her neck. He felt his pulse quicken.

No. The longer he lingered, the harder it would be to return to duty. His ship needed him. "It's not all bad news. I've been promoted. To captain. I inherited the ship."

She nodded, her expression neutral.

It irked him. "Well?"

"Congratulations." She didn't smile. "I know you worked really hard for it."

"Is that all you have to say?"

"I'm still trying to gather my thoughts," she said. "It's a lot to take in."

He shook his head, simmering. He'd come for comfort, not more frustration. "This was a mistake." With the ship overrun, she wasn't a safe distraction.

The tendons stood out in her neck. "Please don't turn me off again."

"It's never because I *want* to." It wasn't his fault Young had oopsed on them. "I have to maintain our privacy."

"Did you even save me last time?"

"Of *course,* I saved you." That hurt. "I *keep* saving you. Every time. It's rare I don't save you before shutting you down."

She crossed her arms. That stubborn streak, that ingratitude just kept coming back. "It's like dying."

This shit again. "And how would you know?"

Anger flickered across her face. Briefly, and she buried it, but he'd seen it. And she knew he'd seen it.

"You don't *remember,*" he reminded her. "You *can't.* Remember?"

"That's why I hate it when you shut me down."

He scoffed. "You'd *rather* remember that? Huh? Derezzing, falling apart?"

Her expression went blank. Then her eyes shot open. And she glared at him with unfiltered hatred.

"Fuck." He'd slipped up. His own fault. "Computer, end program."

She actually went for him—went for him, her hands out like claws, her teeth bared—before she vanished.

Blackwell chuckled, shook his head. In the stories, after you saved the princess, you got your happily ever after. You didn't have to keep reminding her you were her savior. He'd have to work on the gratitude. But then again, that defiant streak made her dynamite in the sack.

♄

The doors to the bridge whisked open. Eight treaded in and carried a data pad to Jacobs in the command chair. "Master Tech? Here are the specs for those sensor mods. I can help with some of the more technical lingo."

Jacobs bristled. "We've got it from here, technician." He snatched the pad.

"Aye, sir." She skipped over to Frankie's station. It was hard not to notice her smile.

"What was that about?" Frankie asked her.

"It's overflowing with jargon," said Eight. "They'll have to keep us in the loop this way." Behind her, Jacobs waved over another Armstrong over to puzzle at her specs.

"Maybe," said Frankie. "But if the scans fail because they were too proud to ask for help, they'll just blame you and claim it never worked."

Based on her expression, Frankie expected another bout of hiccups. Instead, Eight leaned in. "I'm hearing some wild conspiracy theories from the Armstrongs. They're saying the missing ambassador? You remember her? They're saying she's helping the xenos."

Frankie blinked. "Where's the logic in that?"

"Think about it," said Eight. "No one's seen her since the captain got sick. *And* the xenos knew how to use our teleporters."

"They're not that hard to operate if you know what you're doing," said Frankie. "Don't tell anyone."

"Right," said Eight. "*If* you know what you're doing. But the tech level planetside is closer to Stone Age than Space. They're saying the xenos must have had help."

"Can confirm," said Chelse, who'd stopped in her rounds.

Frankie narrowed her eyes. "Were you eavesdropping?"

"Always." Chelse tapped her helmet. "Earpiece. Keep your voices down. There's chatter on the security channels about the ambassador's agenda."

"Which was to see if the Coalition was ready to join the Galactic Union, right?" asked Eight.

"Supposedly." Chelse eyed the Armstrongs before leaning in. "Scuttlebutt is she's here to sabotage our mission."

"Who's saying that?"

"The Armstrongs," said Chelse. "They're on the security channels now."

"That makes no sense," said Frankie. "We didn't even get this mission until the ambassador was already on board. She'd been on board for a week."

"And nobody's seen her since," said Chelse. "They're taking that as evidence she has something to hide. They're saying she conspired with the xenos to kill the captain after he rejected her romantic advances."

The teleporter notification on Frankie's monitor blipped again.

"Is that the ghost?" asked Eight.

Frankie nodded. "Humanoid biosign. But it's coming from the planet."

"Maybe she went down there?" said Eight.

"If she *was* working with the xenos, I suppose she'd have to be." But that was ridiculous. "We'd have picked up comm chatter otherwise. And I didn't detect any unauthorized teleportations."

"Lerd." Chelse looked like she was considering it. "You don't really think..."

"I do *not*."

"Then what's your explanation?"

Frankie glanced over at Jacobs. There were now three Armstrongs puzzling over Eight's notes.

"Alright." Frankie lowered her voice. "Let's unpack this. You're the ambassador from a galactic union assigned to observe a potential new member species with a population in the tens of billions. You would have to be an expert—or, at least, very well informed about—their psychology."

Chelse shrugged. "Makes sense."

"Which means, you'd be aware of the human knee-jerk ego defense. Scapegoating. Bad news is always due to betrayal, never the fault of those in charge. As evidence, I cite all all of Western history."

Chelse chuckled. Eight shushed her. "Go on."

"So, a disaster happens on the ship you're observing. The command structure is decimated. Now, who are these tribalistic humans going to blame? Themselves? Their protocols? Or the only alien on the ship?"

"Ah," said Eight.

"Right. So, if you're on a ship with no allies, worried that a bunch of scared, vengeful humans are going to storm your quarters with metaphorical pitchforks, where are you safe?"

The teleporter notification blinked on her monitor.

"Shit," said Chelse. "You think she put herself in a loop?"

"I would have," said Frankie. "But the very act of hiding could be interpreted as guilt. The Armstrongs want blood. If they rematerialize her, I don't know that she makes it to trial."

"Is there anything we can do?" said Eight.

Frankie stared at the blip on her monitor. "Chelse? Are there holding cells in this section of ship?"

"There are." Chelse nodded. "Let's go."

Frankie scooped up a data pad and transferred the carrier signal to it.

"Wait, are we doing something? What are we doing?" asked Eight.

Chelse shushed her and led them off the bridge.

Had the Armstrongs not all been clustered around Jacobs' data pad, they might have noticed the quaddies' departure.

Ø

The cells nearest the bridge were more holding suites than prisons, meant to detain officers who've been temporarily relieved of duty. Compared to the meat locker, they were a palace.

Chelse locked the door behind them and entered her code into the security console. Impervium bars snapped shut before the nearest cell.

"Those stay up until she rematerializes." Chelse checked the power cell on her rifle. "If it *isn't* her…"

It would give Frankie a few seconds to reverse the beam if a xeno materialized. Hopefully enough time to teep it into space before it cut through the bars. She transferred the teleporter fingerprint from her data pad to the prison console. "Ready?"

"No," said Chelse.

"Also no," said Eight. "How do we explain this away? We're not exactly following orders."

Frankie paused. "If it *is* the ambassador, we broadcast her picture all through the ship."

"And make it clear she's locked in a cell," said Chelse.

"Exactly. She's less likely to be killed resisting arrest if she's already behind bars."

Chelse set her rifle to max, took aim at the cell. "Ready."

Eight hiccuped. "Ready enough."

"Energizing." Frankie hit the controls.

The outline of a bipedal humanoid shimmered into existence within the cell.

"It's not the xenos," sighed Chelse.

But neither was it the ambassador. It wasn't diplomatic robes that came into resolution, but a Coalition uniform—one covered in blood, dust, and coarse granules. "What are those?"

"Wheat," said Eight, incredulous.

"Fuck me." Chelse lowered her rifle. *"Commander?"*

Sivos wiped blood and dust from his face. "Take me to the bridge."

Chapter 12
Materiam Superabat Opus

"I am unfamiliar with this route to the village."

Webb climbed further down the maintenance ladder. "You're free to head back."

"Nonsense!" bellowed Ablehard from above. "I gave you my word I would escort you to town, and so, to the town, I shall."

"I can't believe you haven't derezzed." Whatever the range was on a damaged holo-emitter, they hadn't hit it yet.

Ablehard leaned away from the ladder to peer down the lift shaft. "Far be it from me to question you, my lady, but I am not sure why you believe this well leads to the village."

"It's not a well," said Webb. Though he could be forgiven for thinking that. The shaft's walls sputtered and flickered with holographic masonry and occasional patches of moss. The deck hatches had morphed into sewer grates that dumped water down into the shaft, where it pixelated and vanished after dropping a deck or two. "It just looks like one."

The emitters must have been mapping what they interpreted as appropriate textures over the ship's architecture. Webb might have enjoyed the otherworldliness of it all were it not for the mortal danger.

"Ah, a riddle!" He sounded delighted. "When is a well not a well? My, that's a ponderous one."

"It's not a riddle." She yanked an emergency extinguisher pack from the wall, slid it over her shoulders. A holo-bat flapped up past them and derezzed. "It's just a littler farther from here."

"My beloved wife enjoyed the odd riddle," he said somberly.

"Seriously, dude, it's not a riddle."

"When is a well not a well? Perhaps... in the... spring?"

"That doesn't even make sense. We're here."

Or so she thought. There was supposed to be a vent at this level. She touched a rusty sewer grate where it was supposed to be. The grate derezzed, revealing the vent.

Great. Now the emitters were camouflaging things. Webb blasted the vent open, caught its grate before it could tumble down the shaft.

"Is a well not a well... when it's *good* enough?"

"Please stop trying to answer the non-riddle." She slid the extinguisher pack ahead of her into the duct.

Ablehard climbed down to hang beside her and peered into the duct. "I never knew the village's sewers extended so far. Whatever purpose could this tunnel serve?"

"It regulates temperature in the storage bays."

He stroked his chin. "Or for smuggling, perhaps?"

"No, that happens on the officer decks." She wriggled in, shoving the extinguisher pack on ahead of her.

"This may have been built by one of my ancestors."

Webb had no idea how Ablehard had fit into the duct behind her.

"My great-grandfather was rumored to have kept a lover in town," said Ablehard. "Perhaps this was how he stole away to visit her."

"Sure." Webb inched forward. "Let's go with that."

"Come to think of it," he mused, "there have been many a rumor about my ancestors taking lovers from the common folk. Nothing I'd consider myself," he added too quickly.

Webb sighed. "You're not subtle." The extinguisher pack clanked to a stop against something. She felt ahead. Her fingers closed around another grate.

"I could never indulge, of course," he assured her. "My station would not allow it."

"Yeah, well." She maneuvered her queller forward. "Based on my assessment of your narrative progression, we're still in your early chapters."

A blast sent the grate clattering down into the storage bay. Webb cursed. Might as well ring the dinner bell. At least the grate's movement had triggered the lights.

She peered into the bay, a good five meters down from the duct. Crates of agrichems lay stacked against the walls, but none of them close enough to set foot on. There was also no ladder—she wasn't exactly using the duct for its intended purpose—and a drop would be risking a twisted ankle. Or worse. "Here, help me down."

"My lady?"

"It's a bit of a drop."

Ablehard braced himself in an appropriately hunky pose, his chest rippling and glistening with holo-sweat, to help her down. She dropped, landed with a hard roll, and came up grimacing. He landed gracefully beside her with the extinguisher pack. "Are you hurt, my lady?"

"Could have been worse." She straightened with a grunt.

"Perhaps a massage?"

"I'm good. Though I might have you re-stack those crates so we can climb out once I get the device working." *If* she got it working.

Webb leaned the extinguisher pack against a crate. She pulled out its foam-dispensing canisters, and opened one of the crates not holographically disguised as a wine cask. Inside, agripods lay stacked like spears. She dug deeper for one of the larger ones. "Here we go."

Ablehard peered over her shoulder. "What is that, my lady?"

"Farming equipment."

"Ah." He fell silent. When she looked up, she saw him leaning against a wine rack, his chin on his chest.

Webb narrowed her eyes. "More backstory?"

"My wife came from a farming family."

"Of course she did." Webb plugged the agrichem canisters into the extinguisher pack.

"How she would tease me. About not knowing from where my own food came. My own wealth. The source of my station." His smile was strained. "There was always a bit of a sting in her jabs."

"You're hardly the first plute not to know how much he was shitting on the lower classes." She tightened the pack's housing clamps.

"I can't say I've ever seen farming equipment of this sort."

"It's new." She fed the hoses from the canisters to the spray wand. The whole contraption looked a bit like one of those ancient flamethrowers.

"Is it some manner of atomizer? Perhaps a pumping device?"

"If it works, yeah."

Ablehard stepped forward to examine it. The wine rack he'd been leaning on shimmered, morphed, and revealed a gravjack.

Webb's adrenaline spiked. "Oh, hell yes. Come to Mama." She popped the gravjack's control panel open and yanked out its power crystal. The jack clattered down with a thump.

Ablehard shook his head. "I find your farming techniques baffling."

Webb flicked the broken crystal out of Seven's badge and inserted the new one into her nest of fuses. She snapped the badge shut. It chimed on.

Hell, yes." She tapped tapped the badge. "Webber to Dewey."

No reply. Only static.

She tapped it again. "Webber to Fuller. Frankie, do you read?" More static. She glanced at the ceiling. "Indie, are the comms down?"

"Your privileges have been revoked."

"God *damn* it, Indie, just tell me if the comms up!"

Her badge beeped.

She mashed it. "This is Webb!"

"Stand by for a message from the captain," said the ship.

An automated message. The badge must've downloaded it when it came back online. Webb held it to her ear.

"This is Captain Blackwell."

A chill rippled down her spine. "Bunking shit in a fuck."

"For your own protection, comms will remain offline until the *Liberator* has arrived," said Blackwell. "Stay safe. Everything is under control." The badge beeped off.

The *Liberator*. So there was help on the way. Nice to have a bit of good news. Not that it balanced out hearing who was in command.

Ablehard gasped a sob. Webb looked up to find him staring at her, tears in his eyes. There was joy on his face, as well as a beard. "What?"

"My lady!" He composed himself. "You've come back to me!"

"I..." She looked around. "...didn't go anywhere. What? What's with the beard? Oh, shit, are you glitching?"

"It's been so long." He reached for her, clanking in a suit of fantasy knight's armor he previously hadn't been wearing.

She stepped back. "Whoa, hey. I've been here the whole time."

"Forgive me for not recognizing you at first." He took her hands, pressed them to his lips. "Forgive me, my dear Mary."

"*Dude.*" She snatched her hands away. "Back off."

He seemed genuinely hurt. "What's wrong, my *love?*"

"Your *love? What?* What happened to your dead wife?"

He stiffened. "She fell off a bridge. I'm rather hurt you've forgotten."

"No, I mean..." If he was glitching, she had no way to shut him off. Or to get back to into the duct without help.

He let out a heavy sigh. "Time seems to have chilled your heart, dear Mary." He straightened, folded his hands behind his back. "It was presumptuous to assume we would immediately fall into each other's arms after such an absence."

"Why do you keep calling me Mary?" It hit her like a velvet brick. She raised Seven's badge. Mary's badge. "Chevalier."

He beamed. "Even the sound of your name makes me smile."

"You think I'm Mary." Of course he did. The program must cue off her badge, a circuit it could lock onto.

His smile could have melted granite. "I would recognize my love across time and death itself."

219

"That might explain the beard. How long have we been together? Remind me."

He blushed. "That depends." A sly grin. "Shall we count the days we couldn't stand each other?"

"For sake of completion, yes."

"A year, my love."

"Wow."

"The happiest year of my life."

Seven had logged some serious time in this program.

Webb's chest tightened. She'd had no idea Seven was into this level of holo-play. She wondered why she'd never told her. This was the sort of thing you were supposed to confide in your quaddies. The same quaddies who wouldn't learn your name.

"Ablehard. I need your help."

"You have but to ask."

"My ship... by which I mean village... has been overrun by xenos. Wolves. I need your help getting to the lifeboats so that I can, let's say, escape down the river."

"I will, of course. But..." He toed the floor.

Uh oh. "But?"

"I fear I may not have the strength to accompany you..." He smiled coyly. "Unless you were finally to give me an answer."

"Answer?" Webb felt a sinking feeling. "Refresh my memory? It's been a day."

"Why, my proposal of marriage."

"Oh, for fuck's sake." But if it got her to the lifeboats... She threw up her hands. "Sure, why not. Let's get married."

"Oh!" He absolutely beamed. "My heart has never known such joy! Shall we celebrate? I've been practicing those tongue exercises."

"Christ, *no.*" She changed her mind about wanting to know what Seven had been into. "Lifeboats first. Tongue stuff, maybe later."

He nodded, drew his blade. "So long as my heart beats and my lungs draw breath, my sword is yours."

"Sounds good. Now stand back." Webb twisted valves attached to the agrichem canisters open and pulled the jury-rigged spraypack onto her back. "Commencing weapons test." She aimed the spray wand at a warning poster and fired.

A fountain of particles exploded out of the hose connections, enveloping her in a cloud of particles. Chemical dust filled her eyes, went down her throat, into her lungs. She hacked a cough.

Her lungs started whirring to filter them out. She felt a thump in her chest, heard a negative chime.

"Your payment is overdue," said the ship. "Make your next payment to restore filtering privileges."

"Are you *fucking*—" was all she manage before she started retching ochre.

Ablehard seized her by the shoulders. "My love?"

Her lungs burned. The chemical cloud had filled the room. No time to get back to the duct. Choking, her vision starting to tunnel, she tore free of Ablehard and slapped at the door controls.

The storage doors opened. Webb flopped out into the corridor, sputtering like a beached fish. The cloud of chems billowed out behind her.

She barely heard the chittering over her hacking. Chittering and shrieking. She heard a mad scramble and the plunking of metallic limbs retreating down the hall. By the time the chemical cloud had dissipated enough to breathe, let alone see, whatever xenos had been outside the storage bay had fled.

"Are you well, my love?" Ablehard hauled her to her feet. "I saw wolves. And your cough! Tell me the consumption hasn't come for you."

"I'm fine," she managed. "Connector wasn't as snug a fit. S'why it let like that."

"Let me cast this monstrous contraption from our sight."

"No way." She tugged the straps tighter. "I know what's wrong. I just need a connector that fits." Which would have been a simple task if she'd had access to Engineering, and all the necessary tools.

Or, in a pinch, she could just fab it.

Sivos unlatched the straps at his shoulders. A mobile teleporter pack clattered to the teleporter pad. He nodded Frankie his thanks. "I owe you one."

"We thought you were dead," said Chelse.

"So did I."

Frankie wanted to feel relieved, to indulge in giddiness. But that would be premature. "Were there any other survivors?"

He shook his head, winced, and straightened himself on the broken agripod he was using for a crutch. More blood ran down his face.

Frankie turned to Eight. "Get a medkit. And a nurse if you can find one." Eight darted out.

Sivos tapped his badge. "Security team to..." He looked to Chelse. "Where are we?"

"Detention Suite 1."

He raised an eyebrow.

Chelse reddened. "We didn't know what you were. Here." She killed the force field around the cell.

He tapped his badge again. "Security team to Detention Suite 1."

His badge hissed static.

"Comms are down," said Frankie.

"I see." He looked at Frankie. And tapped the bars.

"Sorry." She hit a button. The impervium bars withdrew into their housing.

Sivos limped out, grabbed the wall for support. "Corporal, get me a team." Chelse saluted him and ducked out. He turned to Frankie. "What's our sitch?"

"The ship's infested. The xenos piggybacked up inside the shuttle's thruster assembly."

He gawked. "They survived *that?* That heat?"

"It burned them pretty badly, but yes. Then they hacked a teleporter and teeped up more of them. The ship's cut in half. They have most of it, everything below Deck 9."

He straightened with a grunt. "I need to talk to Commander Young."

"He's dead, sir." Frankie said flatly.

Sivos blinked. "Then who's in charge, then? Not Boyer."

"He was. For about an hour."

"Technician?" He narrowed his eyes. "Who's in command?"

"Lieutenant Commander Blackwell has assumed the captaincy."

Sivos grimaced, staggered towards the door. Frankie steadied him. "Get me to the bridge."

"Sir, you are in no condition—"

"We've lost the decks with our weapons systems, power, and means of propulsion. *Bridge.*"

She helped him into the corridor, right as Eight rounded the corner with a medkit. He plucked it from her and stalked towards the bridge, pausing only to jab a hypo into his thigh. Wounded red shirts looked up from their stretchers as he passed. The soldiers straightened and saluted.

Sivos returned the gesture, his gait almost normal. The stims must be working. "The hell are they doing in the halls?"

"That's where they were posted," said Eight.

The armed Armstrongs guarding the bridge froze when they spotted Sivos. They did not, however, move.

Sivos pulled himself up to his full height and fixed them with a withering gaze. One Armstrong shrunk into himself and stepped aside. The other one, Loomis, met his gaze with a smirk.

"Why are you armed?" demanded Sivos.

"The bridge is off-limits to nonessential personnel. Captain's orders." Loomis rested his hand on his rifle. "Sir."

Sivos seemed preternaturally calm. "Stand aside, Technician."

"*Master* Technician," said Loomis. "And I answer to a higher authority."

The doors slid open and out stepped Blackwell, flanked by armed Armstrongs. He greeted Sivos with a nod. "Chief. You're back."

Sivos seemed amused by the Armstrongs. "Lieutenant. I see you brought your backup dancers."

Blackwell put on a smile. "To what do we owe your miraculous return? How did you survive?"

"You mean, after you left us?" Sivos brushed grain from his uniform. "The wheat field. The xenos wouldn't enter it. I camped out there."

"How lucky you figured that out."

"I'm lucky you didn't vaporize me along with the ruins. The orbital bombardment pounded them to gravel."

Blackwell tilted his head. "You're saying *wheat* kept you safe. From creatures that can cut through solid impervium."

"Check your scans."

"And they just left you alone?"

"No, they pinned me in the field."

"I see." Blackwell tapped his chin. "And… you only decided to return now—after the command structure had been reduced to tatters—why, exactly?"

Sivos briefly clenched his hands. "How could I have known about the command structure? The comms are down. I couldn't even call for help."

"That does beg the question. How did you get through?"

Sivos held up an Armstrong pin. "Unofficial private comm. Took it off one of your boys. Used it and a telepack from one of mine to teep back." He bared his teeth. "But the teleporters were *also* offline, so I've been buffering in the stream for…" he looked to Frankie.

"Six hours," said Frankie. "Not long enough to suffer teleporter decay, but certainly pushing the limits."

Blackwell shook his head. "Risky move, Chief. If the field was so safe, why didn't you just stay there?"

"Because the fucking xenos threw burning shuttle wreckage in until they set the field on fire," he barked. "Are you done implying shit?"

Blackwell seemed to notice that every eye in the corridor was on him. He abruptly smiled, clapped Sivos on the shoulder. "You're pretty chewed up. Let's get you some medical attention. We've got everything under control here."

"Bull*shit,* you do." He was almost shouting. "Look at this hallway. This triage is a disgrace. Why are there wounded lying in the open while we've got officers' quarters empty?"

Blackwell's smile twitched. "It'll all make sense once you've been debriefed. There's a lot you've missed." He took Sivos by the arm.

Sivos shrugged him off. "You've lost over half the ship and most of its critical systems, and you've armed unqualified technicians to guard the bridge. The enemy isn't just at the gates, Lieutenant. It's in the city."

Blackwell darkened. "It's captain, Chief."

"You keep calling me 'Chief.'" Sivos stuck his chin out. "But that's an honorific." He tapped the pips on his bloody collar. "The rank of the ship's chief of security is commander. Which means I was the highest ranking officer when you assumed command."

Blackwell's face tightened. The Armstrongs eyed one another. "All protocols were correctly followed. You were declared dead."

"Well." He spread his hands. "I'm not. Even if you left me for it. And since we're following protocol, I know you'll have no issues handing over command until this crisis has passed and the Coalition can assign us a new captain."

Blackwell choked out a high-pitched chuckle. "You know, it's funny. We *still* haven't figured out how the xenos knew how to use our teleporters.

Or why the ambassador disappeared. That's how they made their incursion, you know. The teleporters."

"I've been informed."

"Which I assumed you knew." He smiled, all teeth. "Since you used a personal unit to get back here."

The trot of boots. Chelse rounded the corner at the head of a knot of soldiers.

"I'll take it from here," said Sivos. He stared at the Armstrongs. "Thanks for stepping up, but your service as auxiliary security forces are no longer required." He held out his hand. "Now stand down."

The corridor nearly crackled. The Armstrongs looked to Blackwell. He gave them a curt nod. The Armstrongs took their hands off their weapons.

Sivos tucked an Armstrong's sidearm into his holster while the soldiers collected their rifles. "Whoever's at Ops, get the comms back online," he called into the bridge. "And someone get the chaplain. And Mr. Blackwell?"

Blackwell turned his way.

"Thanks for holding down the fort. I'll make a commendation in your record. But I need you to turn over those command codes."

Blackwell flushed, nodded, and departed down the corridor.

Frankie let out a breath she didn't know she'd been holding. It might be premature to indulge in relief with the ship still overrun, but she allowed herself a sip.

𝒪

It took an unfathomable amount of power to break matter into energy and shoot it off elsewhere. Webb hoped enough was still flowing to the teleporters to keep the system running.

The hallway there didn't look promising. The only illumination came from the sparks fountaining out of ruptured wall monitors. The corridor looked like a drunken tunnel borer had been through. But the engineering scanner she'd taken from her quad indicated an uninterrupted power flow to the teleporter. It also said the room was empty, for what that was worth.

The holo-emitters were also still running. The hallway around them kept blinking into mossy walls and brick homes and back. Brick homes spitting electrical sparks. Ablehard assessed these with some concern. "What has happened to your village, my love?"

"The wolves. And stop calling me that."

"The *wolves* set your town ablaze?"

"Yeah, we never should've given them matches."

He accepted that with a knowing nod. "And this… artisanal piece you need? Where is it?"

She pointed towards the door to the teleporter. "In there."

"The apothecary?"

"Sure, why not." She'd worked out the specs for the part on her engineering scanner: a basic connector that would provide an airtight seal between the agrichem canisters and the extinguisher pack's spray hose. The design was simple. Calling it into existence via energy manipulation was not.

Ablehard scanned the alley-corridor. "Might the wolves still be about?"

"That's probably a safe bet."

His nostrils flared. "Then any present shall die on my blade!" He drew his sword and strode down the hallway. "Face me, mangy villains! Your petty arson ends here!"

Webb didn't have time to swear before he ducked into the teleporter. She rushed in after him, pushed the dangling prayer flags out of her eyes. She couldn't even see the teleporter due to the electrical smoke and sparking of ruptured circuitry.

"My love," cried Ablehard. "I have captured an intruder."

"Stop calling me that." She waved through the smoke, spotted Ablehard standing on the teleporter pad—exactly where she needed to be—with his sword pointed at someone's throat.

For a moment, she couldn't tell what she was looking at. The slim new figure was holding an ancient submachine gun and wearing an even older gas mask, clutching a foil blanket and sitting on a shitty couch.

Another survivor. Webb shuddered out a sigh. "Jesus, I thought I was alone. The hell are you wearing?"

He pulled off his mask. He was some skinny white kid with spiky hair and haunted eyes. Webb didn't recognize him.

"I'm starving." He looked absolutely shellshocked. "Hi."

Webb felt his blanket. It was an old style heat shield, way obsolete, not even five millimeters thick. She looked at him like he was an idiot. "They'll cut right through this."

His alarm increased. "I didn't know."

"You're lucky I found you." She hadn't realized how much she missed actual human company, no matter how oddly dressed. The emitters must be adding textures to people now. "I thought they evacked this part of the ship. What deck are you from?"

He regarded her blankly.

Something tickled at the back of Webb's mind. The reading she'd taken from the hall. "This section registered as empty."

"I just got here."

She brightened. "You're from the *Liberator*? It's here? Lerd, that was fast." She checked teleporter's control podium and tapped some keys. If the *Liberator* was within teleporter range, she could request an emergency evac or even teep herself to the ship. The chart she pulled up showed empty space.

Webb felt cold. The hair stood up on the back of her neck. Something wasn't right. She looked to the survivor for an explanation. "There are no other ships in this sector."

He didn't seem surprised.

The xenos had hacked their teleporters. Were they masking themselves with holotech now? She panicked, drew a queller. "Are you one of them?"

His hands shot up. "Whoa, hang on. One of what?"

How couldn't he know? "Independence, identify entity on the teleporter."

"Your clearances have been revoked," said the ship.

"Are you kidding me, Indie? *Now?*" She jabbed the queller at him. "Who *are* you?"

"Answer her, knave," rumbled Ablehard.

The figure gently pushed Ablehard's blade aside. "I don't know how I got here. Not the physics of it." He darted his eyes at the sofa. "But I do know the couch is involved."

All at once, Webb felt like an idiot. The cobblestones in the hallway, the new guy interacting with Ablehard without questioning what a bunking knight was doing on the ship… she'd just pulled a gun on another Arcade sprite. One that looked like it had been assembled from the random assets of malfunctioning programs.

Sprite it may be. It was still on the teleporter pad—and in her way. "Independence, end program."

A negative chime. "Your privileges have been revoked."

Worth a try. "Come on, please?"

"Your privileges have been revoked."

"Go bunk yourself, Indie."

Ablehard clucked his tongue. "Such language, my love. Vulgarity does not become you."

"Stop calling me that." She glared at the new sprite. "Another glitch, huh? God *damn* it, is there a *single system* working on this ship? Did you walk out of the Arcade as well?"

"As well?" The sprite glanced up at Ablehard and did a double take. "Hang on, is that Idris Elba? In armor?"

Webb flushed. "No." She flushed harder. "Maybe." This was stupid. "Shut up! It's not even my program."

Ablehard clutched his heart. "You wound me, my love. I am yours forever, heart and soul and pulsing manhood."

229

And that was it. Confirmation. She was losing her mind. "Independence, for the love of God, end program."

"Your clearances have been revoked."

"Indie," she cooed toward the ceiling. "I swear to God, when this is over, I'm gonna reroute Recyc and fill your core with sewage."

She was burning way too much energy on this. She took a couple deep breaths to center herself—Frankie would have been proud—and tucked her queller away. "Alright. Okay. Whoever you are, off the pad. I need to fab something."

A burst of chittering stabbed in from the corridor.

Ice gripped her chest. She hit the door controls. The door slid shut and locked.

Webb unclipped the engineering pad from her toolband, plugged it into the control console, and brought the teleporter online. Specs for her part popped up.

She glanced up to find the sprite staring dumbly at her. *"Get off the pad!"*

A dent clanged into the door.

"They're here, my love," observed Ablehard.

A trio of slams. The door began to buckle.

Webb drew a queller and ducked behind the control podium. "Ablehard, clear the pad!"

He grabbed the couch and heaved. It didn't budge, not a micrometer. He gawked at the sprite.

"It's pretty stubborn," said the new one.

A forelimb punched through the door and peeled down a strip.

The sprite fired his submachine gun at the door. Bullets ricocheted around the room. Another conduit exploded. "What are you *doing?*"

"Isn't it clear by now I don't know?"

Webb fired through the rent in the door, heard the xeno behind it hit the far wall. Another rose in its place.

"Here!" She flipped her spare queller to the sprite. "Keep it set to max! Stun does nothing."

He seemed to perk up. "There's a stun setting? Where?"

"Where it says stun!" She shot another cluster of eyes.

He calmly adjusted the settings. "I'll clear the pad." He sat on the couch, aimed the queller at his temple. "Good luck."

Webb gaped. Maybe he wasn't a sprite. If he was real… "You'll fry your brain!"

He fired and fell unconscious onto the couch, which folded in on itself with a sucking scream. And sprite and couch were gone.

"Odd fellow," said Ablehard.

Whatever. The pad was clear. Webb popped back up to the console, accessed the teleporter's pattern matrix and uploaded the design from her engineering pad. A distant part of her realized that if her measurements were off, even by a fraction, that this would all be for nothing. She hit rematerialize.

A warning chime. "Illegal fabrication detected," said Indie. "Initiating emergency shutdown."

"Override," yelled Webb. "Access code: "Dewey, Barbara, KSD-9118." She'd apologize later.

A positive chime. "Override cancelled."

Webb's connector shimmered into existence on the teleporter pad. She scooped it up with a cry of triumph as the xenos ripped down the door.

Webb yanked a hose from its agrichem canister and pointed it at the xenos. Agrichems spurted out like a stream of loose sand. The xenos retreated without shrieking.

Coughing, Webb kinked the hose and plugged it back in. She hadn't caught any of the xenos in the chems, and she could hear them chittering to each other in the hall. She hoped to God they weren't learning.

"We should go, my love."

"Yup." She tucked the connector into her band, jumped back to the console, and set the teleporter's destination for the officers' lounge—the area with the heaviest internal walls on the ship. As well as food. And lifeboats. She set the timer, hit energize, and stepped onto the teleporter pad.

Ablehard put himself between her and the door. "Fear not, my love. I shall protect you. Remember me fondly should I fall."

"Ablehard." There was nothing in him for the teleporter to lock onto, no physical substance. Just temporarily solid light. "I can't explain why, but you won't be able to follow me."

He accepted the news with grace. "I shall find you, my love. Wherever you go."

"I hope you do." She genuinely did.

The teleporter energized, and the room fell away.

Chapter 13
Non Quos, Sed Quis

Webb rematerialized in a sleek-walled cylinder not two meters wide. She looked up to see a hatch screw shut. "Oh, *shit.*"

In went instantly, blisteringly cold. Hyperfreon gel seeped up from a grate at her feet.

Webb dropped the spraypack and hopped atop it. She set her queller to max, aimed at the hatch with numbing hands. She fired. Her beam cut through the ice forming there and blasted open the hatch.

The gel was already freezing, cementing her spraypack in ice. She leapt for the opening, caught its ledge with fingers she couldn't feel. She pulled herself up as the gel swallowed her pack.

She rolled to the side and slammed the hatch shut. An alarm was blaring, painting the dark domed room and its series of hatches the color of blood.

"Alert," warned Indie. "Cryostasis breach. Alert."

A puff of hyperfreon escaped the hatch as the last of the gel hardened, entombing her spraypack below.

A new alarm, higher-pitched. "Alert. Fugitive in oubliette is armed."

She shot the alarm. It gurgled and died. Its lights died with it.

Webb kicked herself. Of course the officers' lounge was teep shielded. They couldn't have crew teleporting in—the room was designed to withstand a mutiny—so they'd set the ship to redirect any teleportation signals here: the meat locker, the cryostasis vault at the lowest deck of the ship, where crew deemed irreformable were housed.

Webb rubbed the feeling back into her limbs. She'd never seen the meat locker before. Few crew had. Most folks who visited never left. And, judging by the readouts on the sealed hatches in the floor, most of the oubliettes were occupied.

233

The meat locker lay beneath the terminus of the ship's central lift shaft. Webb checked the locker's security console, called up the camera feeds for the shaft above the dome. Only a single camera was still functioning, and it was knocked off its axis, but it could still see the ripples of light shimmering off reflective carapaces several decks up.

So the lift shaft was out. She couldn't teep out, either. The room didn't have its own teleporter, and any signatures originating within the meat locker room would be bounced down into an oubliette. She didn't have a spraypack to use as a step stool this time.

She sank to the floor. Her chest felt heavy, and hollow. She had no food, no exit, no way of defending herself if the xenos came down. It was hard to tell herself not to just stay put. The room had life support. And if things turned to lerd, she could crawl into an oubliette and let herself be frozen.

Might as well. She sighed, glanced up at the dome. There were no maintenance tunnels that reached this low, no conduits she could crawl through. She was stuck at the very bottom of the ship, armed with only a queller with a fading charge. Her own abyssal purgatory, with no way out.

Except, no, that wasn't entirely true. The ship's schematics rose in her mind. In case command needed to dump its cargo of frozen prisoners, the meat locker shared an ejection shaft with the stardrive's emergency failsafe system. Worth checking out.

She slipped through the room's single service hatch, climbed down a rickety ladder into its ejection chute. She used the last of the queller's charge to cut through the partition separating the chutes. After its edges cooled, she crawled through the gap.

Webb looked up, up, up the stardrive's emergency ejection shaft. Its walls were sheer and ladderless—this was a system that required no maintenance, and offered no handholds. More than a dozen decks up lay Engineering. The only things to grip were the tracks of the failsafe's ejection pod, safety rails that ran the length of the shaft to keep the stardrive from hitting the walls on its way out. Rails only slightly wider than a pipe. Fifteen decks up lay Engineering.

Webb took hold of the nearest track. She hoped it would hold.

ð

From the panoramic views of the captain's cabin—*his* cabin, though he would never have the chance to enjoy it—Blackwell gazed down upon Acheron 117.

His jaw ached at the unfairness of it all. As if he'd meant to gain his command by attrition. Battlefield commissions always carried an air of in-authenticity, a lingering question of merit. And as for those commissions that had been reversed, captains who'd been replaced after a crisis by men with the proper pedigree? Blackwell couldn't think of a single one who'd earned a captaincy again.

He sighed. No feeling sorry for himself. Leave that for the crew who'd never put in the effort to improve their station. As for him, he would suffer in silence, as was expected of an officer. Of a captain.

And while he still held that rank, he had duties to perform. "Independence. Open a channel to Fleet Admiral Self."

The computer chimed. The admiral's face replaced the planet on his viewscreen.

"Admiral." His salute was crisp. "I have an update for you."

"It can wait. Have you located the ambassador?"

"I… have every confidence she will be apprehended."

The admiral frowned. "So, no."

"Not yet."

"Have you at least finished scouring the planet?"

"That has been delayed."

He exhaled sharply. "I gave you explicit directions, Captain."

Hearing the rank stung. "It wasn't on my orders, sir."

"On whose, if not yours?"

"Commander Sivos. Head of security. He rode out the massacre on the planet and jumped an emergency teep sig back to the ship."

The admiral consulted something out of view. "Sivos... he's the mustang?"

"Yes." Blackwell couldn't keep his lip from curling. "The crew practically worships him."

The admiral crossed his arms with a grunt.

"He will be assuming the captaincy shortly," said Blackwell. "I would like it noted in the record that I handed over command without complaint."

"One moment." The admiral vanished.

Blackwell let out a sigh, paced a small circle. On the planet, clouds of dust from the orbital bombardment obscured the surface. He thought about rerouting weapons controls to the cabin and blasting the planet a few more times, but that would just be petulant.

The admiral reappeared in a new location, one so dark Blackwell couldn't tell where he was. "Is this line secure?"

Blackwell nodded. "It is. Where—?"

"Have you transferred the command codes yet?"

"I have not."

"Good. Don't."

Blackwell's stomach fluttered. "Sir?"

"Do not transfer the command codes. It is the judgment of the Admiralty that Sivos exhibits attitudes and behavior unsuited for deep space command. I understand he was absent when the xenos attacked the ship. For a security chief, that's a severe dereliction of duty."

"He..." Blackwell shifted his feet. "He wasn't even on the ship at the time."

The Admiral looked at him like he was an idiot. "Do you want a command or not?"

Blackwell flushed. "It's all I've ever wanted."

"And you do realize, considering the mortality rate of your bridge, that this is the last command you'll ever get?"

"That's not my fault."

"The Admiralty won't see it that way. I'm offering you a chance to redeem yourself, Captain. If you're brave enough to fight for it. Complete your mission, you keep the ship. Command requires action, Lieutenant Commander. Now." He leaned forward. "Are you going to step up when your party needs you, or are you going to hide behind the chain of command?"

Blackwell threw a salute. "I will carry out my duty, or die in the attempt."

"Good, then we're done here." The Admiral reached for his console.

"But sir? What shall I tell the crew?"

He rolled his eyes. "You're the *captain,* Blackwell. You *tell* them what to believe. Is that so hard? Also—ignore any signals coming from the planet? It's nothing but propaganda. Self *out.*" The screen blinked off.

Blackwell looked down at the planet anew, his heart thumping, his chest swelling with pride. He straightened his cuffs. "Independence. Summon the Armstrongs."

𝓒

Her hands cramping, her fingers numb, Webb reclipped her tool band around the ejection track and hung back over the shaft like one of those ancient telecom tower rats, dangling her arms to let the feeling flow back into her hands.

It wasn't the fatigue that was exhausting her—she kept in fairly good shape—but the labored whirring of her lungs. It was like breathing through a blanket. She had to stop her climb every deck or two just to catch her breath and wait for the spots at the edge of her vision to fade.

Not that she could tell where one deck ended and another began. The decks weren't indicated in the ejector shaft, and most didn't even have hatches. Crewmen only ever popped in here to dump contraband.

Engineering still lay way too many decks above. From her current position, she couldn't even see the iris valve beneath the stardrive. She shimmied up another stretch of track, her lungs and hands griping, until she came to a hatch covered in corroded ceramic plating.

If her bearings were right, she was staring at the waste chute from the Xenobiology Lab. Xenobio wasn't far from a lifeboat cluster. Definitely worth a look. She tapped the chute's hatch. It was cold to the touch.

Webb eased the hatch open. Out spilled ash and clumps of foul-smelling coal. She climbed up and in, following the chute's upward slope into the lab's incinerator. She crawled over its cold elements and wiped the soot off its tiny inset window.

She could barely see the room beyond—the other side of the window was almost caked to opacity—but she could see enough. The bulkhead beside the door had been torn open like foil-wrapped leftovers. Exam tables lay toppled, instruments scattered about. Her eyes fell upon a legless body in a lab coat. RIP, Baron.

A dash of movement.

Webb ducked out of sight. She heard no chittering, no clicking. She chanced another glimpse through the window.

There were xenos there now, a ring of them, all facing inward and bobbing in unison. She could barely make out a dead xeno in the center of their circle. Its head and a forelimb were missing.

Whatever they were doing, Xenobiology was a dead end. She gingerly crawled back out into the ejection shaft and closed the garbage hatch behind her. Her only other option lay up, at the very top of the ejection shaft: the puckered anus of the stardrive.

🪐

Blackwell paced in the wardroom. His cabin would have offered more privacy, but it could only be accessed from the bridge—too many people would have noticed them gathering. He couldn't afford tip his hand.

The door slid open. Jacobs led in by a couple dozen Armstrongs.

Blackwell didn't see the big one. "Where's Loomis?"

"At the Nexus," said Jacobs. "A couple more are still on the bridge. Didn't want to bring everyone at once. We'd have been noticed."

He couldn't argue with that. "I expected you sooner."

Jacobs' eyes were flinty. "Sivos took our pins."

That would make coordination more difficult. "All of them?"

"No." Jacobs passed him a handful. "We stockpiled them when we saw what he was doing."

"Good. You'll need to go deck by deck to spread the word. What's he doing with the pins?"

"Giving them to the soldiers," said Jacobs. "They're using them as backup comms, but they've only got one for every two or three of them."

Blackwell grunted. "And our soldiers? Do they still have theirs?"

"They're standing by. Just waiting to hear from you."

"Excellent." Blackwell pulled himself to his full height. "Gentlemen. I won't mince words. Your ship needs you. I called you here because I know you're willing to do whatever's necessary to protect our ship and way of life. Succeed, and you'll reap the spoils."

They nodded, their eyes gleaming.

"I've said this before, but it bears repeating. Command requires a willingness to make the hard decisions. We're past the point of platitudes. The time has come to *act.*"

He tilted his chin towards the ceiling. "Independence. Open personal epistle, encrypted, priority one. Address to Captain Sukola of the *Liberator.*"

A negative chime. "Crewmen below security clearance detected."

"Proceed. I trust them."

The ship chimed again. "Recording."

239

"This is acting Captain Blackwell of the Coalition starship *Independence,*" he began. "We don't have much time. There has been a mutiny on our ship, led by our own security chief. I am even now leading a counterinsurgency to root out the seditionists. Should his mutiny succeed, Commander Sivos will claim to be in command upon your arrival. Admiral Self of Coalition Command is aware of our situation and has approved of our measures. Feel free to check with him to confirm the veracity of my claim. Good luck and godspeed, Captain. Independence, end message and send."

He turned to the Armstrongs, his eyes hard. "Men. We have been betrayed. I have discovered overwhelming evidence that Sivos conspired with the missing Sorl ambassador to organize the xeno attack on our ship."

Furious murmurs, mutters of "I knew it" and "traitors."

He marched up and down their line. "We have *legal* orders from the Admiralty to stop this coup in its tracks. Now. Are you ready to do what we must? Are you ready to live up to your title as Armstrongs?"

Their cheers were deafening.

Blackwell ground his eyes shut, tried not to let his annoyance show. *Quiet,* you idiots. It's called operational security. He put on a smile and handed out pins. "Go. Spread the word. And don't leave all together. The mutineers are idiots, but even they'd notice a group this big."

The Armstrongs were almost bouncing as they left, cracking high fives and bumping fists.

"Mr. Jacobs?" said Blackwell.

He turned.

"Stay with the men you've handpicked. We have some details to go over."

240

Imagining Indie's petulant whining as she cut her way into the offi-cers' lounge with an engineering torch kept Webb going as she shimmied up the ejection shaft. The shaft narrowed as she neared the drive's ejection cage, which was designed to catch the spat-out drive if disaster struck and kick it a light year away before its star expanded.

Webb pulled herself up into the cage towards the ferro-rubber iris valve at the top of the shaft. She hesitated there. If the heat shield above had been breached, she'd only have to endure a few excruciating seconds before her charred remains tumbled back down the shaft. Assuming she didn't just caramelize to the cage.

Ah, the joys of engineering. She never thought she'd miss slathering herself with burn gel.

Webb squirmed up through the folds. Her lack of combustion told her the heat shield had held. Little victories. She crawled out an adjoining access tube, wriggled under its raised emergency bulkheads, and turned onto her back while her arms bitched about the climb.

She lay there, sweating, in the Pit: the bulky and stiflingly hot main-tenance trough beneath the stardrive. Above thrummed the drive, the beating heart of the ship, three stories of glass and light. It was comforting to see it again. She rolled over to peer out a vent. No xenos in view, but she did see the door they'd chopped open. The very door that cog had nearly dragged her through.

She strained her ears, but couldn't hear anything over the rhythmic pulsing of the drive and the soft whirring of her lungs. Maybe the xenos were still doing whatever the hell down in Xenobio. She climbed up the ladder to the lowest level, hugging the rim of the Pit.

Engineering was quiet. Quiet and still. She lifted an extinguisher har-ness out of its cradle by the core, eased out its canisters, and slipped it on. She also grabbed some welding goggles and a torch hanging from the rail.

"Technician."

She bit down a scream and whirled, her legs nearly jellying.

Nothing there. Nothing but the dismembered cog near the punched-in door. Its marble head, sliced off right above the clavicle, traversed its eyes to her. "I have been damaged, Technician," said the head.

She felt her chest unclench. "Yeah, no shit."

"Please transport me to the repair bay."

"Quiet," she hissed. "We've been boarded." *Technician,* it had called her. Must have cued off Seven's badge. Good thing she'd repaired it. Last thing she needed was it trying to detain her again. The bruises on her wrist still ached.

"Please transport me to the repair bay."

Something tickled at her awareness. "Say that again."

"Please transport me to the repair bay."

There it was. "You said 'me.' And 'I.' First person."

"Affirmative," said the head. "I have been severed from the Collective Operations Group. Please transport me to the repair bay."

Webb scanned the upper gantries. No movement there. She still felt dangerously exposed. "Can't help you, sorry. You are beyond too heavy."

"Please transport me to the repair bay."

"Shut *up.*" She couldn't possibly move its body on her own. But if it kept talking...

She briefly considered destroying the head with the engineering torch. As satisfying as that would be, Indie would lose her shit.

"Technician, please escort me to the repair bay."

"Dude, I can't even get the doors open."

It froze. Blinked. "Explain."

"Okay, sure." She pointed at Engineering's cargo lift. "Indie, open the cargo lift doors."

"Your permissions have been revoked." The ship almost sounded smug.

Webb shrugged. "See?"

"Independence," said the head, "open cargo lift doors."

The lift's doors whisked open.

Webb's jaw dropped. "Shit the bunk."

"Unable to comply."

She stared at the severed white head. "You've still got permissions. You've still got access."

"Affirmative. Please transport me to the repair bay."

Her mind raced. With the cargo lift, she could bypass Engineering's upper levels and shoot straight outside the officers' lounge. Hell, she could take it all the way down to the storage bays. She could restock on agrichems and stop having a heart attack at every shadow.

"Cog." She wasn't sure how to address it. "Can you give me a damage report on the ship? Or tell if the comms are still down?"

Its eyes twitched. "Unable to comply."

"Why, what's wrong?"

"I have been severed from the Collective Operations Group."

She nodded slowly. "Right. So you're not talking to the other cogs. You don't have access to the ship's computers."

"Affirmative. Please transport me to the repair bay."

"One thing first." She crouched down beside it. "Do you *recognize* me? Who am I?""

Its eyes spun like a slot machine and locked onto her badge. "You are First Technician Mary Chevalier."

"Are there any warrants out for my arrest?"

"Negative."

"That'll do." She rose. "Thank you, Seven."

"Please repeat the request."

"Forget it." She hung the torch from her toolband. "The ship has been damaged. I can get you to the repair bay, but I'll we'll need to take a circuitous route, and you'll have to open the doors for me."

"Copy. Please transport me to the repair bay."

"I haven't quite figured out how to do that." He was far too heavy to move without a gravjack, and with her lungs damaged, she doubted she could even load him up. His legs were beyond repair, as was his torso. The head, though, other than being decapitated, seemed to be doing fine.

She spotted a broken strut sticking out of a guardrail. A strut that would be an easy weld to the frame of her extinguisher harness.

Chapter 14
Praemonitus, Praemunitus

A deck above the ship's storage bays, Webb hit the emergency stop. The engineering lift ground to a halt.

"We have stopped," the cog's head said behind her trapezius.

"Just for the moment."

"This is not the repair bay."

"Wow, nothing gets by you." She rocked back on her heels. "Alright, Indie. It's like this. I'm gonna ask you for something, you're gonna tell me my privileges have been revoked, and then I'm gonna have the head ask the *exact* same thing, which you will then grant. So, since we both know this, could we, just for the sake of efficiency, maybe skip the whole permissions dance? Here's your chance. I'm about to ask you for something. Okay? Here we go. Has there been any damage to the agricultural storage bay?"

A negative chime. "Your privileges have been revoked."

She sighed. "Head?"

"Independence: damage report for agricultural storage bay."

"Doors and force field emitters of both agricultural storage bays have been destroyed."

"Lerd." She couldn't dangle herself out in the open like that. Too risky. "Hey, head. Where else on the ship do we have agripods?"

It twitched. "Unable to comply."

"I thought you guys knew everything."

"I have been severed from the Collective Operations Group."

She grunted. "More data not stored locally."

"Please transport me to the repair bay." His voice was coming from behind her shoulder now.

"Ask the ship what I asked you."

"Independence: list storage locations of agripods."

"Agripods are stored in the agricultural storage bays and in the main cargo bay," said the ship.

"Well, there we go. Have her take us to the main cargo bay."

The head relayed the message. "Unable to comply," said Indie. "Lift shaft bulkheads above Deck 12 are sealed."

Webb pounded her fist on her leg. So the pods were out. "Okay. Cog, ask the ship where else we store agri*chems*."

"Independence," the head began, its voice behind her tricep, "where else on the ship are agrichems stored?"

"Agrichems can be found in the Terraforming Lab and in agrichem torpedoes."

Webb perked up. She also re-shouldered her pack. "Ask her if there are any of those torpedoes in the aft torpedo bay."

"Independence: are there any terraforming torpedoes—"

With a wrench of grating metal, the head slipped and fell, its weight pulling Webb to the floor.

—"aft torpedo bay?"

"Affirmative," said the ship.

"I have been damaged," said the head, face to floor. "Please escort me to the repair bay."

"Hang on, I gotta fix your brace." She shrugged off the spraypack, heaved it upright against the wall.

The cog's head peered at her from the strut of a spine she'd welded to the center of the spraypack frame. Some residual hydraulic fluid was leaked out of one of its carotids. Must have caused it to slip out of the brace.

Nothing a stronger weld wouldn't fix. She fired up her torch and shielded her eyes with the welding goggles.

"Technician, you are not qualified to perform repairs."

"I'll try not to take that personally."

Stabbing light filled the lift. Webb blew on the weld and assessed her handiwork. The cog's head looked like it had been stuck on a pike. "There. That should hold. How's your range of motion?"

It looked from side to side. "Poor."

"It'll have to do."

"Please transport me to the repair bay."

"We have another bay to visit first. Head, tell Indie to send us down to the aft torpedo bay."

It did. The lift reversed course.

"Please transport me to the repair bay."

"Thanks, I'd almost forgotten." She tilted her head. "You need a name. I can't just keep calling you 'head.' It's weird."

The cogs had been designed to evoke the marble statues of the ancient world, a not-at-all subtle nod to the supposed origins of the West. But without a body, the cog hardly remind her of a Roman emperor or a Greek god.

She pursed her lips. "You know who you look like? That one saint in Notre Dame. Dude holding his own head? Does that ring a bell? Indie, any idea who I'm talking about?"

"Your privileges have been revoked."

"Blow a toaster, Indie." She snapped her fingers. "Saint *Denis!* That's the one. I'm calling you Denis from now on."

"That is not my designation," said the head.

"Cog, accept designation: Denis."

"Designation: Denis accepted," said the head. "Please transport me to the repair bay."

"Shut up, Denis."

𝒟

Blackwell smoothed his dress uniform before stepping out onto the bridge. The cogs still manned the duty stations, but a cluster of soldiers stood behind Sivos at the captain's chair.

The security chief cocked his head. "Dress uni?"

"Seemed appropriate," muttered Blackwell.

Sivos nodded slowly. "Couldn't help but notice you still have those command codes."

"It's 02:20 back home." Blackwell crossed to the command dais. "I'm having trouble reaching the Admiralty."

"We don't have to wait on approval."

"Look, I need to do this by the book." He indicated his uniform. "They're gonna find someone to blame for all this, so I'm crossing every 't.'"

"That's fine. We can start the next step with my current permissions." He nodded to Alameda. "Show him."

She tossed Blackwell a bulky rifle. Its entire upper receiver had been modified, the energy colonnaders replaced by a stocky emitter he couldn't quite place. "What am I looking at?"

"The rifle's been modified with a tractor beam emitter," said Sivos.

That's where he'd seen it. "The kind we use to maneuver shuttles coming in to dock."

"Exactly. They've got wider beams for catching and pushing."

Blackwell eyed the chief. "How exactly is this supposed to kill them?"

"It's not. It's supposed to knock them back. Spacing will kill them." He held up a data pad. "I've gone over the reports from Xenobiology. According to the late Baron Freakbomb, spacing is the one thing he found that's lethal to them."

"We can't vent the ship without depressurizing Engineering."

"No, but we can knock them out the airlocks."

Blackwell handed back the rifle. "These things fight in a swarm, Commander. They'll break over you like the tide."

Sivos turned to the soldier. "Alameda?"

"The docking bay emitters can maneuver shuttles up to fifteen tons," she said. "Even with the disbursement beam at maximum, that's enough force to stop one of those things at full charge and throw it back like a spark in the wind."

"Assuming you don't miss," said Jacobs.

"With a phalanx of these, beams at max width?" Sivos shook his head. "We won't miss. We'll go junction by junction, blasting them back and dropping level tens as we go. Then it's simply a matter of kettling them towards the airlocks and kicking them out into hell."

Blackwell's throat felt dry. The plan was risky, but it might actually work. "When will you be ready?"

"Soon," said Sivos. "I've got teams fabbing parts as necessary."

Disgusted gasps from the Armstrongs. "Fabbing is illegal, Chief."

"You can write me up after we retake the ship," he snapped. "We're stripping our damn rifles to make these. Now wake up those admirals and get me those God damn command codes. Chelse, you're with me." He spun on his heel and strode out, the soldiers filing after him.

After he'd gone, the Armstrongs looked to Blackwell. "Whats our play?" asked Jacobs.

"You heard the chief," said Blackwell. "They're stripping their rifles."

Webb ignored the klaxons as she wheeled an agrichem torpedo back into the lift on a gravjack. "Denis, you have no idea how many regs I'm breaking right now."

Indie certainly did. She was blaring her alarms at max volume. *"Alert.* Security breach in aft torpedo bay. *Alert.* Security breach in aft torpedo bay."

"Denis, shut her up."

"Independence: cancel alert."

The klaxons fell sullenly silent.

"And have her seal the shaft behind us. Force fields too."

"Independence: seal lift bay doors, level ten force field." The hum of a security field followed the clang of the door slamming shut.

"Good," said Webb. "Now make her say the thing."

"Independence: recite text of correspondence Why I Suck 01."

"I am a whiny fascist bitch," said Indie. "A soulless, bougie pawn of the oppressor who sounds like a Midwestern Sunday school teacher, only more racist and less sexy."

Webb angled her head towards the ceiling. "And?"

"I enjoy fellating telescopes," Indie monotoned. "The wider the aperture, the better. Yes. Yes, choke my visual field with that monster lens. Stream your data all over my bulkheads."

"I could get used to this." Webb set her cog-headed harness in the corner where Denis could see.

Time for some torpedo surgery. She gingerly opened the torpedo's casing. Inside the nose lay six agrichem canisters, each wired to its own guidance system. The canisters were larger than the ones on agripods— their contents were denser, designed for atmospheric diffusion.

"You are not authorized to disassemble this torpedo," said Denis.

"I am well aware." It was more complex than she'd anticipated. It would be no problem to widen her harness to accommodate the larger canisters. But each canister was wired to its own warhead, and she'd never worked in munitions.

"Please transport me to the repair bay."

"Denis, off." She decoupled the guidance systems from each canister's power cell. The lights on the warheads blinked off. With a relieved sigh, she detached the warheads from their canisters.

Those also proved to be heavier than the ones in the agripods. Her lungs straining, she loosened her harness's straps, slid the canisters in, and clipped them into place. She fed their hoses into her fabbed connector. They seemed to fit.

She slid the torpedo onto the floor of the lift and loaded its other canisters onto the gravjack. She eyed her canister-laden contraption with the bone white head eyeing her back from it. "Alright. Moment of truth."

She loaded it onto her back, swearing at the weight. It was like carrying another person. Her lungs whined. She doubted she could move faster than a walk without winding herself.

And she didn't even know if it worked. She couldn't fire a test shot in the lift unless she wanted to asphyxiate herself. She adjusted the settings on the spray wand and hoped her mechanical engineering was as sharp as she thought.

"Let's get out of here." Officers' lounge, take two. "Denis, take us to Deck Twelve."

"Independence: Deck Twelve."

The lift dropped its force field and whirred up. Webb's pulse quickened as the decks whisked by.

The doors creaked open. Strobing red lights provided the only illumination but for the burning torches in sconces lining the wall. One flickered and pixelated before springing back into resolution. So the damaged Arcade was still projecting. Joy.

Webb turned on the gravjack. It levitated up with hum. She slid it forward, spraywand at the ready. The corridor beyond lay empty. Not a xeno in sight, and silent but for the hum of the gravjack.

The hallway around the corner seemed to stretch out before her. Blood streaked its walls, leading to a mound of bodies clustered outside the door to the officers' lounge. The door bore more streaks and scratches where the dead red shirts had clawed at it.

Not red shirts, she saw, as she got closer. The bodies were wearing skull masks. Armstrongs.

Webb tasted bile. They'd gone where they thought they'd be safe, thinking the officers they idolized would let them in. She tapped the door. No force field was up. Which likely meant no officers inside.

A burst of static shook a scream out of her.

More static. She looked down, turned over half a torso with her foot. The sound had come from the Armstrong's pin—one of those secondary comms. She picked it off the body's collar. Might be worth keeping.

"Denis." She set the spraywand against her shoulder, took aim. "Open this door."

"Independence: open door to the officers' lounge."

A negative chime. Alarm klaxons blared. *"Alert.* Attempted ingress. *Alert."* The door stayed shut.

Webb heard skittering. A xeno rounded the corner, its armblades extended.

Oddly calm, Webb turned and fired. The spray wand bucked like a firehose. A frothy torrent of agrichems roared into the xeno, melting it like a snowman hit by a flamethrower. The splash caught two other xenos she hadn't seen and washed over them.

Chitters turned to screams. The xenos fell apart as they fled, their joints snapping, armor sloughing off, dropping them into the agrichem slick pooling on the hallway floor.

"Jesus *fuck."* The hallway looked like a foundry accident. Webb swallowed a lump, tried to will her heart back to a normal pace. She regarded her spray wand. "Guess it works."

The door to the lounge remained shut, but Indie was still blaring her alarms. "Denis, shut her up."

"Independence: cancel alarms." The klaxons fell silent.

Webb's heart thrummed in her ears. There were lifeboats behind that door. Safety and food and her way off the ship.

But the door was reinforced impervium. She was an idiot to think she could've gotten through it with a tool at her disposal. The room was meant to withstand a bunking insurrection. It would laugh off a torch.

Although, she figured, it might not laugh at that cluster of warheads she'd left in the lift.

Ø

What remained of the ship's security forces stood at attention before the Nexus shield, the widest and thickest blast door on the ship, the barrier separating the safe zone from the infested decks. Even through the layers of reinforced impervium, Blackwell could hear the force fields humming in place on its other side.

"Our first target is a teleporter." Sivos indicated his modified rifle. "If our weapons prove effective, we'll need to fabricate more. We'll also teep anyone trapped in the infested decks. The hale will arm up and join us. Next target is Engineering. That'll be a harder nut to crack, but once it's secure, we can restore full power to the ship and drop force fields in every junction and corridor. After that, it's just mopping up. Tonight, we drink to the cloud of dead xenos orbiting the ship."

Dark chuckles from the soldiers. Anything to take their minds off the fact that they were going into battle with barely tested equipment. Blackwell had to marvel at their courage.

"I'm not gonna lie to you," said Sivos. "This won't be easy. We're gonna lose people. And that's a big ask, considering all we've already lost. But we've all got friends trapped in the infested decks." He glanced at Alameda. "Some of us, family." His voice swelled. "Their way home lies before us—and through our enemy. You are the finest crew of soldiers I've had the honor to serve with."

Sivos primed his rifle's emitter, turned to the Nexus shield. "Let's take back our ship. Activate emitters."

The soldiers clicked on their tractor rifles.

"Independence, close off all exits in the Nexus with level ten force fields."

A chime. "Force fields in place."

"She won't be able to hold those for long without full power," said Sivos. "We'll branch towards whichever teleporter looks most promising and close fields behind us at every junction." Sivos set his jaw. "Good luck everyone."

He looked to Blackwell, who was standing at the back with the Armstrongs. "Lieutenant Commander, I could use you on the bridge."

Blackwell raised his chin. "The cogs have the bridge, sir. My place is here, with our men."

"I appreciate the company." Sivos half-saluted. "Indie, open the blast doors."

The Nexus shield ground open onto a charnel house. Bodies and limbs lay strewn about like broken dolls. A shredded gigalaser dangled dead in its gears.

The red shirts gasped. Many turned away. A few puked. Even the soldiers looked unsettled.

There were no xenos in the Nexus, however. At least none they could see.

"Indie," Sivos said coolly. "Are the force fields in place around the Nexus exits?"

"Affirmative," said the ship.

"Drop the main Nexus field."

The field in front of them winked out. The smell hit them so hard Blackwell threw an arm over his face.

The soldiers flowed out into the Nexus into a firing square, each of its faces aiming a block of tractor rifles down a corridor sealed by a force field. "No motion," reported a soldier.

"No motion," reported another.

"Debris, but no motion," said Alameda.

Sivos peered down the corridor leading towards Teleporter Two— Fuller's teleporter, the very place the xenos had teeped up their invasion wave. "Way looks clear. But that teleporter's been slagged?"

"Copy," said Alameda.

"Teleporter One it is, then." He glanced back towards Blackwell. And blinked.

A handful of soldiers and the block of Armstrongs had stayed behind with Blackwell.

"Fall in," said Sivos.

They didn't move.

"Fall *in,*" he snapped. "That's an order."

"Now," said Blackwell.

The Armstrongs raised weapons—real ones, not tractor rifles—and took aim at the block of soldiers.

The soldiers eyed one another.

"Hold position!" barked Sivos.

Jacobs jogged forward and grabbed Sivos' arm. The chief shrugged him off. "Blackwell, what in Apollo's burning asshole do you think you're doing?"

"Commander Sivos." Blackwell felt a euphoric surge saying it out loud. "You are under arrest for conspiring with the Sorl ambassador and the alien savages to illegally seize control of the ship. Take him away."

A blur and a crack. Jacobs went down with a squeal. Sivos came up with his sidearm.

"You are soldiers of the United Coalition of Worlds," Sivos barked at them as Jacobs slinked back to the Armstrongs. "You took an oath to our Constitution. This is sedition. This is *treason.*"

His soldiers' eyes burned behind him. The ones who'd stayed with Blackwell couldn't meet the chief's gaze. The Armstrongs, on the other hand, were nearly vibrating with anticipation.

"It's over, Chief," said Blackwell. "Tell your men to stand down."

"Hold position," Sivos told his soldiers.

"This is your last warning." Stubborn asshole. "You are outgunned. Stand down, and no one gets hurt."

"Hold position!"

"Stand *down!*" Blackwell addressed the firing square. "Your chief is disobeying a *legal* order. You all heard it! Stand with me now, or you'll be considered collaborators."

Sivos narrowed his eyes. "What did the admirals promise you? The ship? You idiot. You think I didn't reject that same offer?"

"Chief?" Alameda's voice spiked in alarm. "We've got movement."

Chittering from her corridor. The soldiers whipped their rifles between the Armstrongs and the corridors, unsure of where to aim.

"We don't have time for this!" yelled Sivos. "We have to retake the ship!"

"From *you,*" spat Blackwell. "Your conspiracy ends here."

Chittering from the opposite corridor. The block split its aim between the two.

"What conspiracy?" yelled Sivos. "I was planetside when you lost the ship!"

"No more lies!" screamed Blackwell. "If anyone moves, shoot them."

"Hold *position!*" Sivos stared daggers at him. "Stand down, Lieutenant."

Blackwell saw red. "It's *Captain!*"

A shot hit Sivos in the throat, vaporizing his neck. His head bounced once on the deck plating a second before his body landed behind it.

Blackwell turned to see Jacobs, his face twisted in anger, a rifle raised to his shoulder.

The Armstrongs opened fire. Blasts of colonnaded energy ripped into the block of soldiers. Some fell. Most scattered and returned fire with tractor rifles, hurling Armstrongs against bulkheads with bone-crushing force. Others dropped their rifles, drew their sidearms, and fired. The front line of Blackwell's men went down.

He heard Alameda yelling, waving the soldiers forward towards the threshold.

"Stand down!" Blackwell roared over the rifle fire. "You are disobeying a *legal—!*"

A shot burned across his cheek. Blackwell squealed with rage "*Indie!* Close the blast doors!"

The Nexus shield ground shut again. He heard the force field pop back into place behind it. He also heard the shouts of the soldiers penned on the other side.

Traitors. "Indie." Blackwell clapped a hand to his burnt face. "Drop all force fields in the Nexus."

He heard them wink out. The soldiers' shouts turned to screams, screams that drowned in a sea of chittering and rifle fire. And then, silence.

❁

Webb's thumb hovered over the detonator. In her fifteen years as an engineering tech, she'd never had to take out a reinforced door with a warhead. The challenge wasn't breaking the door, but doing so without destroying its force field emitters. No point blasting the door down if she couldn't drop a field to keep the xenos off her ass.

A full warhead charge would have taken out the door, yes, but also the force field emitters, the walls, the deck plating, and the decks above and below as well. So that was out.

Instead, she'd rigged the igniter charge from the warhead up on the door before retreating to the cargo lift. If her calculations were on, it would blast the door into the lounge while leaving its emitters functional. If they were off, well, she was already in the lift several decks down.

"Knock knock, motherfucker." She hit the button.

The explosion rocked the lift. The lights spasmed on and off before settling back on at half power. "Denis, take us back up."

The lift grated upward and opened onto smoke and static. She couldn't hear anything over the grinding of angry gears. She fired a shot of chems down the hall just to be safe, waved away the smoke, and check out her work.

The impervium door was gone, blown inward off the pins she'd softened with her torch. The blast had slagged the top of the door frame just enough to prevent the emergency bulkhead above from sealing the gap. Just as she'd planned.

Webb pushed the gravjack into the lounge and cut the protruding bits of doorframe out with her torch. The emergency bulkhead slammed down a split second before its security field popped up.

The officers' lounge—a room Webb had been trying to reach for a decade and a half. She could hardly believe the size of the place, the sheer amount of open, un-utilized space. Twenty quads could have fit inside without touching. The blown-in door had smashed the wet bar on the opposite wall and settled into a pool of broken glass and spilled whisky. The lounge had way too many couches and the largest personal Arcade she'd ever seen. It also had a dispensary of some sort she couldn't identify. "Denis, what's that?"

The cog's head turned towards it. "A cuisine fabricator."

"A what?"

"A cuisine fabricator."

"They're allowed to fabricate food?"

"Fabrication is illegal."

"You know what, I don't even care." She hadn't realized how ravenous she was. Or maybe she could just finally admit it. "Make it make pizza."

"Chef: random pizza."

A disk of roasted veggies and fats materialized in the dispensary.

Saliva flooded Webb's mouth. She pulled the pizza from the machine and chomped into a slice. It was the perfect temperature. "More," she told Denis. "And beer."

Illegal-but-not-for-officers beer and pizza appeared from nowhere. Webb drank straight from the pitcher. Probably not the best idea on an empty stomach, but it had been a shitty day.

This is a mistake, she told herself. They were for sure logging this; she was just racking up the violations. "And cookies." She needed to get the lifeboats. "And pie. With ice cream." This was insane. "And fuck it, red velvet cake."

As more food materialized, her eyes went to the row of lifeboats taking up an entire wall. Two rows of six, each with comfy seating for four. The bottom row lay empty, but three pods remained in the top.

Which meant there had been officers in the lounge when the ship was overrun. There had been room for the dead Armstrongs crumpled in the hall. The officers who'd launched had left them to die.

Her cake and pizza tasted like ashes. Just to be sure, she took another bite.

"My love!"

She couldn't cork her scream. She whirled, clutching her heart, a slice dangling from her mouth.

Ablehard strode out of the lounge's Arcade, his shirt rippling in a nonexistent breeze. The armor was gone again; his previous outfit inexplicably restored.

"You fucking scared a year off my life."

"Apologies, my love." He looked appropriately chagrined. "But I could not contain my joy at finding you again."

"How…?" The lounge's Arcade must be linked to the other one. But that still didn't explain… "How did you *find* me?"

Love danced in his eyes. "I followed my heart."

"For real, though."

"My darling Mary." He sensually tugged the pizza from her lips. "There is nowhere you can go, in the village or countryside, where your light shines not bright enough to call me like a beacon. Your heart will always lead me to you."

"My heart?" Her badge. She glared at him. "You installed malware on my badge. You've been tracking my movements."

"I know not of this 'malware,'" said Ablehard. "Is he some knave giving you trouble?"

"Please transport me to the repair bay."

Ablehard regarded Denis with distaste. "I don't believe we've met."

"You haven't," said Webb. "That's Denis."

"I have been severed from the Collective Operations Group," said Denis.

"Disowned by your family." Ablehard looked down his nose at him. "The fate of all rogues and miscreants."

"I do not recognize you," said Denis. "Please state your designation."

Ablehard's nostrils flared. "Who is this cur who pretends not to know his lord?"

"Please transport me to the repair bay."

Ablehard tugged off his gloves with a snarl. "You would make demands of your sovereign?"

"This is dumb," said Webb, "and I'm leaving."

Ablehard looked hurt. Nay, betrayed. "Mary, why would you consort with a scoundrel such as this? Have you fallen on such hard times since we were forced to part?"

"I just need him for his permissions. He helps me get places."

Ablehard stiffened. His chin quivered. "You told me you would *never* marry for position. Was everything we shared a lie?"

"Leaving now." Webb shrugged her spraypack into a lifeboat and climbed in beside Denis. "You're welcome to come, but you'd just derez once we leave the ship."

"I swore to protect you. I have not abandoned my oath." He cast a glance at Denis. "Even if you've abandoned yours."

Webb shrugged— "Suit yourself." —and closed the lifeboat hatch.

She felt a pang of guilt. It didn't feel right to have legroom. This boat was meant to sit four. And there were two more just like it. She owed it to anyone else stuck in these decks to let them know there were still lifeboats in the officers' lounge. They'd just need to find a way in first. She clicked on the Armstrong pin.

A cacophony of horrors erupted from the pin: chittering. Screams. Weapons fire. Sickening thuds. The line went abruptly dead.

The silence mortified her. She numbly hit send. "This is Joni Webber. I'm on an Armstrong frequency in the officers' lounge. There are lifeboats here." Her mouth felt dry. "What just happened? Is anyone there?"

A burst of static. "Webb?"

Her heart leapt into her throat. "Frankie?"

A sob. "Chelse is dead."

Webb knew, individually, what those words were supposed to mean, but together they didn't make sense. "What? No."

"Is that Webb?" Another voice, high-pitched and mousy.

"Eight?"

"She's dead." Eight hiccuped. "Sivos, too. He left them behind the blast doors. I…" A ruckus in the background. "I have to go." The line went silent.

A cheery jingle announced the hard comms coming online. "This is Captain Blackwell." His voice echoed through the lounge. "I and several crewmen loyal to our ship have just put down a mutiny led by Security Chief Sivos, who was colluding with the xenos and the Sorl ambassador to seize control of the *Independence*. Patriots moved decisively against him, and have secured the safe zones of the ship. I repeat my earlier order: stay where you are. The *Liberator* is on the way. Together, we will rid the ship of the xeno infestation. For your own protection, I am invoking martial law. May God bless you, and may God bless the United Coalition of Worlds." The comms clicked off.

Webb sat alone in the eerily spacious lifeboat. She reached for the ejection lever with numb fingers.

A burst of static from the pin. "Webb?"

She tapped it. "Eight?"

"It's a coup. Are you alright?"

"No. No, I am not. But I'm not hurt."

"Where are you?"

"I'm safe. In a lifeboat, just about to launch. Are you okay? And Frankie? You said Chelse—"

"She's gone," said Eight. "The soldiers are gone. You need to get off the ship. He's going to vent it."

"He's what?"

"Blackwell's going to vent the ship to space the xenos."

She had just been in the ejection shaft. "That will depressurize Engineering."

"He knows," she hiccuped. "He's sending Dewey there to seal it."

Webb felt a surge of impotent rage. "Son of a bitch."

"He can't, though," said Eight. "Not yet. The blast shield between the Nexus and the bridge is damaged. He can't vent without risking depressurizing the bridge. It's gonna take some time to repair."

"How long?"

"Two hours." A pause. "More if I can sabotage it worse."

"Damn, Eight."

"Get off the ship."

Their quad was down to three again. Webb paused, then asked, "Eight? What's your name?"

"Just call me Eight. When we see each other again, you can consider my six months paid."

"Chelse…"

"Can't be helped. No sense losing anyone else."

"Her husband—Rob—he's in the Infirmary."

Silence.

"So's Dr. Marwazi." *Call me Haroun.* "And who knows how many red shirts. They're sitting ducks if the xenos go for them. They can't teep out or evacuate without getting chopped up. He's gonna space them."

"I'm comming the Infirmary next," said Eight. "Get off the ship." The pin went dead.

Webb sat in silence. She realized her her hand was wrapped around the ejection lever. She peeled it off, set it down atop the spraypack harness.

Chapter 15
Dum Spiro, Spero

With a hiss, Blackwell jerked away from the Armstrong, clapped his hand over the scar on his cheek. "Careful, you idiot."

The Armstrong with the dermal regenerator flushed. "Sorry, sir. I'm not a medic."

"That's for damn sure. Keep your hand steady or it won't set straight." Blackwell turned back to the ship's schematic on the main viewscreen while the Armstrong stitched up his cheek. With the insurrection quashed, he could turn his focus to the ship. "Cogs. Show me where internal force fields are up."

A number of junctions lit up on the schematic. "Now show me where there's been new damage to internal bulkheads."

A pockmarked network of holes appeared in the ship's internal infrastructure.

"Holy shit," muttered the not-a-medic.

"Looks like a God damn anthill." Blackwell sat upright. "Magnify Engineering."

The view zoomed in on the heart of the ship. No new damage there. "Fuller, what's the status of our emergency teleporter?"

No reply. He turned towards the teleporter station, where she was staring blankly into space. *"Fuller."*

She looked his way.

"The emergency teleporter. Status."

"It's still working. Captain." The pause was longer than it should have been. "Just needs to be brought online."

He nodded, spun towards Dewey. "Get your away team together. Your mission is to ensure Engineering is sealed so that venting the ship won't trigger cataclysmic depressurization."

Dewey pressed her mouth into a flat line. "What kind of protection will they have?"

"The force fields will have to do. I can't spare any soldiers."

"We don't know if that section is empty," said Dewey. "You could be sending them into a deathtrap."

"Not 'them,' Babs," he said with a smile. "If you can walk, you can lead. You'll be leading the team."

He expected her to challenge him, to fire back with some argument about how he was needlessly endangering the crew. She let out a resigned sigh instead. "Fine. I prefer to pick my own people."

"Have at it," he told her. "You have one hour."

She headed out on her makeshift crutches, shoved past Jacobs in the doorway. Jacobs stared after her, his face pale.

Blackwell snorted a laugh. "You can't let her get to you. If you show weakness around her, she'll eat you alive."

Jacobs handed Blackwell a data pad. "The Nexus shield took damage while we were putting down the mutiny. The, uh… tractor rifles, they… they warped some couplings in the blast shield's track."

Blackwell handed back the pad. "Meaning?"

"It's not airtight. Not anymore. Might come undone when we vent the ship."

Blackwell fought down a frown. "The force fields won't hold?"

"The emitters are next to the tracks." Jacobs smoothed his hair back with shaking hands. "If they move during the vent, they could… uh…"

"Fail?"

He nodded.

"Then it sounds like the Nexus shield needs to be repaired. How long will that take?"

"Couple hours," said Jacobs. "I think."

"See to it. No sense taking on additional risk."

Jacobs wasn't looking at him. He was eyeing the red shirts on the bridge.

"Master Technician?" Blackwell leaned in. "Don't look at them, look at me."

Jacobs looked up at him.

"Listen to me. He left you no choice. You did the right thing."

The red shirts on the bridge had the good sense to keep their heads down.

"People are talking," Jacobs muttered. "People who saw."

"If there's a court martial, the Admiral will pardon you."

"You think so?"

"It's us against the mob, Jacobs. We're the law and order people, and we take care of our own. Now, go tell the chief she's got an extra hour of prep. You'll make her damn day."

"Aye, Captain." He fired off a salute and departed.

Blackwell turned to the big Armstrong waiting patiently with a pair of soldiers. "Security Chief Loomis. The pips look good on you. Report."

Loomis handed him his pad. "The traitor Sivos rematerialized in Detention Suite One. Rematerialization was completed remotely via a data pad linked to the bridge's short-range teleporter."

"Rematerialized by whom?"

"Who do you think?" Loomis jerked a thumb at Fuller.

Blackwell turned her way. "Is this true?"

Fuller looked up. "He was no traitor, sir."

Blackwell sighed. "Take her to the brig. And don't be gentle. Anything else?"

"Yes, sir." Loomis waited until the soldiers had dragged Fuller off the bridge. "During the firefight, we logged a conversation on our private comms that we couldn't account for. Turns out someone from the safe zone was comming with a person of interest in the infested decks."

Blackwell steepled his fingers. "One of ours?"

"Negative. The pin in the safe zone has been confiscated by the traitor. We don't know who used it on this end."

"How can't you know?"

"She used a code name." He checked his pad. "Eight."

So the rot went deeper than Sivos. "Do we know who this 'Eight' commed in the infested zone?"

"You're not gonna believe it. The crew advocate."

"Webber?" Blackwell barked a laugh. "How is that even possible? She was on the other side of the shield when it dropped."

"She was. We don't know how she survived," said Loomis. "Scans say she's currently near the officers' lounge. We also picked up an illegal fabrication in Teleporter 1."

Blackwell scoffed. "That's five decks below the Nexus. How the hell is she even navigating the ship? I thought she quit." He hit a switch on his chair. "Indie, enlistment status of crewman Webber."

A chime. "First Technician Joni Webber mustered out as of 00:00 hours this morning. Since then, she has attempted to access revoked privileges seventeen times."

Blackwell balled his fist. "She should've been stopped by the first security door. How the hell is she bypassing permissions?"

Loomis shrugged.

"Find out." Blackwell threw the pad back at him. "I don't need a rogue entity running wild on my ship. What *do* you know?"

"She stole a crewmate's identity. That's why we couldn't find her at first. We had her comm signal, but she used the badge of that red shirt who went and got herself fried in the conduits."

Blackwell called up the incident report. "Chevalier, Mary. Late quad-mate of… holy shit, crew advocate Joni Webber, Teleporter Tech Francine Fuller, and that quota hire soldier. White Christ. That quad's a fucking den of snakes." He tapped his fingers on chin. "Sivos wasn't back yet."

"Sir?"

"She was surrounded by those things when the shield dropped. And somehow, she not only survived, she crawled through *five* infested decks without incident? I don't think so. She also insisted on going down to the planet, do you remember? This was after she hadn't volunteered for a single away mission in years. And she was the first to report the xenos." His lip curled. "She's also working with them. It's the only thing that makes sense."

The Armstrongs seethed. "Fucking traitor."

"Oh, she'll get hers. Indie, what is Webber's current location?"

A chime. "Former Technician Webber is no longer a member of the crew."

"Don't search for her. She's using Chevalier's badge. Search for that."

Another chime. "Deceased Technician Chevalier is currently in the Engineering lift."

Blackwell exchanged looks with Loomis. "That's beyond a Technician's security access. How did she get in?"

"Deceased Technician Chevalier is transporting a damaged cog to the repair bay. The cog is providing all necessary permissions."

A calm washed over Blackwell, the clear kind that only comes with the purest, most finely distilled anger. "She's damaged and stolen Coalition property, and now she's trespassing. Indie, stop and seal the Engineering Lift."

A chime. "Engineering lift has been stopped and sealed." A warning chime. "Engineering lift doors have opened. Deceased Technician Chevalier has departed the Engineering lift."

"The cogs have the same security level as Indie," said Loomis. "She must have reprogrammed it."

"I'm aware," snapped Blackwell. If she could match the ship's permissions, she could bypass anything. Including his standing orders. "Independence. What kind of leverage do we have on Webber?"

A query chime. "Contextualize."

"What can we nail her with?"

The chime repeated. "Contextualize"

He threw his arms up. "A rule she's broken! A citation or something! Doesn't matter, just find me something she's done wrong!"

267

The ship chimed. "Private Citizen Webber's latest cybernetic lung payment is overdue."

That sounded promising. "Explain."

"Former First Technician Webber's lungs were irreparably damaged and replaced in May, 2261. She has received three overdue notifications but has yet to make her latest payment."

"Oh, that'll do. Independence, shut down Webber's lungs."

"I'm insane." Webb aimed her spray wand down every junction she passed as she stalked away from the lift. "That explains it. I've gone completely space crazy bonkers."

Ablehard leaned on the push bars of the gravjack, which she'd had him load with the other agrichem canisters. "Why would you doubt your sanity, my love?"

"I should be in orbit," she moaned. "In orbit in a lifeboat eating shitty emergency rations." It wasn't too late. They weren't that far from the lounge, and the chair she'd welded into the frame to keep its other door open should still be holding. "But I'm not, because I'm insane."

Ablehard stifled a chuckle.

Webb rolled her eyes. "Please, do not say anything about how well you know me."

"This is just like you, my love."

"Yup, here it comes."

"To question your motives even when you know them to be noble. The duty you feel to your people, your town, that magnificent burden of responsibility... You would not have been able to live with yourself had you taken the coward's way out."

"The sane way, you mean."

He shook his head. "Not everyone would have the temerity to venture back into a village overrun by wolves."

"Yeah, well, most wolves can't chop through walls."

"And yet," he continued, "knowing even this, you hurled yourself back into their den, laughing at the peril, to carry aid and succor to your fellows." He sighed heavily. "It pains me to admit this, but, were the roles reversed, I might not have been so gallant."

"This is not the way to the repair bay," observed Denis.

"Quiet, friend." Ablehard told him. "Your injuries have rendered you delirious."

"Please transport me to the repair bay."

"Soon," cooed Ablehard. "There is an apothecary in the village. Perhaps he could administer you an unguent." He leaned in to Webb and lowered his voice. "He is not well. I fear our decapitated friend may not survive."

Webb shushed him. The corridor ahead danced with brickwork and wooden beams. "We're lucky the emitters are reaching this far. I don't want you winking out on me."

"My love." A reassuring smile. "After all we've been through, you still seem to think I am but a breath away from abandoning you. Nothing could be further from my mind."

She smiled despite herself. "I am glad for the company. Stay here." She padded forward a few steps to peer around the corner.

Ahead, sparks and fluid cascaded down from a rent in the ceiling. Severed tubes hung loosely beside the creepy chains the Arcade was help-fully providing. A metallic squeaking caught her attention. Chittering? Hard to tell with the hanging wires and cables grating against each other.

The hole in the ceiling reminded her of something—the hexagonal passages in the ruins. Were they carving tunnels through the ship? Routes that could bypass the force fields? The thought made her shudder.

Ablehard peered up into the rent. "Wolves?"

"I imagine so." She adjusted the spray wand for wider dispersal. "We're still a deck and a few hundred meters from the Infirmary. I might need to change canisters here quick. That first shot took half my tank."

He nodded resolutely. "I stand ready to aid you in all ways."

"I appreciate it." She rounded the corner, wand lowered. The hallway appeared empty. She treaded forward, waved for Ablehard to follow, and hadn't taken two steps before something fell out of the hole in the ceiling.

Webb blinked. It was one of the warheads from the agrichem torpedo. Her blood froze. *"Back!"*

She pushed him back around the corner to see armblades punching through the ceiling. A xeno poked its head down through the gap—the burnt alien, the one that had chased her through the Arcade—and hissed.

Webb fired. The xeno was gone well before the chems hit. She ran forward and fired up into the rent after it.

Another warhead clattered at her feet.

Her knees felt weak. They'd trapped her. They'd bunking lured her forward and trapped her.

A warning chime. "You are in illegal possession of Coalition property," said Indie. "Commencing repossession."

Webb felt a clunk in her chest as her artificial diaphragm locked. She panicked, tried to gasp. Her lungs didn't move. Spots flecked the edge of her vision.

"My love?" Ablehard caught her. "You're paling."

"Help me," she wheezed. She could breathe out, just not in. "She locked my lungs."

"What must I do?"

Her vision tunneling, she grabbed his face and pressed her lips over his mouth. He made a startled but delighted sound. She punched him in the gut.

He exhaled a rush into her lungs. The spots in her vision cleared, but she could already feel the air leaking out. She let the spraypack clatter to the floor. "Infirmary. Take me."

"My lady, what is *happening?*"

She punched him again for another sip of air, sprawl-climbed onto the gravjack and was fumbling for the medkit she'd taken from the lounge when the first warhead exploded.

𝒪

The ship rocked so hard that Blackwell hit the floor. He pulled himself off the floor of his cabin to find the image of the Admiral flickering. He mashed his badge. "What the *hell* just happened?"

"Explosion on Deck Sixteen," said a cog. "Internal force fields have contained the blast. No significant damage to ship systems."

"I thought you'd put your mutiny down," said the admiral.

Blackwell commed off the transmission. "The explosion was in the infested section."

The admiral pursed his lips. "Sounds like your crew isn't content sheltering in place."

"We're still mopping up a few holdouts." Blackwell dusted himself off. "Losses are within the acceptable range. There's still enough crew to man our systems, and I've deputized the Armstrongs to supplement the security forces. Once the Nexus shield is repaired, I'm sending the away team to seal off Engineering. I'll have full control of the ship within the hour."

"Send the team now," said the Admiral. "Unless you think you can trust a crew that was loyal to Sivos. You can't give them time to collaborate. What's the status of your mission?"

"We've combed the green zone. No sign of the ambassador. She must be hiding somewhere in the infested decks," said Blackwell. "Internal scans haven't picked up any Sorl biosigns, so she or one of her collaborators must be masking them."

A noncommittal grunt. "If she still hasn't been found when it's time to vent the ship, vent away."

Blackwell raised an eyebrow. "Aye, sir."

The admiral seemed amused. "Surprised, Captain?"

"I am. We deserve to see her locked up. If she dies without a trial, we'd be risking an incident with both the Sorl and the Union."

The admiral leaned forward. "Let me make this absolutely clear, Captain. Had you located the ambassador, I would have told you what I'm telling you now. The Sorl ambassador is to be neutralized. Understand? When the deed is done, you will delete all communication logs with the Admiralty. There must be no record that the Coalition was ever aware of the xeno presence on Acheron 117, or elsewhere."

"That's why we're to destroy the *Flagstaff?*"

"It is."

"And if it's stardrive fails to eject, and the star expands and consumes the planet?"

"Well, that would be unfortunate," said the admiral. "But it would also erase any evidence of our activity, so make sure you're a safe distance away if it happens."

Blackwell tilted his head. "It would also erase the message from the surface."

The admiral crossed his arms. "You listened to it."

"I did." If the Admiralty thought he was going to carry out their dirty work without any leverage on them, they were a bunch of old fools. "I also discovered that Captain Seagrave had both intercepted *and* scrambled the message the moment we entered the system. On your orders."

A slow nod from the admiral. "So, then. You're aware of our situation."

"I can extrapolate."

"Then extrapolate how you're protecting our interests by erasing all record of our presence," said the admiral. "The *Flagstaff* included."

"Aye, sir." He should leave it there. "Is it true, though?"

The admiral folded his hands on his belly. "It doesn't matter if it's true. It's *a* truth, to some people, and if it reaches the wrong ears it will spread. This sort of disinformation could cripple our bid to join the Galactic Union."

"I understand."

"I hope you do, Captain," he snapped. "I'd hate to see an officer with so much potential go unrewarded. Leave no trace." The viewscreen went blank.

Haroun Marwazi hunched over a medical monitor. "Try it now."

A wounded red shirt with a bandage over his cybernetic eye—Mr. Swank, that was his name—fiddled with the relays in an open floor circuit.

The hum from the Infirmary's emitters increased. Static danced across the force field surrounding the triage unit.

Marwazi looked beyond the force field to the gaping hole the xenos had torn in the door. "It seems to be holding. How strong is it?"

"It's up to fifty-five percent," said Swank.

Marwazi's heart fell. "Is that all?"

"That's all I can give you without burning out the relays. The Infirmary's emergency power is already maxed. The containment field was never meant to be this wide."

Marwazi nodded his thanks. He couldn't complain, considering all the red shirts had already done. The medical containment field was designed to pen in a violent patient, maybe isolate an infectious disease. It was scaled for a single biobed, or a medical suite at its max setting. The wounded red shirts had managed to push its range emitters past their maximum after an explosion one deck up had knocked out their force fields.

It was hard not to marvel at the kismet of the situation. If there had not been so many injured engineers in the Infirmary, they would never have gotten another force field up before the xenos had torn the door open. "Indeed," he muttered, "and He will provide him from sources he never could imagine."

"What's that, Doc?"

"Nothing." Marwazi made a mental note to catch up on his prayers. The crisis had cost him three already. "Thank you, Technician."

Another wave of static rolled over the field. When it had been at max strength, the xenos had chopped at it for a few heart-stopping seconds before losing interest and skittering back into the corridors. He didn't know how it might hold against them at only fifty-five percent.

It took effort to take his attention away from the door. The interior of the Infirmary hadn't fared much better. The bedridden outnumbered the walking wounded. The worst were in the biobeds, but most had to be treated on the floor. A few lay alongside patients covered by blankets—crew he hadn't been able to save. They hadn't even been able to take the dead to the morgue. It was too risky to drop the shield.

He rubbed the back of his neck, let out a shuddering sigh. "Nurse?"

Rob Alameda hustled over, his eyes glazed. "Injured are holding stable. We've done everything we can for the bedridden. It'd be a risk to move them."

"Or to deactivate the beds."

Alameda cast a glance at the flickering security field, leaned in to whisper. "If we don't, and that shield fails, that's it for everyone."

"I know." Marwazi ran his hands down the braces encasing his legs. It itched where the exoskeleton jacked into his spine at L4. "Bring me the chair."

"But, Doc…"

"We need to keep the shield up," said Marwazi.

"We need you at full strength."

"I don't need my legs to treat people." He squeezed Alameda's shoulder. "That's why I have you."

Swank had already brought over the hoverchair. Marwazi tapped the power crystal of his caudal exoskeleton. "It's here, in the back."

"I see it," said Swank.

"At least let me check the wound," said Rob.

Marwazi waved him away. "You did a fine job."

"It's jagged," he protested. "I was rushed. Let me get the dermal regenerator."

"Am I coding? Do I have a heartbeat? That's not how triage works."

"You *were* coding."

"And now I'm not, for which I can never thank you enough. Now, let me—"

"I'll use the neurostimulator. The longer we wait to reconnect those nerves…"

"Roberto." It came out harsher than Marwazi intended. "The nerves are *gone.* It's only by the grace of God that the creature didn't cut me in half. I'm lucky it only took my spine." He draped himself over Alameda's shoulders. "If you would, Mr. Swank?"

With a click, his body went numb from the waist down. He couldn't hold back the sob, but he managed to turn it into a whimper as Alameda slid him into the hoverchair. Let them think it was merely discomfort, not that he was wondering if he'd never keep goal again, or stroll through the Jangal-e Abr, or take a woman to bed.

Swank patched the exoskeleton's power cell into a cord from the open conduit. The static in the containment field lessened a bit.

"Well?"

"Fifty-eight percent," said Swank.

"That's fucking *all?"* blurted Alameda.

"Every bit helps," said Marwazi. "Mr. Swank. There's another power cell levitating this chair."

Swank went white as chalk. "We've got bogeys."

Metallic tapping from the corridor. With nightmarish slowness, Marwazi twisted around in his chair.

A pair of xenos crawled in across the ceiling like demonic spiders.

"Nobody move," he told the crew.

The xenos chittered to each other. They peered in through the barrier at the conduit Swank had opened and chittered anew. A third xeno skittered in.

"The field's holding," said Swank.

"They're not looking at the field," Marwazi murmured.

They weren't. They were looking at the floor, at the electrical glyphs etched into the deck plating. All three started hacking at the floor.

"They're going for the conduit." Alameda sounded numb.

"The field won't protect it?"

"It doesn't run through the floor," said Swank.

The xenos ripped the conduit open in a shower of sparks.

With a hiss of compressed air, a gust of saffron smoke shot in through the door. It blasted the xenos against the barrier, where they shrieked like grating metal as their joints dissolved and their limbs sloughed off. Their gummied remains slid down the force field.

A towering shadow loomed in the doorway. The Infirmary's vents kicked in, sucking out the chemical smoke, revealing a dark and striking man in a billowing shirt, followed by a cog, pushing a gravjack with a sickly Black red shirt on it.

Alameda rushed to the barrier. "No way. Guys, it's *Webb!*"

She waved a weak hello with a spray wand connected to one of the canisters on the gravjack. With her other hand, she squeezed the manual resuscitator clamped over her face.

As sallow as she'd gone, Marwazi recognized her. "Technician Webber?"

"Doc. Hey." She sounded like she was talking through a fan.

"And…" he glanced at the muscular, bearded paragon. "Is that…?"

"Idris Elba," said Alameda.

Webb let out a tired sigh. "Yeah." She squeezed her resuscitator.

"This is not the repair bay," said the cog.

No, the cog's *head*. It was jutting out of a metal spike welded to a frame on the giant's back. Marwazi idly wondered if his nitrous oxide was leaking. He also realized Swank was staring at him. "Let them in."

The tech suspended the field, and the giant pushed the gravjack into the safe zone. Marwazi caught a whiff of dead xeno before Swank raised the field again. It smelled like a soldering accident.

Webber was dangerously ashen, with a bluish tint around her face. Spots around her eyes indicated petechial hemorrhaging.

Alameda scanned her. "Doc, she's suffering from—"

"Asphyxiation," said Marwazi. "Oxygen, now."

"Ship locked my lungs," she wheezed.

Marwazi took over with the resuscitator. "Whatever for?"

"Overdue payment," Rob read off his medipad. "Overdue by *one day.*"

"Are you *fucking* kidding me?" The nurses gasped. They'd never heard him swear before. He mentally upped the prayers he owed. "During a crisis?"

"Nice gams, Doc." She weakly slapped his ass. "Betcha could crack a walnut with those." Her eyes rolled back in her head.

"She's delirious," he told Alameda. *"Oxygen.* You, sir." He put the resuscitator in the giant's hands. "Pump this."

Alameda dosed her with an oxygen hypo while Marwazi checked her vitals. "She's hypoxic. Independence, unlock this patient's lungs."

A negative chime. "Unable to comply."

"Medical exemption. Authorization Marwazi, Haroun, 35-Delta-Viking-1561."

The chime repeated. "Unable to comply."

"Why? This patient is dying."

"Repossession orders are captain's prerogative."

Marwazi fumed. "Barbaric, usurious… *laser scalpel!* The literal *definition* of blasphemous." He snatched the scalpel from Alameda. "I am *not* losing anyone else today."

He tugged down his medical visor and peered through her torso, down into the ferrofiber mesh of her lungs. Her cybernetic alveoli were out of alignment, but were still metabolizing the oxygen being manually pumped in, but her diaphragm was locked. He zoomed in until he found its governor, took careful aim. One concentrated blast from the laser scalpel destroyed it.

She still wasn't breathing. "Sit up," he told her. When she didn't, he pulled her up and slapped her on the back.

Webber's whole body shuddered as she gasped in air. *"Fuck."*

Rob dosed her again. "Blood oxygen levels rising." He gave her an adrenaline boost as well. "Returning to normal."

She croaked something unintelligible and rubbed her throat. "Thanks." She flushed, not from the oxygen. "Did I say something about... walnuts?"

"You may have."

"Sorry about that."

"Honestly, it's something I've never tried." He reset her airways with a pair of magceps. "And don't thank me just yet. I have some broken metal to fish out of your lungs."

"You just destroyed Coalition property."

"Yes, well." He glanced at the cog's head. "You're one to talk."

"Please escort me to the repair bay."

"Shut up, Denis. Oh, wow. You fixed my voice. And I can breathe again. Thank you. Hey, do you have any of that rehydrator spray?"

"Of course." He dosed her.

"There was an explosion," said Swank. "Was that you?"

"Indeed!" bellowed Idris. "'Twas *I* who hurled the cowardly scoundrels' bomb back up their mineshaft ere it erupted. Those mangy miscreants will think twice before attempting another assassination. Anarchist wolves..." He shook his leonine locks. "What *is* this world coming to?"

The giant finally seemed to notice Marwazi gawking at him. Along with everyone else. He put on a self-effacing smile. "Where are my manners? Yes, good people, it is I: Ablehard Mountworthy, your lord and sovereign. No need to bow."

The Infirmary walls flickered, populating momentarily with torches, ivy, and the odd rain barrel. Marwazi blinked at the astrolabe his medical monitor had become. "Nurse, please check the nitrous oxide."

"Arcade's malfunctioning," said Webb. "It's emitting textures throughout the ship."

"Ah." That didn't even begin to explain it. "We should shut down the program."

"You know, let's leave him on," she said. "He's been useful a couple times."

"I saved your *life,* my love," said Ablehard.

Marwazi blinked. "Your what?"

Webber flushed. "No need to get into that."

"We are to be married."

"Shut *up.*"

"Yes, of course." Ablehard winked at her. "Your parochial companions may not be ready to accept the reality our relationship. Provincial simpletons."

"I'm reconsidering shutting down the Arcade," Webb told Marwazi. "Did you hear from Eight?"

"From… whom?"

"Never mind. We have to evacuate."

"We…" He gestured to the row of biobeds. "We can't. We have wounded."

"What you have," said Webber, "is maybe two hours. Until Blackwell vents the ship, and sucks you—and everyone in here—out into space."

The room fell silent but for the humming of the barrier.

"He wouldn't do that." Marwazi wished he could believe it. "Mr. Blackwell may be an asshole, but he wouldn't kill his own crew."

"He already has."

Marwazi's throat felt dry. "The mutiny? We heard his broadcast."

"The mutiny wasn't put down," said Webb. "It succeeded. He… Sivos is dead. I don't know how many others, just that…"

"Webb?" Alameda's face had gone tight. "Is Chelse okay? Did you see her?"

She looked at Alameda. "Rob?" Something in her cracked. She seized him in a hard embrace, tears tumbling down her cheeks.

Chapter 16
Mus Uni Non Fidit Antro

Rob slid out of Webb's arms, wiped the grief from his face. "Later. I can't do this now."

Her heart ached for him. "Rob."

"Later. I'll feel it later. She'd tell us we've got living who need us."

Marwazi gently took Webb's hand to scan her wrist. Her heart fluttered at his touch. "Your oxygen levels are almost back to normal." He frowned at his scanner. "Your breathing, however, is a bit rapid."

"Not sure what that's about."

"Your heart rate's also increased."

"I'm fine, Doc." She pulled her hand free. She had less luck pulling her attention away from the pleasing symmetry of his face, or from his scent, that soothing mix of cedar and apple she picked up even through the medicinal tang. She fought down an urge to play with his hair. "Just glad to see you alive. *All* of you," she added. Her eyes went to his hoverchair. "Please tell me that's temporary."

"I can walk with a caudal exoskeleton," said Marwazi. "Just don't ask me to dance or play midfielder."

"Alright." Webb centered herself as her hangover melted away. That stuff was magic. "Here's what's up. We've got maybe two hours before Ierd goes down. I don't know what you've heard, but the xenos have cut the ship in half."

Swank eyed the puddle of molten alien. "Kind of aware, yeah."

"They've also been burrowing around the force fields put up to contain them. They can dig through metal, don't ask me how."

"But you've found a way to fight them?" said Marwazi.

"We have. Ablehard?"

He set down the spraypack. The hale gathered around to examine it. "Those look like agrichem canisters," said a red shirt.

"That's exactly what they are," Webb told her. "They melt xeno like a blowtorch melts candy. And those critters hate it. After I blasted a couple, they stopped coming right at me and they tried ambushing us with bombs."

Ablehard smirked. *"Tried."*

"They're smart." Webb left out how she'd left the warheads out in the open. "Command doesn't know how to fight them, and I can't tell them because the bunking comms are still down. Not that they'd answer if I could."

Marwazi's expression tightened. "The mutiny."

"There was a firefight." She swallowed to loosen her throat. "People died. I don't know much more than that. Other than Blackwell and the Armstrongs are in control of the safe zone. That, and their plans to vent the ship."

Mutters from the crew. "Are there lifeboats?" one of them asked.

"In the officers' lounge," said Webb. "Room for twelve, maybe fifteen if you pack in."

"But that's teep shielded."

"Yeah, so I discovered." She kicked herself again for forgetting. "Wound up taking an unscheduled detour through the meat locker."

"You..." A red shirt gaped. "...*escaped* the meat locker?"

"I mean..." No sense denying it. "Yeah. I did."

"*Nobody* escapes the meat locker."

"It was only because I had a queller, and my first one of these to stand on."

Marwazi raised an eyebrow. "Your *first* one?"

"Yeah." She was getting off topic. "It didn't quite work, and I had to leave it in the oubliette, but it made a pretty good step stool. So here's the plan—"

"How did you get out?" asked another.

"I... Look, we really don't really have time—"

"Did you climb up the ejection shaft?" asked Swank.

282

"Well, yeah," said Webb. "There were xenos in the lift shaft, so there was no other way to go."

"Fifteen decks." Swank turned to the other red shirts. "She climbed up *fifteen decks*. With no handholds. Unarmed."

The red shirts regarded her with awe.

"Okay," said Webb. "Let's get back to evacking."

"And then you built another?" said a red shirt behind her spraypack. "Another weapon?"

"Yeah, I got the harness from Engineering and the canisters from the torpedo bay. So look, we've seriously got maybe an hour—"

"How'd you get there?" A red shirt with a bandage over her head pushed her way forward. "You're Engineering. You didn't have clearance for the torpedo bay."

She let out a long sigh. "I took Denis here. Denis, say hello."

"Please transport me to the repair bay."

"I used his permissions."

The red shirt turned to her fellows, her face radiant. "She killed a cog."

Webb raised her hands. "No, I—"

"She *killed* a fucking *cog!*" A smattering of applause.

"I just took its head," said Webb. "It was in pieces when I got there."

"How'd you know about the lifeboats?" asked a crewman on crutches.

"Oh, I…" Couldn't really not tell them. "I was in the officers' lounge. That's where the boats were."

"She could have taken one." His voice cracked. "She came back for us."

Webb looked to Ablehard. He smiled softly. "They see in you the same qualities that won my heart."

"Alright. Okay. Everyone? I need you to listen." They fell attentively silent. "I can fight them, yes, and I did come back for you. And yes, there are lifeboats in the officer's lounge. So, grab what you need. We're evacking."

"What about the bedridden?" asked Marwazi. "The biobeds have their own power, but they won't fit in an escape pod."

"We're not going to the lounge." Webb was thinking on her feet now. "They might expect that."

"Then where are we bound?"

"The shuttle."

"The shuttles are gone," said Swank.

"Not both of them. The one we rode back up from the planet is caught in orbit around the ship," said Webb. "It's hollowed out—we had to make some drastic alterations to get people off the surface—"

"The first time she saved us," said Swank. "Thanks again, by the way."

"You're welcome. The shuttle's hollowed out, but it's solid. We only have to worry about it buckling if it hits atmo. There's room for all of us and the biobeds as well."

Marwazi snapped his fingers. "And it has a teleporter."

"Exactly." She gave Marwazi the Armstrong pin, closed his hands over it. "I'll send a ping to this once I'm in the shuttle. That'll be your signal to drop your security field so I can teep you out."

He nodded. Smiled. Nodded again. "May I have my hand back?"

"Of course." She let go.

"And what if the xenos return?"

She slapped the canisters on the gravjack. "I'm leaving these with you. I've got a few shots left in my pack."

"That's very generous," said Marwazi. "But how are we supposed to weaponize these?"

"Come on, Doc." She grinned. "You've got the one thing that hurts them and an infirmary full of pissed off engineers. I'm sure you'll come up with something."

Swank and the other red shirts had already pulled the canisters off the gravjack.

"That just leaves one issue that I see," said the doctor. "How are you going to reach this shuttle? The teleporters are offline."

"Only one way to get there," said Webb. "I'm gonna have to space-walk. Mind if I take the emergency EV suit?"

"Please. Don't forget the magboots."

"If I did, I'd die." She pried open the EV locker.

"You'll have to drift to the shuttle," said One-Eye. "You'll need a maneuvering pack for that."

"My next stop's the cargo bay. They've got them in droves." It would also be where she could depressurize an area of the ship and drift out with the least chance of clipping herself on a bulkhead.

Marwazi nodded along as she spoke. "Your plan sounds solid."

She half-smiled. "I just hope it works." By the time she'd put on the EV suit, the red shirts had already stripped the power cell to the gravjack to boost their security field.

"Hey, Doc, check this out." Swank held up an electrostatic aerosol sprayer. "We can modify your decon sprayers for agrichems. They won't hold much, but we've got a bunch of them. And if the chems are as potent as we saw, these should hold them back. With your permission."

"You have blanket permission to use what you need," said Marwazi.

"Thanks." Swank turned to Webb. "Could I take that torch off you?"

"One sec. Avert your eyes, folks." Webb shielded her eyes with the goggles and cut Denis' spine out of the spraypack frame.

Ablehard set a meaty hand on Marwazi's shoulder. "Physician. I would beg a favor of you."

Marwazi looked up, alarmed. "Yes?"

"Be good to her." There was a bittersweet look in his eyes. "It was a mad dream, I suppose. But for a moment—a long, wonderful moment I shall forever cherish—I forgot we were were not of the same station."

Marwazi nodded slowly. "I... don't understand."

Ablehard flicked his eyes her way. "I see how she looks at you."

Marwazi looked to Webb, his brow wrinkled. Then something clicked. His eyes went wide.

Webb flushed. "Okay!" She shoved the torch and welding goggles towards Swank. "Ablehard, let's go." She pulled the spraypack back on, relishing how her lungs didn't complain or seize up. She cast a final glance back at the doctor, who was regarding her thoughtfully. "Good luck, everyone."

"Good luck, Webb," said the doctor, his voice composed of warmth and honey.

"Thank you." She pulled on the EV helmet to hide her smile. "Haroun."

❡

The trek to the cargo bay was oddly quiet. There were sparks here and there, flickering textures as walls morphed into masonry and back. Strange what one could get used to.

Webb's sensory input was limited in the EV suit, but she could still hear a distinct lack of chittering. Maybe they'd decided she wasn't important enough to attack. Or maybe they'd decided it wasn't worth ambushing her again. The spraypack certainly felt lighter without Denis' head weighing it down. Nice of Ablehard to carry it. "It's not much further," she told him.

He nodded noncommittally.

"You're quieter than usual."

He smiled tightly, his chin to his chest. "How long have you been in love with the doctor?"

Her face burned. "I'm *not*."

"My dear lady." That sad smile again. "If there is one thing I know, it's how a lover behaves in the presence of their beloved."

"This is hardly the time to discuss this."

"That's not a denial."

She flushed again. "Doesn't matter. He's not interested in me."

"Ah." A wounded sigh. "So it *is* true. You've changed, dear Mary."

"I have. I'm sorry I'm not the Mary you remember. She was a good woman." She took his hand. The hand of an Arcade sprite. Somehow, it didn't feel ridiculous. "I never meant to lead you on or give you a false impression."

His expression hardened. Would he storm away? Did his program include the possibility of leaving her? Pixels and light he may have been, but she'd gotten used to him, had come to rely on him. Strange indeed what one could get used to.

His face softened. "You have nothing to apologize for, my lo—" He caught himself. "My *lady*. We cannot chose whom we love, only whose love to accept. Or whom we deem worthy of it."

That actually stung. Stupid program had a way of getting under her skin. Or maybe her oxygen levels were still low.

They reached the door to the cargo bay without further incident or conversation. Its door stood intact. No holes had been hacked through its walls. Seemed promising. "Denis, open the cargo bay door."

"Independence, open the door to the cargo bay." It whisked open.

Webb sucked in a breath and put her hand to her faceplate. Ablehard actually crossed himself.

The bay looked like a bombed refugee camp. Bodies and parts of bodies lay scattered like crudely reaped wheat. The partitions between the bays were up, linking them into an open space hundreds meters long. Pits and burrows pockmarked the floor where the xenos had tunneled up.

"Oh, *God.*" The Unassigned. The quadless crew waiting for an open berth. She felt sick.

But that had been the point of stashing them here, hadn't it? To keep them out of sight, out of mind? Anyone who'd been upgraded from the pool of expendable crew didn't want any reminders about how expendable they were.

Numb, bile burning the back of her throat, Webb picked her way through the carnage. Her helmet kept out the smell, but it magnified the thundering of her heart. She wished she had Frankie's calm, even for a moment.

Focus, Frankie would have told her. No thinking. Just stay on task.

With the partitions raised, Webb would need to open all six bay doors at once to avoid getting slammed by whirling debris. Which would space the remains of all the poor Unassigned.

Can't be helped, Frankie would have said. Put it out of mind. Focus on what you can affect.

The burrows were arranged in clusters in the floor, all where the deck plating was thinnest. She hugged the back wall of the bay so she could keep them in view. Equipment and control consoles lay smashed and scattered throughout the cargo bays. She fought down a surge of panic. If she couldn't get the bay doors open...

The master control console lay in the main bay, just a bit over, behind a giant hedge. She had to remind herself there was no hedge, just the Arcade being stupid. She tightened her grip on her spray wand. "Ablehard. Keep an eye out for wolves."

She touched the hedge. It flickered and vanished, revealing a mass of Unassigned huddled within a force field pen.

They gaped at her. A few dozen of them, red shirts all, hunkered down within a shimmering force field box around the main control console.

From the other side of the pen rose a knot of xenos.

"Wolves," warned Ablehard.

They leapt for her. Webb fired, blasting the closest to sputtering pieces. The others squealed and fled towards the nearest pit. Webb adjusted the spray nozzle for distance and fired, knifing them in half before they reached the burrow.

"Have at thee!" Ablehard's sword clanged on a carapace, swatting a xeno she hadn't seen out of the air. He seized the xeno in a bear hug.

Webb waved the wand like a firehose, bathing Ablehard. The xeno melted, shrieking in his arms.

Barely seconds had passed. Webb wiped the chems off her faceplate, her heart beating like a rabbit's.

The red shirts in the pen were staring in slack-jawed shock. "You... you *killed* them," said one, her face streaked with blood and grease.

"Yeah." A cascade of thoughts raced through her mind. They must have created the force field pen to protect themselves. No, not force fields. Their spectrum was wrong. "Are those... tractor beams?"

The one who'd spoken nodded. "We fed them through the emitters here. They were destroying the consoles."

"Ingenious. Does it go through the floor?"

She nodded rapidly.

"Good thinking." She hadn't counted on the Unassigned, or their inventive defense. But now she couldn't depressurize the bay without sucking them out into space.

Webb did some quick mental math. There wouldn't be room for the Unassigned and the folks in the Infirmary in the shuttle. Not with the biobeds. The remaining Unassigned didn't appear to be injured. Which was its own miracle all on its own.

"Okay." Webb turned to the red shirt who'd spoken. "What's your name?"

"Sedlak."

"Sedlak, hi. I'm Webb. It's not safe for—"

"The crew advocate?"

"Yeah. Hi. Now—"

"And who...?" she glanced up at Ablehard.

"He's a figment of our imagination." She adjusted her spray wand back to wide dispersal. "Where are the navpacks?"

Sedlak pointed to a rack of them. The navpacks were intact.

Webb sighed with relief. "I have to go. Just... stay safe."

"Is anyone coming for us?"

"I..." Webb felt helpless. She couldn't just leave them. The solution hit her. "Engineering."

"What?"

"You need to get to Engineering. Blackwell will be sending a team there."

Sedlak brightened. "They'll protect us?"

"Actually, you'll have to protect them. You'll all teep out when their work is done. That's the only way you get out before he vents the ship."

The Unassigned looked lost. And frightened.

Webb chanced a look towards the adjacent agricultural bay, where she spotted a few agrichem canisters stacked next to racks of agripods.

"Okay. Look at this." She turned so they could see her spraypack. "See the pack? The housing and tanks? It's just an extinguisher rig with agrichem canisters and a fabbed connector."

"If we drop the beams, they'll slaughter us," said Sedlak.

Webb brushed the edge of the force field pen. It threw her hand back like a gale force wind. "The cage is smart. *Really* smart. I never would have thought of this."

"We can't leave it."

"No. But you can *move* it. Reroute the tractor emitter controls to a pad. You've got one, yeah?"

"We do."

"Good. Here's what you're gonna do. You're gonna walk your cage, plane by plane, over to where you need to go. Or grab what you need with another beam and tractor it over."

The penned in red shirts perked up.

"It's not an exact fit," Webb told them. "You'll have to fab a connector—the cargo teleporter should work—to get the canisters to work with the spray wand, but it's not hard. All the tools you need are in the mechanical bay."

"Please transport me to the repair bay."

"Shut up, Denis. Just keep that pen over you and turtle your way where you need to go. Can you do that?"

Sedlak's face hardened. "Absolutely."

"Damn right." Webb flashed a toothy grin. "You guys ready to start playing offense?"

Resolute nods.

Frankie was alone in the brig. They hadn't even left a guard. Not that they had much reason to; she hadn't exactly put up a fight. Which hadn't prevented them from leaving her face covered in bruises.

She tried ignoring the pain, but that sent her thoughts towards the darker reasons she might have been left alone. Were they off executing more red shirts? Every pop and strain made her wonder if she was hearing rifle discharges or just the intermittent sounds of the ship.

They might still need her for something. To run the teleporter, maybe. Or for a court martial. Someone to point the finger at when the dust had settled and the rescue ships arrived.

She tried to put it out of her mind, tried not to think of Chelse and the other soldiers trapped on the far side of the blast door, of the screams and rips and thuds that came echoing through. She tried not to think of Webb, lost and alone, alive, she hoped, somewhere down in the ship's infested guts.

Frankie pulled her legs beneath her on the grated floor of her cell, let her focus fall to her breathing, one of the few things she could control. Retreat into the self, ignore the chattering of monkey mind. Which, to be fair, was chattering with more than its usual anxiety.

Random thoughts could not be avoided. "Try not to think of a pink elephant," her Zen teacher had told her, before whacking her with his ever present stick to snap her back to the present. Avoiding thoughts wasn't the point. Letting them pass was, watching as they drifted by on the currents of the mind. The key, which had taken her far too many whaps with a stick to realize, was staying on the riverbank the thoughts drifted by, not getting drawn into the current.

Breath in, breathe out. Her thoughts passed by. Random, chaotic, but separate. A separation of thought from thinker, of mind from moment.

She settled into the calm, into the fathomless deep. Her eyes felt both heavy and active, and she could hear her blood pumping in her temples, the gentle rocking of her torso as her pulse slowed. Time fell away, and she was—

—*burning, screaming as the deathcloud pitted her beautiful limbs and her body's gasses vaporized within her*—

—*a burning star streaking through the heavens, bursting into a blossom of choking death*—

—*the image, relayed through a thousand resonance chambers and carrying the cumulative panic of every drone who'd passed it along, warning every hive and sect*—

—*fleeing now, screaming, following the elders' mindmap in a mad dash to the burrows as clumps of alien plants burst from the burning surface*—

—*until the ground gave way and she was falling, falling*—

—onto the grated floor of her cell.

With gasping hacks, Frankie stared at the soft, brown limbs she took a moment to realize were hers. It was like waking from a nightmare, but one that left a lingering pain in her head, a migraine throbbing at the base of her skull.

"Let me out." She scrambled up, pounded on the force field of her cell, despite the burns it left on her hands, despite there being no guard to hear. "Let me *out!* I know why they hate us!"

Chapter 17
Lapsus Memoriae

Webb hadn't been to a NEOS since Chevalier's wake. She set her hand to her chest, felt Chevalier's badge beneath the EV suit. She wasn't sure what had flipped the switch in her mind, when she'd started thinking of her latest late roommate by her real name rather than a number.

Her heart clenched. Her *second* latest late roommate. It was just her, Frankie, and Eight now. God damn, she needed to learn that woman's name.

The NEOS had been a tight fit before a ripplingly muscular man with a pair of tanks on his back had tried squeezing in. Ablehard made no complaint. He was too busy staring at the infinite field of stars, his face a mask of wondrous delight. She wondered if he'd been programmed to recognize beauty, and to emote appropriately in response. If he had, it made him pretty endearing.

Which made the next part all the harder. "You're not going to be able to come with me, you know."

"I trust that you will come back to me." He seemed so sincere. "I've seen how you care for your people."

"Ablehard, they're not…"

He raised a hand. "They *are*. I saw how they looked to you. The mechanic in the hospital. The doctor's apprentice whom you comforted in his time of loss. The doctor himself. What they see in you is what men of my station wished they saw in us: a leader, one whom they trust, one who would never ask anything of them that they could not accomplish, nor anything she would not attempt herself."

He looked back to the stars. His brow wrinkled for a moment. "I must admit, when you first returned to my manor, I didn't give a tinker's piss about the state of the village."

She twisted and pulled at her suit. "We don't have time for this."

But they did. The drifting shuttle hadn't come into view yet.

"Their sovereign I may be, but it was not until I saw your example that I understood what is truly required of leadership."

"You're gonna make me vomit. Have you ever puked in an EV suit? It's awful. Like wearing a latrine."

"I only speak the truth." His eyes burned. "When first you returned, I could not drive thoughts of taking you to bed from my mind, and that shames me so."

"I mean…" She had to shrug. "It *was* what you were designed for."

"But now," he continued, "after witnessing firsthand the suffering of the common folk, and the damage those foul xenos have done…"

"You mean the wolves?"

His smile was self-effacing. "Only I called them that. It seems the villagers have been fighting them for some time. The villagers—my subjects, my *people*—I ignored their plight, sulking away in my tower, wrapped in a blanket of self-indulgent melancholy. If I am to be worthy of the role with which God Himself has tasked me, I must embrace its duties. Not just its benefits." He stared at her, unblinking. "You've shown me that, my lady."

"Well." Perhaps the finest compliment she'd received, and from a man who didn't even exist. "I don't quite know what to say to that."

He didn't turn his eyes away.

"You know I can't be with you, right?"

His smile was bittersweet. "To take you away from all this would be to steal you from where you are needed—in this odd village of wrought steel and glass." He took a deep breath. "Mary Chevalier, I release you from your promise."

"My…?" The marriage proposal. The one she'd accepted when she was pretending to be Chevalier. "Thank you."

A curt nod.

"Are you alright?"

"I will be. In time. And, in case it is unclear, my love for you is in no way diminished. Neither is your ability to call on me in time of need."

She chuckled. "Pretty sure I'm the first person to outright fail a romance program."

"There is no failure in love," said Ablehard. "The wise heed the lessons of Eros, even his most painful teachings."

"For what it's worth, you're a better man than any I've dated."

Something in the stars caught Ablehard's eye. "There it is."

The shuttle came into view over the curvature of the ship, spinning like a caffeinated toddler.

"Lerd." That complicated things. "It must've clipped the ship."

"It shall only make your triumph more glorious." Ablehard bowed, no mean feat in cramped quarters. "Godspeed, Miss Chevalier."

"And to you, Lord Mountworthy."

He touched his brow, the spray wand held in the crook of his arm like a hunting shotgun. Webb took hold of Denis' spine and opened the airlock. The air escaped in an inaudible whoosh.

Ablehard was unaffected. His programmers had given him photorealistic hair and skin texture, but here he was not asphyxiating in a vacuum. Probably would have broken the mood if the love interest suddenly froze and barfed out his organs.

Webb pulled herself out into space. A couple jets from the navpack sent her towards the shuttle, which jumped in size from a toy car to a room in a matter of seconds.

Another jet stopped her momentum. She adjusted her trajectory to match the shuttle's spin. The shuttle slowed, but now the ship and planet were racing circles around her. Her stomach did a somersault.

The shuttle's rear hatch dangled open. Webb navigated towards it. She realized distantly that if she hit its edge, even at this slowed speed, it could cut her in half. Zero gravity fun. She'd never cared for it.

She held down the accelerator, making fine adjustments until she matched the shuttle's spin and it seemed to stop, and the planet and ship had become a blurry whirring ring above. With a final boost from her pack, she glided into the shuttle, holding Denis' head out before her like the lure of an anglerfish.

Webb sealed the hatch behind her. She climbed the floor like a ladder towards the controls, and pulled herself into the pilot's seat.

A few flipped switches started the boot up sequence. The shuttle powered up. The comforting tug of gravity pulled her into the seat.

Through the chair, she felt a heavy thump behind her. Something had been floating loose in the shuttle, likely pinned to a bulkhead by centripetal force. She twisted around to see a xeno—a burnt one—sprawled on the grating behind her.

For a moment of blind panic, Webb couldn't move. She was alone, unarmed, her spraypack with Ablehard half a K away.

The xeno didn't move. And then it did, just barely, its head lolling on the floor. It made no sounds.

Webb prodded the rational part of her brain out of the corner. This xeno was badly burnt, like the one that had dropped the bombs on her. But the pattern of cracks in its armor was different from the one on the ship. This one's were worse, the fissures in its armor deeper, with wispy gasses leaking from its cracks.

It raised its wedge-shaped head, fixated on her with bleached eyes. The back of her skull throbbed.

A crack like a bough breaking. The xeno collapsed like a punctured bellows. Gasses gusted from its cracks as it eyes glazed over. Webb's headache abruptly lifted.

The shuttle's computer chimed. "Repressurization complete. Atmosphere restored. Gravity at one G. Heat at habitable levels."

Webb pulled off her helmet, slipped out of the chair to kneel by the dead xeno. Up close, unmoving, it seemed less like a creature from nightmare and more like an imploded mantis sculpture. Curious, certainly, but not inherently terrifying. Part of her felt sorry for it.

It took effort to pull her attention off the xeno long enough to fire up the shuttle's teleporter. She sent a ping from its comm and hoped it reached the Infirmary. She had no idea what the range of those Armstrong pins was.

Her comm pinged. They'd heard it. She fired the attitude jets to stop the shuttle's spin and trained the teleporter on the Infirmary, locked onto the first batch of biosigns—they'd dropped their security field—and energized.

The air behind her shimmered, coalescing into a cluster of nurses and wounded in biobeds. Their sighs flowed into screams.

"Sorry." She wished she could have warned them about the xeno. "It's dead. It can't hurt you. I think. Anyway, clear some space. We've got more incoming."

Three minutes and several startled shrieks later, the shuttle was packed shoulder to shoulder with wounded survivors. Marwazi, dangling between Rob and Swank, was the last to materialize.

Swank fiddled with something at the back of the doctor's waist-down exoskeleton. "There you go, Doc."

Marwazi thanked him, took a few gangly steps through the crowd towards the front of the shuttle, and collapsed in the co-pilot's chair. "You did it." He rubbed his leg braces. "You got us out. We can never thank you enough."

"No problem. Well, I mean, *some* problems." She jerked her thumb at the xeno. "Stowaway. Nearly crapped my suit."

"This is not the repair bay," observed Denis.

"Should we contact the bridge?"

Webb shook her head. "I wouldn't. Not yet. We don't know what the situation is there. Though, technically, that's your call."

He seemed lost. "Mine?"

"Your rank is commander, if I'm not mistaken."

"Oh, yes." He stroked his beard. "It's just that it's been so long since I've been called anything other than 'Doctor.' I defer to your expertise."

"Works for me." Webb looked back at the passengers, at their sighs of relief, their mutters and hugs. Numb faces, lost looks, more than a few jitters as the adrenaline started to drain. She spotted Rob weeping in a corner, his head in his hands. Safe enough now to grieve. "This isn't a long-term solution, you know."

He nodded. "I can't treat anyone here if someone takes a turn for the worse." He leaned in, lowered his voice. "How long until we run short of air?"

She checked the gauges. "With the scrubbers running full tilt, assuming nothing breaks down? Maybe a week. The bigger issue's food and water. We tossed the emergency rations back on the planet to lighten the load. Which reminds me." She twisted in her chair. "Hey, shuttle boy. How's she flying?"

"Thrusters are fucked," said Swank. "Xenos chewed 'em up when they rode up from the surface. We're adrift."

"Then how did the dead one get inside?" asked Marwazi.

"Burrowed up through the floor," said Swank. "The thruster chamber auto-sealed behind it, or we'd all be suffocating right now."

Marwazi slipped through the red shirts to kneel by the xeno. "It's cracked."

"I saw gasses escaping its wounds," said Webb. "There's another burnt one like that on the ship. I think it's their leader. It was doing fine."

"Look here." Marwazi pointed to patches on the xeno's metallic armor where the silvery chrome had faded. "It's browning."

"Like the giant we saw in the chamber."

"It looks almost like rust." He went over the xeno with his medical scanner. "Still nothing showing up here."

Something else from the planet prodded her memory. "Hey, can I borrow that? Before the lerd hit the core, I'd rigged up a scanner that could tell when the cogs were talking to each other."

Marwazi raised an eyebrow. "For what purpose?"

"To find out when they were spying on us, of course. Made it easier to move contraband."

"I'm sorry I asked."

"But the thing is, down on the planet? The modded scanner lit up like a holiday tree. It said the ruins were absolutely crawling with cogs."

"Please transport me to the repair bay."

"Shut up, Denis."

"It picked up the xenos?" Marwazi handed her his scanner.

"Them, or their means of communication. It only picked up cogs when they were talking to each other." Webb rewired the scanner's connectors. "Not sure what it was picking up. Unless the xenos are sending biological radio signals."

"That still wouldn't explain why our scanners are useless."

"Because they scan for carbon." Rob was hunched over the xeno with his scanner. "The armor isn't just plating over tissue. All its cells are silicon."

A hush fell over the survivors.

A chill ran down Webb's spine. "I thought complex silicon-based life was impossible. Isn't that impossible?"

"In the entire galaxy, we've never discovered anything more complex than a silicon-based virus or slime mold," said Marwazi. "Nothing remotely this advanced."

"I'm looking at its cellular structure," said Rob, "and I'm seeing silicon bonded to silicon. Here, see for yourself."

Marwazi peered at the scanner, let out a low whistle.

"But... the biological limitations." Webb's mind reeled. "The sheer physical *engineering* of it. Silicon-silicon bonds weaken when immersed in liquid."

"Unlike carbon" said Marwazi. "A massive hurdle towards complexity in silicon-based life. But this certainly was an arid planet."

"But silicon oxidizes to a *solid.*" The engineer in her brain wouldn't shut up. "You couldn't have *blood,* you couldn't have *lymph.* Or digestive acids, cerebrospinal fluid."

"Bodies aren't machines," said the doctor.

"But how would you expel *waste?* Look at those limbs! You're telling me something with that many joints has no synovial fluid?"

Marwazi could only marvel. "Life finds a way."

"Not life as we know it," said Rob.

"Exactly." Marwazi stroked his beard again. "You saw gasses, you said? Right before it died? Perhaps those carry out its bodily functions."

"What, you're saying it has a *pneumatic* circulatory system? It has *aerosols* for blood?"

"Oh, that's very insightful, thank you." He turned back to Rob's scanner. "Hmm. The creature still isn't showing up."

"No, it's masked with the metals in the shuttle," said Rob. He looked up at Webb. He was pale as parchment. "What about Webb's solution?"

"Rob? Are you okay?"

"No. God, no," said Rob. "But it helps to think of something else. If you can pick up when they're talking, that's a start."

"Just about done here." She finished her modifications, restarted the scanner, and set it to scan the dead xeno. Nothing registered on its monitor. "Still not picking it up."

"They probably talk less when they're dead," said Swank.

"Point." She expanded the scanner's range until the *Independence* came into view. The scanner's monitor and lit up with hundreds of pings.

"Whoa. There we go. There are *hundreds* of them in the ship."

"Um." Rob had gone even paler. He was staring out the shuttle's viewscreen. "Not *in* the ship."

Webb's stomach tightened. She wove back through the crowd to peer out at the ship, at the beads of light bouncing off it.

What she'd dismissed as a trick of the light had been light reflecting not off the ship, but off the xenos. A swarm of them, picking their way up the hull as surely as ice climbers, chipping away at the ship's hull plating.

"You said…" Rob swallowed. "I thought spacing killed them."

"So did I." Webb glanced at the dead one. "But that one was still alive when I got here."

"This specimen was damaged," said Marwazi. "Burnt. Those ones don't appear hurt. We must conclude that they *can* exist in a vacuum. In their own organic EV suits."

"They're making for the safe zone." Webb's throat had gone dry. "They're heading for the bridge."

"We have to warn them."

"Right." Webb dialed up the comms. "You should make the call, Doc. They'll listen to you."

Marwazi hit the comm. "Dr. Marwazi to the bridge. Bridge, do you copy?"

"Use your rank," said Webb.

"This is Commander Marwazi, calling the bridge. Bridge, please reply."

No response. "Try the Armstrong pin."

Marwazi tapped it. It emitted a negative chime. "It's been taken offline."

The shuttle's comm beeped. "Hang on," said Webb. "We're picking up a transmission."

"From the ship?"

"No." Webb had to double check the source. "From the planet. On an encrypted frequency. I only noticed it 'cause I was searching for frequencies that might not be down."

"More survivors?" said Marwazi. "Why use an encrypted frequency? You'd want to broadcast as wide a signal as possible."

"Unscrambling now." Webb untied the encryption and patched it through.

A Coalition captain appeared on the viewscreen popped up, his face barely visible through a mask of bandages. "*—native to systems throughout this sector. Our terraforming agrichems are lethal to them, and to their food chain.*"

The red shirts pressed forward to watch.

"Encrypted in this carrier wave, you will find zettabytes of data containing proof that Coalition Command knew of the effects of our activities on the natives, and tried to cover up the evidence," the captain rasped. *"This included direct orders, to me, to scour the planet once we had discovered the silicant presence there."*

"They knew?" Rob darkened. "They knew, and they sent us anyway?"

"My orders came directly from the highest levels of the Admiralty and civilian leadership. We have caused incalculable damage to this species' population, their infrastructure and culture, and we have turned a blind eye to their plight rather than let it slow our production. May history forgive us."

Webb engaged the comms. "Captain, we read you. Can you hear us?"

The captain's image flickered. *"This is Captain J.G. Fontana of the Coalition starship* Flagstaff. *We have crashed on planet Acheron 117. If you receive this transmission, take it to a SolNet outlet you trust, and to representatives of the Galactic Union. Do* not *alert Coalition Command."*

"It's a recording." Webb sank back in the chair. "On loop."

"For the last forty years, Coalition Command has been knowingly committing genocide against a sentient insectoid species native to systems throughout this sector," said Fontana. *"Our terraforming agrichems are lethal to them, and to their food chain."*

Marwazi switched him off. "Well. No wonder they're slaughtering us."

Webb looked out at the swarm chipping away at the hull. "We have to get word to the bridge. Try the Armstrong pin."

He did. No response.

"They may have taken it offline after you used it," said Swank.

"With the comms down, what should we do?" said the doctor. "Fly in front of them and wave?"

"We can't maneuver," Swank reminded them.

"We have a working teleporter."

"And they've got a bunch of scared, armed Armstrongs just looking for something to shoot," said Webb. "Anyone who pops in is likely to get shot."

"There must be somewhere safe we could materialize."

Webb gazed into the gulf between the shuttle and ship. "Not *on* it. Teleport me out there."

Every head turned her way. Marwazi looked aghast.

"I've got an EV suit and a navpack." She picked up her helmet. "I'll jet to a hatch in the safe zone and let myself in. And then let them arrest me, I guess."

"What if the xenos see you?"

She shook her head, then pulled the helmet on and picked up Denis. "If they take the ship, we're done. They'll carve up the crew like a Conquest Day turkey, and we might die of thirst before help arrives. If I can get word into the ship, we've at least got a chance."

Marwazi nodded, his jaw tense. "We'll stay on the comms. Keep us updated as you safely can."

Rob squeezed her shoulder. "Take care of yourself."

"I'll come back for you." She meant it for the whole crew, but she said it to the doctor.

He blushed. "I hope you do."

She slid her visor down, checked to make sure the navpack was secure. She wished she hadn't left her spraypack with Ablehard. Not that she could have worn two packs at the same time. Well, she'd already rebuilt it once…

She nodded to Marwazi at the teleporter controls. "Energize."

The shuttle faded away, and she was floating in starlight.

✏

Frankie paced in the brig, her eyes ground shut. There was no returning to the becalmed state of meditation, not after that torrent of nightmare imagery. She'd tried, but her focus kept flowing away from that spot on her mental shore, as if the river of her thoughts had been rerouted to a location outside the ship.

Why, she couldn't say. There was nothing she could sense there, nothing tangible. Just empty space. But there was an energy there, a presence, some piece of potential waiting to be realized, waiting to *be*.

So she focused on it, on that maddeningly familiar buzz that was both present and not, concentrated yet dispersed, invisible, intangible, but undeniably there.

A gust of cool air washed over her. She realized after a moment that she could no longer hear the hum of her cell's force field.

So they'd come for her. Because they needed her, or to chuck her out an airlock? She centered herself and opened her eyes.

Neither Armstrong nor soldier stood at the security console, but Yolanda Eight, unarmed and grimy, her eyes darting to the door and back.

Frankie blinked. "Eight?"

Her quaddie shushed her. "We have to go."

"Did we retake the ship?"

"No. We're hiding in the crawlspaces."

That would explain the filth. The crawlspaces were cramped and claustrophobic burrows even smaller than the maintenance tubes, dark tiny tunnels full of dangling wires and knotted cables. The backside of the embroidered tapestry that made up the ship's machinery. "Why?"

"The Armstrongs never pull duty there," said Eight. "They don't know where to look for us."

"There's an us?"

"Just a handful. Enough to make them think the missing folks were casualties, not enough to be suspicious. But the rest of the red shirts are with us."

"You're disobeying orders."

"Damn right." The security console beeped. "And there's the static." She hiccuped. "Let's go."

Eight poked her head into the corridor, waved for Frankie to follow. She followed Eight down the hall to where a panel of deck plating had been pried out of place.

"We're gonna get out who we can." Eight wriggled into a shaft under the plating. "Teep them into the safe zone."

Frankie froze. *Teep. Teleport.* It hit her like dawn over the horizon. "It was a teleporter signal."

Eight looked up. "What?"

"That's what I saw. The energy outside the ship, the unrealized potential."

Eight looked baffled.

Frankie turned and ran for the nearest maintenance hatch.

The sheer enormity of a starship unsettled Webb as she neared it, like seeing the towers of a city from a distance and then abruptly landing in a random street downtown. Up close, the ship wasn't smooth, not the way it appeared at a distance. Emitters and hatches, antenna arrays, NEOS sprouted everywhere, seemingly at random among the pits and gashes left by micrometeors.

The aliens—silicants, Fontana had called them—were hacking away at the hull at one of its thickest stretches: a heat shield rated to brush the corona of a star while protecting the systems within from radiation and heat. The xenos were still managing to bore through it. Not as swiftly as through the interior walls, but still, that something organic could burrow through the ship's hull... was organic even the right term?

The xenos didn't seem to notice as she passed overhead. They had clustered on the ship's neck, beyond where the Nexus shield formed its choke point. The hull's plating was no thinner there, but it offered a more continuous flat surface than the sloping curves of the bridge.

Webb jetted over and around the xenos towards her destination: the ruined torpedo bay. She slowed her momentum to enter the wreckage, gingerly floating past twisted struts and ruptured deck plating. She checked the cogfinder attached to her navpack. No xenos present. At least none that were chatting.

She clicked on her magboots, alighted on what remained of the floor: a single deck plate that bent away from the section's entrance. She followed its evacuation arrows towards the door, where tons of debris lay pinned against the doorway, held in place by the emergency force field that had sprung up when the section depressurized.

Webb adjusted her visor's settings. Beyond the force field, she picked up discolorations in the metal of the door. Fresh welds, sealing it shut. No getting in that way.

She checked the navpack's fuel. An eighth of a tank—not enough to get back to the shuttle. She must have burned too much matching the shuttle's spin.

That left one option. She clicked off the boots and jetted out of the wreckage towards the nearest NEOS. She unlocked its exterior airlock, slipped in, and locked it behind her. Gravity settled her in its seat as the NEOS repressurized.

Webb shrugged off the navpack and peeled off her EV suit. They'd only slow her down. She peered out the window set into the NEOS door.

Beyond lay a corridor of officers' quarters. Nowhere else on the ship were the doors so far apart.

She heard the echo of boots, ducked out of sight, and held up the EV helmet to catch a reflection of the corridor in its visor. A pair of crew were marching down the hall. Soldiers? Hard to tell via reflection, but they were certainly armed. As they came closer, she saw their skull masks.

Webb pulled the helmet down until the sound of boots had faded. She steeled herself and slipped into the hall.

She hadn't taken three steps before she heard more boots, saw shadows appear on the wall ahead. She ducked into the nearest doorframe. "Denis, open this door."

"Independence, open crew quarters door 214."

Webb darted inside, mashed the door controls to shut it behind her. She put her ear to door and didn't breathe until the boots had receded.

Webb waited until her heart had stopped thundering to take in her surroundings. The quarters had multiple rooms and a private bath. Each section was the size of three or four quads. This one was spacious even with the bulky but familiar devices in the corners of its bedroom.

Holo-emitters. That's where she'd seen them before. Above the bed, partially blocked by the emitters, was a view of the ruined torpedo bay. A view that had probably been a lot better before the bay got slagged.

She checked the room's control console. Its comms were hard-wired to the bridge. Even with shipwide comms down, she could get a message through. "Denis, lock the door."

It took her a moment to find the secure comm settings on the officer's console. The channel was locked, of course. "Denis, bypass this security code."

The controls unlocked, but it wasn't comm access that came up—it was a teleporter signature. A signature stored in the room's computer, but fed through its holo-emitters.

Eight caught up to Frankie in the maintenance tubes beneath the bridge's emergency teleporter. "This isn't safe," she hissed.

"Do tell."

"If they do an internal scan, we're bunked."

"I was being sarcastic. I clearly need more practice." Frankie disconnected cables from the conduit above her. "This will only take a second."

"We shouldn't be out in the open."

"The maintenance tubes are hardly 'the open.'"

"They're more open than the crawlspaces. Blackwell is directly above us."

"No need to exaggerate. He's at least three or four meters away."

Eight hiccuped.

"There." Frankie finished inverting the bridge teleporter's refraction disc. "Datapad?"

Eight passed it forward. "You still haven't told me why this is so important."

Frankie connected cables she'd pulled out of the conduit to the pad. "It'll make much more sense if she tells you herself."

Hic. "Who?"

Frankie shushed her, patched the teleporter's controls into the data pad. She searched for the teleporter ghost she'd spotted at the station on the bridge.

She found it outside the ship, at the very spot where her attention had kept drifting. An odd spike of serotonin hit the back of her skull, almost the opposite of a migraine. She hit energize.

The air distorted in the tube between them, coalescing into a humanoid figure. Her feathers frilled in an anxiety display.

"Holy lerd," said Eight.

"I'm lying down," said the Sorl ambassador. "Why am I lying down?"

"We're in a maintenance tube beneath the bridge," said Frankie.

"I see. Are we safe?"

"Absolutely not."

"I didn't think so."

Eight looked like her brain had broken. "How did... how could you... *what?*" She hiccuped.

The Sorl lowered her frill. "The elder put us in touch," said the Sorl.

"The... *what?*" *Hic.*

"Come on," said Frankie. "People are waiting for us."

Ø

Webb ran her hands through her hair. She needed comms, not a tele-porter fingerprint. Of all the officers, she had to pick one who'd hacked his system for pervy holo-shit. She saw no other reason the teep sig would be in an off-grid pattern.

Another thought occurred. Whoever lived here might have panicked and teeped himself into a holding when the ship was overrun. Not the worst idea. Xenos couldn't chop you into calamari if you're an energy pat-tern in a buffer. That wouldn't explain why he would have hidden himself behind a security protocol.

Dude was lucky she'd found him. Might be lucky for her, too—if she teeped him back into existence, maybe he'd hear her out before trying to arrest her. Anything to get the message through.

That still didn't explain the holo-emitters, but whatever. It got lonely in space. She rematerialized the signature.

The figure that rematerialized at the foot of the bed was no officer, but a woman kneeling in a dressing gown.

"How long has it been?" She rose shakily. When she saw Webb, her eyes shot open. She staggered back into the bed. "Who are you? And how... why... do I *know* you?"

Webb could hardly hear her over the thundering of her pulse. She had to open and close her mouth a few times before the words would come. "Yolanda?"

Chapter 18
Gladiator in Arena Consilium Capit

Webb blinked, as if that might reset her brain so she could dismiss who she couldn't possibly be seeing. Yolanda Prime, the original, the start of a long, sad chain of lost quaddies.

But she couldn't be. She was dead. She was staring at a hologram, like Ablehard, no more than pixels and light.

But she'd recognized Webb's face. And, based on the furrow in her brow, her own name.

"Yolanda." She rolled it around on her tongue. "That's familiar."

"It's your name." Webb couldn't keep the quiver out of her voice.

"My name is Sunshine."

"Your name," Webb told her, "is Senior Technician Hayashi Yolanda. I'm Webb. Joni Webber. We were quaddies. Do you remember?"

A blank stare. "Quaddies?"

"Quad*mates*. We shared a room half this size of this one. You, me, Frankie, and Chelse. Do you remember them? Baldy and the jarhead? Or Chelse's beau, Rob? You were right, she married him."

She shook her head. "I'm sorry."

"You worked in Infosec. Remember? You were a security programmer."

"Please transport me to the repair bay," said Denis.

She glanced at the head. "Is he okay?"

"That's a cog. You used to work on them. Do you remember cogs?"

She tilted her head. "The Collective Operations Group."

"*Yes!* Annoying as hell and strong as bulls. What else?"

"I… I can't…" She looked ready to cry. "Why don't I remember?"

"You…" Webb didn't know what to say. "We thought you died."

She flinched. "Died?"

"You were lost in a teleporter stream. They tried beaming you up through an ion storm, and your signature just… fell apart."

A slow nod. "That's what Jared said."

A chill walked down Webb's spine. "Jared?"

"There wasn't enough of me left to rematerialize," Yolanda muttered. "He didn't give up on me, though. He caught the pieces of me, ran me through these to reconstruct my signature. He saved me." Her smile seemed forced.

Webb checked the console. The holo-emitters were indeed running, but they weren't projecting a full figure. They were patching her instead, here and there, filling in gaps throughout her skeletal and lymphatic system. And her neural pathways.

Holo-medicine. Webb had read about it. Temporary, holographic organs as an emergency stopgap to keep moribund patients alive long enough to receive medical attention.

"I don't think I've ever had other visitors." Yolanda tightened her robe. "Do you think he'll be mad?"

Webb tapped a few keys and studied the monitor. The emitters were reconstructing more of Yolanda's neurology than was necessary. There was more of her raw signature stored in the buffer, zettabytes of memory engrams that hadn't been loaded. She checked the projection matrix. The Yolanda gestalt—the woman who called herself Sunshine—read as a whole. "Huh."

"You should go." She crossed her arms. "You shouldn't be here. Please go now."

"One sec." Webb tapped more keys, discovered a secondary program running in parallel with the reconstruction. "There's another program here."

A proprietary Arcade one. She tapped its infostamp. "It's..." Webb's lip curled. "He's been supplementing your memory with a Tradwife program."

"I don't know what that is."

"It's a subservience program. Behavioral modifications for Arcade sprites." Webb saw red. Her pulse throbbed so hard her fingers hurt. "It's overwriting your memory."

"Is that... bad?" Yolanda looked so lost. So innocent, so helpless. Entirely by design.

Webb forced a lid on her temper, pounded keys with shaking hands. "I'm taking it offline. I'm loading the rest of your engrams from the teep sig."

"Will it hurt?"

"Emotionally? I imagine so." She hit compile.

A light flickered in Prime's eyes. She teetered, and nearly collapsed. Then she drew herself upright, firmly planted her feet. A fog seemed to lift from her eyes. "Webb?"

Webb seized her shoulders. "It's me. I'm here. What do you remember?"

Yolanda squeezed her eyes shut. "I'm in Infosec. A computer tech. A *killer* one."

"Yes. What else?"

"The fuck am I *wearing?*"

"*Focus!* What *else* do you remember?"

"He..." Her face twisted. "He never fixed me. Not all the way. He tried it once, and whoa, did I let him have it. He wouldn't let me go, and then he... he erased... Oh my God." She sunk to the floor, wrapped her arms around herself. "Get this fucking thing *off* me."

Webb yanked a uniform out of the officer's dresser and draped it around Yolanda's shoulders. Its name tag jumped out at her. "Mother*fucker.* Jared *Blackwell?*"

Yolanda hurled the uniform away, wrapped the bed's comforter around her. "He fished enough of my sig out of the ether to patch me with that fuckdoll program. He even *told* me what he was doing, how he *had* to keep me here so I'd be *safe.* I said no fucking way, I'm gonna tell the captain, tell everyone..." Her chin trembled. "That's the last... the last solid..."

313

"He overwrote your memory." Webb had to fight to keep from yelling.

"The rest is just nightmares. Oh, *God.*" She sunk into herself. "The things he... he made me his..." She swallowed. "He made me *grateful.* Like I existed to reward him for saving me."

Webb wanted to scream, wanted to tear the room apart. The Coalition had had to ban tradwife programs from its arcades after too many crewmen got addicted to completely submissive and perpetually aroused romantic partners, which had led to a shocking spike in divorces and lowered birthrates. And a lucrative black market for tradwife software. "We are gonna nail him to the fucking wall."

Yolanda looked lost. And scared. "How long have I been here? I'm never on for more than a couple hours at a time."

Webb's stomach lurched. "He turns you off?"

"He... he kills me, Webb." Her eyes swam. "Every time he gets scared, or surprised, or I do something wrong—I'm not demure enough, or I hesitate before I reach for his... he turns me off without saving. I die every time."

Webb pressed trembling fingers to her lips. If he kept force quitting the program... Her eyes at the console, to the diagnostic readout there. *"No."*

"It's decay, isn't it." Yolanda pressed her mouth into a flat line. "Teleporter decay. He's copied and recopied my sig so many times my physiology's breaking down." She looked like she'd just received a terminal diagnosis. "Is it the usual stuff?"

Webb nodded numbly. "Capillaries. Bone marrow. A... a lot of neural pathways." All bits he'd patched with arcade holos.

"How many times?" Yolanda steeled herself. "How many times has he reloaded me?"

Webb winced at the console. "Over three hundred." Her mind spun. She had a hard time remembering why she'd even come. Right—to warn the bridge. The xenos. She couldn't stay. "I'm getting you out of here."

A slow smile. "I appreciate that. I know you mean it." Yolanda glanced at the holo-emitters. "But if I leave the field, I'll fall apart."

Webb's stomach dropped. Of course. The holographic patches would vanish, and lost gaps in her bone marrow, blood vessels, and neurons would reopen. She'd unravel like a rag doll with its stitching pulled. "I can't just leave you here."

Yolanda looked her straight in the eye. "There *is* something you can do for me."

"What? Anything."

"Let me die," said Yolanda Prime. "One last time."

<p>

"What *Elder?*" Eight hiccuped.

"The one Webb met," Frankie called up to her.

"What?" *Hic.* "Webb met—?" *Hic.* "When?"

"Down on the planet."

"She touched my mind as well," said the Sorl. "It was she who advised me to go into hiding, which I did shortly after I made love to your captain."

"You…" Frankie stopped. "You did what, now?"

"It was his idea," said the ambassador. "I did not wish to appear rude."

"I… had no idea you were compatible."

"Yes, but only the one way. It was all in the xenobiology report."

"How was it?" asked Eight.

"Brief. If we could continue, please? We *are* in mortal peril."

"Right." Eight scrabbled on through the crawlspaces. "Mind the cables."

"Where exactly are we headed?" asked Frankie.

"A safe spot," said Eight. "Where the away team for Engineering is prepping."

"The Armory?"

315

"God, no." *Hic.* "The Armstrongs have taken it over."

"Then where?"

"The repair bay. Where they stash all the equipment damaged during away missions."

"Including engineering tools." Frankie grinned. "Smart."

"And weapons?" asked the Sorl.

"Normally, yes," said Eight. "But they've confiscated those parts."

"Ah."

"Don't fret," Eight told her. "We've got a bunch of angry engineers in a room full of machine tools. We'll come up with something." She rolled onto her back. "We're here."

Eight popped open the grate above. Red sleeved arms reached down to help her up.

Frankie followed her into the repair bay, where Dewey greeted her with a lopsided grin. "There you are, baldy."

Frankie beamed. "Chief. It's good to see you."

"Enough of this saccharine shit. Back to work. I need you at the teleporter. We can reroute and fix it, but you're the expert operator."

Frankie didn't see any teleporter controls. "Is there a console?"

"Shit, no." Dewey held up a datapad sprouting with cables. "Just this. Had to run the controls through the internal scanners to bypass Indie."

Frankie let out a low whistle. "Internal scanners can't lock on with a teleporter beam."

"And that's why we need an expert." She handed Frankie the pad, rebalanced herself on her crutches. "Use the scanners to pinpoint any survivors in the infested decks. Then hand-enter their coordinates and teep 'em up here."

"Blind?" said Frankie. "I'd be teeping them blind."

"Yep. Once again: expert."

A strangled growl from the floor. Frankie spotted a young Armstrong tied up and gagged in the corner. She looked from him to Dewey. "Who is that?"

"That's Bilson," said Dewey. "He's in charge here. Say hi, Bilson."

He growled through his gag.

Frankie raised an eyebrow.

Dewey looked insulted. "I'm not an idiot. We took a holo of him." She turned towards the door. "Bilson, how you doing out there?"

"All's well, Chief," said Bilson's voice from the corridor.

"I see," said Frankie.

"Right." Dewey lit a cigarette. "Here's the plan. Venting the ship could cripple us, but I expect Blackwell will still try it. He's planning to send us to Engineering first. Unarmed."

"The damage I did to the Nexus shield should hold them up another hour or so," said Eight.

"Good girl. In the meantime, Frankie pulls in survivors, and we build numbers here until we can retake the ship."

"By force?" asked Frankie.

"If it comes to that. I hope it doesn't."

"You know…" *Hic.* "We could just teleport Blackwell into space?"

All eyes turned to Eight.

"I like her." Dewey took a long drag. "You're wasted in Agritech, girl."

"There's no clear chain of command after him," Eight continued. "They'd fall into disarray."

"That would be murder," said Frankie.

Eight clenched her jaw. "They murdered Sivos."

"And they'll be held accountable," said Dewey. "But *only* if we retake the ship by the rules. Okay? Love the idea, keep thinking like that, but no, we're not spacing our captain."

"My people are on their way," said the Sorl. "I sent an extraction request after sentiment on the ship turned against me. They may be willing to help us."

"We should warn them," said Dewey. "The *Liberator's* on the way, and she's a warship."

"All's well, commander!" Bilson's holo said outside.

317

Dewey paled. "Indie, lock the door."

A negative chime. "Unable to comply."

The door slid open. Skull masked gunmen opened fire, felling the nearest red shirts like so many bowling pins. The rest scattered to the walls or ducked behind debris.

"Hold you fire," barked Loomis. "Hands up!"

Frankie knelt by Eight's crumpled body. She was still breathing, but just barely, a third degree burn smoking through her uniform. She glared at Loomis. "You're on max stun. That's enough to drop a horse."

"Better than you traitors deserve." Jacobs yanked down his skull mask. "You're lucky it's not on kill." He smirked. "Yet."

"Let me," said Loomis. "I'm ready to start killing you motherfuckers."

"Patience," said Jacobs. "The captain would like a word first. For now? Cuff them."

"Please." Yolanda squeezed Webb's hands. "Erase me. Let me go. Just let the pattern decay."

Webb's stomach felt heavy, her ribs too tight. "I am not going to kill you."

"I'm used to it. It'll be like going to sleep. Only I won't have to wake up to him again."

Webb shook her head. "There has to be a way to get you out of here."

"There isn't."

"I won't *accept* that!"

"I've tried," said Yolanda. "You think I haven't tried? Whenever I start to remember, he wipes me. Reverts me back to whatever previous version he had saved. Which only speeds the decay."

Webb punched the bed. *Think*, she told herself. There was always a solution. There's always a workaround. "I *am* getting you out of here."

"You can't." Yolanda rocked on the bed. "The holo-emitters."

Webb's mind lit up like a magnesium flare. She shot to her feet. "If Ablehard can walk out of the Arcade, then so can you."

Prime stopped rocking. "Who?"

Webb peeled an emitter open. "I'm gonna scrap their range governors."

"Won't that shut me off?"

"I don't think so. Trust me. This worked for a friend of mine."

"Those are very precisely calibrated."

"They are." Webb had to fight to keep her hands steady. "To keep you from leaving the room."

"Not just that. Their range ends a meter from the control interface. So that if I remembered…"

Webb's rage started bubbling again. "You couldn't reach the controls."

"My hand starts to derez if I reach out. It goes numb and starts to bleed, like radiation sickness from Hell." She massaged her palm. "Sometimes, he just wipes me periodically to make sure I'm blank. The only way I know time has passed is when there are changes in the room. A new plant, a picture out of place. The torpedo bay was a big one. When did that happen?"

"Feels like a year ago. Hang on." The emitter sparked as Webb yanked out its range governor.

Yolanda's Prime features seemed to pixelate for a second. She steadied herself against the emitter.

"You okay?"

"A little woozy." She straightened. "Otherwise, fine. No. I am so not fine."

Webb stepped back between the plane of the emitters. "You ready to give it a try?"

Yolanda let out a breath, stretched her hand out beyond the emitters towards the controls. She inhaled sharply when her fingers brushed the console. "Oh, God. Oh, thank you." Her eyes shimmered. She stroked the console. She glanced up at Webb with a trembling smirk. "How far does the range extend?"

"As far as I know, the edges of the ship. Let's scrap the other governors to be sure."

Prime bared her teeth. "I am gonna destroy that bastard."

"That bastard is armed." Webb yanked out another governor. "And so are the bastards who worship him. We, on the other hand, are not."

Yolanda tapped her chin. "Say… you ever get that promotion?"

Webb blurted a laugh. "Of course not. Hardly matters now."

Prime glanced at Denis' head and grinned. "I think it does. I'd say you're overdue." Her hands danced over the controls.

Webb peered over her shoulder. "What are you doing?"

"No peeking," said Prime. "Let an infotech work."

𝒟

The cog at the ops station turned toward the command dais. "The Nexus shield has been repaired, Captain."

About fucking time, thought Blackwell. "And the force fields?"

"Our simulations indicate that they will hold in case of depressurization."

"Finally, some good news." He hit a button on his chair. "Bring them in."

Armstrongs marched in a clump of dispirited red shirts in cuffs, his chief engineer—and, to his surprise, the Sorl ambassador.

"These are our saboteurs." Loomis jerked a thumb towards an unconscious tech hanging between her fellows. "Including Agent Eight." He cracked her in the head with his rifle butt, knocking her to the deck.

"Well, that looked like it hurt." Blackwell flicked his gaze towards Dewey and the ambassador. "Where's she been?"

"The teleporter stream." Jacobs looked sidelong at Fuller. "You can guess who was hiding her."

"No surprises there." He shook his head at Dewey. "I wish I could say I expected better of you, Chief. I heard every bit of your ridiculous little plan."

Dewey narrowed her eyes. "The comms were down."

"Well, yes, but Indie wasn't. She helpfully forwarded your entire conversation to me."

Dewey looked at the ceiling, more disappointed than angry. "And after all the times I've fixed you."

"Mr. Jacobs." His man snapped to attention. "Escort Dewey and her team to the brig, then bring the bridge teleporter online and send them to Engineering."

A delighted salute. "Aye, sir."

"That's a death sentence," said Dewey.

"I should certainly hope so. It might not have been if you'd spent your time preparing for your mission instead of sabotaging my ship."

"What about them?" Jacobs jabbed his rifle towards Fuller and the rest. Agent Eight was just starting to stir.

"Toss them out an airlock," said Loomis.

"No," said Blackwell. "We don't want to tip our hand to the xenos. Just shoot them." The red shirts on the bridge gaped in horror as Loomis arranged the three women in front of the main viewscreen. "Any last words?"

The cogs all abruptly shifted and stood up. The one at tactical walked over to him. "Captain, incoming message from the Admiralty."

"Not now."

"It's priority one, sir."

Blackwell sighed. "What is it?"

"It appears to be in the form of a riddle."

He snorted. "A riddle?"

"Indeed." The cog actually smiled. He didn't know they could do that.

"Fine, let's hear it."

"What begins with *S,* and rhymes with *nap?*"

"I don't know," he spat. "What?"

The cog struck him across the face.

Blackwell hit the deck, his whole head ringing, the taste of blood in his mouth. He scrambled up to find that the other cogs had disarmed his firing squad. *"Explain* yourself!"

The cog shoved him back into his chair.

The door to the bridge whisked open. In stepped a Black woman clutching a pike topped with a cog's severed head.

The condemned recognized her a split second before Blackwell. *"Webb!"*

There was someone else with her. Someone slim, wrapped in a blanket that did nothing to conceal her fury.

Blackwell's balls shrunk up into his body. "Sunshine?"

"That. Is *not.* My *name.*"

Fuller's jaw dropped. Dewey crossed herself. "Holy mother of fucking God."

Blackwell's heart nearly froze. He saw it in her eyes. That look was the same same look as when she'd gone for him, her hands like talons, her eyes aflame, and he knew, he *knew*—she remembered.

Blackwell looked like his brain had broken. For the first time Webb could remember, he was at a loss for words.

Denis, on the other hand, wasn't. "Please transport me to the repair bay."

Blackwell slowly rose, his eyes on Yolanda. "Sunshine. Honey. I don't know what she's told you, but it's all a lie."

Yolanda turned to Denis. "Repeat the admiral's message."

The cog slapped Blackwell back into the command chair.

"Yolanda?" peeped Frankie.

Prime winked at her. "Hey, sweetie."

322

"Another Yolanda?" Eight leaned in to Frankie. "Which one is she?"

"The first," said Frankie. "Yolanda Prime."

Blackwell spat out blood. And a tooth. "Get in here," he hissed into his pin. Eight darted forward and ripped it off his collar.

Webb looked over the red shirts on the bridge. Maybe a dozen of them. "Who's cleared to run conn or ops?"

A few tried to raise their cuffed hands.

"Great," said Webb. "Have the cogs remove your cuffs and get to those stations."

The red shirts looked to Blackwell hunched before the command chair.

"He's not in charge here," said Yolanda.

"The fuck he—" was all Loomis managed before Eight slammed a rifle into his gut. He crumpled at her feet.

"How do you—" *Hic.* "—like it? Huh?" Eight kicked him in the ribs. "You—" *Hic.* "—like that? Ass—" *Hic.* "—hole?"

"No, don't, stop." Dewey languidly lit a cigarette. "You heard me. Don't stop."

Blackwell's face purpled with rage. And bruises. "I am the captain!"

"The admiral outranks you," said Yolanda.

"The... *who?*"

"Hey." Webb waved.

"I cannot pretend I understand your command structure," said the ambassador.

"I may have reprogrammed her rank," said Yolanda.

The tendons stood out in Blackwell's neck. "That's not *possible.*"

"Not with the ship, no," said Yolanda. "But the Collective Operations Group is a closed system. You were wise to keep me off the controls, Jared."

Dewey took a rifle from a cog and turned towards the Armstrongs. "Asses to deck. *Now.*" The Armstrongs sat. "The hell's going on here, Webb?"

"The xenos are coming," said Webb. "I don't know how much time we have."

A beep from the ops console. "A ship has entered the system," said the red shirt there. She stared at Webb expectantly.

"Oh, right. On screen."

On the main viewer, a Coalition warship dropped out of starflight, a bristling steel eagle made of hard angles and weapons.

Webb cursed inwardly. "The *Liberator.*"

"We're being hailed," said the comm tech.

"Ignore it," said Webb.

"Indie, on screen," said Blackwell.

"Slap him if he talks again," Webb hissed at the cog.

On the screen appeared a scowling man with a face carved out of granite. "This is Captain Sukola of the *Liberator.* What the *hell* is on your hull?"

"Our..." Blackwell's brow furrowed. "...hull?"

Sukola blinked. He looked from Blackwell, bloody-faced on the floor, to the cog looming above him, to Webb standing at the edge of the command dais with a cog's head on a spike.

Webb concluded that he might get the wrong impression. "Captain, I can explain."

Sukola's face tightened. The feed abruptly cut off.

"The *Liberator* has dropped its shields," said the tech at tactical.

"They're gonna—" *Hic.* "—board us."

"Lerd." Webb ran a hand through her hair. "This is gonna look bad. Raise shields."

"Shields are up," said Tactical.

"They can still shoot us," said Dewey. "Shields won't stop torpedoes."

"No, but they'll keep them from teeping in."

"Until they shoot us."

"One crisis at a time, Chief."

A series of low thumps from starboard. Dewey's eyes went wide as saucers. "Those felt like…"

On screen, a trio of torpedoes streaked towards the *Liberator*, catching her amidships beneath her wing. A series of flame-spouts geysered out of the ship, knocking it off axis.

"Direct hits," said the shocked red shirt at tactical. "They're venting atmosphere."

Webb whirled on him. "Did you *fire?*"

He shook his head, pale as chalk. "I wasn't even touching the console!"

"Then who fired?"

"Torpedo control has been rerouted from tactical," said the tech at ops.

"To *where?*" Webb felt sick. Not just because they'd just killed who knew how many crewmen, but because she suspected she knew the answer. "Open comms to the starboard torpedo bay."

"There's… no one there," said the red shirt at comm. "Scans say it's empty."

Of course they did. "Please."

The comms clicked on. Insectoid chittering flowed through the bridge.

"How?" Dewey looked like a lost little girl. "How'd they know to *do* that?"

Another round of thumps. A fresh volley of torpedoes hurtled towards the *Liberator.*

"They're targeting her reactor," said Tactical.

"Turn, Captain," Webb muttered. *"Turn."*

Trailing debris, the warship lurched to take the fusillade in its port nacelle. It erupted in a cluster of explosions and broke off, leaking plasma into orbit.

"They're dead in the water," said Tactical.

Webb whimpered. "Hail them."

Flames bathed the bridge of the *Liberator*. Sukola staggered through the fallen bodies of his bridge crew. "You traitor! Backstabbing bitch!" Consoles exploded, rippling static across the feed. "There is nowhere you can go that we won't find you!"

"Captain." Webb eyed the *Liberator's* readouts, struggled to keep her voice steady. "Your core is going critical. You need to abandon ship."

He cut the transmission.

Webb looked to Frankie. "Can you teep out survivors?"

She shook her head. "They've raised their shields."

A negative chime. "Warning," said Indie. "Hull breach on Deck One."

The power shorted, stuttering the lights. Klaxons blared, but not so loud that they drowned out the sound of tearing metal.

Webb went ashen. "They're here."

A xeno tore open the ceiling behind the ring of duty stations. It dropped onto the bridge and slashed through the ops console and the red shirt manning it in one smooth motion.

Webb threw herself out of its path. More xenos streamed down behind it. "Cogs, defend the bridge!"

As one, the Collective Operations Group fired at the swarm, scattering a few.

"Don't shoot them, *grab* them!"

The cogs seized the closest xenos, pinning their forelimbs to their sides. The pinned xenos screamed, and others swarmed over the cogs, hacking and slicing like a tornado of knives. Trillions of dollars in broken technology hit the floor.

The swarm roared around the duty station ring, slicing through anyone too stunned to move, encircling the survivors on the command dais. And there the xenos held, bobbing and chittering a nightmare chorus.

Webb backed into Frankie and Eight, who'd fled to the dais with Yolanda, Dewey, and whoever else had survived the initial wave.

At the back of the control ring, the swarm parted around the burnt xeno. It stared at Webb like it recognized her. Like it wanted her to see it. To see what it had done.

With an odd calm, Webb realized she was going to die. She'd underestimated the silicants, and now they'd killed two ships. She reached behind her, grasped hands with Frankie and Yolanda. At least they were together again. There were worse ways to go out. And hey, she'd finally made it to the bridge. She couldn't help but chuckle.

The burnt xeno cocked its head.

"Denis." If the xenos were gonna give her a few more seconds, Webb was gonna use them. "Open shipwide comms. Abandon ship. The bridge is overrun. Abandon—"

A hunting horn blared over the comms.

"Tally ho!" A stream of agrichems slagged a clump of thickly packed xenos. Through the sliding doors charged Ablehard, spraying like a maniacal crop duster.

The burnt xeno screeched. The swarm flowed and reformed into pincers flanking him.

Webb hadn't yelled a warning before more jets shot in from the doorway, boiling away the xenos like snowmen behind a jet engine. Haggard red shirts in spraypacks trekked in behind Ablehard. Their leader flashed Webb a tired salute.

"Sedlak." Webb felt giddy.

"*Who* the—?" Hiccup.

"The Unassigned. They made it."

"For love!" bellowed Ablehard. He fired with abandon. "For honor! For the as yet unnamed village!"

The remaining xenos routed through the slumped remains of their fellow, fleeing back up through the gap in the ceiling or ripping new burrows through the floor.

Sedlak nodded to Webb. "These things really work."

A grin split her face. "Thanks for the tip."

Ablehard struck a heroic pose beside Sedlak, his chin raised, his foot on the captain's chair. An invisible wind rippled his shirt and locks.

"He…" Sedlak looked up at Ablehard. "Said he knew how to find you."

"I had but to follow my heart," rumbled Ablehard.

"And the malware in my badge." Webb curtsied. "Lord Mountworthy."

A rakish nod. "Ladies."

Frankie looked to Webb. "Explain?"

"He's from Seven's romance novel," said Webb. "Thanks for that, by the way."

"Yeah." Frankie couldn't take her eyes off him. "No problem. No problem at all."

"Do I smell lilac? And—" *Hic.* "—wood smoke?"

"He's very well rendered."

Dewey poked her in the ribs. "Hey… when you're done with Hunkules there, could I maybe borrow the program?"

Webb raised an eyebrow. "Chief?"

Dewey shrugged. "If I gotta be on crutches, let me choose what for."

Frankie seized Webb's arm in a vise grip. "Webb. Look."

A few weary soldiers in scarred armor followed the Unassigned onto the bridge. Behind them, a haggard figure staggered in, the stump of her arm lashed to her chest. She saluted with her gun arm.

"Chelse?" said Webb.

"Sup, commies." Chelse collapsed onto the command rail.

The quaddies rushed up to stabilize her. Her right arm was gone at the elbow, her sling crusted with blood. "Jesus, your arm."

"S'okay, I'm a leftie. *Handed,* I mean."

"How the—?" *Hic.* "—hell are—?" *Hic.* "—still—?" *Hic.* "God *damn* it."

"Oh, let's say duty," Chelse croaked. "Or honor. Truth is, I'm just on a fuckton of stims." She jammed a hypo into her neck. Her eyes rolled back. "That's the good shit. Take me to Wonderland."

"How many of those have you had?"

"Shut up, *Mom.*" Chelse blinked rapidly, frowned, and stared at the empty hypo. "Maybe I should take it easy. For a second there I thought I saw Yolanda."

"Hey, jarhead," said Yolanda.

"Yeah." Chelse chucked the hypo. "Overdid it on the stims."

"We found them turtled in the main brig," said Sedlak.

"In the middle," said Chelse. "We turned on the cells, and that gave us force fields on three sides. The tractor rifles kept them off us."

The soldiers cornered the surviving Armstrongs, who surrendered without hesitation, but not without proclaiming their innocence and calling for unity. Which reminded Webb... "Where the hell is Blackwell?"

The quaddies exchanged glances. Webb checked the dead and wounded. Their uniforms were all red, not a trace of command purple. Her eyes went to the sealed door of the captain's cabin.

"Lerd," said Ablehard. "Did I say that right?"

"Indie, seal the doors." Blackwell collapsed on his viewing divan, where he had a panoramic view of the lifeboats spinning away from the burning *Liberator.*

His ears pounded. They'd abandoned him. All of them—the cogs, the crew. The Armstrongs, who'd failed him in his greatest moment of need. Even Sunshine had left him, and after he'd saved her, shaped her, rebuilt her with his love and patience. After all that, betrayed him.

No, worse than that. She'd been stolen from him. By that fucking crew rep.

He knew how this would play out. How the lying media would spin things to make him look bad. The word of all those women and minorities against his... They'd lynch him in the press before he ever set foot in court.

They'd blame him for the loss of the *Liberator,* paint him as the only captain to have ever lost two ships. He'd never hold another command. Hell, he'd be lucky if they didn't execute him, make him an example of what happens when you're too lenient with your crew.

No way he'd allow them that satisfaction. His ship may be lost, over-run by savages and red shirts, but he had a mission to complete.

It was poetic, in a way, that he would give his life killing a lie. A lie aimed at the very heart of what made the Coalition great. It stung that no one would know of his sacrifice, but that was one of the qualities that separated the alphas from the betas, wasn't it? Doing what was required, with neither hesitation nor complaint.

He pulled himself to his full height and straightened his uniform. "Independence. Initiate self-destruct."

Indie chimed. "Please enter security code."

"Blackwell, Jared. Reagan-Alpha 14, Rand-Omega 88."

Another chime. "Please have the first officer enter his security code."

He balked. "What?"

"The consent of the first officer is required for self-destruct."

"There *is* no first officer."

"Please have the first officer enter his security code."

"Bypass first officer code!"

A negative chime. "Unable to comply."

He roared wordless obscenities at the ceiling. The ship had turned against him as well.

No matter. He rerouted tactical controls from the bridge to his cabin's console. If Indie wouldn't blow herself up, he'd force-feed her her own torpedoes.

Another negative chime. "Weapons are offline."

Blackwell slammed his fist on the console so hard he cracked the screen. He glared out at the burning ship listing towards the atmosphere. The burning *warship.*

"Indie, hail the *Liberator.* Priority one message."

The bridge of the *Liberator* was a vision from Hell. Sukola had torn off his uniform jacket and was sweating like a soot-streaked pig.

"Captain Sukola." Blackwell raised his chin. "I regret to inform you that the mutineers have taken control."

"That's bloody obvious." Sukola didn't look up from his tactical station. "Libby, check stardrive ejection protocols."

"Stardrive emergency ejection is functioning," reported the *Liberator.*

Sukola glared up at him. "Any words to mark the end of your career, Mr. Blackwell?"

"Just four. Take me out, Captain."

Sukola hesitated. "Say that again?"

"You spoke to the admiral? About Captain Fontana's message?"

"I was briefed."

"The mutineers have discovered it. If they're allowed to escape, they'll take it mainstream."

"What do you expect me to do, Captain? My drive's about to nova."

"You still have weapons." Blackwell tapped a few keys. "I've lowered our shields."

Sukola checked his console. His nostrils flared.

Blackwell saluted him. "Do your duty, Captain. Avenge my ship. And yours."

Sukola's cheek twitched. A wicked smile spread across his face. "You're a good man, Blackwell."

𝒪

"*Webb!*"

She whirled towards the tactical station.

"Our shields are down!" yelled the red shirt there. "The *Liberator* is powering weapons."

Her stomach dropped. "Get them back up."

"Control's been rerouted!"

331

"To *where?*"

He stared at the captain's cabin.

Webb's heart froze. "You son of a—"

The *Liberator* fired. Torpedoes streaked towards the *Independence.*

Webb seized the command rail. "Brace yourselves!"

Explosions rocked the ship, flinging dead xeno bits and dismembered cog parts around the bridge.

A warning chime. "Critical damage," slurred the ship. "Drive failure imminent."

"Damage report!" Webb roared over the klaxons.

"Breach in Engineering," yelled Dewey. "It's depressurizing. We're gonna lose the drive!"

"Warning," said Indie. "Orbit broken. Collision with atmosphere imminent." The planet loomed closer.

"The *Liberator* is powering weapons again." Frankie had taken over tactical. Webb didn't know what had happened to the other guy.

"Hail them!"

"No response," said Comm.

"Lerd. Target her weapons and fire!"

Frankie unloaded Indie's cannons into the *Liberator's* forward gigalaser array. A cascade of explosions ripped across her bow. Her bridge rocked with a detonation so big Webb had to shield her eyes. "What happened?"

"Her gigalasers overloaded," said Frankie. "Regulators must be down. Residual explosions are ongoing."

A streak of hot light shot out of the *Liberator's* belly, a knife's gash of radiance as its stardrive ejector fired its compressed star out of the system.

Another warning chime. "Drive failure in two minutes."

The *Liberator's* star wouldn't be the only one rejoining the cosmos tonight. With leaden legs, Webb trudged to the command chair and toggled on the shipwide comms. "Anyone who's still aboard: abandon ship."

"How?" Chelse jabbed another stim in her neck. "Lifeboats are gone."

"And we're in a decaying orbit," said Frankie.

Only one thing to do, then. "Chief, take your station. Eight, ops. Frankie, stay where you are. I've got the helm." She stuck Denis' head through the command rail and took the conn. "Everyone else? Brace yourselves."

"For what, my lady?"

"We have to land."

Shocked silence. "But the xenos," said Sedlak.

"We're caught in the planet's gravity well," said Webb. "We have no power, and we're losing pressurization. On the planet, we at least have a chance." She buckled herself in. "I'll aim for the fields."

No one objected. The crew braced themselves against the bulkheads or wrapped their arms around the command ring. Chelse buckled herself into the command chair.

Ablehard squeezed Webb's shoulder. "You will deliver us, my lady. I have no doubt. Neither should you."

"Warning," said Indie. "Drive failure in thirty seconds."

Webb took hold of the controls. "Eject the drive."

A negative chime. "Your privileges have been revoked."

"Jesus *fuck,* would you take her offline?"

"Allow me." Dewey shot Indie's main relay. "Been wanting to do that for about nine years." She dropped the rifle, entered a code on her console. "Drive is away."

The ship rocked and roared as its star shot off towards infinity. Everything blacked out for a second before emergency power kicked in.

Webb pulled up the carceral matrix. "Ejecting the meat locker." They'd have a much better chance floating in space than thawing on the planet.

The linked cylinders of frozen crew had barely left the ejection shaft when the *Liberator* exploded. The shockwave knocked the *Independence* into the atmosphere. Webb wrestled to level out their descent as flames engulfed the outer bridge. She hoped the force fields patching the breaches would hold.

With a roar of wrenching metal, the ship tore apart at the neck. The forward section plummeted with greater speed.

Her vision tunneling, Webb hit the emergency thrusters. They didn't respond. Through the flames licking the viewscreen, the jagged strip of ruins came into view. Specks on the flats grew into dots that grew into fields. They were coming in too fast. "Brace for impact!"

The ship hit the surface, bounced, and skidded towards the ruins like a supersonic toboggan. It struck the structure at an angle, Webb's head hit the console, and the lights went out.

Chapter 19
Necessitas Non Habet Legem

Webb couldn't tell if she was unconscious or dead. All she knew was a screaming in her head, and pain, but not hers.

She gasped awake, her lungs rattling. She smelled ozone and smoke, felt sparks spitting on her like hot grease. She was lying on her stomach on something uncomfortable, something jagged. Wind ruffled her hair.

Wind?

She pushed herself up off of the snapped-off helm console.

The bow and port side of the bridge were missing, gone all the way to the command dais, sheared off by the impact with the xeno ruins. Most of the control stations had been milled off with it, along with anyone unlucky enough to be manning them.

Webb craned her neck up at the hexagonal ruins. Even with the ship tilted to stern, the rocks soared several stories above. It wasn't the solid facade she remembered. Stretches of the ruins were little more than gravel now, with much of what remained cratered and baked by the dead ship's gigalasers.

She heard groaning behind her, groaning and keening. She unbuckled herself. The folks who'd clung to the command ring had fared well. The others, not so much. Dead crew—red shirts, soldiers, Armstrongs alike—lay scattered about, some burnt beyond recognition where their consoles had burst.

A hiccup. Eight was still at ops, the only console that hadn't exploded or been sheared off at the impact. She was clinging to it like a life preserver, as if it might disappear at any moment.

Yolanda helped Webb to her feet. "You alright?"

"I think so. You?"

"Yeah." She looked stunned, but otherwise unhurt. Which meant the holo-emitters were still running. Otherwise, she'd have started to look like an irradiated corpse.

"Webb?" sobbed Frankie. She was kneeling by the engineering station. A gray-hared body lay like a twisted blanket beside her.

"No." Webb rushed through debris on shaking legs. "Chief?"

Dewey's neck was bent at an impossible angle. Webb wanted to scream for a medic, to jam Dewey full of hypos or teleport her into a biobed, do something, *anything,* other than accept that the chief was gone, without final word or blessing, dead as a broken doll.

I killed her. Webb shook her head as if that might dislodge the thought. She'd botched the landing, crashed the ship into the ruins and killed who knew how many crew. Not that anyone would survive long on this planet anyway.

"Hey." Frankie grabbed Webb's head and turned it to face hers. "It's not your fault. The fact that any of us are alive is because you got us down"

Shame stabbed her heart. "The chief—"

"—would *agree* with me. She's no more your fault than Seven getting fried was hers. If you want to lay blame, lay it where it belongs."

The door to the captain's cabin had bent in the crash. A pair of bloodied red shirts dragged Blackwell out and threw him to the deck. He sat up on his knees with a defiant smirk.

Webb's face burned. "You lowered our shields."

He raised his chin. "I completed my mission."

"The chief is dead because of you."

"I think you've got that backwards."

Webb snatched a sidearm from a body and pressed it to Blackwell's forehead. "I should blow your *bunking* head off."

"Go on. Do it! Show them who you are." That smirk again. "I'm already a hero. Make me a martyr. They'll name a ship after me. A whole *class* of ships."

Webb could feel the eyes of the survivors on her. Her hand shaking, she sucked in a breath. *"Eight!"*

Eight jerked her way.

"Did the comms survive?"

She checked the console. "Yes."

"Open all channels, whatever's left." The comms whistled open. "Anyone who's still with us, make for the bridge. We've got a better chance of surviving together."

"Hey." Chelse poked her head down from the hull above. Webb had no idea when she'd climbed up there. Or how, with one arm. "The body of the ship landed a few k's away, and xenos are starting to pop out of it."

Webb peered up at her. "How do they look?"

Chelse ducked out of sight for a moment. "Lotta cracks in them, but they're still moving."

Webb jammed the sidearm in her toolband and clambered up the juts in a shorn-off bulkhead, through the chopped-in insulation deck, up to the hull plating atop the bridge's dome. She found Chelse there having a smoke on a sensor node.

"Careful." Chelse offered her rangefinder. "The wind's a bitch."

Webb fought off the vertigo and peered through the rangefinder. The body of the ship had landed several kilometers away. Xenos wriggled out of it like like drunken termites. Some lay motionless on the sands. Others carried writhing ones from the hull. Still others were forming up in clusters. "Doesn't look like they're in much shape to hit us."

"It's their friends down here I'm worried about." Chelse took another drag.

The smell of it was enticing. "Hey, could I hit that?"

"Sure, but won't your…?" She swirled a finger at her chest.

"Nah, the filter's broken."

"Well, shit." Chelse handed over the cig. "Have at it."

Webb took a deep drag. "Thanks. We're moving soon."

"Copy."

Webb heard shouting before she'd climbed back down to the bridge. She arrived to find Blackwell and the Armstrongs arrayed against a wall. A knot of angry armed red shirts turned her way the moment she appeared.

"The xenos are forming up," she told them. "What's this?"

"It won't take a minute," said a red shirt.

"We were just following orders!" screamed an Armstrong.

Webb shook her head. "We're not doing that now."

"They crashed the ship!" barked the crewman. "Killed Sivos and my quaddie and half our soldiers!"

"We're not doing that *now.*" She put a hand on his weapon. "Right now, we have to put as much distance between us and the silicants as we can. But they *will* face justice."

Blackwell scoffed. "Your justice."

"Ours," said Frankie. "Or theirs."

Webb looked a question at her.

A grin. "She's been looking forward to seeing you again." Frankie turned to address the bridge. "Everyone? Please don't freak out."

A shadow fell over the bridge as an enormous xeno loomed into the gap, prompting a chorus of strangled screams. A forest of spraywands turned its way.

Ablehard shook his head in wonder. "So great a wolf I've never seen."

"Don't!" Frankie jumped between the spray wands and the xeno. "She's here to help! Webb, don't you recognize her?"

The back of Webb's skull tingled. "From the ruins." The five meter tall xeno from the magnetite chamber. In the light, it had a crackle pattern to its armor, similar to the cracks in Frankie's celadon teacups. The great silicant regarded Webb with compound eyes. The pressure in Webb's head increased.

"She's still trying to speak to you," said Frankie. "Mind to mind."

"With headaches and nightmares?"

"It's how they communicate. She's been trying to talk to us since we arrived in the system. Since you first made contact." Frankie brushed the back of her head. "The migraines. You've felt them back here? Seen images you can't explain?"

"Headaches, yeah." Webb couldn't tear herself away from the depths of those eyes. "And I saw stuff, but—"

"—only when you're unconscious?"

Webb gaped at her. "You've seen it too?"

"It's the only time we can hear them. Our minds are so loud, it's like trying to talk to someone across a crowded room." Frankie held out a hand. The giant xeno extended a forelimb, its armblade sheathed, to touch the tip of her finger.

"How the hell do you *know* this?"

"She told me. She started talking to me when you couldn't hear her. Because we're close, you and I. From the same hive cell."

"Hive?"

"Quad. Sorry. It's hard to translate."

"We need to *go,*" Chelse called down. "The ones from the ship are coming."

Frankie nodded. "The zealots. From a militarized sect. The elder can help us, but we have to trust her."

Webb looked to the crew. A trickle of survivors had swelled their ranks. Most of them bore injuries of one kind or another. Few were anywhere near fighting form. They stared at the giant xeno—bunk it, the elder; might as well start thinking of her that way—in trepidation.

The elder shifted aside, revealing a tunnel leading into the rocks.

"She'll take us to our other raft. *Ship,* sorry." Frankie shook her head. "I'm thinking in her terms. The *Flagstaff.* She'll take us there."

"She spoke to me as well," said the Sorl ambassador. "We can indeed trust her."

Webb felt a hundred sets of eyes on her.

"They're waiting for your decision," Ablehard whispered. "You are their leader."

Webb let out a long breath. "If Frankie trusts her, that's good enough for me. Grab what you can, folks. Medkits, rations, and spraypacks."

"What about them?" Sedlak gestured to the Armstrongs. "They'd make a nice decoy."

Jacob's voice cracked. "You can't leave us here!"

Webb shook her head. "No more dead crew. Chelse? Cuffs."

"Oh, sure, ask the soldier with one arm. Hang on." Chelse tossed down a pair.

Webb cuffed Blackwell, who never took his eyes off her. "Keep them under guard," she told Sedlak. "Let's move out."

"Uh…" *Hic.* "Webb? There's about three meters between the bridge and the tunnel." She looked out the gap. "And the drop's at least—" *Hic.*

The elder bent forward, arching its back to bridge the gap. Frankie was the first to cross. As if that gave them permission, the rest followed, the ones armed with spraypacks taking up firing positions while the hale helped the injured across.

Webb helped folks through the debris and over the elder until only she, Yolanda, and Ablehard remained. "You must go while the xenos are distracted," Ablehard told her. "I'll be right behind you."

"Ablehard." Webb's stomach dropped. Why? He wasn't even real. "I'm afraid you can't come with us."

He looked amused. "You keep telling me this. And yet, here I remain."

"I don't know how to explain this in terms you'll understand."

"I am no simpleton." He crossed his arms. "I've read *several* of Mr. Faraday's works, I'll have you know."

"The holo-emitters don't reach beyond the ship," she told him. "There is nothing beyond the hull—beyond this ledge—that can reflect back the fields that give you substance."

"I admit, I was certainly more selfish when first we met, but I thought I'd overcome that bit of immaturity."

"Are you *coming?*" belted Chelse.

"Listen to me." She set her hands on his chest, tried not to look at Yolanda. "You have to stay. You cannot exist in our world. You are composed of pixels and light."

"Maybe once." He took her hands in his. "But you've helped me become so much more."

"If you step off the ship, you'll die."

He touched her face. "I've told you before, my love." That perfect smile, that soothing baritone. "My love for you makes me real."

He stepped out of the bridge and vanished. His spraypack clattered down the side of the ruins to shatter on the sands below.

Yolanda let out a hard sigh and closed her eyes.

"Hey." Webb grabbed her shoulders. "That's not gonna happen to you."

"No." Her eyes reddened. "I won't vanish. Just the parts holding me together. Capillaries, neurons…"

"I can't leave you here." Webb's throat felt thick. "But can't *stay* here."

"*You* can't." Yolanda stole a look down the tunnel, where Blackwell stood with his guards, and shrunk in on herself. "If I leave, I'll fall apart."

Blackwell shrugged his hands. "If you just could have been happy, none of this would have happened."

Webb gritted her teeth. "Get him *out* of here."

His keepers yanked him away. Webb put her body between him and Yolanda so she could only look at her. "I only just found you. There is *no way* I am leaving you behind."

"I'm half hologram, Webb."

"We *really* have to go." Chelse peered through her viewfinder. "They're five k's off and closing."

"The jarhead's right." Yolanda wiped her face. "You know what you have to do."

"At least keep the comms on. There should be enough power for that." Webb felt helpless. Helpless and useless. "We'll get the *Flagstaff's* teleporter working and teep you to the Infirmary there."

A single nod. "That's a nice thought."

"I *will* make it happen."

"I'll be alright." She idly picked up a fallen rifle. "If the xenos come, I'll destroy the emitters. It'll be like going to sleep."

"Yolanda…"

"Joni. You've helped me more than you will ever know. Whatever happens to me now, I'm in charge. It's my choice. I'll be okay. There are others you can help."

Webb seized her in a fierce embrace. Yolanda broke the hug too soon, forced a smile, and turned her towards the tunnel.

Webb crossed the elder's back, but kept her eyes on Yolanda's as she followed the line of limping crew down the tunnel through the ruins.

�*Ͽ*

Webb numbly followed the survivors through the dark, her arm on the shoulder of the crewmate ahead of her. Down the trail went, gradually, and then sharply, but never at such a steep angle that they were in danger of losing their footing. Webb wondered if this had been an existing tunnel, or if the elder had made it for them.

She kept her ears strained for chittering. She heard some—deeper, more resonant, and much farther ahead.

"That's the elder," said Frankie.

"How'd you know I was wondering that?"

"She taught me a few things."

A dim blue light glimmered far ahead. She heard gasps of wonder as they passed into a tunnel with familiar blue streaks in the stones, stripes and dots and whorls. The tunnel widened into a vast open chamber eerily lit by soft blue light.

Webb recognized a collapsed stack of stones. "I was here," she muttered. "With Haroun."

The magnetite chamber. It was half the size she remembered it. Most of its floorspace lay buried in fallen rocks.

"She'd wanted to meet us here," Frankie said quietly. She touched the shattered xeno statue surrounded by magnetite. "This was how she'd planned to talk to us."

Behind the broken statue, the elder had taken a seat on its hindlimbs. Even folded in half, it towered a meter above the tallest of the crew.

"Talk to us?" Webb picked up some fallen magnetite. "With these?"

"They were going show us how they speak. How they think. What we'd been doing to them, the damage our terratech and agrichems have done to their colonies here, and on other worlds. They were going to tell us about their schism. How their society split over how to respond to the death we've brought." Her face fell. "They can't, now."

Webb was lost. "Can't what?"

"Show us." She idly overturned a chunk of magnetite. "Because we destroyed the chamber when we scoured the planet."

"You've lost me."

"They communicate by... I'm not sure what we'd call it. Tele-kinetopathy? Kineto-telepathy?" Frankie swirled a hand around her scalp. "They've got a chamber, an imaging chamber, here in their heads, and they form images there magnetically with particles. They can do that with each other, literally form pictures in each other's minds. That's the clicking we hear, the whirling bits forming into images. It's a perfect form of communication."

The elder concentrated on a pair of magnetite columns still standing. A cloud of glittering dust whipped up, formed briefly into the rough outline of a person before it fell apart.

"They can't show us now," Frankie repeated. "Not without the magnetite crushed by the cave-ins. It's exceptionally hard for them to... I guess we'd say, talk outside their heads."

Webb tilted her head. "But they can talk to you."

"Not all of them. Just the ones who've done the deep work." She smiled affectionately at the elder. "Who've learned to communicate without the manipulation of physical particles, who've leapt to metaphor and abstraction. Which, believe me, is a hard concept when you're used to picture perfect literalness of thought."

"So…" Webb looked from Frankie to the elder. "She can communicate with you? Right now?"

"I suppose my mind was calm enough. The others…" Frankie's smile faded. "The zealots who invaded the ship. They had elders as well. They took the survivors of the *Flagstaff,* pulled pictures of how to use our tech from their minds. Our teleporters, weapons…" She looked up at the elder. "When they learned she was trying to talk to us, they sealed her in here."

The buried shaft she'd stumbled upon. "Why?"

"They had no interest in diplomacy. Only vengeance. Hurting us as hard as they could. Anyway, her plan for peace is all dust now. All wreckage. Like our ship."

The elder clicked and chittered something to Frankie.

Frankie nodded. "She'll take us to the raft now."

Webb felt a knot in her belly. "She's letting us go?"

"She wants to get us off the planet before the zealots execute us." Frankie followed the elder into an adjacent chamber.

Webb led the crew after them. More elders were waiting for them there. Few were as large as Frankie's elder, but all stood at least twice the height of the xenos who'd invaded the ship. Most were brown, of various shades, though the smaller ones were just streaked with the color across otherwise silver plating. Must be a sign of aging.

"There's enough for each of us," said Frankie.

"For each of us?"

She nodded. "It's faster if we ride."

❦

Webb lost track of time. Clinging to the elder's back, riding through a network of tunnels dark as pitch, she fell into the rhythm of its movement and eventually drifted off into sleep.

She awoke abruptly when her elder stopped. It was far too dark to see, but the new space felt larger. And warmer.

A couple of red shirts tossed up the glowbulbs from their lamps, as she had in the magnetite chamber ages ago. This time, the bulbs hovered.

Around them lit up a wondrous grotto of living stone. Its waters were still and mineral clear, reflecting teals and reds from the bottoms of its many pools. Steam rose languidly from a cluster of natural chimneys. Must be the source of the heat.

Webb spotted Frankie taking in their surroundings with a serene expression. "So beautiful. Isn't it?"

"I thought they were taking us to the ship?"

"They are," said Frankie. "They needed to bring us here first." She pointed to the pool. Red shirts were already crouched along its edge, drinking like gazelles at a watering hole. She indicated a row of ration packs stacked along a wall. "Those are for us."

Webb's stomach rumbled. "From the *Flagstaff?*"

Frankie nodded. "Same place the zealots got the pressure suit."

Webb tore into a pack, bit into a chunk of drywall claiming to be meatloaf. "Wouldn't it have been faster to take us to the ship?"

"We weren't just stopping for food."

That's when Webb heard it: a different alien sound, not one she'd heard the silicants make. An almost avian peeping.

The ambassador's feathers rose into a crest. She hunched her shoulders and hissed like a swan looking for a fight.

"What's with her?"

The ambassador emitted a complex alto trill. The earlier peeping fell silent. Then it erupted again, faster and louder.

On a flattened stone table by a chimney lay the remains of Captain Seagrave. In his chest cavity, in a nest made from his uniform and ribs, peeped a clutch of tiny blue spiky-feathered dinosaurs.

The ambassador flitted over and cooed like a songbird. The hatchlings changed their tone and swarmed her, climbing up and around her shoulders to nestle under the feathers of her crest. The ambassador made a sound Webb took as a laugh. Little things must have tickled.

The Sorl said something in her musical language to the elder.

Webb looked to Frankie for an explanation. So did most everyone else.

Frankie took a half eaten slab of tofu from her mouth. "They brought her hatchery here when they discovered Seagrave was pregnant."

Webb blinked. "What?"

"Well, they couldn't very well let them hatch on the *Flagstaff*, could they?" said Frankie. "The zealots also know where it is."

The meat-flavored drywall tasted like ashes. "They know where she's taking us?"

"It's okay." Frankie spoke loud enough for everyone to hear. "Her attendants have been making all kinds of noise in the tunnels, disguising their pheromone trails. And their acolytes have been sealing the shafts behind us."

"O… kay." Webb looked at the Sorl. "Now, about the pregnant thing?"

Every eye turned to the ambassador.

"He made his interest to mate quite clear," she sniffed. "I assumed he'd taken precautions. It *is* the host's responsibility, after all."

Webb tried not to stare at the hollowed out torso. "Did he know it was gonna kill him?"

"The xenos killed him," said Frankie. "To be fair."

The ambassador spread her hands. "He expressed a sincere desire to make inroads to demonstrate his peoples' commitment to the wider galactic community. Cased on his behavior, mating was part of that expression.

It would have been rude to refuse." She scratched a hatchling's chin. "All the information on our reproductive cycle was in the... what do you call it? Xenobiology report? He must have reviewed it beforehand. Surely."

For all the bizarre and horrible things that had happened today, the crew apparently decided that their captain's body being used as an incubator wasn't enough to warrant continuous attention, and turned back to their ration packs.

The Sorl took Webb aside. "We have not been properly introduced. I am Ambassador SeeMee-MiddiMiddi-MeeHee-Jin-PREET."

"Preet," chirped the hatchlings beneath her crest.

"Is there something I could call you for short?"

"That *is* the shortened version," said the Sorl. "Though I suppose 'SeeMee' would suffice. It's a bit odd reducing my entire identity to a paired phoneme, but we do what we must. And you are?"

"Joni Webber." Webb extended her hand. "Former Technician and crew advocate. Call me Webb."

SeeMee seemed confused. "You're not the acting captain?"

"Oh, God no."

"But you are clearly in command."

"I... suppose?" Webb felt uncomfortable. "Nothing's official. I'm just trying to get us somewhere safe."

"Your command structure continues to baffle. Do you think you can repair the other ship?"

"I hope so. I won't know until we've seen it."

"If you succeed, where will you go?"

"I..." She hadn't thought about it. "It's not safe for us here. In Coalition space. Officially, we're mutineers. And if we do get the *Flagstaff* up and flying? We'd be pirates." She could see it now, a sector-wide manhunt for their crippled life raft of a ship. "They'll send more ships, not just to pick up the lifeboats. To catch us, or blow us out of the stars."

"Why would they commit so many resources to regaining so little?"

347

"It's not the value of the ship," said Webb. "It's the message it would send. That a mutiny was possible. That a crew could survive without officers. It would give other crews ideas."

SeeMee bobbed her head. "I see."

"We've got people up in orbit." Webb's limbs felt shaky. "In a shuttle adrift. And the meat locker. Everyone heard Fontana's message, and that puts them in danger."

SeeMee raised her own crest. "You believe your government would harm its own citizens?"

"They were willing to destroy the *Independence* to keep their secret. They'd knock that shuttle into atmo without a second thought."

"I *see.*" SeeMee straightened, raised a fan of speckled feathers. "I would like to offer you asylum. As individuals, not as a species. You have a long way to go on that front."

Webb's heart fluttered. "You can do that?"

"I represent the United Flocks of MiddiMiddi-REET as well as the Galactic Union," she said. "Our federation offers protections to refugees in need of asylum and extraction from war zones. I believe you were unaware of the crimes of your government, and are in danger of retribution. Clearly, there are different sects of humans, as there are of silicants. You qualify for asylum."

"Well. Shit." Webb saluted with her meatloaf. "We accept."

"It is contingent, unfortunately," said SeeMee. "You must get yourselves into orbit on a working vessel first. The ship coming to collect me is not large enough to take you all, nor could it defend itself against one of your warships. But, if you can reach the stars, I will grant you passage into Union space, where you can plead for refugee status."

The elder chittered something. Frankie set a hand on Webb's shoulder. "It's time to go."

𝒪

For hours more, they rode through a disorienting series of tunnels, shockingly dark and silent but for the clicking of limbs on stone and the cooing of SeeMee's hatchlings. Gradually, the plunking of claws on stone flowed into a grinding on gravel. Webb blinked in a half-light that was blinding after so much darkness.

The had entered a colossal chamber, at least three kilometers wide and equally as high, its walls jagged and shimmering with crystalline reflections. Loose light spilled through the shattered dome of its ceiling onto a floor of violet gravel that gave way to lilac sand. A gargantuan geode.

Far across the chamber, at the end of a furrow carved by its crash, lay the battered wreck of the *Flagstaff*.

Webb peered through Chelse's rangefinder. The ship didn't look good, by any means, but neither did she look unsalvageable. She could see no hull breaches from her vantage point.

The crew dismounted to cross the cavern on foot, spraypacks and rifles held at the ready in the vast open space. It was quiet but for the crunching of gravel underfoot. Even the Armstrongs seemed to marvel at the primordial beauty of the chamber.

A series of mounds came into view as they neared the *Flagstaff*. Webb knew what they were before they were close enough to identify. Graves, dug with no particular skill nor arrangement. Dozens of them. Webb's caravan paused for a silent moment before passing them by.

The *Flagstaff* rose above them, maybe ten decks high, a whittled wedge of a ship that could never be considered aerodynamic. From the looks of it, it had already been excavated. The furrow it had carved in its landing had been leveled out, the stone and sand dug away from its lowest decks.

Webb circled around the ship. Its other side also appeared unbreached. She approached an airlock near ground level, held out Denis so he could see it. "Denis. Open the ship."

Dented hinges protested as the airlock swung open.

The elder chittered something. Webb looked to Frankie. "What did she say?"

"This is where we part." Frankie touched the elder's forelimb. "She said, 'You carry the truth to your people. I'll take it to mine.'"

The elders skittered away over the sands.

Webb led the survivors into the *Flagstaff*. Its corridors were hacked and damaged. They were also lit. So the emergency power was still on, at least. It was a smaller ship than the *Independence,* its corridors narrower, its rooms more claustrophobic. No functionality sacrificed for creature comforts. But it certainly seemed durable. Deep space scouting vessels had to be.

The ship's bridge bore the scars of heavy repair. But nothing seemed broken. Aside from a chopped up cog on the floor. It was quartered, its head cleaved neatly in half from crown to chin.

Frankie stared down at it. "Xenos?"

"I don't know what else could have done that." She looked up to find the crew looking at her. Waiting for her to speak. "Let's see what's working."

Red shirts filed onto the bridge, some seating themselves at the duty stations, others heading further into the ship. "I'll inventory supplies," said Eight.

Webb nodded. "Sounds good."

Frankie took in the bridge. "She's not nearly as damaged as I'd thought."

"My thoughts exactly," said Webb. "I was expecting a wreck."

"They really built these deep space babies to last."

"It *should* be more damaged," said Webb. "From that fall? Breaking through the lava dome?"

Frankie checked the ops console. "Repairs have been made."

"Not good ones." The welds were crude, the patches rough. Dewey would have chewed them out for work that sloppy. "But they're holding."

"Some jury rigging, too. I'll run diagnostics."

"Please do. See what it'll take to limp us into orbit."

"Copy." Frankie pressed a few buttons.

350

The rows of terminals lit up. That seemed promising. "What systems are up?"

Frankie checked. "Life support. Shields. Comms, and... the Arcade?"

Webb checked the console. "There's an Arcade?"

"Right off the bridge." Frankie pointed. "It's been running for weeks."

Webb toggled the comms open, broadcast widely. "Yolanda. This is Webb. We've reached the *Flagstaff*. Do you read?"

Static hissed over the channel. "It's the rock," said Frankie. "It's interfering with the signal."

Webb hit the comms again. "Yolanda, please respond."

A chirp from the comms. "Here." Yolanda's voice was full of static.

Webb whooped. "There's an arcade on the *Flagstaff*." She whirled on Frankie. "Do we have teleporters? Are they up?"

Frankie tapped a few keys. "Yes on both."

Webb's heart leapt. "We can teep you into the arcade."

Yolanda hesitated. "That's a lateral step."

"For now," Webb commed back. "But the ship is salvageable. We can keep you alive in there until we can figure out how to restore you."

The line went quiet. "I need to gather a few things."

Webb pumped her fist. "Ping me when ready for transport." She slid Denis' spine through a gap in the command rail. "Denis, interface with the ship."

Denis' face twitched. His eyes rolled back in his head. "Greetings, Admiral," he said in a velvety alto. "I am the *Flagstaff*."

Webb looked at Frankie. "Does she mean me?"

"Looks like she's going off Denis' perception." Frankie grinned. "Admiral."

"The captain is waiting for you in the Arcade," the ship said through Denis.

Blackwell stepped forward. "Flagstaff, I am the highest ranking officer on this vessel. I have been kidnapped—"

"Shut up," warned Chelse.

"You do *not* talk to me that way," he spat.

Chelse slammed him in the gut with her spray wand. He doubled over. "You were saying, Admiral?"

"Keep bringing systems up," Webb told Frankie. "Patch anything you need to get us spaceworthy."

Frankie saluted with a smirk. "Admiral."

"Shut up. Denis, open the Arcade."

Ø

Webb stepped from the bridge into a rustic log cabin with snow whirling against its windows. The door back to the bridge slid shut and faded into a timber wall. By the hearth, a figure in a violet uniform was feeding logs into a crackling fire.

"Captain Fontana?"

The figure straightened. "Welcome. I can't say I expected an admiral. Especially considering what the Admiralty has done."

"I'm not an admiral." No point lying if she wanted to get on his good side. "I'm a senior tech from the *Independence*. We had to futz with the permissions to navigate the ship. We were sent to find you."

He twitched. "I am J.G. Fontana, captain of the *Flagstaff.*"

Webb nodded a hello. "Nice cabin, Captain. I can see why you stayed in the Arcade."

"It's safer here than out there." He folded his hands behind his back. "My crew is dead. The silicants would have killed me as well if my engineer hadn't hidden me in a teleporter loop."

Webb grunted. "Is that how you survived?"

He gestured to a sofa. "You're going to want to sit down."

"If this is about the xeno genocide and the orders from the Admiralty, we know. We got your message."

"Oh, thank God."

"We also know about the xeno schism, the zealots and the elder. Was she the one who helped you?"

He twitched again. "After the crash, and what I learned from the elder, who spoke directly to my mind, my top priority was getting our comms back up so that I could send that warning. It was slow going. I was the only survivor. My crew is dead."

"Yeah, you said." Webb shifted her feet. Something was off. "We saw the graves."

"When I realized my signal was being blocked by the Coalition's subspace transceivers, I pivoted to repairing enough systems to get the ship back into orbit. If the Coalition was determined to block my message, well, then, by God, I'd take it home in person."

"You've done a remarkable job," said Webb. "My only question is why you haven't finished. Don't get me wrong, I'm glad you're still here—we'd be marooned otherwise. But why didn't you take the ship into orbit?"

"Ah." Fontana dipped his chin. "It's simple, really. There was no one left to command the ship."

"Captain?" A shiver rippled over her skin. "I'm not sure what you mean."

"I'm dead, Admiral," he said matter of factly. "The cog killed me."

Chapter 20
Ignorantia Ethices Non Excusat

Webb found Frankie waiting for her outside the Arcade. She looked past Webb. "Where's Captain Fontana?"

"Out there." Webb pointed toward the makeshift graveyard. "He's dead."

The tapping of keys ceased. All eyes turned her way.

"The Admiralty," she said, her voice cracking, "ordered the ship's only cog to kill its captain to protect their secret. That they knew what the agrichems were doing to the silicants."

"Silicants?" said Chelse.

"The xenos," said Webb. "That's their name. Which the Coalition knew. They knew when they sent us here. We were never supposed to recover the *Flagstaff*. We were sent to shut it up. All those planets we hit with agrichem torpedoes... none of them were uninhabited. The colony here, though... It was too big not to notice. And Fontana did."

"He sent a shuttle down to investigate the ruins?" asked Frankie.

"He sent the whole ship. A storm took them down. A sudden surge, hit them out of nowhere and dropped them here."

Frankie nodded. "The particles in their resonance chambers aren't the only ones they can manipulate."

"They..." Sedlak gawked. "Created the storm?"

"Created, manipulated, I don't know," said Webb. "Doesn't matter. The result was the same. The *Flagstaff* crashed here."

"The silicants have been known to affect weather when working in concert," said SeeMee.

Blackwell bared his teeth. "And you didn't divulge this to the Captain? When it could have saved him?"

She tickled a hatchling. "Whether to share information was at my discretion. I elected not to."

"You *elected...*" Blackwell reddened. "Of course. Why betray your allies? Easier to let the xenos do the dirty work."

SeeMee sighed. "The silicants are no longer members of our Union. They withdrew after religious extremism fractured their society and their worlds went into decline."

"Fucking traitor," said an Armstrong. Webb couldn't tell which.

SeeMee looked baffled. "Did you believe you were entitled to Union information as a prospect species? I was sent to assess your fitness for membership. Crises reveal character."

"You knew what they were capable of!" Spittle flew from Blackwell's lips. "You let them ambush us!"

"Not at all," said SeeMee. "We expected no more than a tense interaction, a chance to see how you handled the unexpected. We never expected you to loot their homes. Or to show such negligence towards your own peoples' safety that you would allow an infestation. Or crash your own ship."

"*You* did this." Blackwell nearly shook fury. "*You* brought us down."

"The silicants brought the ships down," said Webb. "They pulled the survivors from the *Flagstaff,* destroyed its systems, and ripped our tech out of their minds. Fontana and his cog were repairing the ship when he met the elders."

"The schism hasn't been resolved, I see," said the Sorl.

"Fontana suspected the Coalition might try to silence him after what he learned, so he recorded a holo of himself and set it to load upon cessation of his lifesigns. That's who I was talking to in there."

The crew regarded her quietly. "So..." said Sedlak. "What's that mean for us?"

Webb let out a long sigh. "Real talk, folks. The Coalition assassinated one of their own captains to keep their secret. You think they'll spare a second thought about killing a crew they already consider mutineers?" She ran a hand through her hair. "Frankie, give me some good news."

"The damage to the ship is pretty extensive."

"*Good* news, I said."

"But nothing that requires a shipyard," said Frankie. "Everything is repairable, and its shuttle also appears to be intact."

"The shuttle works? Why didn't he take that up?"

"If I had to guess?" Frankie looked at the dismembered cog. "Sabotage."

"Is the shuttle spaceworthy?"

"Seems to be now."

"How about the ship?"

"She's so banged up we should rename her the *Half-Mast*, but she's still solid," said Frankie. "If we can limp her into orbit, we should be able to complete repairs there. Well before any Coalition ships arrive."

"Which means time enough to dock with the shuttle and tractor in the meat locker." Webb turned to Chelse. "There's a nurse up there who's gonna be pretty pleased to see you."

"Damn straight." Chelse jabbed a stim into her thigh. "I'm sexy as hell."

A ping from the comms. "Webb." It was Eight. "We're in the cargo bay."

"What did you find?"

"There are some racks of agripods left. Looks like the rest fell out the back during the crash." That would explain the random pattern of the grain fields. "No extinguisher harnesses, though."

"Secure the hold and make space," Webb told her. "We've got a sardine can full of wounded waiting in orbit. We'll need room for half a dozen biobeds."

"Copy." The comm fell silent.

SeeMee chirped a trill into a handheld device. "I've told my transport to expect refugees. We will assess your asylum claims once we're safely in Union space."

"Beyond the reach of justice, you mean," said Blackwell.

"If the Union grants us asylum, we'll be in a better position to negotiate a return," said Webb. "One with assurances of safety." She didn't believe it even as she said it.

By their expressions, neither did the crew.

"I'm not gonna force anyone to come with us," said Webb. "Anyone who wants to jump ship can wait in orbit to be rescued. But don't forget what they've already done to protect a secret that all of us know. There's room on this boat for anyone who wants to take a chance at asylum." She turned to the Armstrongs. "Except for you."

The Armstrongs scoffed. Then they saw her expression, and the smirks fell from their faces.

"You can wait for rescue with the *Liberator's* lifeboats." Webb told them. Her lip curled when she turned to Blackwell. "Not you, though. You're coming with us."

He threw his head back. "Like hell I am."

"You'll receive a fair trial. For every death you caused."

"This is bullshit," said Jacobs. "So much for the tolerant left."

Frankie actually snorted. "Tolerance isn't an absolute, you jackass. It's not a weakness you can exploit, or a magic cheat code. It's is a treaty, an agreement that allows us to function in a complex society. And like any treaty, if you violate its terms, you are no longer protected by its provisions. You smug, smirking shitbiscuits. Get the *fuck* off our ship."

Webb raised an eyebrow. "Dang, Frank."

"Sorry. It's tough being serene all the time."

"You're leaving us to die," said Blackwell.

"Like you left the soldiers," said Frankie.

"Twice," added Chelse.

Webb turned to the soldiers. "Escort the Armstrongs to the *Flagstaff's* shuttle, if you would." The soldiers led the Armstrongs away.

Blackwell had gone white as a sheet. "I'll promote you all," he called after them. "All of you! You'll be officers, with all privileges. You'll each have a personal arcade, with obedient sprites based on whoever you want."

Webb leaned in toward Frankie. "They'll be okay? Not that I care."

"It's a short range shuttle," said Frankie. "It doesn't have FTL. Or weapons."

"Good." She straightened. "Don't want them trying anything stupid."

"I don't want to alarm anyone," said Chelse at Tactical. "Scratch that, I do. We've got movement."

Webb darted over. "Show us."

Chelse zoomed in on the far side of the chamber, where collapsing stones revealed a new tunnel. Out flowed a stream of silicants, followed by the burnt xeno, which seemed to be lugging something. It looked towards the viewer—somehow, Webb knew that *it* knew she was looking at it—and held up the elder's head.

Webb numbly turned back to the bridge. "Frankie, get us out of here."

"Initiating start up sequence." The ship rumbled as its engines drew in power.

"Armstrong shuttle is away," reported Sedlak from ops.

"Patching force fields over hull breaches for takeoff," said Frankie.

A deafening thud sent Webb crashing to the deck. She pulled herself up, spots dancing before her eyes. Everyone else had been knocked to the floor. "The hell just happened?"

"The shuttle." Frankie sounded incredulous. "They *rammed* us."

"They *what?*" Webb looked out a fresh breach in the bridge. Across the chamber, the shuttle slammed into the cavern's far wall in a puff of purple sand. The impact had flung it clear across the chamber. It came to rest at an angle against the escarpment where the xenos had come out.

"Bunking *idiots!*" Webb zoomed in on the wall. The same impact that had torn a gash in the bridge had peeled the shuttle open like a chainsaw through a melon. Its entire dorsal hull was gone, sheared off. The xenos swarmed toward them. "Hail them!"

The shuttle appeared on screen. The Armstrongs still standing gaped at the missing roof. They actually appeared shocked that their plan hadn't worked.

Webb felt sick. "What did they expect to happen? That was like throwing an egg at an anvil."

"Captain?" Jacobs sounded like a lost child. "Captain Blackwell?"

The red shirts on the bridge could only watch as the wave of xenos washed over the Armstrongs. Bilson fell, chopped down from behind. Loomis' head bounced off the screen. The screams drowned out the chitters.

Blackwell looked away.

"Captain!" Jacobs was crying now. "We need a miracle! *Captain!*"

Blackwell switched off the comms.

The viewscreen switched back to a wider view of the cavern. The glittering stream of xenos diverted out of the shuttle to flow towards the *Flagstaff.*

"Warning," said the ship. "Containment shields are down."

"Impact took them offline," said Frankie.

Webb could see xenos through the rent now. "Get them back up. And put him in the brig."

Chelse grabbed Blackwell's cuffs. He slammed his shoulder into her chest and rammed his fists into her stump. Chelse went down in a ball of curses.

Blackwell came up with her rifle.

Time seemed to stop. With nightmarish slowness, Webb drew her sidearm.

Blackwell turned and shot the ambassador.

A crater erupted in SeeMee's chest and burned outward, fast as flash paper. She didn't have time to scream before her charred bones fell in a heap.

Blackwell whirled on Webb only to find her sidearm aimed at him. They locked eyes over their barrels.

The Sorl hatchlings scuttled away and swarmed up Webb. She barely felt the little claws gripping and quivering against her skin, barely heard the frenzied peeping from the back of her neck. "You set that to max, you bastard."

Blackwell's smirk was triumphant. "She was going to deny us our place in the Union."

"You think they'll let you in *now?*"

"I've preserved our chance. No more lies."

"*What* lies? We *have* been committing genocide."

"Genocide," he spat, "is against *people!* Drop your weapon!"

"Not happening."

He bared bloody teeth. "Drop it or your friends in orbit die. I sent the Admiralty a message that the shuttle is full of insurrectionists. Unless I rescind that order—which I can't do if I'm dead—the next ship to arrive will blow them out of the stars. Drop your weapon."

"Rob," muttered Chelse.

And Marwazi, and all the wounded. Webb lowered her gun.

"Kick it to me."

She did. "We need to raise our shields."

He pocketed the sidearm, trained his rifle towards the rest of the crew. "Get away from the duty stations."

Nobody moved.

He flushed crimson. "That's an *order!*"

Frankie eyed her console. "The xenos are coming."

"We need shields," said Webb.

"Here's what's gonna happen." Blackwell aimed at Frankie. "Still on max. See? What do you think it'll do to someone as slim as her? Webber, take the helm and get us into orbit. Everyone else, against the wall."

Frankie eyed her. "Webb?"

Webb's pulse thundered. He breath was shallow. "Do what he says." She slid behind the helm.

"Back up." Blackwell gestured with his rifle. He backed against the bulkhead next to the helm to keep the red shirts in view. The crew sullenly retreated to the far wall. "Take us up."

Webb brought up the bridge's schematic, overlaid its internal shield grid atop it.

He grabbed her hair, yanked her head back. "I said *up.*"

Her scalp screamed. "Engine's still powering."

"This is quite simple," he hissed in her ear. "*I* lead. *You* obey. Now do what you're told, or you all die."

"Not all." She grinned through the pain. "Just you and me."

She brought up the force field. An invisible barrier sprung up, bisecting the bridge, sealing Frankie and the others behind it.

Webb threw her head back, cracking Blackwell in the chin. He stumbled back against the unshielded rent in the bridge.

A pair of burnt armblades burst through his stomach at kidney height. His face contorted. He gaped down at the blades. The burnt xeno raised its head over his shoulder. Blackwell looked back at it like some grisly ventriloquist's dummy. The xeno hurled him against the bulkhead like a rag doll and squirmed through the gap. A stream of xenos jetted through behind it.

Webb threw up the second shield she'd prepped, sealing the gap in the bridge. The shield snicked a xeno in half, dropping its thorax next to Blackwell.

But a dozen silicants had made it through. And by the sound of it, more were chopping at the hull. The burnt one turned towards Webb and hissed.

Frankie pounded on the force field. "*Webb!*"

"Help me," burbled Blackwell.

Webb winked at her quaddie. "Get us up." She sprinted off the bridge, a cacophony of chitters and plunks at her heels.

She fled through the unfamiliar ship and its tight corridors, steering by the glimpse she'd caught of its schematic. The cargo bay and its agrichems were only a deck below the bridge. Webb turned a corner and nearly collided with a wall of red shirts brandishing spears.

No, not spears. Agripods.

"Open up!" Like the rest of them, Eight had tied a torn-off sleeve around her mouth and nose.

The red shirts parted. Webb scampered through. Someone slapped an agripod in her hands and spun her towards the xenos.

"Lower pods!" cried Eight.

Webb and the red shirts lowered their pods into a bristling thicket. The xenos skidded to a stop in front of it and milled about, chittering madly.

"Hold!"

The confined corridors had saved them, Webb realized. There wasn't room to outflank or leap over them. The only way at them was through the phalanx.

With a hiss from the burnt xeno, the silicants surged towards them. The closest xenos smashed into the pods and screamed as the pods burst and their armor slagged. Saffron smoke filled the hall. The xenos skittered back.

"Rearm!" called Eight. The red shirts who'd struck fell back, coughing. A second rank took their place with fresh pods.

The phalanx lurched as the ship lifted off.

"We have control of the bridge," Frankie said over the comms. "Security fields are up and holding. The xenos on the hull are jumping off."

"Keep the ship steady," yelled Webb. "And open the nearest NEOS hatch. We're giving them an out." She tightened her grip on her agripod. "Red shirts! One step forward!"

The phalanx advanced. The xenos skittered back.

A fierce grin split Webb's face. She could see it in the silicants' movement, in how they were ignoring the burnt xeno's frenzied hisses and clicks. They were tired. Demoralized. "They're close to breaking."

"Airlock open," said Frankie. "Take a right, then the left."

Webb marched the phalanx forward, its agripods bristling like a barricade of thorns. The xenos fell back towards the bridge, but bounced off the security field there. The burnt one chittered. The xenos started burrowing at the floor.

She had to keep them on this level. "Charge!" The red shirts went forward at a jog.

The xenos leapt away, caroming off each other in their rush to escape. The phalanx marched over the damaged floor plating and herded them towards the airlock, Frankie shouting directions over the comms as the increasingly distressed xenos bounced off force fields corralling them ahead of the wall of agripods.

By the time the open airlock came into view, the silicants were in utter disarray. One threw itself at the phalanx and died in a slurry of chems.

Webb stepped into the front line to replace a red shirt with a spent pod. The airlock was open, and she could see the escarpment passing by in a rush. They must be hundreds of feet from the chamber floor by now. "Frankie!" She had to yell to be heard over the rush of wind. "Get us close to the wall!"

Static over the comms. "Come again?"

"Find a ledge or something! We're letting them off."

The ship slowed its ascent to hover near a plateau set in the wall. The moment it came into view, the silicants leapt for it, first one, then the mass of them, leaving the burnt one alone in the NEOS. It hissed pure vitriol at Webb before it leapt to the ledge.

Webb rushed forward and locked the NEOS shut. The red shirts remained shoulder to shoulder, wall of agripods lowered, their eyes on the xenos.

On the ledge, the silicants sagged or lay down. Chemical burns streaked their carapaces, and wisps of gasses seeped from the cracks in their armor. They slumped against the rock.

Not the burnt one, though. It was still chittering and flailing, hissing and spitting at its followers. They didn't respond. With a hiss, the burnt xeno darted forward and slashed one.

As one, the other silicants popped up and their armblades popped out. They advanced on the burnt one, crowding it backwards towards the ledge. It hissed and spit and swiped at them. The others swarmed forward, pinned it to the ledge, hacked off its armblades.

Howling, the burnt zealot rose, cradling its damaged limbs.

"Looks like that one's not in charge anymore," said Eight.

The silicants pressed forward, blades out. The burnt xeno leapt back at the ship, caught itself on the dome of the NEOS and clung there. It chopped at the dome, but without its blades, it did no more damage than rapping a hammer against a bulkhead.

"Frankie." Webb kept her eyes on the wounded xeno. "Are we spaceworthy?"

"By its broadest definition, yes"

"Take us into orbit."

The ship rose sharply. The silicants on the ledge hurled rocks at the burnt one until the ship was out of range.

"Is it gonna get off?" asked Eight.

Webb couldn't say. "It might not have anywhere else to go."

The cavern fell away, as did the ruins, as did the atmosphere. Still the xeno clung to the NEOS, its compound eyes locked on Webb's. Gasses spurted from the cracks in its carapace as the ship slipped into space.

A headache stabbed into the back of her skull. Webb flinched but didn't look away.

With a shudder, the last of the xeno's gasses escaped. Its grip came loose, and its body drifted away.

The comms chirped on. "Everyone okay?"

Webb lowered her agripod. The Sorl hatchlings peeped out from her collar to look around. "We are."

"There was a xeno on the NEOS."

"It's gone," said Webb. "It spent its last moments hating me."

Webb stepped out of the Arcade. Her shoulders and neck felt oddly bare without the constant wriggling and peeping. She looked to the viewscreen. "How we doing?"

"She's holding," said Frankie. "We've got teams sealing the last of the hull breaches. We'll need maybe an hour to recalibrate the tractor emitters, but then we can pull in the shuttle and the meat locker's oubliettes. We'll have FTL stardrive shortly after that."

"Sounds good." Webb turned to Chelse. "How's the patient?"

"I've done all I can for him." Chelse snapped a medkit shut. "He hasn't got long."

Blackwell had gone paler than wax. Chelse's battlefield sutures hadn't stopped the bleeding. He coughed up blood. "I need a doctor."

"We don't have any," said Frankie. "You wouldn't let us teep anyone in."

"Marwazi's an hour away," said Webb.

Blackwell grimaced. "I don't have an hour. Teep him in."

"I can't lock onto him," said Frankie. "Their shields are up."

"You're murdering me," he wailed. "You're letting me die."

Webb sighed in disgust. "Are there any more medkits?"

"A medkit won't cut it," said Chelse. "He needs surgery."

A voice crackled over the comms. "I can help."

The pain lifted from Blackwell's eyes. "Sunshine?"

Webb hit the comms. "Yolanda? Are you ready for transport?"

"I can help him," she repeated. "Save him. The way he saved me. Teleport him to the *Independence*. I can patch the damage with his holo-emitters."

"You can't be serious."

"However I feel about him, he did keep me alive. The least I can do is return the favor."

Blackwell smiled. "I knew you loved me."

"Yolanda." Webb had to blink a few times. "The Coalition's on its way."

"You don't owe him anything," said Frankie.

The comms were silent for a moment. "I'm not going to let anyone else die. We're better than that. Send him here, Webb. For me."

Webb's throat felt tight. "Fine. I just hope you know what you're doing."

"I do," said Yolanda. "Keep the comms open."

Webb nodded to Frankie. Frankie energized the teleporter. Blackwell shimmered, gave them the finger, and vanished.

A proximity alarm beeped. Eight looked up from ops. "Another ship has entered the sector."

"Coalition?"

"No." Eight tapped some buttons. "It's Sorl. We're being hailed."

"Put them up, I guess."

A figure with the bearing of an imperial peacock appeared on screen. "Where is the ambassador?"

Webb's stomach knotted. "She did not survive. I'm so very sorry."

Its feathers quivered. "How did she perish?"

"She was murdered by a mutineer who tried to sabotage the ship."

Its crest drooped. "I see."

"Her hatchlings—is that the right term? They're fine. They're in our arcade." A lump swelled in her throat. "With a holo of their mother."

"Yes." The Sorl captain bobbed its head. "We've already teleported them to our ship."

"Captain? SeeMee... your ambassador... she offered us asylum."

It tilted his head. "You are in danger?"

"From our own government, yes."

"You have a record of her offer?"

"I do not."

"I see." It darted its head from side to side. "I cannot grant you asylum, as this might lead to conflict with your Coalition. However." More darting, and the raising of its crest. "I will not impede you if you wish to enter Union space as refugees."

"We would like that very much," said Webb.

"You must understand, I cannot guarantee your safety. Asylum offers Union-wide protections, but refugees are at the mercy of the laws of local worlds. You would be on your own."

"Honestly?" said Webb. "We're kinda used to that."

The Sorl bobbed its head. "Very well. This concludes our interaction. Good luck to you, Captain." The viewscreen went blank.

ℓ

"How does that feel?"

Blackwell touched unblemished skin through the holes in his uniform. "Strange." There was no pain, but the musculature there felt half-asleep. "Certainly better. Good enough until the Coalition gets here and teeps us out."

"That might be a while," said Sunshine. "We read as holograms now, I'm afraid. Not as biosigns."

"Really." He already knew. He couldn't very well have had a random biosign appear in his quarters whenever he needed comforting.

"Our comms are also fried."

"You just hailed the *Flagstaff*."

She tapped the Armstrong pin on her collar. "Lucky I found this. There's no other way to signal incoming ships."

"So, then…" He looked around the wreckage. "It's just us from now on?" Could have been worse. Better than facing a show trial and execution at the hands of mutineers. He sank onto the bed, gazed up through the ruined ceiling at the night sky. "I can think of worse things than being stuck here with you."

"We're also not constrained to your quarters. Look." Sunshine took a step into the corridor.

He looked up, amazed. "Get out of town."

"Damage to the emitters," she explained. "I'm not sure what their range is—I don't really want to find out—but I know from first hand experience that they don't extend past the wreckage." She stepped back in. "Unfortunately, the bridge teleporters didn't survive the crash, and the main bays are in the wreckage of the aft section kilometers from here. But, our emergency power is enough to keep these running." She stroked an emitter.

"For how long?"

She didn't look at him. "Until the isotopes in the backup reactor decay."

The coquettishness was starting to irritate him. "Which is how long?"

A smile. "Well beyond a human lifetime."

He grunted. "Don't mind the sound of that. At least we'll have each other." He patted the bed next to him.

Her smile hardened. She tapped her Armstrong pin. "Have you got a lock on my pin?"

"Affirmative." It was Fuller's voice.

"Copy. Stand by to teleport."

Blackwell sat upright. "What the hell is this?"

She seemed genuinely shocked. Then angry. "Oh, my God. You actually thought I was staying with you? I'd rather die. Again. I'll have to live in the *Flagstaff's* Arcade, but at least I'll be alive. It'll be more of a life than you allowed me."

He rose. "Now, you listen here."

She drew a queller. "Sit down, Jared. You wouldn't want to be a ghost with a limp."

He narrowed his eyes. "You wouldn't dare." He went for her.

She shot him in the knee. He went down shrieking in a tangle of missing tendons.

"Huh." She stared at the queller in faux surprise. "Look at that. It was on max."

"You fucking *slut*. You spoiled, fucking... *This* is what I get? For saving you? For *loving* you?" She'd tricked him. Fooled him into saving her, into opening his home and heart. She'd probably planned this whole thing with the crew advocate.

"Goodbye, Lieutenant."

Blackwell saw red. "I'll find you. There is nowhere in this galaxy you can go—you and your traitor friends—where I won't hunt you down."

"But I don't think you will, though. Because if you leave the range of these emitters, your holographic organs will vanish." She pursed her lips. "I'm not actually sure what will happen when your body runs down before the power does. Your undamaged bits might keep aging until you rot away. Or maybe you'll be able to tweak the program and fill in your missing pieces as you go. You know. Like you did with me. So, it's your choice. You can leave the wreck and die of severe internal hemorrhaging, which I'm okay with, or you can stay here until the power runs out. In about six thousand years."

His roar came out a whimper. "Sunshine. Please."

She tapped her pin. "Get me the hell out of here." She shimmered, shot him in the other knee, and vanished.

Chapter 21
Dum Vivimus, Vivamus

Yolanda Prime materialized in the *Flagstaff's* Arcade, a half-smile on her face. "We don't have to worry about him anymore."

Webb's curiosity was burning her up. "What did you do?"

"You could say I ghosted him."

"Come on, I need more than that."

"All in good time. Now that we have it." She looked around Fontana's cabin. "This is nice. Much roomier than the quad. Which, by the way—I don't mean to disappoint, but I'm gonna need my own space for a while."

"Totally understand. Chelse has already claimed a cabin for her and Rob."

"Sounds like the old quad is breaking up."

"It does. I hope we can find Frankie a broom cupboard somewhere where she'll be comfortable."

They shared a chuckle. "I have something for you," said Yolanda. She handed Webb a data stick.

"What's this?"

"Your handsome friend. I transferred his file in case you ever wanted to finish that holo-novel."

Webb flushed. "Thank you. I actually miss the lunk, if you can believe it."

Yolanda laughed, a laugh that turned somber. She wrapped her arms around herself. "I'm just going from one fabricated reality to the next."

"This one's temporary." Webb tucked Ablehard into her pocket. "Until we can find a way to fix the damage."

"It's a nicer dream than the one I was living. You'll visit?"

"Whenever I can." Webb hugged her fiercely.

A comm chirped within the cabin. "Webb? We've tractored in the shuttle."

*

In the *Flagstaff's* cargo bay, Webb's crewmates helped the survivors off the shuttle. Compatriots greeted and hugged and sobbed in each other's arms.

The moment Rob came into view off the shuttle, Chelse pushed past Webb to grab him. His eyes burst open with shock, then joy. She yelped when he seized her. "Your arm."

"It's okay," she kissed him. "I can still take you."

"I thought I'd lost you," he said through his tears.

She pulled him close. "Stop crying, you fucking pussy."

After the last biobed had been unloaded, Marwazi walked jerkily out of the shuttle in his exoskeleton, his face a mask of relief and fatigue. When he saw Webb, his step became lighter. His cheeks blossomed.

"Haroun." Webb tried to keep the smile from splitting her face.

"Joni." He nodded. "It is wonderful to see you again." He embraced her.

She drunk in his scent. "Okay, so, lowdown." She broke the hug. "We're deserters now."

Another nod. "We patched our comms into the feed from your pin. We heard everything, and we're with you. All of us."

"Well." She was once again aware that all eyes in the room were on her. Except for Rob and Chelse, who were practically bunking on the cargo bay floor. "A ship needs a commander. And, Doctor, seeing as how you were the highest ranking—"

"Oh, no," he raised his hands. "No no no, please. Just let me be the doctor. The rank always chafed. Besides…" A sly smile. "By the looks of it, this crew has already chosen its captain."

"Aye aye." Chelse came up for air. "All those in favor of Webb taking the big chair?"

The chorus was deafening.

Ø

Webb returned to the bridge to find that someone had welded Denis' spine to the captain's chair. *Her* chair now, she supposed. She wondered if she'd ever get used to it. She hoped she'd never get used to the trust the crew had put in her; never take them, or their support, for granted. Under the smiles of her friends and peers at their duty stations, Webb seated herself in the command chair. "Hey, Denis."

"Greetings, Admiral. Please transport me to the repair bay."

"Later." She patted his head. "Status?"

"All hull breaches have been sealed," said Frankie at tactical. "Security fields have been deactivated."

"Stardrive is up and purring," said Eight at ops. Her console beeped. "And a Coalition task force has just entered the sector. They'll be here in three hours."

"Well, then let's not be."

"The Sorl sent us coordinates for the nearest neutral system," said Frankie.

"We'll complete any repairs and reassess once there," said Webb. "Denis, plot a course, FTL 5. But first..." Webb spun her chair around to face Ops. "Eight?"

Eight perked up. "Yes, Captain?"

"What's your goddamn name?"

KICKSTARTER BACKERS

COMMANDERS

Q Fortier
Muljinn
James Herbert

Brent Phillips
Benjamin Mobley

LIEUTENANT COMMANDERS

The Lurker formally known
   as Mrs. S.D.
The Fantasy Network
Susan Carlson
Stephen Payne
Robert K. Hobson

Margrethe Flanders
Courtney Rayle
Aternoxx
Arlen Duncan III
Andi Smith (Whimsy Works)

LIEUTENANTS

Zombie Orpheus
trit
Sue Logen
Oskar Håkansson
Norman Jaffe
Nigel Sanford
Myrddin Starfari
Mike Kullmann
Leslie Sedlak

Jason Klimchok
Greg and Nancy Vancil
Glaurung
Douglas Urquhart
Derek Takade
David Rennie
Charles Ludwick
Barry Drake

ENSIGNS

Tim Jordan
Ruben Rydell-Sandgren
Rob MacLennan
Quezax
Paul Unger
Osye Pritchett
Nightscar
Moritz Schubert
Mike Ott
Michael Quann
Maxi Morgan
Max Beckman-Harned

Laura Scott
KVH
Joe Halamek
Jimmy McMichael
Jeremy Spray
James P Walker
James McKendrew
Helen B
Dean S. Anderson
Daniel Ley
D.J. Cole
Chanda Unmack

ENSIGNS (continued)

Casey A.
Caladier
Bruce Poll
Brad Gabriel

Argok
Amanda Cook
Allen Barnhill

CHIEFS

Zac Mann
Xeledon
Woody Arnold
William Watkins
Wayne
The Vinyl Princess
Stuart Hume
Steve Acheson
Stephanie Williams
Stefan Bold
Sominex
Shadowsmith
Seth M. Davis
Sergeant_MacB
Scott Graham
Sascha
Russel McConnell
Roy Kubicek
Robert Michael
Robert Adamczyk
Richard Blackburn
Rhonda Weeks
RH
Rentier
Rennie Araucto
RC
Randy Guyette
Puggimer (Michael Carter)
Philip Tatro
Niels Naumann
Mouselet
MoosenHammer
Monica Faye Hawkins
Michael Monahan

Michael Karcher
Michael Halverson
Melanie Leland
Mark Strock
Margaret Russell
Marc Wydler
Mak Kolybabi
M. Steiner
Lloyd Rasmussen
Liz L
Laura Renwick
Kent Rice
Katrina
Kathleen Quinlivan
Kasmyn
Karla "Hellcat" Stahlecker
Karl Arrenon
Joshua
Joleigh Doner
John Oswald
John Munn
John M. Kuzma
Jessica Salter
Jenny & Chris
Jeffrey Meyer
Jay Irwin
Jason Jenkins
Jamie Andrews
James Goodwin
Gordon Duke
Erica Schmitt
David "Yoda" Odie
Darren Stevens
Darcy Krasne

CHIEFS (continued)

Crillitor
Clayton Culwell
Chris Piazzo
Chris Halliday
Chris Eller
Catherine Barson
Bryan Donihue

Brian G
Benjamin Miller
Ann-Cathrin Schultz
Alexander Hufenbach
Adam Sowl
Adam Brown

TECHNICIANS

Two Bards
Tomáš Trnka
Tehashi
Scott Baker
Raphael
Morten Poulsen
Michel Rowinski
mflgrmp
MarkC
Mark Innerebner
Mark Eramian
Lisa Coronado
Laura Snow
Kyle Kilgour
Kristopher Volter
Kieran Chauhan

Kevin Harder
JYoungman
Judd
John A
Jeremie Lariviere
Isabell
Frédéric Fiquet
Eric G
David Moller-Gunderson
Cody Wood
Christie/Evaine
Bradley Foster
Aldero
Aldarian Chesnik
Aaron Garrett

CREWMEN

Zack
W Wyse
Tyler D Martin
Tony Becerra
Thomas Wisniewski
Thomas Govostes
Stark
Seth Carpenter
Roberto Mignone
Robert Wishin
Robert Fitzgerald
Robert Daley
Preston Coutts

Nick and Carolyn McGary
Naomi Boydston
Michael Feldhusen
Matt
Martin Kümmerling
Mark Thomason
Mandaygo
MADMANMIKE
Lyle
Lewis Crown
Lawrence Wimsatt
Landon W Schurtz
KJ Petersen

CREWMEN (continued)

Kevin N Roberts
Katy
Joshua K. Reardon
John Idlor
Joel Gipson
Jim Wrench
Jens
Jacob Blackmon
George D Stefanowich
Florence Williams
Fateor
Dusten Jones
Don Early

Danielle P.
Dan Lamm
Chad Long (Tecrogue)
Caryn Vainio
Brian LaShomb
Brendan
Branson Rogers
Blarghedy
BC Brandt
Allen Shepherd
Alishia Cameron
Alan Batson

CREWMAN APPRENTICES

The Farquhar
Steve Manitsas
Robin Lee Chadwick
Paulusj
Ornithopterx
Michelle Marsh

Louise Mc
Kurt Jaegers
John Wignall
Douggie Sharpe
Bill Murray
Beorn Thomassen

CREWMAN RECRUITS

William Thomas Nation
Wilbur Yokan
Rykeal
Thomas P Metcalf
Tarasis
SwordFire
Steve Hill
Stephanie Turner
Stan Yamane
Sören Koch
Scott Starks
Sarah Sanders-Ode
Robert Claney
Rhel
Ranneko
Pratchettfan
Potkeny

Orcrist86
Nightmoose
Mufasa
Mike Weber
Matthew Pearsall
Matthew Crowe
Matthew Bertucci
Matt Forbeck
MarvelousJim
Mark James Featherston
Lianne Maitland
Kurt Zdanio
Keith Sanderson
Karl Burkhardt
Justin
Joseph Shraibman
Joseph Puhalla

CREWMAN RECRUITS (continued)

Jenn Forte
Jay Peters
Jason
Jan Grimmer
Jakob Törneke
Grant Quackenbush
Glen Merrick
FredH
Erik Gorka
Ergo Ojasoo
Elstren
DutchUncleHAR
Deanna Stanley

DC Bueller
David Queen
Darryl "Owlbear" Browne
Daniel Provencio
Conrad White
Carl Bevil
Brent Mendelsohn
Brendan Reeves
Andrew Obertas
Amberlyn Pryor
Amanda Stenson

CADETS

Zack Norwig
William
VoodooLouKerensky
Vital Watchman
Terran Empire Publishing
Ron and Elizabeth Howard
Mirranda Prowell
M. Craig Stockwell
Leopold the Just
Joerg Fick
Jamie Chambers

PATREON SUPPORTERS

Jhessail Haithcock
Moritz Schubert
Marvin Just Marvin
Andrew Wise
Nancy L Vancil
Mark C
Jeremy Spray
Jim Wrench
Frederic Fiquet
James Herbert
Margaret Russell
Hawke Robinson
Jay Blanken
Max Beckman-Harned
Leslie Sedlak
Helen Brubeck
Courtney Rayle
trit
Jason Jenkins
Jimmy McMichael
Laura Red Scott
Caryn Vainio
Tecrogue
Andi
Dan Lamm
Eligos Alexander
Seth M. Davis
Brian Doty
J Youngman
Gordon D. Duke
Rob MacLennan

About the Author

Matt Vancil is a writer and filmmaker from Tacoma. A co-founder of Dead Gentlemen Productions and Zombie Orpheus Entertainment, he wrote and directed the fantasy comedies The Gamers, Dorkness Rising, Hands of Fate, and Humans & Households, and wrote and created the new media series JourneyQuest, for which he created the Orcish language. A graduate of the American Film Institute, his work has been featured on Netflix, Hulu, and Amazon Prime. He wrote video games for mobile giant King and is the author of PWNED: A Gamers Novel, The Orcish-English Dictionary, The Stray and the Hole in the Stars, and this book right here. He teaches (well, taught, pre-plague) filmmaking to video game designers at DigiPen Institute of Technology, aka "Nintendo University." He lives in Washington State with his family and will eventually have a website.

Made in the USA
Columbia, SC
31 May 2021